Dedalus European Classics
General Editor: Mike Mitchell

IDA BRANDT

Herman Bang

IDA
BRANDT

Translated by W. Glyn Jones

Dedalus

Dedalus would like to thank The Danish Arts Council's Committee for Literature and Arts Council England, London for their assistance in producing this book.

Published in the UK by Dedalus Limited,
24-26, St Judith's Lane, Sawtry, Cambs, PE28 5XE
email: info@dedalusbooks.com
www.dedalusbooks.com

ISBN 978 1 907650 73 4

Dedalus is distributed in the USA by SCB Distributors,
15608 South New Century Drive, Gardena, CA 90248
email: info@scbdistributors.com   web: www.scbdistributors.com

Dedalus is distributed in Australia by Peribo Pty Ltd.
58, Beaumont Road, Mount Kuring-gai, N.S.W. 2080
email: info@peribo.com.au

Publishing History
First published in Denmark in 1896
First published by Dedalus in 2013

Printed in Finland by Bookwell
Typeset by Marie Lane

The Author

Herman Bang (1857–1912) was from an aristocratic Danish family. His homosexuality led to a smear campaign against him and his exclusion from Danish literary circles. He worked as a theatre producer and as a journalist, having first tried unsuccessfully to be an actor.

His first novel *Families Without Hope* was banned for obscenity. He specialised in novels about isolated female characters.

The Translator

W. Glyn Jones read Modern Languages at Pembroke College Cambridge, with Danish as his principal language, before doing his doctoral thesis at Cambridge. He taught at various universities in England and Scandinavia before becoming Professor of Scandinavian Studies at Newcastle and then at the University of East Anglia. He also spent two years as Professor of Scandinavian Literature in the Faeroese Academy. On his retirement from teaching he was created a Knight of the Royal Danish Order of the Dannebrog.

He has written widely on Danish, Faeroese and Finland-Swedish literature including studies of Johannes Jorgensen, Tove Jansson and William Heinesen.

He is the author of *Denmark: A Modern History* and co-author with his wife, Kirsten Gade, of *Colloquial Danish* and the *Blue Guide* to Denmark.

His translations from Danish include *Seneca* by Villy Sorensen and for Dedalus *The Black Cauldron*, *The Lost Musicians*, *Windswept Dawn*, *The Good Hope* and *Mother Pleiades* by William Heinesen and *My Fairy-Tale Life* by Hans Christian Andersen.

He is currently translating *The Tower at the Edge of the World* by William Heinesen.

"At times I feel almost as though someone else were adding the figures up."

I

The porter had come for the three patients who had been working in the basement. He went over and shouted to the second of them, the man with the abdominal support, who was wandering up and down, up and down along the wall by the stove. He gave him a loud shout, straight in his face:

"Time to go."

"Yes." Patient number two stopped and looked at the porter. "Yes," he said again, nodding and spinning around like a dog about to lie down. He always did this before embarking on even the smallest thing.

Then he got his dressing gown on like the others, and the three moved off. The porter's keys could be heard rattling in the corridor as he locked the door – first at the top then lower down.

Nurse Brandt put the washed cups together in a corner of the small kitchen table and went into the ward to "listen". But the two old folks in there were asleep, breathing deeply.

And all was quiet in Ward A.

Nurse Brandt climbed up on the chair in the anteroom – she had to do that in order to reach the window – and moved the flowers a little so as to make room and then sat down on the sill.

"Brandt's quite mad," said Nurse Brun in the women's ward. "She flies up like a scared chicken."

Ida Brandt leant her head back against the wall – she was always rather tired towards evening after her first time on day duty – and she looked out through the big window: the "Lakes" looked so calm, a single strip of red glowing in the sinking sun.

Ida Brandt took out a letter, but she sat there holding it in her

9

hand for a long time as the red flush on the lake gradually slipped away and faded before starting to read:

Horsens, the 1st of October

My dear,
You will receive this letter five days late. I know. But on the other hand, you don't have five terrible children, two of whom last week broke the front leg off the writing desk. They just wanted to pretend it was a boat, my dear, while I was doing the cleaning. But the leg has been glued on again now, and this morning I managed to hang the last winter curtains, and so now you can have my birthday wishes: God bless you, my dear; you know that all of us here in the "Villa" wish you that.

So you are really twenty-eight now. Oh how time flies. When I pass your old window, I often feel it was only yesterday I used to see you sitting there on the mahogany chair and looking out like the good girl that you were. Everything about you was good, Ida, your eyes, your hair beautifully combed with its two pigtails, and everything. You used to look out at us giddy kids from Miss Jørgensen's school as we came running down the street with our schoolbags, playing 'tick' in the gateways until there wasn't a whole pleat in our skirts.

At last you would come out on to the outdoor steps and stand holding carefully on to the railing as though afraid of falling into the water until your mother called out 'I-da', and in you went with stiff pigtails and a rather old-maidish walk and your mother closed the door.

There was always something about your mother that put a damper on things.

I would pause to catch my breath in our doorway. I knew perfectly well that mother was watching: 'Oh that's where you are?' (I had sidled in through the door). 'Let me have a look at you' – and I had to turn around.

'Take your fingers out of your mouth, Olivia.'

'Now I've told you before, this is the last time you're going to

10

have fur edging on your coat...' I pulled a face; there was always a bit hanging loose here or there; I don't know how it was, but Regine and I simply became untidy.

'All right, you can go now.'

I ran with my schoolbag straight into the doorframe.

'I wonder whether that child will ever learn to walk on her own legs'

And I was out in the street.

'But...' came the voice from the window again, 'you'd better get Karen to put a brush on your hair...It's a disgrace to you.'

Hair was the worst thing. It always ended with Karen having to stand with the brushes in front of Mamma, brushing and brushing:

'No,' Mamma would sigh. 'It's impossible to make that hair look tidy. Just you look at Ida Brandt, she can keep hers in order.'

I stood there as stiff as a poker, and Karen brushed away: you were always the paragon of virtue.

And do you remember when Mamma visited your mother together with me – I don't think they had really known each other very well before that – and they were talking in the living room and we were sitting in your two little chairs in the bedroom between your mother's bed and the window and I suddenly took hold of both your pigtails and banged your head against the edge of the bed?

You didn't resist and you didn't make a fuss, but you simply started to cry – quite gently...Do you know what, my dear: I think I was fond of you from that moment because you had cried so quietly...

Ida Brandt lowered her friend's letter to her lap. She gazed out at the Lakes without seeing them. It was as though she could see everything at home, the house, the living room where the furniture had never been rearranged, and the bedroom with the two small chairs on which she was to fold her clothes, garment by garment, before going to bed; and her mother, calm and broad with the heavy curls in her hair and the gold chain around her neck.

Then she read on:

I so well remember the Wednesdays, when I used to come across to your house at five o'clock to fetch you out. Once I was indoors, your mother would call from her window seat into the bedroom, where you were doing your homework:

'Ida...'

'I-da.' You always stuck you fingers in your ears when you were reading, you were so keen: 'It's Olivia Frank.'

Continuing to knit with her big needles, your mother would nod and say, 'Sit down, dear.'

And I would sit down by the door – in your home one always sat in the middle of the chair – until you had all your clothes on – your waistcoat and your little scarf and then your cape and big scarf – and then we curtsied to your mother.

'Have you a handkerchief, Ida?' she would ask – I always felt for my own handkerchief – 'Take care of yourselves...'

And we went past the window, side by side.

In the evening, the cloth was taken off the table – I can see your mother moving the lamp from one table to the other – a job she always did herself and then we played patience while your mother had a game of whist with the maiden ladies. At half past eight, when I was to go home and your Sofie came in with the redcurrant wine, we were given an apple each while my outdoor clothes were brought into the warm room...

Mamma used to say, 'Olivia is better behaved for a whole day when she has been at Ida Brandt's.'

But on Sundays you came to our house from first thing in the morning. Do you remember how Sofie used to bring you and say that 'madam sends her compliments' as she took your outdoor clothes off one by one as though she was undoing a bundle? No one scared Mamma like your Sofie.

'I don't know,' she used to say, 'but her eyes are everywhere as though she is looking for the tiniest speck of dust on the furniture.'

Mamma had a tendency to become flustered in the presence of other people's maids.

In her most polite voice, Mamma would say, 'Could I offer you a cup of coffee, Sofie?'

And Sofie would drink it, sitting primly on the chair near the black bookcase, without saying a word.

Do you remember the day we were out playing and you tore your blue muslin dress on a nail?

You simply sat there, quite quietly, all the time smoothing the tear over your knee without saying a word, and I stood just watching and then I started to help you, with both my thumbs, as though we could glue the tear until I whispered, 'We must tell Mamma'.

And we ran up to Mamma, and when we were just inside the doorway I said:

'Ida's torn her dress.'

When I said 'torn' I started to cry, but you stood there as quiet as ever.

'Where?'

Mamma took hold of your dress by the seam and held it out from you like a banner:

'Yes, what did I tell you?' She let go of the skirt. 'What must Mrs Brandt think about this crazy family?'

You stood there, trembling but not crying, and Mamma loosened the hair behind her ears with her crochet hook:

'We must send for Miss Finsen,' she said, just as dismayed as we were. 'Take your dress off...'

Karen ran to fetch Miss Finsen and you put on one of Mamma's nightdresses while you waited, and Mamma went on about 'this house' and my dress, which I could tear without there being a problem...

'There's Mrs Brandt,' I shouted from the window.

Mamma let go of the dress:

'She's going to church,' she said, as though relieved. And we both watched your mother's straight back as she crossed the market place.

'It's Mr Hansen preaching the sermon,' said Mamma.

'No,' you said in a weak, thick voice – it was about the first thing you said – 'It's Mr Schmidt'.

Mamma put her hands down on her lap.

*'In that case they won't be going home before half past twelve,'
she said with conviction.*

*When Miss Finsen came, she declared that she could take half a
width out and then alter the pleats in the back.*

*'It won't be seen,' she said as she measured and examined the blue
material. Miss Finsen, poor woman, had a pair of eyes as though
she was always wondering how best to cut a length of material of
difficult material.*

'No, you won't be able to see it.'

*'Do you think not? Do you think not?' said Mamma, who always
listened to Finsen as though she was speaking in Latin: 'Well,
provided it won't be seen...'*

It was not to be seen.

*'Turn round, dear,' Mamma said to you once you had the dress on
again. 'Once more...No, it can't be seen.'*

*'Thank goodness for that, Finsen.' Mamma put her hands down
on her lap.*

'Let's have a cream cake now.'

*Cream cake was Mamma's regular treat for seamstresses. A tiny
bit of pastry was always left behind on Finsen's lower lip, in the
crack she had acquired by biting threads.*

*I went with you that evening when Sofie came. You grabbed
my hand rather tight when we got to the street. When we reached
the cellar steps, I said: 'They are playing cards; I saw the ladies'
shadows on your white curtain.'*

'Yes,' you whispered in a tiny, frightened voice.

*We went inside and you took off your outdoor clothes and we
curtseyed to them all, first I and then you, and your mother said over
the cards: 'Has Ida behaved herself?'*

'Yes.' That was the first lie you ever told, my dear.

*'Good, then you can go to bed. You know that you have to do your
practice at seven o'clock on Mondays. Good night.'*

You received a kiss on the forehead and then went off.

*'Goodbye,' I said almost like an explosion. And I ran home to
Mamma so that I was quite out of breath:*

14

'They didn't see anything.'

'Oh, thank goodness for that,' said Mamma, sitting down heavily on the sofa.

'Well, it does Ida good to be a bit naughty occasionally,' she said. I had surreptitiously taken hold of my homework from by the window.

'I say, Olivia,' said Mamma, 'are you starting on your homework now?...Do you think Ida Brandt steals candles to read in bed?'

∞∞∞

Ida Brandt closed the letter and sat for a long time smiling and leaning her head on the window frame. The street lamps were being lit one by one over on the other side of the Lakes. She heard Josefine bring the supper and then go again, and she heard the old people in Ward A starting to turn in their beds.

She sat there for just a moment longer.

But suddenly, the keys rattled in the door in the women's ward, and she jumped down with such a start that she overturned the chair. It might be the professor: he came at so many different times and the lamps were not lit.

But no, it was Mr von Eichbaum from the office, who said:

"May I go through, Nurse?"

"Yes, do."

She lit the lamps; she had been so scared that she was quite out of breath.

Mr von Eichbaum stayed while she lit them.

"You know it's damned curious," he said in his slightly nasal voice, "how much I've been thinking about Ludvigsbakke since I ended up in this confounded office."

"Yes, but it was so lovely there," said Ida in a voice almost as though she were looking at it. "There was such a beautiful view over towards Brædstrup."

"Yes, it was nice," he said, smacking his lips. "Those were the days."

He remained there while she fetched the ladder and climbed it to

15

light the gas lamp above the door to Ward A.

"No," he said as he watched her; there aren't many to compare with His Lordship."

They exchanged a few more words as she came down again and went into Ward A. The gentleman in there, who was sitting in the black easy chair, raised his head and watched her through his big, gloomy eyes as she lit the lamps on his table.

"Who is he really?" asked von Eichbaum when she returned.

"I don't know," she said. "A doctor." And half laughing she said: "He is the only one I am frightened of."

Eichbaum laughed. "But damn it all, he looks pretty quiet."

"Yes, but I don't know, he's almost like a ghost."

"A ghost?"

"Yes," said Ida, apparently slightly embarrassed. "The ghost of somebody or other."

Mr von Eichbaum continued to laugh; he did not take his eyes off her.

"Oh well, good night, nurse."

Mr von Eichbaum nodded and let himself out, and Ida crept up the ladder to light the lamp above the door to the "Hall". The sound of a high-pitched plaintive voice could be heard from the women's ward. It was Miss Benjamin; she was always restless as evening approached.

Ida Brandt could not refrain from smiling as she stood there, humming gently as she divided up the butter for supper: she was thinking of Olivia's letter.

And of Ludvigsbakke.

The patients working in the basement came up again and started wandering around in the anteroom, going to and fro in some curious way without heeding each other, while their clogs clattered ceaselessly across the floor.

Bertelsen, a tall man who had "come to a standstill", went over to the washbasin in the kitchen to wash his hands, a pair of reddish, clammy hands – he had to wash them every ten minutes as though to cleanse them of some thousandfold sin.

"Come on, Bertelsen, you're clean," said Nurse Brandt.

"Yes," he said, suddenly stopping washing as though no longer remembering to do it. He went over to the table, stood there and looked at her for a while – as far as he was able, for his eyes never rested on one single thing:

"But what am I supposed to be here for?" he said suddenly.

"Will you tell me, what I am supposed to be here for?" His voice was raised as he repeated his words.

"You have to get better, Bertelsen," said the nurse as she continued to prepare the sandwiches.

"Better!" His laugh was more by way of a snarl, and all his compact teeth could be seen. They gleamed, and it was as though they were the only things in his face with any colour to them:

"Better here, where I'm locked in."

"And you must have something to eat," she said. "And then that will be another day gone, Bertelsen."

"Yes, I'm coming," she shouted into the "Hall", where the two patients had already seated themselves at the tables at the end of the beds, impatiently banging on the floor with their clogs. "I'm coming."

She listened first at Nurse Petersen's door; she was still fast asleep, and her breathing could be heard even out there.

"Nurse Petersen," she shouted. "Time to get up."

The loud breathing stopped, and at long last there came a sleepy, "All right." Nurse Petersen was the night nurse. Ida took the food into the ante-room, where the man with the abdominal support was still shuffling around.

"You must have something to eat, Schrøder," said Ida, facing him directly as though speaking to someone who was deaf.

"Hm." He merely looked at her.

"You must have something to eat, Schrøder," she repeated.

"Hm."

"I mean *now*." She continued to speak clearly, as though the man had difficulty in hearing. "Because the *doctors* are coming now."

And, holding him in front of her, she guided him over to the table.

The doctors could already be heard on the stairs, and the keys sounded in the door. It was the registrar and two junior doctors, followed by Nurse Helgesen carrying the case notes. She carried them like an officer in a court of law clutching some legal document.

The patients rose from the table, and the three old bedridden patients watched the doctors through strangely half-glazed eyes.

"Nothing to report?" asked the doctor.

"No, doctor."

The doctor went into Ward A alone and shut the door.

Quam, one of the junior doctors, sprang on to the table in the ante-room and brought his feet together.

"Heaven preserve us – what a shift – eleven new admissions and one of them pumped."

"Was it opium?" Nurse Helgesen spoke to the junior doctors in a businesslike manner as though to colleagues.

"Yes, he's a locksmith's apprentice. They say it's a love affair, and now they've dragged him up and down the floor for almost five hours – two men. Heaven preserve us." Quam yawned: "Just fancy, human beings can't learn to take things calmly. What do you say, Nurse Brandt?"

Quam jumped down, for the registrar was emerging.

"You can let the patient have a little fresh air," he said; he was already at the door to the women's ward.

Quam followed him at the end of the procession; he always wore white sports trousers on the days when he was on duty, and on reaching the doorway he shook his legs as though he wanted to shake the dust off his feet.

Ida provided the three old men with food; she had a gentle way of her own when raising them up in bed.

Nurse Petersen came out of her room, energetic and out of breath.

"What time is it, nurse?" she said to Ida – the lower part of Nurse Petersen's body performed ten elegant oscillations at every step she took.

"My watch has stopped."

"It's getting late," said Ida. It was always getting late when Nurse

Petersen emerged in the evenings.

"Oh yes, thank you for waiting." Nurse Petersen took out her keys – she was for ever making small movements with her fingers – "I'll be quick with my tea."

Ida just nodded; she was so used to having to wait for the others for half an hour after her duty. She sat down under the light in the Hall and started to sew.

How well she remembered him, of course, now she thought about it, at home in Ludvigsbakke – him and his mother, who always sat right up at the end of the table – she always sat up beside His Lordship at table.

And she went for walks on the dot, and had the two stone benches in the approach to the steward's house where she rested.

"Hm," she always said: "And here we have little Miss Brandt," as though she discovered her anew each time.

The three patients sat playing cards at the end of the bed with their woollen trousers concertinaed high up on their legs. But Schrøder wanted to go to bed.

He was sitting in his bare shirt on the edge of the bed, his legs hanging down as though his bones were all loose.

"Bedtime, Schrøder," said Ida.

"Yes," he replied, though he continued to sit there with his head drooping down.

Ida had to get up before Schrøder managed to lift his legs with some difficulty, as though this was something that required serious thought. "There," she said, smoothing the blankets with both hands. "It's a lot better when you lie down, isn't it?"

She continued to help with the blankets while hushing Bertelsen; he was always so aggressive when playing cards. Then she heard Nurse Petersen's keys and started putting her sewing away; all she had to do now was open the door to Ward A.

The gentleman in Ward A was sitting by the table and only looked up briefly to start writing on his big papers again. He wrote nothing but numbers and more numbers, slowly as though he were printing.

"I will just open the shutters," said Ida, as she opened the big window.

But he made no reply and just went on writing. Here, in Ward A, Miss Benjamin was the patient who was heard most clearly, for she was right up against the wall.

Nurse Petersen was standing outside at the peephole when Ida came out.

"He's one I wouldn't mind getting rid of," she said. She came from Flensburg and still spoke with an accent – and they both remained at the peephole. The gentleman in there rose slowly, and he seated himself quietly up on the windowsill.

He sat there without moving, staring out into the night, at the stars.

"Good heavens, he just always sits there working things out," said Nurse Petersen.

"Dr Quam says he wants to discover the laws," said Ida.

"Poor man," said Nurse Petersen, who understood nothing at all, and she gave a maidenly toss of the head before leaving the peephole.

Ida opened the door to the noisy ward and went in. Two porters were supporting a lifeless body between them; its arms were draped over their shoulders as they dragged him along.

Josefine, sitting on the bench beneath the windows and trying to get two men to eat something, nodded in the direction of the porters.

"What a job! They've been at it for five hours."

The porters turned just by the door leading to the "good" ward, as Ida came in, and one of them, looking at the hanging head, said:

"He's actually quite a respectable chap."

"Yes," said Ida, looking at the face with lips open like those in a mask – and the porters turned round and continued to drag the body around.

In the quiet ward, the doors to the individual rooms were open, and the patients were dozing on their beds. In the dining room, with her opera glasses before her and buttoning her gloves, sat Nurse Friis, who was off that evening and going to the theatre.

"Ah," she said. "There we have our assistant nurse."

"Give me a hand, will you?" she held out one hand towards Ida, who always had to "give a hand". "I'm going to be far too late."

Ida buttoned the glove while Nurse Helgesen, who was sitting, arms crossed, in her favourite position behind the urn, said in her very clear voice:

"What did that blouse cost?"

"Thank you, nurse."

Nurse Friis looked at herself one last time in the little mirror in the corner; she was still wearing the coat she had received as a twenty-two-year old ten years ago, and her hair had to be waved in her own quite special way around her temples.

"I got it from a cousin in Aalborg," she said, referring to the blouse.

Nurse Krohn and Nurse Berg, who were drinking their tea at the other end of the table, said: "Oh dear, now we shall have to start thinking about winter clothes."

And they started to talk about hats.

"I make my own," said Nurse Helgesen behind the urn.

Then a large female figure appeared in the doorway.

"There's a fine smell in here," she said, putting a white hand up to a broad nose while looking at Nurse Friis. This was Sister Koch, the senior nurse in the women's ward.

"Yes," said Nurse Friis, who was ready at last and had taken hold of her opera glass. "I don't like to smell of carbolic outside the hospital."

"Good night."

Sister Koch came in and sat down over in the corner with her hands on her knees like a man.

"May I be here for a bit?" she said.

And Nurse Helgesen, who had nodded to her, said from behind the urn, "Nurse Friis is very fond of clothes."

Nurse Berg and Nurse Krohn continued to talk about hats, and Nurse Koch, scratching the grey hair tied up at the back of her neck in the much same way as one ties a piece of rope said:

"Buy yourselves a couple of fur hats, ladies, they don't wear out."

The two laughed and went on discussing hats: they had more or less to suit the way you did your hair; and they started to talk about hair while the two senior nurses asked about the new patients.

"There were eleven today," said Nurse Helgesen.

"Yes and quite a lot of bother," said Sister Koch.

Nurse Berg could not imagine herself without a fringe.

"Aye," she said, "if one had Brandt's hair. Good Heavens, Brandt, I can't understand you don't try to wave it a bit."

"It's always been like this," said Ida.

But Nurse Berg wanted to try to wave it and started to ruffle Ida's fringe with a pocket comb. "I can hardly recognise you," she said, going on ruffling: "otherwise you just look as though your hair's been plastered down with a wet comb."

Nurse Krohn, sitting watching, with both arms on the table, said: "Oh, did you see the new man in the office? My word, that's some back parting he's got."

They discussed Mr. von Eichbaum, and from over in her chair Nurse Helgesen said: "Mr. von Eichbaum seems to me to be a very nice person..."

Sister Koch pushed her glasses more firmly on her nose as though to see better.

"Well," she said, "he gives me the impression of being something of a philanderer."

"I know him," said Ida, sitting there quite quietly with her ruffled hair. "I knew him at home in Ludvigsbakke." She always said "Ludvigsbakke" rather more gently than the other words she spoke.

But, drumming her fingers on the table as though dancing a waltz with them, Nurse Krohn said:

"The man wears straps on his trousers."

Sister Koch spoke about Ludvigsbakke, which was in the part of the country from which she came, and about His Old Lordship and Her Ladyship.

"But surely she was already dead by that time."

"Yes," replied Ida. "Her Ladyship was dead."

"She was a lovely woman," said Sister Koch. "She still used to hoe her own flowerbeds when she was eighty, with farmhand's socks pulled up over her shoes."

Sister Koch laughed at the thought of Her Late Ladyship and her woollen socks.

"But that must be almost thirty years ago. Well..." – Sister Koch shook the front of her skirt. This was a habit she always had when she rose – "we all of us come to that."

"Are you going upstairs, Brandt?"

"Yes."

"Then I'll go up with you," said Sister Koch. "Good night."

They let themselves out on the stairs near the quiet ward and stopped at Sister Koch's door.

"Yes," said Sister Koch in a quite different tone, and they stood by the door for a moment. "It was a splendid place." She was thinking of Ludvigsbakke. "Good night, Brandt."

"Good night."

Ida went up and made her way across the loft to her own room. She lit the lamp, which was covered by a butterfly-shaped cloth (there were so many little things scattered about in the room that she and Nurse Roed made while on night duty to decorate their rooms), and she stood for a time in front of the chest of drawers looking at the picture of Ludvigsbakke with the tall white house and the lawn in front of it with the new flagpole, and all the children sitting on the steps all the way up.

There was Mr von Eichbaum as well. Yes, it was he, she thought it was a long time since she had noticed him. But she could well remember that the picture was from the year when he had come home from some school in Switzerland and spent his time stretched out on the lawn.

And His Lordship was standing by the flagpole.

She went across to the writing desk and let the flap down and took out a couple more pictures. That was the one of the lake and she stood there holding it and smiling: hmm, it was from when it was dry and the water was low as well, and all the gentlemen and Agnes Linde waded out with bare legs, splashing around among all the fish. How they enjoyed themselves. But a pike had once bitten

Agnes Linde on the calf so that they had to send for Dr. Didrichsen.

There was Mrs von Eichbaum sitting under the white parasol.

She closed the drawers again; they were full of so many of mother's old things, and while she undressed she took Olivia's letter out and put it over by the bed. She had a habit of taking letters to bed and keeping them under the pillow as though to have them with her.

She sat up in bed and looked through all the sheets of paper. Olivia always started with quite small writing, which then became bigger and bigger and went all over the place:

Aye, those were the days, and who can understand what became of them...Here I can see us in church, at our confirmation, when we all wore white dresses and were flushed with crying and with our hair all smoothed down. Old Mr Bacher, poor thing, he's going downhill, and they all go to Mr Robert for their confirmation classes now; he had twenty-seven last time round.

But goodness knows how often you had to test me on hymns.

Mamma always said: 'I always think that Ida is the smartest of the confirmation candidates...there is something special about that girl with the way she holds her head, looking down a little...rather different from the others.'

And the dress you wore the next day was blue with tiny white dots.

We attended our first ball that Christmas. I had slept with gloves on for three weeks:

'You simply can't go to a ball with those hands,' said Mamma. 'Ida helps in the house, and yet she has nicer hands than you.'

We went there in Jensen's carriage, you and I on the back seat, with two skirts up over our heads, sitting on the canvas ones while Mamma squeezed into the front seat and your Sofie sat proudly up on the box with your shoes, all wrapped in paper.

Every mother gave her own orders and tidied us up. And there we stood, in the middle of the floor with red arms and all frightened and smiling, while Mrs Ferder rushed all over the place:

'My word, Mrs Franck, yours are lovely,' she went on; she had an

open packet of pins fixed on her breast to straighten up Inka's dress. There was a loud knock on the door: 'Open up, open up'. It was Nina Stjernholm in her fur coat.

'Good evening, good evening, children, children, I'm far too late,' she shouted, shaking her head and making her curls fly all over the place, and then she shouted to Mamma:

'Dear Mrs Franck, where are the fillies?' And she scrutinized us and pushed fat Mrs Eriksen aside: 'Charming, charming,' she said as she bustled about.

'Have you a partner for the first dance?' she said turning to us.

'Ida hasn't...'

'Good, then stay with me, Miss Brandt; I've got a couple of new lieutenants from Fredericia...and I will take His Lordship.'

The master of ceremonies knocked on the door and asked whether the ladies were ready, and the music started.

We danced. I heard Captain Bergfeld say to Mamma:

'That quiet young lady is so charming.'

That 'quiet young lady' was you, my girl, and the captain was a connoisseur.

Oh, yes, those wonderful early days: when summer arrived and the 'sewing club' moved out into the grove and we sat there in a circle, behind the pavilion, beneath the trees, while one of us read aloud.

But then came the autumn when your mother was taken ill.

You were over at our house, I remember, when Sofie came running across and shouted for you from out in the corridor. You had got up from the table and you left, without a word, without saying goodbye, running along the street after Sofie. You met Miss Fischer and took hold of her and spoke to her and then went on, faster and faster.

I stood at our window and wanted to go after you, but I don't know...I was afraid, so frightened...that perhaps she was dead already, and I said to Mamma:

'Are you not going to go with her?'

And we put on our coats and went along and arrived in your living room, where all the furniture had been moved because they had had to lift your mother and carry her; and the doctor came and the room was full of people until the doctor said they should go, and Miss Fischer came running in with a bowl full of ice, and she was crying and kept on saying:

'But she would never do as anyone advised her to do; she would never follow anyone's advice.'

I stayed with you that night, and we sat and kept watch in the living room and heard all the clocks ticking and announcing the slow hours with the bell whirring and striking.

And we heard the night nurse whisper to Sofie and change the ice, and we sat there again, listening to the clocks.

But you, poor thing, sat up for many nights after this.

Goodbye for now, my dear. May the new year bring you much joy. You know that we in the Villa all wish you that.

And then a kiss to mark the occasion, although you know how I hate all this kissing between friends. The children are shouting to me to give you their love.

Yours,

Olivia

Ida turned round and was about to put the letter, which she had slowly folded, under her pillow when she heard three sharp knocks on the door.

"Open up," said a voice from outside.

It was Nurse Kjær and Nurse Øverud from the women's ward, who darted in and quickly closed the door again.

"We've got something to drink," said Nurse Kjær in little more than a whisper; she was carrying a brown bottle: "to celebrate her sister."

"Of course," said Ida. "They were getting married today."

"Yes," said Nurse Kjær. "She's married now," (they all three continued to speak quickly and in subdued voices as though the *crème de cacao* was something they had stolen): "Well, Sister Koch had gone to bed..."

Still in a half whisper, she said: "Øverud, where are the glasses?"

Nurse Øverud carefully took three small glasses out of her pocket, and the two sat down on chairs in front of the bed with the light shining down on Ida's duvet.

"Good health," said Kjær.

All three of them took a drink, while keeping the bottle on the floor as though to hide it, and Nurse Kjær said slowly as she sat there holding her glass, "There are forty of them there today."

"Well," she continued (she had acquired the same habit of moving her hand up towards her nose as Sister Koch), "it was certainly about time they got married...they'd managed to stick together for five and a half years now while Poulsen was working in the post office...Then last summer while I was at home I was sent up into the woods to find them. Poulsen had the Sunday off (Kjær laughed), as he had every third Sunday, and *there* he was, asleep with his head on Marie's shawl, while Marie, poor creature, was tiptoeing quietly around picking raspberries, aye, aye," she said and chinked glasses with Nurse Øverud, who was laughing.

"It's not easy to stay awake when you have had to drool over each other for five years."

"But is it right they are going to move to Samsø now?" asked Ida.

"Yes, with sixteen hundred and a pension."

They sat for a while, and then Nurse Kjær said in a quite different tone:

"Henriette wrote that the girls were going to decorate the church. It is so beautiful" – she paused for a moment – "that church at home, when it is decorated."

The last time Nurse Øverud helped to decorate the church, she told them in her Funen lilt, was for Anna Kjærbølling's wedding.

"Anna Kjærbølling, you know her, of course, Nurse Brandt. She comes from Broholm."

"Yes," said Ida. "She has two delightful children."

"Yes, two lovely children."

Nurse Kjær still sat looking at the wall.

"And I think, too," she said slowly, "that children are the best thing of all."

There was a moment's silence while they all three stared into the light with changed and, as it were, sharper faces.

"Oh well, let's wish them all the best," said Nurse Kjær as she emptied her glass.

"Yes, all the best," said the others, chinking their glasses with hers.

Nurse Kjær suddenly rose:

"We must go over," she said, walking across the floor with the bottle; but her thoughts were still with her sister, and in the same voice as before, as though she was watching them go, she said: "And they will be on Samsø tomorrow."

"Good night."

"Good night."

Ida locked her door again, and she heard them hurrying across the loft as she returned to her bed. She was so wide awake now, although her head was heavy. She was thinking of Olivia and her children and of Nina with her four tall boys, whom she had seen last year, and about her father and her home – at home in Ludvigsbakke.

She could see the big white wing of the bailiff's farm and the rooms in which everything was so clean and tidy and so quiet, and then there were the flowers, four in each window and four in the painted flower pots; and father's shells, which she was never allowed to touch, were resplendent in the corners.

And she saw the office as she knocked on the very bottom of the door when she was quite small and went in and said that dinner was ready. Her father was sitting at the green table in his long canvas coat and wearing his old straw hat – for he always "covered up" when he was in the office – and she clambered up in the big armchair and waited: all "father's birds" were perched around them, in their big cases, behind glass.

Until mother opened the door:

"Brandt, dinner is waiting."

"Yes, dear. Is Ida here?"

And he absent-mindedly caressed Ida with a pair of loving hands: "Yes dear, yes my dear."

They went in. Ida toddled along beside her father, who held her so close to his knee that she stumbled over his boots.

"Brandt," said her mother, "that's no way to walk with the child."

After dinner, father sat down in the sofa with a handkerchief over his face; mother sat in her chair by the window. Before long they were both asleep.

Ida tiptoed around quietly – she wore carpet slippers at home – and left the doors ajar. Then she sat down on a stool while her parents slept.

After dinner, Ida went with her mother to have coffee at the Madsens in the school. This was up by the main road to the north, along which carriages would be driving. One of them was that of the pharmacist's wife from Brædstrup.

She had bought herself a sewing machine in Copenhagen now.

Yes, Mrs Madsen had been over to see it. But *she* thought that things would last better if they were sewn by hand.

Her mother nodded.

"But you know they have to try everything out at the pharmacy," she said.

Ida sat on a small chair, learning to knit, and she had her own little cup.

When Ida and her mother went home, they took the road leading past the farm. Only two solitary candles were burning, one in Miss Schrøder's room and one in the steward's wing.

There was the sound of a voice: "Good evening." It was Lars Jensen, the farm foreman; he rose from a bench.

"Good evening," replied mother.

And they went on their way into the dark avenue leading to the bailiff's house.

At home, they could hear laughter in the hallway. It was the forester and his wife who had come over for supper. Mother went in to prepare things, and Ida curtsied first to Mrs Lund, quite a small, frail lady who had given birth to eleven boys and whose eyes had grown bigger at every birth, and then to her husband.

"Well, and how is the young lady?" he said, lifting her up in both arms just in the midst of her curtsey and swinging her in the air. Lund was a man of enormous girth, and he laughed until he turned red right up to the back of his head.

"Lund, Lund, you're so rough," said his wife. "You're only used to romping about with boys."

"Oh," said Lund as he continued to swing her around, "It's good for her, so it is. It gets her blood circulating."

They went in to have something to eat. "Oh," said Mrs Lund (for nowhere were there so many beautiful things on a table as at the bailiff's). "How wonderful it must be to be able to look after everything as you do, Mrs Brandt."

Things were rather all over the place at the forester's; eleven was a somewhat large number of heirs to see to.

They exchanged news from the neighbourhood and talked about the sewing machine. Lund had been in to see how it worked.

"You must go and have a look at that great work of art," he said.

"But surely it works by hand?" said Mrs Brandt.

"Yes, but heaven knows how long it will last."

"You know, Lund," said his wife with a faraway look in her eyes, "it must surely be lovely to have one of those in a home where there are so many to make clothes for."

Lund just laughed:

"Aye, née Silferhjelm," – the pharmacist's wife had her distinguished maiden name placed below Mogensen on her cards – "could surely manage to sew the few skirts she needs by hand."

"But there are people," said Mrs Brandt as she handed a dish around, "who must be the first to have things."

"And then when you haven't anything else to think about," said Mrs Lund, "it is quite reasonable."

Mrs Lund, who always spoke in a tone as though she were trying to quieten someone down, changed the subject to the price of butter:

"Now Levy has reduced his price by four *skillings*."

Mrs Brandt failed to understand that, for she had maintained her price all the time.

"Well," said Mrs Lund, shaking her head – she had four small curls at the back, tied with a velvet ribbon – "but it is presumably because things do not always turn out like that for us at home... heaven knows how that happens."

"Let's have a schnapps, Lund," said Brandt who was doing little but look, first at one and then at the other. "Has Ida got anything to eat?"

Ida was allowed to spread her butter herself with a blunt-edged knife. "You have to *accustom* children," said her mother. "It is good for them."

"Cheers, Lund," said the bailiff, and they went on to wonder when His Lordship could be expected. It would scarcely be before the end of June, in a couple of months.

"When the woods are past their best," said the forester.

Ida was to go to bed after the meal. Her father put her on his knee when she said good night and bounced her up and down.

"My, you do bounce that child around," said Lund with a laugh, and Ida said good night to the others, one after the other in turn.

The forester and his wife left at ten o'clock.

"Let me take your arm," said Lund, for it was dark.

"She's a prickly one, you know," he said. "She can't forget we've known her as the housekeeper...and all that went with it."

"But they're very helpful, Lund," she said.

The forester said nothing to that. His only comment was: "She takes up a lot of space at the end of the table."

"And how nice everything is," said his wife. She was always full of profound admiration when she was in other people's homes.

The Lunds made their way home.

But Mrs Brandt went around putting away the silver.

...Ida was to have a children's party, and that must be now, before His Lordship came.

The children had chocolate to drink on the Mound adjoining His Lordship's garden.

The girls sat in a row, all in starched dresses – with the two from the inn at the end of the table in tartan winter dresses and wearing earrings – all drinking and eating.

Mrs Brandt, who was going around, wearing a white shawl and pouring out the cocoa, said:

"I don't think you have anything, have you Ingeborg?"

Ingeborg was the judge's only child and she was wearing net mittens decorated with small bows.

Not a sound was to be heard.

Ida, who was the smallest of them all, went around showing her dolls to those who were finished, and the forester's two youngest, Edvard and Karl Johan, who had chapped hands ("Heaven knows how that happens," said Mrs Lund: "but all the dirt in existence seems to land on those boys' hands") went for the dishes of cakes all of a sudden as though they had to grab at everything they were eating.

"Sofie," said Mrs Brandt, looking down along the silent table, "I do not think they have anything down there," as though it was only a matter of filling them up.

"No thank you," said Ingeborg, when Mrs Brandt offered her more, "it's so late to be having tea."

The two from the inn had turned their cups upside down.

Brandt appeared at the bottom of the Mound – his trousers so easily found their way into the backs of his shoes as he walked:

"Aha, this is a party," he said as he came up. "Have you all got something?" he said. "Aha," he went around pinching their cheeks, diffidently saying their names for he did not know what else to say, while the little girls shuffled and looked down at their skirts.

"But then you'd better play some games," he repeated.

"Then they had better play games," he repeated to his wife.

"But perhaps some of the children would like some more," replied Mrs Brandt.

"No," said the eldest of those from the inn sharply, behind his cup, deciding it for them all.

"Then you must go and play," continued the father in the same tone; he did not know what they were to play.

"We could have a game of handkerchief into the ring," said the judge's daughter Ingeborg, while the little girls sat there, flushed and quiet.

"Well, yes, but little children must be allowed to make a noise," said Brandt. "Children must make a noise, they must run around." And suddenly, quite put out, he said:

"I'll fetch Schrøder, my dear." And he went.

"The forester's two mumbled something about not knowing what was meant by handkerchief into the ring, and they went over and sulked by a tree.

"Right, you can start," said Ida hanging over the edge of a bench beside Ingeborg and handing her a handkerchief that was far too small to be thrown into the ring.

Brandt ran through the garden and in through His Lordship's gate. Up in the main building, all the doors were wide open and there was a smell of starched curtains and cleanliness.

Miss Schrøder was standing on a stepladder in the middle of the sitting room in her stocking feet; when hard-pressed she was fond of taking off her shoes:

"Lord, Mr Brandt, you've come to *fetch* me," she shouted, letting her arms fall.

"Yes, Schrøder my dear, you'll have to go over there...they can't get things going," said Brandt, pushing his glasses up and down; "there's no one who knows what children do to enjoy themselves." He pulled both trouser legs up:

"I think there are fifty of them," he said.

"Good heavens, of course I'll come." And Schrøder put her hands up to her hair: "But I've got all this to do."

Schrøder looked around; there were curtains on all the chairs: "And they'll be here tomorrow!" She came down from the steps and flipped her shoes on. "This heat's terrible on your legs," she said. Heat was always a problem for Schrøder, and from the first day in June she was forever on her way down through the garden with a sheet; she used to bathe in the pond: there's nothing in the world like water, she said.

"Oh good Lord," she looked at the curtains: "then we'll hang them up tonight."

Down on the Mound they had started rolling lids.

"Good heavens," said Schrøder, surveying the group: "this is a bit tame, isn't it? Let's have something with a bit more go in it."

She lined the children up and they started to march. Ida took her hand, and when they had marched a little way, the judge's daughter Ingeborg came and took her other hand.

"Look," she said to Ingeborg. "I am wearing bronze shoes."

The forester's boys went after the girls from the inn and smacked their bottoms, for they were the last in line.

Before long they started playing postman's knock down by the pond. Brandt had gone with them and he had great fun getting in the way of the children wherever they tried to run.

"That's more like it," he said.

"Yes," said Schrøder, pushing up her sleeves, "but I've got curtains to hang at twelve windows."

Mrs Brandt and Sofie, both of them straight backed, carried the dishes of sandwiches through the garden and up on the Mound to set the table.

Ida was so happy. She twice ran across to Schrøder and kissed her hand, without saying a word.

∞∞∞

His Lordship's family were to take a trip into the woods in two carriages; they had turned out of the drive, and His Lordship was in his element in the young ladies' coach. Mrs Brandt went across to the house with the local newspaper.

Schrøder was in the pantry, where she had been packing the picnic.

"Ugh, I haven't a stitch on under this," she said, touching the front of her print dress: "And now we can start to tidy up in the guest room."

She hurried out through the kitchen, where three smallholders' wives from the tied cottages were attending to the workers' supper, and then on across the corridor to the guest rooms.

"Oh," said Schrøder, "this is a mess if ever there was one."

All the doors between the rooms were open, and no one had closed their suitcases. Dresses and shirts lay here and hung there. Schrøder talked away as she hung things up and moved things around.

Mrs Brandt said nothing, but went around lifting the skirts as though to judge the materials they were made of.

"Yes indeed, it's all right for some," she said.

"Well," said Schrøder, turning around; she had gone ahead: "These Copenhageners often don't have much in the way of underclothes...You can tell that from how often they have to have them washed while they're here."

Mrs Brandt did not reply or carry on the conversation – it was never Mrs Brandt's custom to ask anything – she merely used her grey eyes while Schrøder ran about in front of her and carried on and chatted:

"Aye, heaven knows how it's going to turn out for Miss With and Falkenstjerne but they're suited to each other, you know, tall men with short wives, that always works..."

"And she's a lovely girl," said Schrøder.

She closed a trunk and launched herself into the idea:

"Miss Adlerberg," she said, "has a waist, you know, such as it was nice to have at one time. When you could get Miss Jensen to pop over from Brædstrup in the middle of the day..."

Miss Jensen was the seamstress in Brædstrup, and she sometimes did a fitting for someone in the guest rooms during the summer.

"That's a 'Garibaldi'," explained Schrøder as she entered the innermost room, where two strong trunks were closed and locked and the dresses were hanging on the hooks, wrapped in tulle.

"Miss Schrøder, Miss Schrøder," shouted Ida outside the window.

"That's Ida," said Schrøder, reaching out and lifting the "little thing" in through the window before unrolling a long, broad black moiré train out of a length of tulle that stretched right across the floor.

"That's her dress, and what a train. It's lined."

While Ida stood looking up at all that silk, Schrøder laughed and held the skirt over her like a cloak; but Mrs Brandt examined the lining:

"The lining is old," she said.

"Yes," said Schrøder. "But you know it really is wonderful what they can get out of it."

Schrøder always expressed wonderment at the Copenhageners.

"And now we'll go on," she said.

When they reached the last window, she suddenly put Ida out on the gravel path again.

"Cause otherwise you'll never grow up," she said with a laugh. "And besides, we must count the washing."

"Well, I suppose *I* cannot be of any use," said Mrs Brandt, who was already in the corridor.

"Oh no," said Schrøder. "I'll manage it myself."

She stood on the stairs for a moment looking at Mrs Brandt's back as she walked across the open space:

"I think it's going to thunder," she said, breathing out heavily. "I wish it would."

The three smallholders' wives were going about quietly in the kitchen. They only had black woollen socks on their feet even though it was a stone floor.

Over at Brandts, Mrs Madsen had arrived from the school. They otherwise saw little of each other during the summer.

"We know perfectly well," she said to Mrs Ludvigsen, "that we in the 'farm' are good enough company for them in the winter."

Brandt was walking restlessly to and fro: his knees always let him know when it was going to thunder. And the clouds were certainly gathering over Brædstrup.

Mrs Madsen had indeed already put out some curds, she said, for Madsen had been on the lookout for thunder as soon as he got up that morning. He could feel it in his wound.

Madsen had been wounded by a sabre during the first Schleswig war and was the chairman of the Veterans' Association.

∞∞∞∞

That evening, Schrøder stood right down on the road to keep a look-out for the carriages, for it was already lightning down beyond Brædstrup, and Mrs von Eichbaum was always so frightened of driving, and now there was a storm approaching as well...

The bailiff's girls ran past her shouting and carrying sheets from the bleaching ground, and in the home farm she could hear the steward shouting to them to close the hatches, when the two carriages appeared down on the road at as great a speed as the reins could stand. His Lordship was in the barouche with Mrs von Eichbaum.

The maids in the main building closed the windows, and as soon as he reached the entrance His Lordship started shouting that the hatches should be closed, while the steward came running out wearing a big cape.

The guests, who were nervous and stiff, alighted by the steps. Mrs von Eichbaum, as pale as a sheet, went into her sitting room and lit the lamp behind the drawn blinds. She was always afraid when "the elements were angry".

His Lordship, going through the rooms to make sure the windows were all fastened, shouted that they should all gather together; and Schrøder ran through the rain across to the bailiff's, and he came back with her. Ida toddled along with her head poking out of a long cloak, and Mrs Madsen was there, too, for she had not dared to go home.

"Indoors, indoors," Schrøder shouted.

But Miss Rosenfeld had put on a bathing cap and was standing out in the middle of the lawn, catching the rain in her hands.

"Go indoors," shouted His Lordship, and laughing and bending her back she ran in under the glass roof.

"*Here*," said Miss Adlerberg, catching hold of her. They were all sitting or standing on the garden steps now, looking out through the rain towards the silent flashes.

"Here," she said, forcing Miss Rosenfeld down on a travelling

37

rug.

They all spoke in quiet voices, looking out at the heavens that were becoming darker and telling of thunder and lightning.

"Aye," said Brandt in his slow voice, "when Aggersøgaard burned down, as I'm sure Your Lordship will remember, it was a full hour before we got the cattle out..."

He said nothing for a time; there came a flash of lightning brighter than the others.

"But," he went on, "both the baron's carriage horses got away from us...it was dreadful."

"Yes," said His Lordship, standing alongside Brandt. "And we were both standing here when the old flagpole was struck."

"Yes, Your Lordship."

And in the same voice, His Lordship added: "And that was the year my late wife died."

Mrs Madsen nodded: she remembered *that*.

The lightning became brighter and there were more and more flashes and in the light from them they could see the cattle out in the fields and the houses in Brædstrup. Everyone was silent and no one spoke any more except Miss Adlerberg, who whispered to Mr Feddersen from the Ministry:

"We roll the blinds down at home and light the lamps and dance," she said, having made a fan of her gardening hat.

The rain came on heavier and sounded like the rat-tat-tat of drums on the roof, while the poplars in the drive swayed and bent as though they were about to break.

"Here we go," said the bailiff quietly as the first rumble was heard above them.

Lieutenant Falkenstjerne had sat down on the steps at Miss With's feet; she grasped his shoulder.

"Listen." And in a fragile little voice she said: "Mother and I always go down into the cellar at home."

There was another flash and Schrøder was speaking half aloud when the crash came.

"It's over Ringgaard," said His Lordship, who knew every patch of ground and every distance in the region.

"Yes, Your Lordship."

They had not finished speaking before there was more lightning. The flashes came from two sides like bright, interrupted beams, and they saw the flat field where the cattle were running in great circles to escape, and the entire heavens, where the black-edged clouds rolled up towards them like chariots.

No one spoke any more; only Miss Rosenfeld, who was sitting there with her head cocked attentively, whispered:

"How beautiful it is, how beautiful..."

Meanwhile Mrs Madsen sat there all the time moving her lips and Ida had bowed her head beneath her mother's arm and there was another flash of lightning.

They saw a horseman come in through the gate and a man in a cape came running across the courtyard. It was the forester coming from "Her Ladyship's wood" and not daring to ride any further on account of the horse.

The thunder drowned his voice, and it was so dark that it was scarcely possible to see his face as he said:

"There's something on fire to the west of Brædstrup, there were some huge flames..."

"Was it at Christen Nielsen's?" said His Lordship. And they muttered some half inaudible words as to whether he was insured.

"It is not very nice," said Miss Adlerberg to the student; she had folded her hands around her gardening hat.

Schrøder let go of young Karl von Eichbaum and suddenly ran across to Mrs von Eichbaum's door. Through the keyhole she could see her sitting motionless and pale in front of her candles.

Miss With had not let go of Falkenstjerne's shoulder, and he could feel her hand ice cold beside his cheek. When the lightning came he could see her face, as pale as a sheet, while her eyes looked as though they were green.

"Miss With, Miss With," he said.

There came a new flash of lightning and a new crash of thunder as though some huge iron body was being flung against the ground at their feet:

"I suppose that was the end of another oak tree," said the forester, who was thinking about his forests all the time he sat there.

No one spoke and no one would have been able to hear. When the thunder died away for a moment, they could hear the cattle lowing out in the field and the sheep bleating pitifully.

"It's over at Christen Nielsen's," said Brandt. They caught a brief glimpse of the light from the fire, behind the cattle sheds, in the darkness.

"Keep an eye on the home farm," His Lordship said to Brandt.

There was a flash of lightning like a shining, white gimlet before their eyes, and the bailiff ran and flung out both his arms like one blinded and then ran again as the report came, a clap of thunder like a thousand things being smashed and crushed; Ida, tearing herself away from her mother, rushed frantically across to her father, shrilly screaming:

"Daddy, daddy," and she hid herself up against his legs.

Falkenstjerne had taken Miss With's hands: "Miss Emmy," he said, using her Christian name for the first time.

"Miss Emmy."

"Yes, yes," she whispered, not knowing what she was saying, while he maintained his hold on her hands.

All was quite still for a moment, and the only sound was that of the heavy rain falling.

Then, putting her hand to her forehead, in a gentle, almost deferential voice, Miss Rosenfeld said to Feddersen, to whom she otherwise hardly ever spoke:

"It was so lovely."

They all sat in silence as though still waiting. But the flashes grew paler over the fields and the rumbles grew less. It was as though a refreshing cool air was coming up from the ground, and the rain died down.

Then, in the western sky, they saw the stars again.

Mrs Madsen sat telling Feddersen all about Madsen's wound and His Lordship and the forester went down the road to have a look at the fire at Christen's Nielsen's.

The rain was gentle and kind. They heard it falling on the roof like a fond murmur, and its drops filled the night like a radiant mist.

Then Miss Rosenfeld, who was sitting with her head in her hands, started to sing quietly.

Falkenstjerne still sat with Miss With's hands in his:

"Won't you join in?" said Miss Rosenfeld, turning her head towards them. And in low voices, almost humming, the girls sang:

> *Fly, o bird, fly o'er the lake's gentle wave*
> *Soon the black night will be here.*
> *Gone is the sun from hind forest and cave*
> *Day has now left this fair sphere.*
> *Fly you now home to the mate of your heart,*
> *And to your golden-beaked brood;*
> *Then when you come at the morning's bright start,*
> *You must tell all that is good.*

"Look," said Brandt. Ida had fallen asleep in his arms, with her head against his shoulder:

"Look at the child," he whispered, bending down towards Miss With. He looked so happy as they continued their singing, and the forester joined in, singing at the entrance in his quiet bass voice:

> *Fly, o bird, fly o'er the lake's gentle waters...*

The song came to an end.

Out in the night the rain had ceased and they all went down the steps – Falkenstjerne and Miss With walking side by side – and stood breathing out in the cool air.

Then Schrøder came along with a huge tray. They really needed something, she said, after that fright.

They walked up and down the paths for a time. Then there came the sound of laughs and screams from down on the road. It was His Lordship who – old rascal that he was – had snatched a kiss from

Miss Adlerberg.

Shortly after this, the party broke up.

Brandt was still carrying Ida. He tiptoed on his long legs so as not to wake the child.

After they all retired, Miss Rosenfeld came out of her door and went quietly upstairs. She opened a window in the gable and sat down by the windowsill with her hands around her knees.

There, she saw the dawn of a new day.

∞∞∞

It was the nineteenth of August, and the whole of Ludvigsbakke was on the go. It was His Lordship's birthday tomorrow, and he would be seventy years old.

Schrøder was making pastries and baking. There was steam all around her. She had locked the kitchen door with a huge, rusty old key.

"We can't have anyone meddling in here," she said.

The key was in the pocket of the print dress and was flapping around her legs.

The girls were making festoons in a corner in the grove and running past the bailiff's Mound with clothes baskets full of greenery. Mrs Brandt sat there holding Ida rather like a sentry standing at ease until Miss Rosenfeld went up the slope to the Mound and lifted Ida over the fence:

"*We*'ll look after *her*, Mrs Brandt," she said.

Down in the grove, they were laughing and chatting so they could be heard far away as they fixed oak leaves and asters to the clothes-lines.

Miss Adlerberg was wearing gloves for the work:

"For this dreadful stuff cuts into your fingers," she said, taking off her gloves about once every ten minutes to show Feddersen the red marks.

Ida went around bending down and picking up all the asters that had been dropped and putting them in Miss Rosenfeld's lap.

"Thank you, dear," said Miss Rosenfeld.

The pharmacist's wife, overflowing with flounces and sitting beside Miss Adlerberg, said:

"Yes, it is dreadful on the hands. Franz (that was the pharmacist) will simply not allow me to do anything...because of my hands."

"A little glycerine will put it right," said Miss Rosenfeld.

"Thank you dear."

It was Ida who was continuing to collect flowers with stems that were far too short.

Brandt arrived; he was going back and forth with all ten fingers as black as coal from the gunpowder he was using to make rockets and Bengal lights down in the office.

"Yes," he said. "They were really good last year. They all went off except one...But when His Excellency received his new title, Eriksen, my managing clerk, had made a Catherine-wheel...that was rather nice."

Brandt stopped in front of Miss Rosenfeld.

"Ah, you have the child," he said with a smile, stroking Ida's head with his black fingers.

"You ought to look after that cough, Brandt," said Miss Rosenfeld.

Brandt had had a nasty cough recently.

"Ugh," – the maids puffed and shook their skirts.

"How many yards have we got now?"

And one of them swung the festoon like a skipping rope while the other started to sing:

> *In the woods when gunfire sounds*
> *And when the hunter's horn is heard*
> *And when there's barking from the hounds,*
> *Where birds do lie and die unheard*
> *And other beasts with wounds profound*
> *Lie bleeding on the ground.*

The forester's family had arrived up on the Mound, where Mrs Brandt was ensconced.

Mrs Lund had come up here: she wanted to present a bunch of flowers.

"And my roses," she said. "Heaven knows how it comes about... but they seemed to be doing so well, and they are producing no more than buds...And those in the churchyard, there are so many of them and they look splendid, but I didn't really think I could use them on an occasion such as this."

So Mrs Lund was welcome to such as Mrs Brandt had, but that was not very many.

"Oh well," said Mrs Lund in some relief. "His Lordship will look at the will more than the deed."

The forester clicked his heels and said:

"Aye, I'm a sober man, mother, but on the twentieth I'm going to get drunk."

"All right, Lund," said his wife, "provided you don't make a speech."

Mrs Madsen arrived down in the gooseberry walk. She did not know what to turn to: Madsen's top hat needed to be ironed, and she simply didn't have an iron to use."

"That's a bit of a problem then," said the forester: "Madsen, the representative of the armed forces."

The veterans were to arrive at twelve o'clock.

The girls came from the grove in a single big group, and the pharmacist's wife, holding a white parasol, waved to those assembled on the Mound. Ida shook hands with everyone before going up.

Mrs Madsen wanted just to walk around down in the meadows adjoining the grove, and the forester and his family accompanied her. They went over the stile and looked at the wreaths and garlands lying on the ground.

"It is really beautiful, it is really beautiful," said Mrs Lund, who was sitting on a bench – she always wanted to sit down.

But Madsen, who was going round estimating every single piece, said:

"There were about a hundred and thirty yards at Her Late Ladyship's funeral..."

At eleven o'clock, His Lordship went around with a candle to close all the doors. This was the family custom. He was wearing a skull cap – during the day he wore a ginger wig very much like that worn by the farm manager – and tested every lock.

The girls, who had hidden in Miss Adlerberg's sitting room, sat giggling in the semi-darkness as he went past.

Then Falkenstjerne knocked on the window from out in the garden, and they opened it for him.

"We've saved the vine," he whispered.

Laughing quietly, the girls jumped out one by one, holding on to their skirts.

"And the lamps?" one of them whispered.

They all tiptoed silently along the house until they suddenly flew like the wind across the lawn, for the dogs started to bark.

"That's Hektor," whispered Miss Adlerberg, grabbing Feddersen by the arm.

"Ssshhh".

They reached the trees. Miss Rosenfeld went slowly behind all the others.

Five lamps were lit beneath the beeches. They sat down at the table and started to make festoons. Miss Falkenberg sat on the stile looking out into the night that lay over the meadows like a great dark cover.

"Emmy," called someone quite quietly. It was Falkenberg.

"Yes."

And the two of them, standing close to each other, looked out into the darkness.

When morning came, Falkenstjerne and the gardener hung the festoons on the front of the house; they were both whistling. Old Brandt, who had raised the flag, was busy with the pennants. But he was off colour and went around coughing.

He stood for a time looking down towards Brædstrup, where the flags were being raised in front of the farms; the morning breeze was fresh as it caught the red banners.

"It's so beautiful," he said. "And then the stacks – aye, this is a lovely place."

He made off towards the bailiff's wing; he wanted to have something warm. But when he arrived there, he said:

"I think I'll lie down a bit." He was shivering and could scarcely stand on his legs.

"Yes, Brandt," said his wife, who was bathing Ida in a zinc bath. "But you *must* get up to present the candlesticks."

"Yes, Mariane," said Brandt, half asleep.

The carriages were already starting to drive in through the entrance, and Sofie ran back and forth to announce who they were. Mrs Brandt was in her underclothes, doing her hair, and the whole bedroom was awash with her white petticoats. She got her skirt on and her bodice buttoned while Brandt lay half asleep in bed, waking up and then dozing off again.

They could hear more and more carriages arriving and large numbers of footsteps on the gravel path.

"Here comes the band from Horsens," shouted Sofie, running out to the fence in her stocking feet.

"And Brandt does nothing but lie there," said Mrs Brandt as she put on her lace sleeves and best bonnet in the garden room.

The band sounded loud and high spirited, and there was the sound of many voices.

"Well, Brandt, here come the veterans," said Mrs Brandt; she had his clothes over her arm and spoke all the time as though to shake him out of his lethargy.

"Where's the child?" was all Brandt said.

Ida, who had been crying because her curlers were too tight, came in wearing a white dress.

"Now not too close to the bed," said Mrs Brandt as she smoothed Ida's skirt. But her father took hold of the tip of her belt and held it in his hands.

"Aye, I suppose I ought to get up," he said, smiling at her all the time – but oh such a weak smile.

They continued to hear steps and instruments and a voice giving orders: that was Madsen. Then came the band again. It seemed to Brandt that they were so strangely far away.

"Here comes His Lordship," shouted Sofie; she opened the door wide with her cotton apron in her hand, for it had come undone in her fright.

"Now we've got the County Council, Brandt," said his wife, who had gone on walking to and fro more and more ponderously. She put the clothes down on a chair.

"Yes, Mariane," said Brandt, sitting up in bed. But Mrs Brandt had run out to receive the guests: this was where they were to congregate.

"Ida, Ida," she shouted.

Ida, who was still standing a little way from the bed, said as though to wake him up:

"Daddy, you must get up now."

"Yes, dear. I'm coming."

He heard His Lordship's voice in the garden room, and he got up to sit on the edge of the bed. He had such a pain in his side.

Then the door opened. It was the forester in full dress.

"What the devil, Brandt," he said; but he suddenly came to a halt. "What's wrong? You look awful."

"No," said Brandt. "I'm not well."

"I can see that all right. And your wife said it was only the usual thing."

Brandt sat there for a moment.

"No," he said and his head sank on his chest. "I can't go over there."

The forester went out and fetched the doctor, who came in wearing tails and adorned with his decorations. "What's wrong, old friend. Are you going to stay in bed on this happy day?" he said. But he suddenly became serious when he saw Brandt. "Lift him up," he said to the forester and hurried to listen to Brandt's chest and back.

The music had stopped outside, and Madsen's voice could be heard through the noise.

"Now Madsen's there with the flag," said Brandt with a smile.

The doctor continued to listen to Brandt's back while the forester stood at the foot of the bed, leaning forward as though he, too, wanted to listen. "I need someone to go to Brædstrup," was all the doctor said, and he went out.

He sat down to write a prescription in the sitting room, surrounded by all the guests, while Mrs Brandt stood beside him and the members of the County Council were all talking in loud voices about the day and about the speakers and the festivities.

"If Brandt has anything wrong with him it is always bad," said Mrs Brandt.

The doctor made no reply; from the bed, where he seemed to have settled down a little after seeing the doctor, Brandt said:

"And how are things going to be arranged this evening?" He was thinking about the fireworks.

They heard the members of the County Council go out through the garden. They had suddenly fallen quite silent.

"There's no need for anyone to bother about me," said Brandt. "I'm feeling better now."

"All right," said the forester.

He went into the sitting room, where his wife still sat on a chair.

"Let's go then," he said quietly. "We mustn't frighten His Lordship."

They went out together with the doctor, and their footsteps could be heard dying away in the corridor until all was quite quiet. Mrs Brandt went around tidying up in the sick man's room, dressed in black, her full silk dress rustling.

"But one must never give up," she said, tidying his pillows.

She stood by the bed for a moment and then in the same voice said:

"Now the pharmacist is going to present the candlesticks."

The sick man only shook his head – perhaps it was a fly – and said:

"Aren't you going to take the flowers over...?"

"We'll have to, of course," said his wife.

But out in the sitting room Ida started to cry because her father was not going to come.

"Come, come," said Mrs Brandt, wiping her face; but the child continued to cry a little as they went through the garden.

Then it fell completely silent while Sofie sat knitting behind the door, and all that was to be heard was the buzzing of flies and the ticking of the grandfather clock, which suddenly sounded tough and hard.

The sick man lay there, moving about in the bed. Having a temperature made one so restless.

Now he could hear His Lordship's voice – Sofie ran in stocking feet across to the fence – and he raised his head a little as though he was listening. Now he was welcoming His Excellency.

But Brandt could not hear anything, and there were so many images in his mind, coming and going, from all his days and from the time when he came here and Her Ladyship was still alive and from the time when Ida was a baby.

How fragile she was then and red and tiny...And she had known him before she knew her mother.

Brandt suddenly took hold of the rope hanging there for the purpose and pulled himself up; now they were shouting three cheers for His Lordship.

Then he fell back and dozed a little.

When he opened his eyes, Miss Rosenfeld was sitting by his bed with Ida on her lap. Ida was scared and held her tight.

"We just wanted to come across and see how you are, Mr Brandt," said Miss Rosenfeld.

"Aye, Miss Rosenfeld," he said, not taking his eyes off Ida, "this is where I am."

"Yes."

The sick man continued to smile and moved his burning hands over to where Ida sat.

"But won't she be creasing her dress?" he said, shutting his eyes.

They heard the clock strike, slowly, as though not in a hurry, and Miss Rosenfeld gently took Ida's hand out of that of the sick man.

They tiptoed out, Ida holding on to Miss Rosenfeld's dress, and they sat down on the sofa. There was nothing to be heard. Only the solid ticking of the clock.

"Miss Rosenfeld," whispered Ida, "Is father going to die?"

"Oh dear, child, my dear child," said Miss Rosenfeld. She stroked Ida's hair; the child had started to weep, without a sound.

They heard footsteps on the garden path. It was Mrs Brandt, who entered in front of His Lordship. He was wearing the decorations betokening his knighthood and his cheeks were flushed.

"What's this I hear?" he said in a rather loud voice. "Have we someone ill here?" And Mrs Brandt, who preceded him to the sickbed, said as though to wake her husband (there seemed to be a trace of anger in her voice throughout that day):

"Brandt, it's His Lordship."

Miss Rosenfeld heard His Lordship say, in a festive tone:

"My dear Brandt..." But then he suddenly lowered his voice; he sat down on a chair, moved a little way away from the bed, vaguely troubled as all old people are when confronted with illness:

"But what on earth is wrong? What on earth is wrong?"

"Well...I suppose the pharmacist has presented the candlesticks," said Brandt, attempting to take hold of his hand.

Ida had tiptoed gently out. Miss Rosenfeld was out among the redcurrant bushes and called softly to her, but there was no reply. Then she found her sitting on a wooden bench just outside the window, huddled up and quiet like a little dog. And Miss Rosenfeld sat down beside her, crouching in almost the same way.

They heard His Lordship return through the garden and Mrs Brandt go into the sickroom. Now she sat down at the foot of the bed, holding her broad cloak out in front of her as though in an attempt to block the way.

There came the sound of gentle footsteps in the living room, and Mrs Brandt rose. It was Mrs Lund, who came on tiptoe, hesitating at every step.

She stopped again and put her hands on Mrs Brandt's hips.

"Lund and I think it's so dreadful," she said.

And when Mrs Brandt said nothing, she went on: "Couldn't we help with something?"

"No, thank you," said Mrs Brandt, who was still thinking of Miss Rosenfeld as she had sat over in the sofa before. "I think we can manage it *ourselves*."

Mrs Lund left in a curiously hasty manner and went along the garden path to find her husband the forester waiting for her.

"Did you see him?" he asked.

"No," was all she said; it was as though she was shedding silent tears. And (the two of them always understanding each other without uttering a word), Lund said:

"Yes, she's as stiff-necked as they come." He felt something like a desire to hit something with his clenched fists.

Mrs Lund had her handkerchief out.

"Oh, Lund," she said. "I suppose that's just the way she is."

Mrs Brandt remained in the sitting room. She then closed all the windows firmly and went inside again – on guard.

Evening had fallen and it was dark in the sickroom, where a small lamp burned and the doctor came and went; there was a striking red glow on the curtains.

"It's so bright," said the sick man as he turned his head.

"It's the torches," said the doctor.

"Aye, it's lovely," said Brandt.

The forester was sitting outside on a bench. He had got himself drunk on the twentieth of August.

"How's it going?" he said.

"Not very well," said the doctor.

When they reached the avenue, they met Miss Adlerberg with Mr Feddersen from the Ministry of Foreign Affairs.

"We are taking a walk," said Miss Adlerberg – it was rather dark in this avenue – "How is he?"

The doctor shrugged his shoulders.

"But it's very unfortunate," said Feddersen, "for His Excellency. In some way or other you can sense it everywhere in the house."

It was quiet in the sickroom, and the only sound to be heard was that of Mrs Brandt's knitting needles, as regular as the ticking of the clock, and occasionally the music from over where they were dancing.

Then Brandt called out.

"Mariane," he said, taking her hand:

"It's a pity for you..."

But it was as though his wife's hand with her countless rings had weighed his down, and he let go of it as he closed his eyes.

"Sickness will take its course," said Mrs Brandt as she tidied the sheet; Brandt still lay there clutching it with his thin fingers.

"I'd like to speak to the lieutenant," he said.

"Yes, all right," said his wife, feeling down his legs, which were cold up above the knees. She stood there for a long time, motionlessly looking at the old man whose body was seen to be so thin beneath the blankets, and then she sat down again.

So now she was going to be left on her own.

...The lieutenant was running around down on the lawn; he was busy with the rockets. They were to be set off now after they had finished dancing. The music came to an end and Falkenstjerne shouted up to the bailiff, who was standing at a window: the first rocket went off like a thin red line that divided into two...

The guests stood at the open windows as the rockets whistled and made slender tracks up in the air, and the gentlemen from Horsens, standing with their hands in their trouser pockets and smoking big cigars, exclaimed in admiration and a dumpy little lady who had tied a handkerchief around her bare neck to protect her from draught, said:

"Good heavens, fancy stopping dancing just for *that*!"

At the upstairs window, Miss Rosenfeld had lifted Ida up in her arms. Ida stayed with her throughout the day, saying nothing, just following her, with cold hands, like a weak little shadow:

"Ooh, just look," she said.

Another rocket went up as Feddersen came past with Miss Adlerberg.

"They are not going very high," he said.

And Miss Adlerberg, laughing as she walked, with her train over her arms, said:

"They are a country product."

Miss Rosenfeld turned round quickly with Ida, and she heard His Lordship say from over by the window:

"It is delightful, really delightful..." and, looking up in the air, he added:

"And he *was* such an excellent man."

Miss Rosenfeld was walking with Ida across the open space when she suddenly felt tears on her hand.

"Why are you crying?" she asked.

The child made no reply.

The forester was up in the ballroom, standing in the corner by the bottom window: the rockets were still being let off in the night, for there were many of them, though they were only small.

"Oh dear, love," he said. "How sad it all is."

Quite quietly, Miss Rosenfeld took Ida into the sick man's room, where Mrs Brandt sat enthroned in the same place.

"We just wanted to say good night," she whispered.

And while Mrs Brandt got up, Ida bent down over her father (her eyes had the same expression as those of a sick child). Brandt opened his eyes.

"Is it Ida?" he said.

"Did she see the fireworks?"

 oooooo

Ida slept in Miss Rosenfeld's bed that night.

Miss Rosenfeld sat at her window. The guests had gone, and the night was dark. Then a carriage drove rapidly out of the bailiff's gateway down over the road, through the darkness, like a shadow...

All the dogs barked furiously.

When they came down in the morning, His Lordship went across to the piano and quietly closed it and took away the key.

Old Brandt was dead.

All the guests dispersed, far into the woods and the garden. Miss Rosenfeld sat alone with Ida on her lap.

Over in the bailiff's house, Mrs Brandt went around and took a large number of sheets out of her deep cupboards.

∞∞∞

Mrs Brandt was in her sitting room, pitch black and mighty, waiting for the carriage that was to bring Mrs Reck, the wife of the newly appointed bailiff, who was to inspect her house. The embroidered rugs were out on all the floors, and there was a garland of dried flowers around Brandt's portrait. Ida was over at Schrøders.

Then Sofie opened the door out to the corridor:

"There she is," she said. It sounded like a command to stand to attention, and she remained standing, tall and in black, behind her mistress, who opened the outer door.

"Yes, I'm Mrs Reck," said a confused lady, who was small and slender and held the train of her dress in her hand.

"I'm pleased to meet you," replied Mrs Brandt, slowly holding out her hand. She had retained the handshake of a peasant girl, merely touching the other's hand. And now her hand was icy cold.

"Help Mrs Reck," she said to Sofie.

And Sofie took Mrs Reck's cape with her bony hands.

They went into the rooms.

"Oh, aren't they big!" Mrs Reck burst out. She blushed immediately. She had stood still for a moment, quite frightened in face of the long floors of a rural residence.

"Yes, the house is quite roomy," said Mrs Brandt, offering Mrs Reck a seat opposite her. Mrs Reck was not herself aware that she twice dabbed her forehead with her handkerchief, while Mrs Brandt said something about the cold weather and about the drive there.

"Yes," said Mrs Reck, "it was rather cold."

She thought she had said something about Mr Brandt and that it would certainly not be easy for Reck (she was quite flustered, and somewhere in her head she was thinking about the floors).

"No, it certainly won't be easy," she said once more and heard Mrs Brandt say:

"Of course, Brandt and I were both born and brought up near here."

Mrs Reck hesitated a moment.

"Of course," she said then. "Reck and I are both townsfolk."

Mrs Brandt had undoubtedly *seen* that, but all she said as she got up was:

"Can I offer you some refreshment?"

And they went into the dining room.

Mrs Reck thought she had never seen so much food, and she ate and ate as though she dared not do otherwise, while Mrs Brandt offered her more and more without taking anything herself, like someone barricaded behind her own food.

She spoke of the big debt they had incurred on alterations. "We have had to cope with it," she said, continuing to offer refreshments in the same cold, dry voice and with her eyes never moving from Mrs Reck, as though she would have liked to choke her guest with the food.

"Yes," said Mrs Reck, "we know a lot has been done here."

Mrs Brandt replied:

"There were stone floors when we came."

Mrs Reck thought that there could well still be stone floors as far as she was concerned.

After the meal, they went around the house, Mrs Brandt leading, opening, closing, showing everything from downstairs room to downstairs room, bedroom to bedroom.

Mrs Reck, who was cold in her thin town dress, said:

"Thank you, I've seen it now...but thank you, I really have seen it now, Mrs Brandt."

But Mrs Brandt went on, showing everything: cellar, milk cellar, potato cellar, lofts, the whole house, refusing to let go of Mrs Reck – the entire perfect house that she had built up and which she, the widow, was now to leave.

She talked about the beds, their own beds, the servants' beds, the beds for visitors. Mrs Reck said:

"Yes, it means buying a lot."

"Here are the cupboards," said Mrs Brandt when they came down into the corridor.

She opened her cupboards, showing the linen, the pillows, the pillowcases, the curtains, making a show of her peasant affluence, speaking a little louder, her mouth twitching a little in a sudden attack of widow-like playful malice.

Mrs Reck was thinking to herself:

"No, she shall never cross my threshold," and said:

"Well, Mrs Brandt, if only I were half as able."

"Well, one has to look after one's house," said Mrs Brandt, shutting her cupboards and putting on some wooden-soled shoes: they were to go and see the garden. When they arrived there, they encountered Ida along with Schrøder, who wanted to see the new mistress.

"I'm the housekeeper," she said, shaking hands with Mrs Reck with a red hand. Mrs Reck felt something akin to relief and, bending down over Ida, who was with her mother, she said in a kind voice:

"So this must be your granddaughter, Mrs. Brandt."

"My daughter," replied Mrs Brandt, and they all flushed suddenly, while Mrs. Reck made matters worse by quickly saying to Ida:

"What a lovely garden you've had here."

"Yes," said Ida, withdrawing the hand that Mrs Reck was holding.

No one said any more before they were back in the corridor, where they found the pharmacist's wife, who had arrived in the pony chaise and was dressed in a sealskin coat. To the accompaniment of a torrent of words, she began wildly to embrace Mrs Reck without vouchsafing the others a glance:

"Oh, my dear Henriette (they had been at school together), dearest Henriette, I am so delighted, my dear, to have someone here I know (they had hardly seen each other for twelve to fifteen years), I really do need that.

"Yes, dear Mrs Brandt, I'll just take my coat off. Dearest Henriette, we have dozens of things to talk about."

She led the way into the sitting room, holding Mrs Reck by the waist, while continuing to talk about the house and about how delighted she was and about what would have to be bought.

"You know, my dear, it *can* be made so lovely here...Well, Mrs Brandt, you know how often I have said that I could not exist even for an hour in these rooms, with all the furniture stuck up against the walls as it is now."

"We have always made modest demands, Mrs Mogensen," said Mrs Brandt, offering her a seat. Ida and Schrøder stayed in a corner.

Mrs Mogensen went on: "There are really only three rooms here. I suppose your piano is a Hornung, Henriette? Yours is German, of course, Mrs Brandt...But then no one has played it very much."

She stood in the doorway between the two main rooms, talking without cease, pointing and advising, deciding where to put furniture, getting rid of the old things, giving Mrs Brandt such benevolent looks, as benevolent as though she were striking her:

"*That* is where you can put *that*, and *that* can go *there*. Dear Henriette...it can be quite delightful in here – "

Mrs Brandt offered them coffee in the silver pot that had been presented to Brandt to mark 25 years of service.

Mrs Reck, too, became quite enthusiastic and spoke about her furniture and curtains and the doors, while Mrs Mogensen moved the silver coffee pot to make a plan of the Recks' rooms on Mrs Brandt's tablecloth.

She asked for a tape measure. "Because you must have the measurements," she said, and Ida brought the tape measure while Mrs Reck measured up, standing on a chair, walking to and fro across the floors, cheerfully asking Mrs Brandt's advice.

"Don't you think so, dear Mrs Brandt, don't you think so, dear Mrs Brandt," she said repeatedly as she hung invisible curtains, arranged alien furniture and took the entire house to pieces bit by bit. Mrs Brandt continued to make brief replies and Schrøder stood panting over her cup: she felt the cakes turning into great lumps in her mouth.

"Yes, you know, I think it can be made quite nice here," Mrs

Reck concluded, jumping down from a chair.

Shortly afterwards, Mrs Mogensen took Mrs Reck home with her to the pharmacy in her pony chaise.

While still standing in the doorway – Mrs Reck was in the chaise – she said goodbye.

"Yes, dear Mrs Brandt," she said, gently placing her hands on hers, "it must be rather difficult..."

She stood there for a moment looking straight into Mrs Brandt's face and said once more as she touched her arm:

"Really difficult."

And then the carriage was gone.

Schrøder hurried to get away: she was not keen on being there alone.

"Well," she said: "That was that. Now the pharmacist has finally got the measurements of the bailiff's house."

Schrøder went.

Mrs Brandt washed the china herself, collecting it piece by piece in large stacks. But then, all at once, she sat down on the chair near the sideboard. Mrs Brandt wept.

Ida just stood in front of her; she had never seen her mother really weep like this.

Then she gently touched her knee. And Mrs Brandt picked the child up while still weeping.

But that afternoon she went down past the pharmacy, veiled and in mourning, carrying a wreath. She was on her way to the churchyard...there were the sounds of music in the pharmacy.

∞∞∞

It was starting to grow dark, but Schrøder continued to walk about in the garden, bending down over the remaining snow and searching; there were always snowdrops around here – the first ones.

But they were so frail and difficult to find.

She had found ten or twelve, delicate and cold. She would give them to Mrs Brandt before she left.

She went inside into the stripped, bare rooms. Ida was toddling around, wrapped in a shawl and had nowhere to lay her head. It was dark and there was straw on the floors.

"Is it you, dear?" said Schrøder, attempting to adopt a happy tone.

"Yes," said Ida.

"Good Lord, but it's cold," said Schrøder, feeling her hands.

"Mother's in there," said Ida.

"In there" was the bedroom. Now they had packed and tidied up for a week, room by room, as though they were losing a bit of the house with each passing day. There was a candle in a jar on the bare window ledge in the bedroom. Otherwise there was only the bed and the servants' old wardrobe. Christen Nielsen's wife was sitting on the edge of the bed, and Mrs Brandt was going around clad in a black shawl.

Christen Nielsen came and spoke slowly in a low voice with his hands on his stomach: "Well, there you are, the butter and the hams and that's that."

Mrs Brandt went around packing the last things as he spoke: now she had surely seen to everything and made all the necessary arrangements...For when all was said and done, it was cheapest for her to buy from the estate when she *had* to buy things. They owed her that at least.

"Aye, aye," said Christen Nielsen's wife.

"I suppose that's it," and she got up from the bed.

"Yes, I suppose so," said Schrøder, putting the snowdrops on the edge of the bed. Ida took them; her mother had put gloves on her, and she held them tight while the other three stood there quietly, looking at the candle in the jar.

They heard the carriage turn up at the door, and Sofie came in, wrapped up so that only her nose was to be seen. She took the candle, and they all went in through the rooms. Mrs Brandt had dropped her veil over her face. But Ida went along holding the twelve snowdrops in her gloves.

Lars was out in the yard with the horses. They were the old ones. But the carriage was His Lordship's phaeton, for Brandt's barouche had been "sold privately".

Mrs Brandt gave orders, behind her black veil.

"I won't be a moment," said Schrøder, running over towards the main building.

There was a host of sacks and jars that had to stand upright, and Mrs Brandt continued to give orders from behind her black veil. The steward came out, and they all helped, though no one spoke except Mrs Brandt, and Ida was helped up into the carriage, followed by her mother.

Schrøder came running back. She had a parcel, she said, something for Ida...Schrøder's voice broke a little. It was the house that Miss Rosenfeld had drawn during the summer.

"And Ida was to have it...to remember it all by," she said, weeping as she handed it up into the carriage.

Then Sofie was up there, and Lars said slowly:

"Have you anything else, madam?"

There was nothing else. Ida sat there, looking strangely small alongside her mother, and Schrøder continued to weep.

And then they left.

The other three stayed on the steps and watched them go; and now the carriage disappeared.

Without saying anything, Schrøder took the candle that was flickering in the corridor window and held it up in the doorway, lighting up the bare rooms. Then Lars lit a lamp, and Schrøder extinguished the candle between two fingers.

"It's very painful after all," said Lars.

They went out and locked the door to the corridor. Then they left.

"It's not easy when the breadwinner dies," said Christen Nielsen's wife.

And then they went off each in their own direction.

∞∞∞

But then the years she spent as a child in the town came back to her, and her confirmation and the first year as a young adult, that bright year, and then the sickness and the long days...

∞∞∞∞

Half awake, Ida could hear Sofie fiddling by the chimney and her mother's difficult breathing beside her – it was as though the sounds of that breathing were to fill the entire house – and almost in her sleep and quite mechanically she put her bare feet out on the knitted rug.

She must get up now. Hans Christensen was there with the milk.

She did not light a lamp, but tiptoed gently around in the dark to dress. She just looked at her mother sitting up in the bed like a broad shadow shutting out the dawn light behind the curtains.

Down in the kitchen, Hans Christensen had already arrived – he was so wrapped in scarves that only his eyes and the tips of his ears could be seen – and she gave him the milk money that lay counted out on the shelf.

"Yes, it's cold this morning," he said (his breath emerged from his scarves like a long cloud):

"The pond's frozen solid now out by our house..."

He took a couple of steps in his clogs to make it sound as though he was going, while Ida managed to pass him the coffee cup and Sofie moved some things over by the chimney in case madam should wake up and hear that they were giving Hans Christensen coffee.

"Goodbye," said Hans Christensen when he had finished, and he lifted the latch ever so gently.

Ida had taken the frozen butter over to the fire to soften it: there was less of it now. Just as she thought, for she had heard stocking feet in the loft yesterday evening.

She went into the sitting room and started to take the covers from the chairs and to do the dusting while quietly moving the little low-legged lamp from one piece of furniture to the other. This was really her best time – it was almost as though she were stealing it – these mornings while her mother was asleep and she could potter about, quite quietly, engrossed in her own thoughts.

Oh, there was plenty to think about...there was always the question of money and the problem always had to be hidden...Now Hans Ole's widow was dead, too. So they probably would no longer be provided with meat; there soon would not be any of the old folks left in Ludvigsbakke. And how could you expect the young folk to remember them...

Now Christian from the mill was out of work again – so they would use almost twice as much now – but it was reasonable enough that Sofie should stick with him when she was so fond of him, poor thing.

Ida stopped in front of the mirror and stretched out to polish it; she had a distinctly virginal way of bending her head.

Then there was to be the christening at Olivia's as well, as soon as the weather was a little milder...She would have to give them a spoon and fork if she was going to be the child's godmother.

She stopped in front of the mirror and smiled.

"Oh, the little chap had such a lot of hair, and his eyes were just like Jørgensen's."

Ida continued to smile; she always thought of so many happy things when thinking of the brickworks and Olivia.

She started to water the flowers and moved them from the floor up on to the window ledge. Her mother's myrtle was very heavy, and its stem was almost like that of a tree. It looked so healthy as it stood there. And Ida plucked every dead leaf off it. She did not know why, but she thought that myrtle was like a reminder of her father.

"Ida, Ida."

Mrs Brandt was awake, and Ida put the plant down.

"Yes, mother."

"I'm lying here *awake*," said Mrs Brandt.

Out in the kitchen, Sofie poured some warm water into two dishes.

"I suppose you do *intend* to get me up," said Mrs Brandt.

"Yes, mother."

Ida started to turn her attention to her mother, tending her and talking to her, tying and untying and telling her the news as she dressed her: they could expect the Lunds today – for they were coming from the wedding – and the pond was frozen solid now according to Hans Christensen.

Ida continued to recite the news; Mrs Brandt simply looked down at her nervous hands:

"You've got your father's fingers," she said: "they are all thumbs."

When her hair was set – Mrs Brandt still had a full head of hair – all the food in the house was brought up so that she could inspect it, in bed. Sofie went there, slow and sullen and brought it in, dish after dish, while Mrs Brandt sat up in bed, with her thoroughly padded hair, carefully inspecting the leavings.

She said nothing, but merely sat silently calculating – Ida looked like a customs officer during an inspection of the cashbox – while Sofie stood by the bed, straight as a pole. Mrs Brandt watched every dish that Sofie took out again as though she wanted to follow its way through the door when it was closed.

"And then we must do the joint, mother, for the Lunds..."

"If they come," said Mrs Brandt.

Ida had again started to attend to her: "But you know they always come when they are in town," she said.

"Yes," said Mrs Brandt. "It's cheaper than eating at the inn."

She had got out of bed and wanted to go into the sitting room. Ida and Sofie had to support her, one under each arm, (Mrs Brandt was never so heavy as when she had to be moved), and she managed to reach the chair by the window. *There* all her gold trinkets lay waiting for her on the table. Ida hung the watch chain around her neck.

"The watch," said Mrs Brandt.

"Here, mother."

She wanted to have Ida's watch in front of her on a frame, beside her purse. They finally had her settled down. The door to the kitchen was left slightly ajar so that she could "listen".

Her mother could not stand a warm room, so Ida was wearing a shawl as she bent over the three new sets of sheets, for the linen was taken care of as it used to be in the "old bailiff's wing".

"Your threads are always too long," said Mrs Brandt.

Ida pulled at the thread.

"Mrs Muus is waving," said her mother.

Ida looked out and flushed as she nodded. Mrs Muus always took a quick and deliberate path close to Mrs Brandt's window and only waved to Ida.

Mrs Muus was the judge's wife, and Mrs Brandt continued to follow her in the mirror and watch her fur coat bouncing against her energetic little backside.

Ida also looked out and smiled. Mrs Muus never reached the corner. She stopped in front of every other house as she went by, swinging her hips and stamping and showing all her friends' windows that she was wearing fur boots.

"Have the Muus's got a housekeeper?" said Mrs Brandt, continuing to watch her.

"I don't know, mother."

"I thought she would be going to the Jørgensens," said Mrs Brandt. "She's a Copenhagener."

And as though in defence of the judge's wife, Ida said:

"But of course, they haven't any children, mother."

Mrs Brandt merely shut her eyes, said nothing and nodded. Sørensen, the local treasurer had appeared at the window of the house opposite and was nodding. Mr Sørensen was going downhill, very much downhill; he could hardly manage to open the newspaper when he wanted to read it.

Mrs Brandt continued to look across at Mr Sørensen. She had the same look in her eyes as when she examined Ida's hands.

Then she turned her head.

"Do they use coke in the brickworks?" she said.

"Coke and coal."

"Hm," said Mrs Brandt. "No, wood is not sufficient in those furnaces, I suppose."

Ida made no reply, and Mrs Brandt said:

"But it's a good thing there is plenty of it."

Sofie was making the beds in the bedroom. She straightened all the duvets as though she wanted to beat them. She was always so energetic with everything when Christian from the mill was out of work.

"It's eleven o'clock," said Mrs Brandt.

Ida knew that; it was time for coffee.

There was the sound of a loud voice from the kitchen. It was Miss Thøgersen, the "housekeeper" to their neighbour, the coppersmith, who was a member of a German "company of confirmed bachelors". She had brought the newspapers.

"Good heavens," she said. "It is bitterly cold today."

Her face was red and blue with cold, and her sleeves were rolled up to her elbows.

"Yes, yes," she said. "I stand in the midst of den Wäsche, and no help do I have."

She emerged in the doorway, completely filling it; the tartan ribbons on her bonnet were fixed with pins and were flapping around her ears like a pair of blinkers.

"Yes, yes," she said, following this with a torrent of words about the washing.

"And you know what a lot of woollens Thønnichsen uses."

Miss Thøgersen sat down on the chair by the door, her stomach resting on her distended lower regions.

"Ach, and now that Julie has got herself into trouble," she said.

Ida was in the kitchen, and Mrs Brandt said that Mrs Thomsen could not be so far gone.

"Ach nein, ach nein." Miss Thøgersen moved across to the basket chair; she moved and collapsed into ten chairs in the course of ten minutes. "But Maren has. She cannot control herself and yesterday they had to send for the midwife."

Maren was her "niece", Julie's maid-of-all work (the three fruits of the coppersmith's life with Miss Thøgersen were all referred to as belonging to a collateral branch of the family) and she loyally ran the entire household except for the ten days when the midwife was needed. That happened, almost to the day, around the first of April.

"Ach ja, ach ja..." Miss Thøgersen went on to give them a detailed account of the circumstances surrounding Maren and the need for the midwife. When she was sitting in the basket chair she always spoke quickly and in a half whisper, while Mrs Brandt remained seated, immovable, but with a singular expression on her face as though she was absorbing Maren's words through an ear trumpet.

"Ach ja, ach ja," Miss Thøgersen finished, placing her hands down on her legs.

"And otherwise she is such a decent person."

With her Schleswig accent, Miss Thøgersen accented her words differently and then she sat there in silence.

Mrs Brandt waited for a few moments. Then, from her raised position, she said:

"Who is it – this time?"

"Gott, Gott." If only she knew.

Miss Thøgersen shook her head.

"But she is so good-natured," she said in explanation.

Ida came in with the coffee; they both had a cup, Miss Thøgersen holding hers as though it were a basin.

From the platform came an admonition:

"Ida, your mouth ..."

Ida often had her mouth open a little when she was carrying something. She offered sugar and went back; she tended to withdraw to the far reaches of the room when Miss Thøgersen was there.

But Miss Thøgersen went on. She had so many concerns.

"And then there was this Gustav who wrote from America – and wanted to come home...But Thønnichsen was not having any of it."

Miss Thøgersen groaned (Gustav was one of the three).

"Ach nein," she said, putting the cup down. "Ach nein, it is not the same as when you have stood before the altar."

Miss Thøgersen had many concerns regarding her family.

The church bells began to ring, and Miss Thøgersen rose from her chair.

"Oh dear, oh dear...and I have to spread sand."

"It's Christensen, the painter," said Mrs Brandt.

"Ach, ja, so sad," said Miss Thøgersen, assuming a quite different voice. "And with four children."

"Will his widow stay in the house?" asked Mrs Brandt.

Miss Thøgersen did not know. "But there are people," she said, "who are kind to a widow."

There was something about the word "widow" that always touched Miss Thøgersen.

"Yes," said Mrs Brandt. "He was a freemason of course."

Miss Thøgersen had gradually moved into Ida's seat by the window, when she suddenly shouted out in horror:

"Gott, Gott, there comes the minister..."

Miss Thøgersen lived in constant fear of clergymen on account of her illegitimate social position.

The minister went past to the house of sorrow and Miss Thøgersen rushed away. Thønnichsen the coppersmith, spread box cuttings and sand on the road for all his more important customers.

"Have you forgotten the cups?" said Mrs Brandt, and Ida took them.

Mrs Brandt watched through the mirror to follow events in the house of mourning.

The blind was down in Mr Sørensen's window opposite to keep out the sun. It was always a source of irritation to him when funeral processions came down the street in the middle of the day.

When they came out of school, the boys shrieked as they ran along the pavement. Olivia's eldest boy was at the front with the remains of a snowball over his left ear.

"Do they let him run about with bare legs now?" said Mrs Brandt. "Oh well, I suppose that's supposed to be a good thing."

"Olivia says she thinks it toughens them, mother."

"Ach, there they are," shouted Miss Thøgersen from outside on the pavement. She scattered the last handful of sand over the gutter plank and then helped with the box cuttings.

Mrs Brandt had already seen the hearse in the mirror. It was the *expensive* one with curtains.

The boys continued to run past on the pavement and the procession approached.

"Oh, look at the children," said Ida.

Christoffersen's two eldest were walking, stiff and shocked, in their new clothes, behind the hearse and in front of the minister, who was holding his white handkerchief up to his nose. The minister could not stand the smell of iodine.

There was a squeal from the pavement as Miss Thøgersen struck out at a couple of boys.

"Fie," she said and went up her stone steps again. "You should be ashamed, getting in the way of that funeral procession..."

The cortege continued to walk past, and the bells were ringing. The last were mourners coming now: two round-shouldered old men wearing grey mittens.

Mrs Brandt looked away from the mirror.

"I suppose it's the masons who are paying," she said.

Miss Thøgersen still stood on the coppersmith's stone steps. Miss Thøgersen wept bitterly every time she saw a coffin.

"It's one o'clock," said Mrs Brandt. Ida had already started to set the table for dinner, on the mahogany table, beneath the mantelpiece clock.

∞∞∞∞

There was a loud noise by the door, awakening Mrs Brandt from her nap. It was the forester knocking the snow off his boots out in the corridor.

"Hello, everyone," he shouted, opening the door to the kitchen. "You have guests from afar."

"Good day, Ida my dear. Good day, Sofie."

"Hello. Hello..." Ida emerged, and her voice took on a quite different sound. Then she opened the door to the sitting room.

"Good day, Mrs. Brandt," said the forester in a rather more reserved voice as Mrs Brandt rose a little from her chair.

"Well," said Mrs Lund as she was divested of a mass of clothes, the innermost layer consisting of two red-striped capes: "It's been a lovely time. But it makes one quite giddy," she said. "And then I always feel a little strange travelling by train..."

Mrs Lund sat down and Mrs Brandt said:

"Are you not going to take your hat off?"

"Oh, thank you. Just for a while." Mrs Lund took off her hat and her grey hair stood on end and made her look like an uncombed poodle. Meanwhile she started telling all about her son's wedding.

"Yes, we celebrated the wedding in the hotel. There's a really lovely hotel at Kolding – and everything is so clean and tidy there. And there were sixty of us, just imagine, all those happy people. Yes, it was lovely to see so much happiness."

"Did she wear silk?" asked Mrs Brandt.

"Oh yes, they do nowadays...and Good Lord, you know it can always be dyed afterwards."

Mrs Lund went on with her account; she spoke rather quickly, for she always became as it were a little out of breath when sitting in the basket chair in front of Mrs Brandt; she told all about the dinner and the guests and the speech...

"It was a jolly splendid do," said Lund, who was walking up and down over by the stove.

"And what about presents?" said Mrs Brandt.

"Yes, people really did remember us – even the smallholders sent telegrams...Oh, do sit down, Lund."

"I need to move about a bit," said Lund, but he nevertheless sat down by the door.

"Yes," he said. "People have been really generous, indeed they have."

"Yes," Mrs Brandt intervened. "People will always remember those who have a bit of money behind them."

Ida, who was setting the table again, said:

"And there were bridesmaids as well, of course."

"Seven," said the forester, slapping his hands against his thighs.

"And then we saw all the boys," said Mrs Lund with a smile: "It's so lovely when the children are growing up."

The forester sat for a while nodding. Then he started to laugh and said:

"And our daughter-in-law went and made merry with all her brothers-in-law after the meal, fooling around in one room after the other, just as though she was at home, and even though she was still wearing her veil."

"Yes, dear; that's the way they are," said Mrs Lund: "They are so much at home there." She turned to Mrs Brandt as though needing to explain it to her.

"Yes," said Lund, "and that was the only thing that brought tears to my eyes...For it was lovely," he added quite quietly.

Ida laughed quietly, almost tenderly:

"How like Henriette that is."

She continued to smile as she stood behind the table, as though she could picture Henriette going around in her veil and fighting with all her brothers-in-law for pure joy.

"Yes, it was lovely," said the forester again.

"You *have* remembered the table?" said Mrs Brandt.

"Yes, mother."

The table was ready and – holding on to the chairs in order to walk over the floor, but not using a stick – Mrs Brandt said:

"Well, I was not sure we could expect you."

The forester sat down heavily on his chair and looked pleased to see so much food.

"It's good to see," he said, "that there's plenty of food in the larder here."

Mrs Brandt sat in the big chair, in front of the dishes.

"Well, at least we can still afford butter on the bread," she said.

"It reminds me of the old house," said little Mrs Lund who, as always when at Mrs Brandt's, took a large amount on her plate and never managed to eat it.

"Aye," said the forester. "It was always good to visit old Brandt."

"Have you remembered to offer second helpings?" Mrs Brandt's lips were trembling a little over her teeth.

"We simply had what suited our condition," she said.

Mrs Lund took still more on her enormously filled plate.

"Oh," she said. "I have so often felt ashamed of my house, Mrs Brandt, when I came to visit you."

Mrs Brandt made no reply, but the forester started to talk about

Christoffersen's funeral.

Mrs Lund continued to tell Ida about the wedding, while Ida sat smiling. She knew all the forester's boys, of course.

"There was a huge cortege, I must say," said Lund. "Aye, Christoffersen was well liked."

"Christoffersen's," said Mrs Brandt, "was always a place where there was plenty to throw around."

Lund gripped his knife rather hard as he cut his ham, and the clocks could be heard ticking.

"Ah well," said the forester. "Cheers, Ida my dear. Here's to *your* turn, my girl..." He raised his glass. "Young ladies must always get to the altar and populate the world, damn it."

"Yes, here's to your turn, Ida," said Mrs Lund. She had loosened the last shawl.

"There's no hurry about *that*," said Mrs Brandt. "Thank goodness, Ida is not one of those who need to be provided for."

"Oh no, of course not," said Mrs Lund. "That was not what I meant. But we always look to the future, Mrs Brandt, to the children's future."

She started to pat Ida's hand, which was quite cold.

"Yes," said the forester, "that's what we're here for."

"Yes, dear, but we often had to leave ours to fend for themselves."

"You never did that, mother."

"Yes we did, Lund. I know it only too well, for there were so many of them, and the little ones had to be looked after while the bigger ones did as they liked...But even so, it's strange to think that they simply saw us doing our best, and now we can as it were always enjoy sharing their everyday lives with them."

"Yes," said Lund.

Mrs Lund continued to stare ahead.

"And the joy, that always comes from the heart, as they say, whatever pressures there are..."

Ida bent her head a little down in the direction of Mrs Lund, and from her sofa Mrs Brandt said:

"Yes, people have to talk so much about the children these days."

"Well, Mrs Brandt," said Lund in a rather loud voice, "I'd jolly well like to know what else there would be to talk about once you've brought them into the world."

There was a knock at the door; it was Niels, the forester's coachman, coming with some parcels, and Mrs Lund went out with Ida into the kitchen.

"It's only a tiny bit, my dear, but I had said they could put it in the coach – a little ham and butter...I just wonder how the butter has stood the journey."

"Oh, Mrs Lund, it's far too much."

"Well then, we'll not say anything to your mother, and then you can arrange things...Your mother simply *can't* get used to buying everything. And that's quite understandable when she has come from such a house as you had..."

"Yes," said Ida. "It really is difficult for mother...and then it would hurt her so much to know that she'd been forgotten by everybody at home...Thank you."

"Oh, heavens, my dear," said Mrs Lund, "who is it up to more than to those who were so fond of your father? But if the butter hasn't kept well, Ida" – they went into the bedroom and closed the door – "you must use it in the frying pan."

Mrs Lund sat on the edge of the bed and Ida sat beside her.

"We're all a little confused," she said, "but it was a lovely time."

She still sat with Ida's hands in hers, and the rooms were beginning to grow dark.

"For you know, it was what you could call such a safe wedding, those two who have known each other since they were children."

"Yes," said Ida – they were both speaking slowly and quietly – "It's so lovely to see when people are happy."

Mrs Lund nodded.

"Yes, so lovely, my dear."

There was another knock on the sitting room door, but they both remained seated. It was Sørensen the borough treasurer and his daughter who were coming from their afternoon walk to the "Grove".

"Are we not going to have the lamps lit?" said Mrs Brandt from the sitting room.

Ida lit the lamps and returned to the edge of the bed, where Mrs Lund was still sitting.

The borough treasurer sat in the basket chair and pulled his mittens off while Mrs Brandt followed him closely with her eyes. There was nothing but bones and veins left in Sørensen's hands.

"Oh, so you've been to a wedding," said Sørensen.

"Yes, we have indeed," said Lund.

"Hmm, yes, everybody's getting married these days..."

"It's the way of the world, Mr Sørensen."

"Yes," and the borough treasurer tapped the floor with his stick. "Well, leave them to it."

He looked up at Lund:

"I'm getting too old, Mr Lund; I don't mix myself up in anything."

The forester said something to the effect that that was probably the wisest course.

"Wisest? Yes, but (and he banged his stick down again) where is it all going? Where is it all going?"

"One just sits here..."

The treasurer was silent for a moment and then he said in a quieter voice:

"That's all there is."

Miss Sørensen had gone into the bedroom and sat down on a chair in front of the bed. She had undone her cloak, revealing a satin-clad breast that rose like a mountain of gold.

"Oh, heavens, of course," she said, "you've been to a wedding. Aye, we all go and think all sorts of thoughts, now we've had an offer for the house again...It's Mathiesen, and he is very keen to have it for a shop."

Miss Sørensen spoke in a whisper, but in an unbroken stream:

"And it would be best to sell it, you know, for when father is no longer with us I shall move to Copenhagen – that's where my sisters are. But as long as father is alive, Mrs Lund, no one is going to make any changes, neither my sisters nor I."

"That is only reasonable," said Mrs Lund.

"That's right, both my sisters and I are agreed. He's an old man when all is said and done, and no one knows how long *he* has to go."

The borough treasurer, who had the ears of an owl, said in the sitting room:

"Oh, they are on about the house again. But," – and he spoke more loudly – "I'm still here."

He banged his stick on the floor:

"Once they have me in the cemetery, they can do as they like. That's all there is to it."

Total silence descended on the bedroom.

"Now you can see what father is like," said Miss Sørensen.

She sat for a few moments with her hands in her clean black lap and then she said:

"But after all, Mrs Lund, we human beings have to think about the future as well."

The treasurer got up from his chair; he wanted to go. The forester went out to the steps with them; he nudged Lund's arm and said:

"Hm, the old girl's tongue is getting a bit swollen in there, isn't it? I suppose she's got fat round her heart as well."

"Yes, she seems to me to be going downhill," said Lund.

Sørensen nodded and looked up at Lund.

"Her tongue's swollen," he said. "Good night."

Lund returned to the sitting room.

"Sørensen's not looking too good," he said.

"He's *old*," said Mrs Brandt.

Mrs Lund and Ida were still seated on the bed. It was as though Ida had woken from her thoughts, and her voice was trembling:

"Oh, fancy if they had to sell everything they have here."

"Yes," said Mrs Lund, who did not really know what sort of thoughts she herself was playing with. "Yes, it's a strange world."

Lunds had to be going; they had also to do some shopping before driving home.

Perhaps Ida could go with them?

"'Cause mother here lets herself be persuaded by any smiling face," said the forester. "And it will do little Ida good to see a few people."

"*I* can perfectly well be left on my own," said Mrs Brandt. "But give me a hand first."

She wanted to move across to the sofa again. Lund offered to help her.

"No thank you," said Mrs Brandt. "Ida is still able to help her mother."

She sat down.

When the Lunds and Ida came out into the street, Lund said:

"Now, my lass, just you go over to your friends the Jørgensens and get a breath of fresh air. We'll see to the rest...So get along with you now. That was the idea."

"And thank you for all those things," whispered Ida as she kissed Mrs Lund.

When the Lunds had gone further along the street, the forester, walking arm in arm with his wife, said:

"Did she get the butter and the ham?"

"Yes, poor thing."

The forester went on a little; then he said:

"No, she damned well sits on her."

"But she's *ill*, Lund..."

"But it's simply not fair to keep the girl there unattached during her best years. She herself knew damned well what she was up to when she was scrubbing the place clean as a dairymaid."

"Now stop it, Lund."

"Oh, it's right enough. And she knew the way both to the bothy and to the bailiff's place when she was the housekeeper."

Lund suddenly started to laugh and lifted his fur cap a little:

"But there wasn't much of her ham left by the time I'd finished," he said.

"Well, you know, she's very hospitable, Lund."

Lund continued to laugh.

"Yes, lass; at least she puts food on the table."

At home, Mrs Brandt had shouted to Sofie:

"Clear the table, of what they have left," she said.

∞∞∞∞

Ida ran in through the wrought-iron gate at the brickworks and rang on the door of the private residence.

Olivia opened the sitting room door to the well-lit corridor (she had heard Ida's voice as she spoke to the maid).

"Oh, it's the young lady herself," she shouted. "How have you escaped from the dower house?"

Ida spoke in a rather subdued voice: "Mother thought I could come out here."

Olivia looked at her for a moment:

"Oh, that's how it is...But do come in."

"Tea, Marie," she shouted through the dining room. Then she put her arm round Ida and started walking up and down, up and down – that was a habit she had learned from her mother – as she started telling a long story.

"Fritz was at a meeting of the town council, and Mrs Kornerup had said she was coming to tea – she was simply determined to form a discussion club. But I refuse to be involved in all these *talk* groups. As Fritz says, it's awful to have to stand and talk about all kinds of things with all those people you don't know...If they are things that concern you personally, there are after all only a few people you can discuss them with..."

"Yes," said Ida.

"But, my girl," said Olivia, "I suppose you don't manage to talk to anybody at all..."

Two toddlers ran in and already shouted "hello" from the dining room, for the children always loved it when Ida came.

"Oh, I have something for them," said Ida, running out into the corridor. She came back with a bag of grapes that she emptied out into a dish on top of the grand piano.

"You're like a magpie, the way you steal," said Olivia.

"Oh, but of course they're your own," she continued coolly as she put a couple of grapes into her mouth.

Ida suddenly flushed. "Surely I can give some to the children," she said; she had one of the toddlers in each arm. "And then off we go up to the Dumpling, up to the Dumpling," she said in a singsong voice as she ran upstairs and into the nursery with both the toddlers.

There was quite a rumpus up on the first floor: the toddlers laughing and Baby Dumpling crying.

"Look at Baby Dumpling, look at Baby Dumpling," shouted Ida, coming down again with the "Dumpling" in her outstretched arms.

"Oh, it's so nice and warm here," she said. She had sat down in a rocking chair and was rocking backwards and forwards with the "Dumpling" on her lap.

"Well," said Olivia, pouring out the tea in the dining room, "I suppose it's moderately warm in your house. There, have a cup..."

Olivia put the teapot on the corner table. "*Well*", she said, putting herself down on the sofa, "and now we'll have the children out. I like best to have them in one of the adjoining rooms, with the door open."

"What a lot of books," she went on, moving a pile of assorted volumes together to make room for the cake dish. "I don't know how it happens, but whatever I don't bring into the house Fritz turns up with instead!"

"Yes, there are always so many new things to read here," said Ida.

Olivia sat with her head leaning against the back of the sofa, looking up into the lamp high above her.

"As Fritz says, it's really a good thing with all these 'new books'. It's as though they teach you to cope better."

"How do you mean?"

"With life..." Olivia continued to stare into the lamp.

They were both silent for a while. Then Ida, leaning forward in the chair and looking at the wall, said:

"But isn't life fairly straightforward really?"

"Well, perhaps."

"Well, I mean," explained Ida, who always seemed to hesitate when expressing an opinion, "I suppose we do what we *have* to do."

She continued to stare at the wall, and Olivia said:

"And then there are the children as well, of course...one might be able to learn something for their sake. Oh well..." – she suddenly smiled all over her face – " I don't think I was ever properly brought up...and she instinctively glanced across at Mrs Franck's portrait above the piano.

"We were simply always together," she said, still smiling.

She sat there quietly and had started to hum softly when Ida, whom something or other had reminded of how things had been at home, suddenly said:

"Oh, Christian from the mill is out of work again."

"Oh, God bless your butter dishes, then." And Olivia laughed. "So I suppose he's lodging 'upstairs' again?"

"Yes," said Ida, looking at her a little despondently. "But what am I to do? I suppose he's nowhere else to go."

Olivia merely laughed. But Ida said slowly:

"But even so, there's so much I have to hide from mother."

Olivia gave a little sigh:

"There is no other house in the world where one learns to lie so brazenly."

Then she jumped up:

"Let's play a duet."

When they were sitting at the piano with the music open before them, she said, without any preparation:

"Oh, we're going to have the Dumpling's christened now...And as Fritz says, it doesn't matter about the weather so long as they put warm water in the font."

They had been playing for a while when there was a ring at the door. It was Mrs Kornerup, who opened the outer door.

"Good heavens, how cold it is."

Mrs Kornerup took off her cloak and threw it over a chair:

"Just fancy people being able to live in such a temperature."

She had a white scarf like a kind of sash curiously tied across the middle of her black skirt.

"Something turned up at the last minute..." Mrs Kornerup seated herself in a high-backed easy chair. Mrs Kornerup loved chairs with Gothic backs against which she could rest her head. "Valdemar received a letter from Neruda just after five enquiring whether he could give a recital here next week."

"My word!"

"Yes, dear, next week. Then *I* had to go out to the Muus'. These people just *won't come* here unless they are guaranteed."

"No, but..."

"And it *must* be arranged," Mrs Kornerup went on. "No one in the entire world has a touch like his...My dear, you can live on his playing for a whole month." She closed and opened her eyes on the words "for a whole month".

Mrs Kornerup, who was the daughter of a district revenue officer from Skanderborg, where she had lived until she married, was brimming over with an energy for which there had never ever been a need, and who therefore exploded in an endless surge of enthusiasm, the object of which changed every month and disappeared without trace, like ether volatilised from an uncorked bottle.

"So Valdemar went up to the Staals," she said.

Valdemar was a meticulously dressed, thirty-year-old lawyer of medium height and with very white teeth, who obediently followed his wife and who, when they were about to go out and he was to close the front door, would ask:

"Eleonora, have you remembered your bottle of malt?"

"Good heavens, no, Valdemar. Do please get it for me."

The agitation to which Mrs Kornerup was constantly and pointlessly subjected put her in a perpetual state of emaciation, as a result of which she lived dependent on an array of medicines.

When artists came to town, Kornerup met them at the station and politely introduced himself to whoever it was, asking whether he could be of any service. The result usually being an evening in the Kornerup home, which consisted of three small rooms equipped with very large furniture, with the most recent literature scattered over the tables – Valdemar was the chairman of the "Readers' Circle" – and with a great deal of fine Copenhagen porcelain on which the usual offering was a dish of boiled vegetables with creamed butter.

Ida brought Mrs Kornerup a cup of tea to counteract the cold.

"But dear Miss Brandt," she said, as though she had only that minute discovered Ida. "How are you? Have I told you that I have twice been together with Karl von Eichbaum at my aunt's?"

"Yes," she continued, giving Olivia a defensive look, "but he is very good looking...My dear, I do believe I must ask him for a photograph."

Asking for a photograph was one of Mrs Kornerup's specialities. Her two albums were full of a whole series of young men of one specific type with very regular features, straight necks and small moustaches.

"He's a good-for-nothing," said Olivia.

"No," said Mrs Kornerup, "I can imagine there is something there that women find attractive."

"But what women?" Olivia entwined her fingers so hard they made a cracking sound.

"I have known him since we were children of course," was all Ida said, quietly.

Ida went in to the children; she always had to be a bow-wow while they laughed and shouted, and she crept around on the floor among the chairs on all fours until she opened the double door out to the veranda and went outside.

She was so fond of the brickworks' garden when it lay there quite white and covered with snow.

It was so quiet here, and the shadows of all the trees fell so silently.

She followed the path beside the house. The snow crunched a little beneath her steps.

There would soon be snowdrops, when the weather grew a little warmer, and the "Dumpling" was to be baptised.

"Ida, Ida," shouted Olivia from the veranda.

Ida did not reply. She was kneeling, behind the gable end, in the light from the big window, digging the snow away with her bare hands. Three or four tender white bells had emerged close to the wall...

"Ida, Ida!"

But Ida did not move.

These were the first flowers of spring. Oh, how lovely it had been when they used to find them at home in Ludvigsbakke, those first flowers.

Ida remained kneeling in the snow, lost in thought. They always said that sort of thing about Karl.

"Ida, Ida."

But Ida made no reply.

"Heaven knows where she's got to," said Olivia, closing the veranda door.

"But she really is so beautiful," said Mrs Kornerup.

"She always has been." Olivia sat down.

"Yes," said Mrs Kornerup, "but when you see her she is always sitting there at the window with her hair combed straight."

And with a sudden leap in her thoughts, she added:

"I suppose she'll be well off when her mother dies."

∞∞∞

When Ida ran up the stone steps at home, Christian from the mill dodged in through the inside door.

Mrs Brandt was sitting in the sofa, idle and ample.

"That took rather a long time," she said. "Where did you all go?"

Rather hesitantly, Ida named various shops and stalls, and Mrs Brandt asked:

"Did Lund go with you?"

"Yes, mother."

"Who were you talking to out on the pavement?"

"The Misses Staal."

"Hm, do those two girls go out alone?"

"Shall I read for you, mother?" asked Ida. She took the newspaper and started to read page four in a clear voice. "Situations Vacant" and "Sale and Purchase". Mrs Brandt listened to this at first with her hands on her lap and eyes that suggested she was glaring through the walls into all the houses where they were seeking appointments or changing servants.

Ida went over to the local news and continued to read in the same tone and without interruption:

"House for sale in Brædstrup."

"Rape in Hatting".

"Who's dead?" asked Mrs Brandt, interrupting her.

Ida read out the three death notices, and Mrs Brandt said:

"Take the serial now."

Her features relaxed, and her eyes started to glaze over.

When Ida had finished reading, she gave her mother the cards to play patience and went out to make tea. It was not long before Mrs Brandt shouted:

"Sofie. Bring me the newspaper."

Mrs Brandt took the newspaper and spread it out over the cards; she read about the rape in Hatting.

Mrs Brandt was in bed, and Ida, with the door open, was in the sitting room, where she could hear her mother's breathing. She thought about "Baby Dumpling's" baptism...Yes, she would simply *have* to get some money out of the big bankbook.

"Ida," came a voice from the bed. "What was in the parcels?"

"What parcels?"

"Niels came with some parcels."

Ida said:

"They were for Mrs Lund."

Her mother's breathing became deeper. It was quite quiet in the house; only up in the loft were there sounds of movement and creaking.

Ida had taken out a book from *her* drawer in the chest of drawers. Evening was the only time when she dared read a little from Olivia's books.

Sofie came in and sat down on the chair by the stove. For a long time, Ida could hear her sighing and sniffing. Then she looked up from her book and put her knitting needle down on the page as a bookmark.

"But can't he find a job, Sofie?" she said.

Sofie started to sniff more noisily when she was spoken to.

"Oh yes, oh yes, but he's no reputation."

Sofie continued to weep – she sounded like a man when she wept:

"But I'd so much like to ask you if I could be allowed to go to Communion...this Sunday."

She sniffed aloud.

"Yes, of course," said Ida. "Of course, Sofie."

That was what Sofie always asked for when things were at their worst and Christian was out of work.

Sofie continued to weep; she was thinking of her own situation.

"Aye, that's it," she said. "That's it, but some people find it easier to get into bed than others."

Ida sat looking into the lamp; she was so used to Sofie's confidences. Then suddenly, in a completely different voice, Sofie said:

"You'll have to get some money this evening. We haven't got a penny in the place."

"Again," said Ida.

"When we never dare say what we're buying...and we have to kid your mother that we're having everything given to us..."

Ida sat silent for a moment. Then she closed the book.

"Yes," she said. "Then it's best we lock up."

Ida locked the door and put the flowers down on the floor and spread the white sheets over all the chairs. There were sounds of a lot of people talking down there in the street...it was folk going home from the theatre.

Hm, how handsome that man had been who played Palle – that evening when she had been there with Olivia – so slim and dark.

She could always see the actors' faces for such a long time afterwards – and their smiles – and how they walked.

He had had such beautiful teeth when he smiled.

Ida tiptoed in. She undressed quietly, listening to her mother's breathing. She was fast asleep now.

Ida lay in her bed and, quite gently, beneath the blanket, she slipped her hand in under her mother's pillow, where her purse lay. In the darkness she took a couple of kroner coins and put the purse back.

Her mother never kept a check on the small coins.

Everything was quite quiet now; her mother's groaning was the only sound to be heard in the house. Ida hid the two coins in her stocking.

∞∞∞

Ida was in the pea bed at Ludvigsbakke; she and Schrøder were picking peas and putting them in a large container.

"There," said Schrøder. "It just struck nine."

She had seen Mrs von Eichbaum, stiff and straight, turn into the path along the pea bed. After Aix-les-Bains, Mrs von Eichbaum was following a course of treatment at Ludvigsbakke, and she followed instructions to the letter.

She came along the path with precise steps, as though she were counting them, past the bed of peas.

"Ah, it's little Brandt," she said without stopping. It was as though, in the most kindly way, she discovered Ida afresh each time she saw her.

"Hmm," said Schrøder as she watched her go. "She ought to see about getting that little lad of hers up of a morning. God knows what she's going to make of him now."

It was a fortnight since Karl von Eichbaum had failed for the second time to get into the Zurich Polytechnic, and now he was resting.

"But he's good looking," said Schrøder.

It was quite quiet in the garden, and each peapod could be heard as it fell into the container, while the white butterflies flew in and out among the vines.

"The air is so lovely," said Ida.

"Ugh, it's going to be hot and I have to stir the mince for the rissoles."

Schrøder was always mixing mince. His Lordship, who was almost ninety years old, could hardly eat anything else. There would soon not be a tooth left in the house, said Schrøder. She herself had acquired six new front teeth during the spring, something that imparted a taut appearance to her mouth – otherwise she was unchanged; and on days when she had most to do, the six teeth came no further than to the glass in which they were kept.

"But I'm not going to have him anywhere where there are young girls," said Schrøder, continuing with the subject of Eichbaum. "He's the sort that has his eyes all over a girl." Schrøder probably noticed how the girls swung their hips when Eichbaum set foot in the kitchen.

"I think he has such kind eyes," said Ida.

There was suddenly a chorus of children's voices screaming and laughing down by the pond.

"Hm," said Schrøder. "Now we'll have to start drying sailor suits again."

It was all the Falkenberg children who were wading in the pond, and Mrs Falkenberg, née With, came down the path – she had to "keep an eye on the children".

"Oh, are you here?" she said (speaking in a somewhat faint, rather outdatedly-girlish voice). "Isn't it lovely here in the sun!"

She seated herself on Schrøder's kitchen stool with her hands in her lap – she always looked as though her wrists were tired.

"Falkenberg is not coming this year," she said.

"Is he not?"

"No, he has written to say that there are some reports." She shrugged her pointed shoulders in her dressing gown; Mrs Falkenberg had actually acquired a child-like figure again by presenting five children to Captain Falkenberg, Knight of the Order of the Dannebrog.

"I don't understand these things," she said. "It is his duty."

"Yes," said Schrøder. "A man has so many things to think about."

"Yes," Mrs Falkenberg nodded. There was an expression in her eyes as though she was sitting there looking in wonder for something that had disappeared:

"They have *their* problems as well."

There were sounds of laughing and shouting from down by the pond and then one boy started to cry.

"That's Edvard," said Mrs Falkenberg, making as though to get up.

"I'll go," said Ida, and she rose.

"Oh yes, Ida dear...would you..." And Mrs Falkenberg remained seated.

Schrøder sat down on Ida's kitchen stool and continued to shell the peas, while Mrs Falkenberg looked on through her pretty eyes.

"Oh, so you have a lot to think about," she said, with her eyes on Schrøder's hands. "Yes, it must be lovely to be strong..."

Ida returned: it was nothing – they were merely quarrelling over the barge.

"Was Erik there?" asked Mrs Falkenberg.

"No, Mrs Falkenberg, I didn't see him."

"Hm," Mrs Falkenberg shook her head. "Heaven knows what that boy gets up to..."

Erik was a gangly seventeen-year-old who spent his holiday in some loft or other surrounded by modern novels and who, on leaving the heated hiding-places where he spent his time, always looked as though the light hurt his eyes.

Mrs Falkenberg continued to sit there, lost in the sunshine.

"Oh dear," she said, "It's a funny thing to have children. It's lovely while they are small but then they have to be sent to school..."

As long as the children were small, Mrs Falkenberg spent the entire day singing with them, but once they went to school it was as though the big door closed behind them."

"It is not easy to keep up with them," she said.

"No, they all go their own way," said Schrøder. "Get hold of this now."

She took one end of the tray and Ida the other and they went.

Mrs Falkenberg stayed where she was. She could stay like this for hours sitting in the sunshine, looking up in the air as though she were staring up into some enormous holes into which everything in life disappeared.

Miss Rosenfeld was reading up on the veranda at the end of the house.

She raised her head and nodded to Ida and Schrøder before continuing.

As Schrøder and Ida entered the kitchen, Karl von Eichbaum put his head in through the other door. "I would like a cup of tea, Schrøder," he said and Schrøder, putting down the peas, murmured something to the effect that there was presumably going to be tea with the meal. But Ida prepared a tray of tea and biscuits and took it out to von Eichbaum, who lay stretched out on the lawn.

"You are always so kind," he said – he had his own straightforward and polite way of speaking to Ida – and he turned over on to his stomach, with his head over his tea.

"Thank you," he said.

Ida offered him the biscuits.

"Is it Wednesday today?" he asked.

"Yes."

"Ugh," said Eichbaum, stirring his tea. "Then I've got another three weeks...and..." – he looked up at her – "God knows what's coming then."

Karl von Eichbaum turned over on to his back again.

"No, it's incredible," he said.

He continued to stare into the sunshine and presumably reflect on "what was coming then".

Ida gave a hand in the kitchen. She was thinking of Karl von Eichbaum: there was nobody he could look to, not really. He used to have Herman Reck...but now he, too, had settled down, in Aalborg, and was no longer at home.

Ida suddenly smiled.

She thought of the time when Karl and Herman were boys and Karl borrowed her few coins to buy cigarettes in Brædstrup.

Karl always used to go in through the window into Schrøder's room after dinner:

"Have you any small change?" he would whisper saucily.

With the help of a knitting needle they would wheedle a few coins out of the piggy bank.

"Thanks," he would whisper before jumping out through the window again.

But on one occasion, when he was a little older, he had also taken four kroner wrapped in paper and intended for tips that he found lying on the bottom of her suitcase...and on that occasion she had wept, for now she had nothing to use as tips when she travelled anywhere.

There was a knock on the ceiling. It was His Lordship, knocking from upstairs in "Her Ladyship's sitting room"; he could no longer get up from his chair and so he called for help by knocking with his stick.

"Oh, is it you, Ida dear," he said. "Are they all out?"

"Yes, Your Lordship."

All visitors to Ludvigsbakke were sent out to get some fresh air.

"Fresh air is good for young people," said His Lordship, "so that they can feel their blood flowing. Young people must have big lungs and strong hearts."

He nodded.

"Would you just open the doors."

Ida opened the doors through the sun-drenched rooms. "Thank you," said His Lordship. Now, seated in Her Ladyship's chair, he could sit in peace and look through all the light-filled rooms he had built and in which he had lived.

He turned his head towards the window; he could see into the bailiff's garden through the opening.

"*They* are a colourful crowd," he said with a nod.

Four ladies dressed in an array of colours were running around on Reck's croquet lawn together with three young men with their trousers rolled up.

"They are not like your father's people, Ida," he said.

"Well, there we are." He turned his head again towards his tranquil rooms: "You see so many things when you grow old."

"But," said the old man, "the world witnesses a great deal of madness, my girl, and yet it survives."

Ida, too, remained there, looking out across the garden towards the bailiff's wing. She so rarely went there now: what a lot of trees they were felling every year...there were so few of the old trees left.

"And how are things at home?" asked His Lordship.

"It is kind of you to ask, but I have not had a letter recently," said Ida.

"Oh, well."

His Lordship sat there in silence, pondering like someone who has lived a long time.

Ida returned to the kitchen, but Schrøder sent her away.

"You're on holiday, my girl," she said. "Go out and get some fresh air. It's so hot in here that you need to take your clothes off."

Schrøder was mixing the mince, and she had taken hers off.

Ida went. She intended to go over to the Lunds. But she stopped out on the main steps: a carriage was just leaving the Home Farm. It was all the children, who were going bathing. The carriage looked like a white nest full of chickens in the sun.

Then the voices moved away, and all was quiet again. Lawn and fields with the cows resting on them like lazy patches, and the houses in Brædstrup – everything seemed to be dozing in the sunlight.

"It is lovely here today," said Miss Rosenfeld, who was walking along slowly, with her book under her arm.

They stood beside each other on the steps.

"Just look how straight the smoke is," said Miss Rosenfeld.

Smoke was rising from the houses in Brædstrup, slowly and straight like pale blue torches in the pale blue air.

Ida and Miss Rosenfeld rarely had much to say to each other. But they often stood together in this way for a short time, looking at the same things. Miss Rosenfeld fetched Ida when she wanted to go for a walk, especially when it had been raining and the trees were still dripping – then they went along together, without saying much, on the damp paths, for a long time.

Ida went down through the garden – she did not really like the road past the "wing" – and she turned in on the path through the forest. The birds were no longer singing, and the only sound she heard was that of her own steps on the soft ground.

At the forester's house, old Lucy was sitting in front of the kitchen door peeling potatoes, and the watchdog, which knew Ida, wagged its tail in front of its kennel.

"Is there anyone at home, Lucie?"

Lucie raised her palsied head.

"They are inside," she said and then sat there and said no more.

All the doors in the house were open and the sun shone on the floors and the well worn furniture. Mrs Lund was sitting in the hall in a basket chair, surrounded by linen, her large glasses on her small face.

"Oh, is it you, dear," she said. "I'm mending sheets, love...We wash and we mend, you know...with all these visitors. But they're welcome, they really are...Oh, could you just give me a hand..."

Ida gave her a hand and threaded needles while thinking how Mrs Lund's hand had really started to shake.

"Oh dear," said Mrs Lund as she pored over the sheets, for there was hole after hole in them. "I think these must be the oldest ones. But during the holidays it's as though they still have a bit of their old home dear, and who knows how long it will go on."

"The children are in the garden," she said and set about her sewing again.

They could hear that; a chorus of bright voices rang out down there. There were a lot of flies buzzing around in the sitting room, and the whitewashed ceiling bore clear traces of where they had been.

"O dear, no," Mrs Lund went on: "His Lordship is failing...and who knows what is going to happen then?"

Ida did not know why she had suddenly had the same thought. But she said:

"But the forests will still be there, Mrs Lund."

"Oh yes, dear, but it will be others felling the trees."

Mrs Lund stared out from behind the big glasses that sat so uncomfortably on her nose.

"And now we've lived here undisturbed for almost thirty-five years."

Old Lucie approached along the path, grumbling and mumbling.

"There," said Mrs Lund, "Lucie's off again now. Oh, it's not easy, my dear. If only she would just sit down. But she wants to be in on everything and she is not one of the cleanest. One minute she is over the food, and the next she's making beds."

Mrs Lund shook her head and Ida smiled, though a little reluctantly. There were those in the area who found it a little difficult to eat in the forester's house because Lucie liked to help with the food.

"But," said Mrs Lund, "as I say to Lund, she must be allowed to die here."

The "student", the youngest of "the boys" poked his head in through the garden door.

"Is it Ida," he said. "Come on, come on out. We're picking cherries."

All the young people were down by the cherry trees, shouting and laughing. Two of the "boys" were up in the branches, picking and throwing down the cherries.

"Is that Ida," shouted one of them.

"Catch." Ida received two cherries in her face as she looked up.

The girls were catching the berries and laughing.

"O-o-h," the cherries flew down.

"O-o-h," how good Emilie Frederiksen was at catching.

"There," one "boy" jumped down from the branch in the midst of the group.

"Here's some more for you," shouted the other, and he threw some cherries down to Ida. But by that time they were all lying down on the grass beneath the trees.

"Oh, it's so nice here," said Emilie, stretching her legs right out.

"Yes," said Ida, almost with tears in her eyes; she did not know how she had fallen into that mood, sad or perhaps as it were uneasy... ever since she had been indoors with Mrs Lund.

Emilie lay there, looking down at her skirt, which bore the stains of three crushed cherries.

"I shall never get rid of those," she said, patting down her skirt.

Ida rose. She would rather go home...such a strange mood had come over her

"Oh well, dear," said Mrs Lund, who went with her to the outside door and stood there, nodding to her. "Remember me to your mother when you write."

As Ida was walking down the road through the woods, Reck's wagonette was approaching. It was full of ladies with coloured parasols.

Miss Constance Reck, sitting on the box and holding a slender ivory whip, stopped the horses and spoke to Ida.

Ida said something in return, and Miss Constance said:

"It is really lovely for Miss Schrøder to have got you out here."

Miss Constance lowered the whip and the parasols moved a little as the carriage moved off.

Ida went on. She was lost in thought and turned down to walk past the bailiff's wing without realising it...

Two of the young gentlemen were standing on the steps leading up to the big new glass-covered veranda; they were each leaning against a doorpost, smoking cigarettes, each with his trousers pulled half way up his legs to display his colourful socks. One of them raised his white felt hat to Ida, as did the other after a brief pause, and after she had passed she heard him say:

"Was *that* Miss Brandt?"

Ida increased her pace. She felt all the time as though something must have happened in the main building, and she said to the maid in the corridor:

"Is everything all right?"

The maid, who was bringing flowers for the table, replied:

"Yes; we are about to have dinner."

And Ida felt quite calm again as she changed her clothes...

She heard a dress rustling out on the garden path. It was Mrs von Eichbaum, who was going for a walk before dinner.

Ida was standing in front of her mirror when the gong sounded.

Sitting at table must surely be the worst thing of all for Karl Eichbaum, she thought.

Schrøder was standing by the open kitchen window pouring the soup into the soup plates when she saw a bare-legged boy coming up round the lawn.

"Who's it for?" she shouted out of the window, past the two maids who were waiting.

It was the telegraph boy. But he was not in a hurry.

"It's for Miss Brandt," he said.

"Who?"

"It was for Miss Brandt," the boy said again, slowly.

"Oh Lord," Schrøder let go of the saucepan. "Oh Lord, then it must be bad news."

"Where is she?" she said immediately afterwards, but then in the same breath: "Oh, let me serve the soup first."

One of the maids took the telegram; she would take it up.

"Are you out of your mind?" said Schrøder and snatched it from her.

"You take the soup in."

Schrøder calmed down again: she would tell John the coachman to be ready in case he was needed; and she went into the servants' room, where he sat waiting for his coffee.

"Then she'll be able to have her meal first," thought Schrøder, and suddenly she began to weep.

"Poor thing," she said.

When she arrived back in the kitchen, in tears, Ida was standing there.

"What on earth is wrong, Schrøder?" she asked. "What is it?" she repeated, in a more worried voice. And when Schrøder, confused, reluctantly held out the telegram to her, she said:

"It's mother..." and she had torn the telegram open and read it.

"Oh dear, Ida, dear Ida," was all Schrøder said, putting an arm around her.

Ida had not spoken. It was as though her eyes failed to see anything as she went into Schrøder's room.

"Dear child," Schrøder went on. "Dearest child...what is it?"

But Ida made no reply, and, scared as she stood there before the pale, stiff face, Schrøder simply went on using the old pet name, dear child, dear child – rocking Ida's head backwards and forwards, backwards and forwards, as though, in fear, she wanted to shake the tears out of her.

"I've ordered the carriage."

"Thank you." And then Ida voiced the only thought she had:

"If only I can manage to see her."

Speaking made her start to weep, and Schrøder said – quite relieved – she had, of course, simply not known whether Mrs Brandt was still alive.

"Oh yes, oh yes, it's not as bad as all that...she'll get over it all right, you'll see, my dear."

Ida simply placed her arms wearily down on the chair.

"You must go," she said. "They are waiting for you up there."

"Oh," said Schrøder, almost angrily, "let them wait."

The door opened; it was Miss Rosenfeld.

"Have you ordered the carriage?" she asked, in a low voice, as though she had entered a sickroom.

"Yes."

She nodded to Schrøder, who went out.

"We'll get off straight away," she said, sitting down quietly and taking hold of Ida's cold hands.

From the kitchen, Anne Marie, the kitchen maid, had crept out into the servants' hall to hear what was going on.

"So I suppose it's all over," she said slowly.

"I suppose so," replied Johan.

Anne Marie stared vacantly ahead, standing straight, in her black socks.

"She'll leave a bit," she said, nodding.

"She'll leave *a lot*," said Johan.

"Aye," and he stretched his artilleryman's legs in front of him: "Is there any coffee?" He drank it and got ready.

"Well," he said, "I suppose we'll take the landau on an occasion such as this."

Ida was fetched and put in the barouche.

Silence fell on the dining table as Mrs Falkenberg attended to His Lordship and left the doors ajar.

"It doesn't sound as though they are enjoying themselves in there. Why not?" asked His Lordship.

"We are enjoying ourselves, Your Lordship."

"Good, but, when people are enjoying themselves, you can usually hear it," the old man said.

Mrs von Eichbaum said she had recently been reading what Bishop Mynster had written in his "Reflections" on the subject of dying suddenly: "They were words to remember".

"But," she added: "little Brandt's future is assured, I suppose."

When the carriage drove up on the gravel path, Ida quietly entered it – her eyes had as it were become very big in her face – and Miss Rosenfeld, who had put her coat on, climbed in and sat down beside her.

"You are not going to go alone," she said.

Karl von Eichbaum had left the table and gone down. He stood, beside the bailiff, over in front of the house by the horses. Then he reached a hand in over the carriage door, without saying anything.

When Schrøder turned to go inside – the coach was right down on the Brædstrup road by this time – she saw the telegraph messenger still sitting on the bench in front of the kitchen windows; he was waiting for his receipt.

Dinner was over and all the dishes were in disarray on the kitchen tables. Schrøder had to have them tidied up before she could start on the servants' dinner. The sun betrayed a large number of grey hairs above her temples as she stood bending over the big bread slicer.

The gardener's assistant came out of the garden. He slowly raked the gravel path, hiding the traces of the carriage that had just left.

The white marker stones flew past the rattling carriage, in which no one spoke. Mile followed after mile, as the horses trotted.

Ida saw nothing and heard nothing. All her life seemed to be gathered in her clenched hands.

One single thought was forcing its way out in words without a sound, as though she wanted to overturn a sense of guilt:

"I had said I wouldn't go..."

She rocked her clenched fists up and down.

"Now I shan't even be able to see her..."

"But...Ida..."

"No, I shan't be able to see her..."

And then they were there.

The horses refused to stand still – two dogs came rushing at them.

Ida saw nothing but Sofie's puffed-up face as she came down the stairs.

"The doctor's here," said Sofie in a whisper.

Ida supported herself on the banister.

"So she's not dead."

"I'll fetch Mrs Jørgensen," said Miss Rosenfeld.

Ida nodded without having heard, and she opened the door to the sitting room; it was dark, and she waited. She could hear the doctor's footsteps in the bedroom.

"It happened at twelve o'clock," whispered Sofie.

But Ida simply groaned.

"And then we sent a telegram," Sofie whispered again.

As though glimpsing a couple of shadows, Ida saw Miss Sørensen, who came in carrying two silver candlesticks, and Miss Thøgersen, who was bringing a cloth.

"Oh," said Sofie, starting to tremble: "this is for the last communion...and she sat down on a chair.

"We're expecting the minister," whispered Miss Sørensen and the two continued to tiptoe around – with so many things.

Ida only listened to the doctor's footsteps.

Then she heard the sound of her mother's heavy breathing, just as she knew it...And suddenly she started to sob, quietly and desperately with gratitude.

The doctor approached her, and she made to get up.

"I heard the carriage," he said, and she looked up into his face.

"It might be best not to go in immediately," he said. "Your mother has been rather irritated..."

Ida continued to look at him.

"In her condition...that you were not here..."

Ida made no reply. She had closed her eyes for a moment, and she failed to notice the hand he reached out to her.

"We will wait until this evening. Goodbye."

Ida had bowed her head. She had understood: she was not to go in there.

She saw Miss Sørensen drag the myrtle across the floor, and she heard the doctor's voice again. "Keep that out of the way," he said and actually struck out at the myrtle.

She merely thought that she was not to go in there.

She did not realise that she had risen and gone across the floor, in to the little sitting room, to the stool, *her* stool behind the big chest of drawers.

Doors were opened and doors were closed; there was the sound of footsteps. Miss Thøgersen came and laid a desperate hand on her shoulder.

"The minister," she breathed, and they could hear Sofie weeping.

"Jesus Christ, Jesus Christ."

But Ida did not move.

There was no sound but the minister's murmur. Then came the sick woman's breathing. Ida heard only that.

"Vater unser, Vater unser," Miss Thøgersen suddenly prayed in her own language, but she got no further.

"The Lord Jesus the same night in which He was betrayed took bread; And when He had given thanks, He brake it and said, Take, eat; this is my body which is broken for you; this do in remembrance of me."

Ida did not pray; she had no room for prayers. She only felt her heart stopped and heavy like a stone in her breast.

"Vater unser, Vater unser..."

"After the same manner also, He took the cup, when He had supped, saying, this cup is the new testament in my blood; this do ye, as oft as ye drink it, in remembrance of me..."

Looking in through the door, Sofie could see, against the candles, the minister bend down over the dying woman and lift her pillow.

"God the Holy Spirit, God the Holy Spirit," she whispered, falling back against the back of the chair. There was silence for a moment, and then Sofie got up again.

"The keys," she said all at once, almost shrieking.

She had seen the bunch slide from under the pillow, slip over the sheet and fall down on the floor.

"The Body of Christ..."

They heard no more, while the night nurse also started to weep.

Ida had folded her hands on her lap:

If she fell asleep, she could go in there; when she was asleep, she could go in...

"The Lord bless you and keep you; the Lord make His face shine upon you, and be gracious unto you; the Lord lift up His countenance upon you, and give you peace."

It became quite silent. Miss Thøgersen had ceased weeping and sat rocking her head to and fro.

"She is nevertheless dying as a respected person," she said, and her tears began to flow again.

Ida heard her name as in a fog, and she stood up. It was the minister, who held out a hand to her.

"You have been away?" he said in a mildly concerned voice.

"Yes, I have."

The minister stood for a moment in front of the tearless face. He tried to think of a text, but failed to find one.

"Aye," he said then, "a mother's a mother. May God give you strength."

Miss Sørensen showed the minister out and crossed the road to go home for a moment. She could not quite forget that episode with the myrtle: she had really only wanted, with the best of intentions, to provide some "embellishment" for the sacred act.

But it was well known that Dr. Berg was a man without much sensitivity.

All was quiet now. The only sounds were those of the clocks' ticking and the night nurse when she moved quietly in some way.

Ida sat in the same chair while Sofie tiptoed to and fro.

"Is she asleep?" Ida whispered.

"She's still awake."

Again, they heard the ticking of the clocks while Sofie lit a solitary candle on which the wax curled up in the form of long threads towards the flame and then fell.

"Is she asleep?" Ida asked again.

"She's awake."

They could hear the laboured breathing and a voice mumbling.

"Is she saying something?" Ida asked.

She had got up. She felt hope almost like a thorn in her breast when the night nurse opened the door.

"Has she asked for me?" Ida could scarcely speak.

The night nurse shook her head.

"She is probably not going to ask for anyone any more," she said. "She is asleep now."

They all three stood listening for a moment in front of the silent candle: she was asleep.

"Then I'm going in," whispered Ida.

Carefully, she took her shoes off and crept in. She looked at her mother's face for a moment. Then, quietly, she sat down on the floor at the end of her own bed without drawing a breath.

Mrs Brandt did not wake again. She died about midnight.

∞∞∞∞

It was cold and empty now. From door to door nothing but the white, dead floors. On the walls only patch after patch, above which were rusty nails.

Ida went from room to room for one last time.

"Well then, you'll close the doors," she said to Sofie.

Sofie stood with her hand on the latch.

"Yes," she said, weeping so the tears streamed down her face as she spoke:

"I don't think I've told you...that the upshot is we're going to get married..."

"Married? But he has nothing, Sofie." (Christian from the Mill was becoming more and more hopeless, and now he was out of work all the time.)

"No," said Sofie, still weeping. "But Hansen's wanted this for a long time...and then he's got his three children to look after..."

"Oh," said Ida, who only now realised that Sofie was not talking about Christian from the Mill; Hansen was a widower; he worked at the gasworks, and he drank.

As though she understood what Ida was thinking, Sofie, continuing to sniff, said:

"And it's not everyone who can be left to live on their own..."

Ida looked at her. She did not herself know why the tears came to her eyes.

"Then I hope it may bring you happiness," she said.

Sofie stared ahead through her tearful eyes, and her voice sounded quite different.

"And I'll be sure of a place to live and a bed to sleep in," she said. "And one's got to live."

She was overcome with tears again, and in despair Ida put her arms around this ageing woman and she, too, wept, though she hardly knew why.

Then, slowly, Sofie closed all the doors, one by one, and left.

She slept at Miss Thøgersen's that night.

Ida had gone to Olivia's house and had supper there on her last evening.

Now she and Olivia were sitting on the veranda steps, looking in the dusk out towards the Sound and Boller Woods, the outline of which was dark and heavy. They had not spoken. Olivia had simply gently slipped her arm under Ida's, and they were standing shoulder to shoulder.

Jørgensen's rocking chair could be heard rocking up and down on the veranda...Rolf, the dog, crept down the steps and lay down at Olivia's feet.

"So I suppose I'll be a nurse," said Ida.

"But why, Ida? You don't need to."

Ida looked out over the darkening sound, and her voice sounded very gentle:

"I suppose it's the only thing I can do."

Olivia made no reply, and they sat for a while in silence.

"And then I'll be of some use to someone."

Ida suddenly thought of Sofie and, still in the same tone, said:

"Now Sofie is going to get married."

"To Christian?" Olivia asked, suddenly in a louder voice.

"No, to Hansen from the gasworks."

"Oh, good Lord," said Olivia. "Is she going to have him to fight with now?"

"Yes," said Ida with a half smile. "I don't think she can live without something like that."

They fell silent again and could hear nothing but the dog's deep breathing as it lay at their feet.

"How quiet Rolf is."

"Yes."

They were both whispering. Not a leaf stirred in the darkening garden.

"It's as though everything knew you were going away."

They sat motionless. But Olivia felt a couple of tears fall on her hand in the dark.

"Let's go up to the children," said Ida.

They stood for a moment more, looking out over the still garden. Then they went in.

Ida ran in first into her own room; then they crept up to the sleeping children. The lamp was burning low beneath the ceiling and the maid sat knitting in a corner.

"How sweet they are," said Olivia.

Ida said nothing, but she lingered for a long time by each of the white beds.

"What are you doing now?" whispered Olivia.

Ida put a small sealed package down under each pillow.

"You do nothing but give things," said Olivia.

Ida stood in front of Dumpling's bed.

"If only I had someone to give to," she said.

They came down into the sitting room and Olivia told Fritz about the parcels.

"I must be allowed to do that," said Ida. "It's my last evening."

"Oh yes, I suppose so," said Olivia with a laugh. "But if you fall in love one day, my dear, you'll give him everything down to your last stitch."

Olivia had gone up with Ida and came back to the quiet sitting room. She and Fritz sat in silence, each in their own chair, in front of the white stove.

"Oh," said Olivia, "if only Ida could be made happy."

Fritz sat for a time looking at the smoke from his cigar and said:

"I don't think she ever will be."

Olivia seemed to ponder this.

"But why?" she asked.

"Because she will never learn to seek her own happiness," said Fritz.

"No."

There was silence again before Olivia said in a voice that betrayed much emotion:

"Do you realise how grateful happy people should really be?"

Fritz merely nodded. But, as though the words were coming from deep down inside her, Olivia said:

"And then death comes even so."

∞∞∞∞

The following afternoon, Ida left on the steamer.

Darkness was beginning to fall – the first day in Copenhagen.

Ida had wandered around among unfamiliar things and had sat at table among unfamiliar people. Now she went out, across squares and along streets. She wanted to see a ship, the *Brage*, which was to sail back home again.

She walked along the quayside, where ships lay side by side. There it was, at the far end. She stood there and looked at it, the big hull and the masts and the cabin doors that were all closed. It was going home to sail the waters over there.

The windlasses were working and there were still people working in the holds. They were going to go along the shore and past the woods and all those lovely meadows.

And Karen would stand there watching for the ship and raise the ladies' flag above the white bathing hut.

Ida stood there for a long time. She hid herself, beneath the eaves of the big warehouse. *There*, it was dark.

∞∞∞∞

Ida was tossing about in her bed. *One* moment, she was dreaming and the *next* she was awake.

The doors were opened and slammed. The porters were bringing patients.

Two long shouts from "the noisy ward" resounded throughout the building and then the doors closed.

Half awake, Ida heard the porters' footsteps and the cries of the difficult patients, as though they were coming from far, far below, from deep down beneath the earth.

II

"Come along, Holm, get those hands of yours washed."

The four patients in the main ward, known as the Hall, were out of bed and standing in the anteroom, each in front of a bowl of water. Josefine put the breakfast down and tapped Holm cheerfully over both his wrists so that his wrinkled hands flew down into the water.

"There," she said, "in with your paws."

Josefine tapped him again and stood there fresh and high-bosomed, with her hands on her hips, while Bertelsen, apathetic and silent, swilled water up around his powerful neck.

"Look happy, Bertelsen," she said. "The sun's shining."

There was something fresh and full about Josefine's voice in the mornings that seemed to be telling people that she had come from outside and that she spent her nights away from the hospital.

"Good morning, nurse."

Josefine nodded in towards the Hall, where Ida was sitting on the sun-lit bed with one of the two old patients, and turned on her heels – Josefine wore rather higher heels in the ward than the rules allowed.

"Good morning, Josefine."

"There," said Ida as she dried the old man's hands, "now you are fine, Sørensen."

The old man smiled and nodded.

The keys rattled energetically in the doors: "Good morning, good morning, what lovely weather." It was Nurse Kjær, smart and rosy-cheeked, who was looking in through the door to the women's ward.

"Isn't it lovely," said Ida, washing down a panel that had been warmed by the sun, while Nurse Kjær hurried out through the kitchen.

"Are you up yet, Petersen?" she shouted, knocking hard on Petersen's door.

"Ach, how schön it is over the Lakes," said Nurse Petersen behind a locked door. Nurse Petersen did not approve of having visitors in the morning while she was taking elaborate care of her thirty-year-old body and dressing in very white and youthful underclothes.

"Speak Danish, my dear German colleague," shouted Nurse Kjær and banged on the door again.

The keys rattled again, and she was gone.

Ida removed the bowls of water; she was busy and worked quickly to butter the bread for them all. Yes, it would be lovely along the lakes today. Her morning walk round them after night duty was the best thing she knew.

She went around, humming and chatting with each patient as she gave them their food until she quietly opened the door to Ward A, where all was still dark.

"Good morning, doctor," she said.

Ida opened the shutters to allow the light to pour in, while the sick man lay there, silent, with his long pale hands motionless on the blanket. She saw to him and he expressed his unswerving gratitude in the same tone (he always said this in a voice as though he felt some profound sympathy with whoever he was thanking) while raising a cautious eye to watch not the sun, but her.

Ida went on cheerfully.

"I'm going to go for a walk now," she said.

The sick man merely nodded.

"Yes," he said. "The sun is tempting."

Ida laughed:

"Yes, after night duty...Good morning."

"Nurse Petersen had emerged and, washed and wearing a starched uniform, was starting her duty. Nurse Petersen looked after the ward as meticulously as the manageress in a milliner's shop.

"I'll be off now," said Ida, opening the door to the corridor, where she was met by the morning air, strong and fresh, pouring in through the open window.

Ida ran up the stairs to her attic room. The rattling of her bunch of keys sounded like the ringing of a set of cheerful little bells as she ran.

Once up in her room, she opened the windows: how fresh everything was, and all the bushes in the gardens were resplendent.

She stayed at the window and suddenly she smiled. She thought of Karl von Eichbaum, who, when she met him yesterday morning, had said:

"Yes, I really think spring is coming."

And they had both laughed, and she had told him about Mrs Franck, who in past times, around the feast of Epiphany, would open her window a little when the sun was shining and sit there with her nose in the chink and say:

"Do you know, children, I can smell spring now."

Ida continued to smile: she had recently been thinking so often of the old days and the year, that lovely year, before mother fell ill; and all the other years seemed almost never to have existed – there was only that time, that sunny time.

It was probably also because she had met them again, almost all of the people from home at Ludvigsbakke: Miss Rosenfeld, who had looked her up, and Karl von Eichbaum, whom she came across every day in the hospital.

Ida looked up at her clock and had to hurry: it had grown so late. She dressed and ran down the stairs and through the garden, closing and locking, closing and locking. There were three maids in the laundry, all singing. When Ida emerged into the big courtyard, Dr Quam was sitting on one of the stone steps, sunning his white trousers.

"Hey, where are you off to in such a hurry?"

"I'm going for a walk."

Without getting up, Dr Quam handed her a rose.

"Take it with you, in the sunshine," he said, and Ida fixed it on her coat.

Dr Quam sat there and watched her. "She has a nice way of walking," he thought as the door closed and Ida went off into the daylight.

The bells could be heard clanging on the tramcars and in the botanical gardens the huge maize tops nodded their heads. Above her, at all the open windows, maids were beating dust out into the fresh air while Ida was walking. How energetically they were beating the rugs, and *there* were two who were talking to each other over the street. Faces and people and every single tree, all so dazzlingly clear on such a morning, as though one's eyes became new.

On the corner at the end of the lakes, the flower lady stood on her steps and nodded.

"Thank you," said Ida, nodding back to her as she inclined a little towards her and put her hand up to Quam's rose: "I have one today."

Otherwise, it was her habit to buy a flower, for their scent was so fresh early in the morning, when they had just been brought by the gardener.

"Oh yes," replied the flower lady. "Isn't the weather lovely today?"

"Yes," said Ida, looking over the shining lake, where the white boats lay motionless beside the bridges as though they were not yet awake.

"It's a good year for flowers, Mrs Hansen."

"Yes Miss, even for roses," said the flower lady, who was a little deaf and had in her eyes something of the wonderment of the deaf, who always look as though they are hearing some strange secret when they hear anything at all. "Even our roses are outdoor grown."

"Good morning."

Ida turned into the road along the lakes, as was her custom. She always walked along the same side of the lakes. She always liked the roads she was used to. There, she knew everything, every cranny, every boat and all the windows, and almost all the people she met as well. And there were some who actually said good morning, just as they did at home.

And now he nodded, too, the toothless old waiter from the "Rørholm" restaurant. This was the result of one morning recently when they had had coffee there – for Karl von Eichbaum had not had any at home because he had got up too late. They were the first customers and sat enjoying coffee and rolls behind an ivy-covered fence that had just been watered. "It's almost as though we were in the country," said Ida. "Yes," said Karl von Eichbaum: "It's nice here."

They had not sat together at table since those days at home.

But he had never managed to get up in the morning. At home in Ludvigsbakke, he had always insisted on having the attic room above the main loft, for Schrøder could not be bothered to go right up there to get him up. And so he lay there until after noon puffing away on the steward's pipes.

Ida was walking past the café when a voice called to her. It was Karl von Eichbaum, who emerged from behind the ivy.

"Morning," he shouted.

Ida spun round.

"Good morning," she said.

"I'm having my morning coffee here."

"Again," said Ida, stopping on the path.

Eichbaum drifted out on to the roadway with both hands in his pockets.

"What glorious weather," he said, standing for a moment to look at the water.

"We ought to have a picnic in the forest, Miss Ida," he said, still with his hands in his pockets.

"Yes, perhaps we should."

They walked a little beside each other, he still on the roadway.

"But then there are no forests in Zealand," he said.

"No, I suppose not," said Ida with a sudden smile.

"But over there, there are *trees*," Eichbaum went on, still thinking of Jutland.

They stopped again, and a couple of young gentlemen of some obviously secretarial occupation went past.

Karl laughed and said: "The gentlemen all turn to look at you, Miss Ida."

"Why?"

Eichbaum laughed again: "Well, why?" he said and smiled.

"Because you look so pretty as you stand there...Goodbye."

Ida nodded and he strolled back, but in the middle of the roadway he stopped again briefly.

Ida went on. She was thinking of the forests. She had after all always thought that the forests at home in Jutland were quite different.

A little further along the road she met Nurse Kaas and Nurse Boserup. They were also taking a walk, but were already on their way home.

"You are late getting out," shouted Nurse Kaas.

"Yes," Ida replied. They stood chatting for a short time; Ida's voice was noticeably bright.

"But I must get on," she said. "Tick!" She tapped Nurse Boserup on the shoulder and ran off.

Nurse Boserup shook her shoulder after the touch.

"Grow up, Brandt?" she shouted after her.

But Ida stopped and shouted back with a laugh:

"I would so much have liked to go for a swim."

Nurse Kaas and Nurse Boserup continued their walk, and Nurse Kaas said:

"Brandt looks nice in that hat."

But Nurse Boserup dug her heel firmly in the ground and said:

"That's no problem when you've got money."

They talked a little about Ida's means, and Nurse Boserup said:

"Yes, that's all very well but in fact she's merely taking up a job that some probationer could do with."

Ida had gone as far as Østerbro, where she was met by the cheerful breeze from the lakes. She crossed the road to a flower shop and bought a potted plant for Nurse Helgesen. She felt such an urge to buy something – to buy everything.

When she arrived back at the hospital and went in to Nurse Helgesen with the plant, Helgesen was sitting at the central table with a large piece of embroidery. Nurse Helgesen always had a never-ending piece of embroidery on the go, with a regular and almost geometric design.

"But it's ridiculous, everything you are buying these days."

"Well," said Ida, "it must be because the weather is so lovely."

She stood for a moment with one of the leaves of the plant between her fingers:

"But isn't it beautiful," she said with a smile.

She went upstairs to the first floor. Nurse Petersen was crocheting by the big window, where the sun was shining on the flowers. The other four were working in the basement, and the two old patients were in the Hall, white and motionless, beside each other in their beds.

"How nice it is in here," said Ida.

"Yes," said Nurse Petersen; "it's quiet in here this morning."

There were no sounds apart from the doctor's footsteps in Ward A, coming and going, coming and going, in perpetual motion.

"Well, good night," said Ida.

"Good night."

Ida went upstairs. She drew the green curtain to keep the light out. But she was unable to sleep. She was so happy and so easy in her mind.

She lay wondering what clothes she should buy now for the winter. She had thought of a pale beige dress. They were always so elegantly dressed for Nurse Fock's birthday, in the evening. Then she could put it on for the first time.

She shook her head. She suddenly came to think of Karl von Eichbaum, how he had hunched his shoulders in his black summer overcoat the other morning when it was blowing a gale: "Ugh," he had said, "and now I'll have to get some winter clothes."

Hm, he probably hadn't any money...

No, and Ida smiled. Of course he had not.

Ida heard them coming up the stairs and the door down there being opened and closed. It was them coming from their work in the basement, so it must be twelve o'clock.

No, for he had never been able to keep any money.

Ida fell asleep.

∞∞∞∞

It was the same day, in Toldbodvejen, in the middle building in the "Family House".

Mrs von Eichbaum – armed with gloves with the fingers cut off – had finished the lamps, and Julius, wearing prunella boots, glided in and out and put them in place. The lamps were Mrs von Eichbaum's sole domestic chore as they also were with her sister, the general's wife. It was a tradition: they attended to the lamps themselves as though they were part of the family.

"I need the table setting for two, Julius," said Mrs von Eichbaum, going out into the sitting room. Mrs von Eichbaum was expecting the general's wife to come in from their country house. The general's wife always stayed out in their country house until well into November. The autumn air did her good – both she and her sister suffered from dry skin.

"Besides," she said to her sister, "you are always there yourself to supervise the way everything is brought indoors from the garden."

The door bell rang on the stroke of twelve, and Julius opened the door.

"Good Lord, Emilie" – it was the general's wife who entered the room – "what glorious weather, my dear...Good morning."

"Good morning, Charlotte, it is so good to be able to have you on your own for a while."

"Julius, you can bring the urn in."

The general's wife sat down on the sofa while Mrs von Eichbaum went in and inspected the table, and the sisters conversed with each other from one room to the other. The general's wife talked about their country residence. She could not believe how delightfully fresh the mornings were.

"And the grapes, dear, grow to *this* size." The general's wife showed with her fingers how big the grapes grew. So she had really thought of trying the recipe recommended by Mrs Schleppegrell, the admiral's wife.

"With refined sugar, you know."

And then she could give her half of them.

"Yes," said Mrs von Eichbaum, from the urn, "they are really so nice for a small dessert."

The sisters continued to converse. They spoke in exactly the same way, in just the same voice, the general's wife just a little faster, both with very open and genteel A's, which as it were broadened all sentences as they spoke them.

"But Emilie," – her voice rose a tone on saying Emilie, and the general's wife let her hands fall down on her lap – "what do you think of Aline?"

"O good gracious me," said Mrs von Eichbaum, coming to the door and standing there for a moment with closed eyes, "I can still hardly bring myself to talk about it. It is incredible that it could happen."

The general's wife repeated "incredible" and went on:

"And we in the family, who have all known her."

"We can eat now, Charlotte," said Mrs von Eichbaum.

They continued to talk about Mrs Feddersen. She was a childhood friend, Mrs von Eichbaum's best, married to a landowner by the name of Feddersen from the estate of Korsgaard, who suddenly and without warning, had left her husband and children for a surveyor who had his own grown-up sons.

"And Feddersen," said the general's wife, "such a calm, admirable man."

Mrs von Eichbaum handed a plate to her sister and said slowly:

"But, Charlotte, it must simply be a momentary aberration."

"Thank you, Julius," – she turned to the butler, who had opened the door – "there is nothing at the moment."

Mrs von Eichbaum continued to eat, but her tone assumed an explanatory or meditative tone.

"There has always been a curious urge to talk in that family, you know...they just had to talk and talk."

"They have that from her mother. She was fond of speaking at revivalist meetings," the general's wife interposed.

"Yes," Mrs von Eichbaum nodded. "All that about spiritual life, you know, and then they talk themselves into such an emotional state...Aline already had a bit of *that* in her young days."

The general's wife agreed, and Mrs von Eichbaum rose and poured the coffee.

"Good heavens, my dear," she said. "Just fancy that people cannot learn to remain silent and suffer in private and get over it."

The general's wife took the coffee cup and nodded again.

If people were to talk of everything," Mrs von Eichbaum continued, "then there would presumably be...There is probably something in every family."

"Of course," said the general's wife.

"And we all have our own cross to bear," concluded Mrs von Eichbaum, staring ahead.

They sat there for a short time. Then, in a rather different voice, sounding almost moved, Mrs von Eichbaum said:

"But of course, *we* must take her part..."

"And say the same thing..."

"Good heavens, Mille," – when they were alone, the sisters occasionally abbreviated their names – "that is only reasonable. I told Anna Schleppegrell yesterday that Aline had gone to Vichy on account of her swollen legs..."

"They dropped the subject of Mrs Feddersen, and the general's wife asked:

"Does Karl not have lunch at home?"

His name had so far not been mentioned.

"Oh no, dear," said Mrs von Eichbaum. "It is such a long way... He has lunch in the office. Ane prepares it, and he takes sandwiches with him. You know, in one of those oilcloth briefcases...It makes him look like a civil servant."

And in the same tone as that in which she had previously spoken of Aline Feddersen's "confusion", Mrs von Eichbaum went on:

"*He* takes his walk in the morning, along the lakes. I don't even hear him."

At which the general's wife said:

"Yes, the mornings are so beautiful this year."

There was a gentle knock on the door. It was Ane who, wearing a white pinafore, wished to say good day to the general's wife. Ane was a small, round, fifty-year-old woman with her hair combed straight back and bright white false teeth.

She so much wanted to hear how things were with the general's wife and out on the estate.

"Thank you, Ane," said the general's wife, and they got up from the table.

"There have been problems with the chimney."

Ane nodded.

"Yes," she said, "and it often happens that they don't know how to fry."

There was always jealousy among the maids in the family.

"And put too much on the fire," said Ane, who had adopted the same broad vowels as her mistress.

The general's wife interrupted her rather abruptly:

"And I suppose your Julie will soon be getting married."

"Yes," said Ane. "The bans have been read twice, and he was so keen to have it soon."

"He is said to be a very nice, sober man," said the general's wife.

"Yes, good morning Ane."

The sisters went into the living room, and the general's wife said something to the effect that they would presumably have to think about a wedding present.

Ane's Julie was the illegitimate fruit of her thirtieth year, when a young, beardless Adonis of a servant had had his fun below stairs. When things in the maternity home had been seen to, Ane had returned to her job, and when Julie was old enough she was placed in a charity school, and every other Sunday, when Mrs von Eichbaum was lunching at the general's, she came to visit Ane, whom she naturally called "Auntie".

Yes, Mrs von Eichbaum had thought of a sugar basin and cream jug as a wedding present.

"He was here the other day," she said. "And good heavens, he is a really nice person – you know, considering – and *there* he sat, very politely on a chair...they always receive some sort of upbringing in the naval dockyard."

"He," was Julie's fiancé, an excellent young man who was an engine room artificer in the navy.

The general's wife sat looking at her sister's work – a very big undertaking, a bed curtain with netted middle sections, the finished areas being wrapped in a great deal of clean tissue paper – and thinking of Julie's illegitimate origins, said:

"Yes, *I* consider it *extremely* honourable of him."

As though they had read each other's thoughts, and as though the distance could be thought to have lessened the illegitimate nature of the relationship, Mrs von Eichbaum said:

"Of course, he is from Ringkøbing."

The mention of this provincial town started a train of thought in the general's wife, and she suddenly said:

"By the way, I have had a letter from Vilhelmine. She writes that they are going to be here this winter."

"All of them?" asked Mrs von Eichbaum.

"No, Mourier is going to stay at home, so only Mine and Kate. But they have thought of renting an apartment, my dear. They can afford it."

Mrs Vilhelmine Mourier was the wife of a merchant from Aarhus, one of the group of friends, whose husband had made a huge fortune by exporting butter to England.

"And Kate," said the general's wife, "is about twenty now."

Mrs von Eichbaum, who had not seen Kate Mourier for two or three years, asked:

"What is she like now she has grown up?"

"Fair-haired and quite pretty...a bit full of herself, I suppose, but that is how they easily turn out in the provinces where they are among the leading families."

"My dear," said Mrs von Eichbaum, "she will get over that with a mother like Vilhelmine."

"A good figure," said the general's wife, who was still thinking about Kate Mourier's exterior.

Mrs von Eichbaum was thinking that she would nevertheless write to Mine Mourier and say how delightful she thought it that they could be living close to each other throughout the winter.

"I think they are going to travel around in Jutland a little first," the general's wife went on. "Mourier wants to look for an estate... somewhere to spend the summer months. That is only reasonable, considering that Vilhelmine has been accustomed to country living since she was a child."

Mrs von Eichbaum made no reply, but a new association of ideas persuaded her to say:

"Did you know that the little Brandt girl, the bailiff's daughter, you remember, is working in the hospital?"

"Oh," said the general's wife, "so that is where she has ended up."

And in a quite indifferent tone she added:

"Does she really need to do that?"

"Good heavens, Lotte, she inherited over eighty thousand," replied Mrs von Eichbaum. The mention of this sum seemed to occupy her mind for a moment, and after a brief silence she added, almost thoughtfully: "Her father was an excellent man."

The general's wife prepared to take her leave and asked to be remembered to Karl; but after she had put on her outdoor clothes in the vestibule, she said:

"By the way, Emilie, could you possibly lend me Petri's sermons?...The roads leading to the chapel are all muddy, and I no longer know anyone there."

Mrs von Eichbaum fetched the sermons, and the general's wife said:

"Thank you, dear...yes, one longs for Petri in the summer. The others do not have the same clarity of thought as he does."

Mrs von Eichbaum nodded.

"My dear," she said, "it is the serenity that he has inherited from his father."

As she opened the main door, a young man in uniform was on his way up the steps.

"Is it for me?" asked Mrs von Eichbaum.

"Yes, it's a bill for you, madam."

Mrs von Eichbaum took it, the corners of her mouth trembling imperceptibly, and the general's wife quickly glanced at her sister through the mirror.

"Oh," said Mrs von Eichbaum as she opened the bill. It is from Mrs Cohn. I have had my grey silk dress cleaned. With some black trimming on the front it can still look quite smart."

"Goodbye, Charlotte."

"Goodbye, Emilie. Well, I will see you on Sunday. I am going to borrow Julius, you know."

When members of the family were giving dinners, they borrowed Julius in turn.

"Goodbye."

The general's wife had descended the steps, and Mrs von Eichbaum went inside to her writing desk in the sitting room, while the messenger waited in the entrance.

Mrs von Eichbaum's money was in the writing desk drawer, divided up into various envelopes, where she had it ready, each for its own purpose. She took fifteen kroner out, and the messenger left. Mrs von Eichbaum seated herself again at the desk and calculated.

After buying an annuity three years ago with the money not used up by Karl, Mrs von Eichbaum had to be very careful with everything.

But at least she still had *the home*.

Mrs von Eichbaum remained seated at the desk.

It was a good thing it had been the account from Cohn and that Charlotte had seen that that was what it was.

But Karl was really settling down now – it was to be hoped – out in that office of his.

Mrs von Eichbaum rose and started on her bed curtain. Her expression was different now; she looked more careworn and older when sitting like that, working and alone.

Julius came into the dining room with the polished knives on a tray and set them out.

At half past four, Julius came in to light the stove, and Mrs von Eichbaum asked:

"Have you lit the fire in my son's room?"

"Yes, madam."

"Thank you."

Mrs von Eichbaum rarely went to her son's room. The only door into it was from the hallway. When Karl came home from Switzerland four years ago, while she herself was at Aix, she had had the door to Karl's room from the sitting room bricked up,

When there were visitors, the gentlemen smoked in there of course.

"And," Mrs von Eichbaum had explained to Mr Petersen, the family builder, "by bricking it up, you avoid exposing your good furniture to all that smoke."

Mr Petersen had bricked it up, and when Karl von Eichbaum came home, the only entrance to his room was from the hall.

Mrs von Eichbaum heard that Karl was in the small drawing room, and she nodded to him from the doorway.

"Aunt Charlotte has been here," she said. "She says it is so lovely out there. She sends her love to you."

She did not speak with such a distinguished voice when addressing her son and the words became as it were narrower in her mouth.

"Thank you," said Karl, sitting down on a chair by the desk. He never stood for long at a time; and then he asked:

"When are they moving in?"

Mrs von Eichbaum was talking about this when Julius opened the door to the dining room with a hushed: "Dinner is served, madam," and they went to the table, where the bottle of red wine, on which there was no label, stood at Karl's place.

"May I pour for you, mother?" said Karl, leaning forward.

"Yes, please. So it is going to be red today?"

There were days when Karl dined out and Mrs von Eichbaum only drank water.

She served the food while continuing to talk about the country seat and the lovely mornings.

"Yes," said Karl in a rather different tone, and he sat for a moment with the glass of wine in his hand.

"The mornings are jolly beautiful."

And they ate a little until Mrs von Eichbaum stumbled on the Mouriers as a subject to talk about. They always had to *find* a subject to discuss.

"They are coming to town this year, according to my sister Charlotte. You know, the Mouriers from Aarhus."

"Oh," said Karl, "the butter merchant."

"My dear Karl," – Mrs von Eichbaum left her spoon in the soup for a moment – "trade is extremely respectable these days."

"Yes," murmured Karl. "They make money, of course."

He had an indolent, troubled antipathy to people who went around making money.

"And Vilhelmine, who is back from Unsgaard – that lovely home of hers."

Mrs von Eichbaum took another bite: "But they are travelling around in Jutland first, looking at country houses."

Nothing more was said for a while until Karl, in order to say something, commented indifferently as Julius was offering him the second course.

"Well, they could buy Ludvigsbakke."

His Lordship's heirs were still lumbered with the estate, which they were unable to sell at a reasonable price in these difficult times.

"I think it would be too big for them," said Mrs von Eichbaum.

"Well, they have the money," said Karl. "And most of it would stay invested in the place."

And Karl suddenly became quite enthusiastic as he poured himself another glass, and he went on talking about "Ludvigs".

"They will never find a better place," he said, thinking of the broad approach road across the fields and the great poplars along the drive and the lawns where the sun shone straight in his face, and the stables where the two horses were left loose in their big stalls.

They'll never find a better place," he said again. "And it's all well kept, both the buildings and the lot."

"Yes, the house makes a good impression," said Mrs von Eichbaum.

Karl thought of the white main building, the steps and the drive down past the bailiff's wing, and suddenly he laughed.

"And Recks could perfectly well get out now," he said, "now that Mrs Reck has got Konstance married."

"Karl," said Mrs von Eichbaum, and then paused. "I do not think Mrs Reck is one of those mothers..."

But Karl continued to talk about "Ludvigs" as he cracked walnuts and peeled apples, and Mrs von Eichbaum sat there animated and with a red patch in her cheeks. She was always so happy when they sat at table for a time.

"And the hunting's fine," said Karl as they left the table.

"I hope you have enjoyed your dinner, my boy," said Mrs Eichbaum, holding his hand in hers for a moment.

Karl remained in a good mood and went on talking, and in the sitting room he said:

"Let me have my coffee in here, mother."

"Mrs von Eichbaum hurried to open the door to the dining room again.

"Julius, my son would like his coffee in here," she said in a clear voice.

"I am sure you want to smoke?" she said.

And as they sat down, each on their own side in the corner sofa, and Karl lit his cigarette, she told him:

"I have heard that Schrøder is in a bad way. I believe she has dropsy."

Karl looked up from his smoking and said:

"You might invite Ida Brandt down here some time, mother. She doesn't know anyone, of course."

"Yes, of course I could," said Mrs von Eichbaum more eagerly: "Some time, she is really quite nice."

Karl looked at the smoke.

"She's sweet," he said.

And shortly afterwards:

"She's really sweet."

Julius brought the coffee, and Karl sat watching him until he had gone again.

"Mother, couldn't you tell Julius to wear some decent boots?"

The prunella boots worn by Julius were a constant source of irritation to him. It was impossible to hear the man coming.

"Good Heavens, Karl," said Mrs von Eichbaum as she poured the coffee. "I think it is delightful that the person waiting on us cannot be heard."

The fact was that Julius suffered from bad feet, which in recent years had prevented him from taking a better post.

"Dear Emilie," said the general's wife to her sister, "we would never keep that excellent man otherwise."

Karl's cigarette went out and, half smiling, he sat there looking at his own reflection in the mirror on the étagère.

Oh, how well he knew that étagère. It had stood in that very place ever since his childhood, with the same Meissen dishes in the same places.

And with a smile, he said:

"Your things keep well, mother."

"Yes, when one looks after them," said Mrs von Eichbaum.

Karl made no reply; but, suddenly overcome by a sort of sense of all the tenderness hidden in this home, which, in spite of him and in spite of everything, had *remained the same*, he reached out for his mother's hand and pressed it gently.

Then he rose.

"I'll stay at home this evening," he said. "I can read something."

When he had gone, Mrs von Eichbaum got up and, as was her custom when Karl was at home, closed the door to the small drawing room. Her hands shook a little as she pushed the bolt down. It was a curious feature about Mrs von Eichbaum, who was otherwise so composed, that her hands trembled a little if she was happy. But that was the only sign that she was growing older.

Karl went into his own room and lit the lamp before putting on a smoking jacket from behind the curtain hiding the bed. It was a large, French bed. Mrs von Eichbaum had bought it when Karl was due to come home.

"For," she said to the general's wife, "people who have been in France..."

"My dear," replied the general's wife, "it is only reasonable. Everyone needs a good night's sleep."

The bed was bought.

Karl seated himself in the easy chair and raised the footrest and took one of the French books. His room did not look as though it was occupied except just in the mornings before it was tidied up, for then there was disarray in plenty with the rifles, some pictures of horses and a couple of old Eichbaum sabres on the walls and the yellow books on the table, which Ane tidied up each day into two piles of equal height.

Karl did not manage to read much. He sat with his pipe and continued to think about the "estate".

Of course these Mouriers could buy "Ludvigs", because they had been fleecing the Brahers and the Vedels of their butter for the past twenty years.

Karl wrinkled his nose as always when he felt some repugnance or surprise.

"It's incredible," he said.

That was his favourite expression. That people could undertake anything at all was to Karl von Eichbaum a matter of such amazement that a large proportion of life's phenomena and results naturally had to seem "incredible" to him.

"But good heavens," he said.

He continued to think of "Ludvigs".

If he had become a gentleman farmer instead of failing all those examinations, then he could perhaps have become the butter merchant's tenant.

Karl pursed his lip.

Hm, the last summer they had spent at "Ludvigs" was the year

Ida's mother died.

There was a knock on the door, and Julius entered with a bottle on a tray.

"Madam asked me to bring the Madeira," he said.

Karl nodded as he poured himself a glass: the Madeira was good. Damn it all, it came from the place itself.

Mrs von Eichbaum's Madeira was brought home by naval officers in the family.

"It's no damned good running around to all those hostelries," said Karl.

With his glass before him, he started to read again. But before long he put the yellow book down on his knee and smiled. He thought that it would really be fun to take Ida Brandt to one of those places, for she had naturally never seen anything of the kind.

Mrs von Eichbaum was sitting at her desk. She had as it were immediately felt a desire to write to Vilhelmine. For the day was passing, and she was in danger of not doing it. And today she had been thinking so much of her and of the time she had spent up at Unsgaaard.

"Dear Vilhelmine," she wrote. "How lovely it is to think we are going to be together again, and not only for a couple of weeks in an hotel, which only makes one feel restless. But to have you here in peace and quiet. I hope you will be able to find something near here. I am thinking of the Lindholms, who are going to Nice with their sick daughter Mary – they always go away with their consumptives when it is too late. You could perhaps rent *that* apartment if we get it well aired and thoroughly cleaned. You know it is quite close to us, and it would be good for Kate so, being close to Grønningen and Langelinie and you must also think of your health. I am really looking forward to the winter, also to seeing Kate; it is so good to have a few young people around us."

Mrs von Eichbaum had closed the letter and was sitting staring into the candles. She was thinking of Karl. Now that he was busy for a specific time every day with something like an office that demanded his attention, he had quite calmed down. But the fault had always been hers. She should never have sent him away from home. Karl, who was so easily swayed.

Mrs von Eichbaum heard Julius in the dining room. She felt it was a long time since she had so looked forward to a cup of tea.

∞∞∞

On the Sunday it was warm enough for the general's wife and Mrs von Eichbaum to take coffee on the veranda. The general's wife said: "You only need a shawl across your shoulders, Mille; you are accustomed to the air in town."

Julius brought the shawl, and the sisters sat together looking out across the Sound. "My nephew does not require coffee," said the general's wife. Karl von Eichbaum had gone down to Bellevue to play billiards.

Mrs von Eichbaum was talking about Vilhelmine Mourier.

"I wrote to her," she said, "and I wonder if they could not rent the Lindholms' apartment..."

"Good heavens, Emilie," said the general's wife. "Do you really think so – in a house where there is consumption?"

"My dear," said Mrs von Eichbaum, "where on earth could one live if one were so nervous? I am used to travelling, and I can only ask you where can one avoid infection? Naturally not using the same bedclothes, and *provided* we make sure beforehand that the house has been properly aired."

"Yes," said the general's wife.

"And it would be nice if they were close to us so we could visit each other."

Mrs von Eichbaum looked out over the water for a moment.

"And lovely for Kate with Grønningen – it would be nice for her when she is so fond of riding."

The general's wife nodded.

"She is a superb horsewoman," she said. (In the family the *e* in superb tended to be pronounced as an *a*).

And shortly afterwards, looking out across the water:

"She has just the same figure as Vilhelmine had in her youth."
The sisters went on to talk of other things.

∞∞∞

That Sunday was the last warm day of the year.

On the Monday it was wet and dirty underfoot, and Ida struggled to make her way on her last morning walk – for she was no longer on night duty from today – up against the wind along the lakes.

When she arrived back home, she came across Karl von Eichbaum, who had just got off the tram.

He was drifting along over on the pavement with both hands in his pockets and the oilcloth briefcase held tight under his right arm.

"Ugh," he said discontentedly, but suddenly he smiled:

"Spring didn't arrive then."

"No, I don't think we shall be going on any picnics in the forest."

"Well in that case," said Karl, thrusting his hands deep into his pockets, "let's go out and enjoy ourselves."

Ida laughed.

"How?" she said.

"We'll go out somewhere one evening to eat. We can take someone else with us..."

"That would be worse," Ida said hurriedly.

Adding, as she blushed deeply:

"With someone I don't know."

"Oh, all right," said Karl in a voice that was suddenly transformed and gentler:

"Then we'll go alone."

They went in through the entrance and exchanged a few more words.

Then, already on the big steps leading up to the office, still with his hands in his pockets, but in the same gentle voice as before, Karl said:

"How old are you, Miss Ida?"

"You know perfectly well."

But Karl said:

"No, I'm sure you're just seventeen."

Ida merely laughed – that was the youngest feature about her, her brief, little, gentle laugh; and they each went their way.

Ida went up to her room. By the time she was in bed, the sun had come out behind the dark green curtains. The room was filled with a gentle, quiet light like that from a matt, green lamp. Ida lay with her eyes half closed.

But she suddenly thought that Karl Eichbaum had been wearing a summer overcoat even today.

Two days later, when she had to take an admission slip across to the office, she met Karl von Eichbaum coming in through the door dressed in a splendid new overcoat. He had been out to lunch. When he had any money at his disposal, Karl von Eichbaum gave "Ane's handiwork" to a porter and had his lunch at "Svendsen's".

They exchanged a few words and Ida gave him an admiring look.

"Yes," said Karl, sticking out his chest, "I'm looking smart today."

"Terribly," she said, suddenly reverting to a Jutland accent. She had been so pleased to see the splendid new coat.

But Karl said:

"You should throw some salt over my shoulder, Miss Ida."

"Yes," said Ida, "that's what we girls always did at home in Horsens."

They were still laughing when a lady entered.

"Hello, mother," said Karl, taking a couple of steps away from Ida.

Then he said: "This is Miss Brandt."

Mrs von Eichbaum held out her hand.

"I am pleased to see you, Ida. Karl has told me of course that you have a position here."

"Yes," said Ida, blushing slightly as she hurried to add: "I have an admission slip to hand in."

"Well," said Mrs von Eichbaum, "you must come and visit me

126

one day – now (she said with a slight smile) that you are working in the same building as my son. He can always let me know one day when you are free."

Mother and son remained down in the doorway while Mrs von Eichbaum gave a message to Karl. Mrs von Eichbaum preferred to go herself rather than send Julius. "One should not," she said to her sister, "send Julius and his like to an office where the other employees, you know, might be in less important posts."

When Karl accompanied her back to the door, Mrs von Eichbaum said:

"I really do think it is delightful that you have the little Brandt girl here, you can always exchange a few words with her. Goodbye, Karl."

As Karl went back up the stairs he met Ida emerging from the office.

"Have you given it any more thought, Miss Ida?" said Karl.

"Any more thought to what?"

"To the idea of going out for something to eat," said Karl. "Because, by Gad, this winter overcoat" – he said, tapping the new garment – "needs to be christened."

∞∞∞∞

Ida turned out the lamps in front of her looking glass and tried to find the door in the dark. She did not herself realise she was walking so carefully on tiptoe. But she did not wish to meet anyone now just as she was going out.

She ran on down the stairs, and suddenly she started: the door to the ward with the restless patients had been opened and closed.

"Ugh," said Quam, as he emerged. "We are never left in peace."

"Well, I'm off duty," said Ida as she ran off.

She went out through the courtyard and the entrance hall, where she nodded to everyone: two porters who were standing by one door, and one in the middle of the room and Josefine who was coming down the stairs.

"Oh, nurse," said Josefine as she eyed her new coat, "so you are off to enjoy yourself now." And she nodded, like the others.

"Yes," said Ida with a smile.

She went out into the street. She could see him over by the lamp post: *there* he was already, on the corner by the Botanical Gardens.

"Here I am," she said, looking up. She was almost out of breath.

"Yes," said Karl. "You are in good time. Good evening."

And they shook hands.

They walked along, while the tramcar bells clanged and the cab horses trotted.

"So what did you say, then?" asked Karl in the rather drawling voice he was fond of using when he was not pleased. "Where did you say you were going?"

"Oh, I said something or other."

"Yes," said Karl. "One can always tell the odd fib or two." And he gave a little laugh.

"For that's something you learn to do already as a child, God help me."

Ida suddenly assumed a serious expression.

"Oh yes."

But her mood changed again, and she exclaimed:

"It was as though they were all saying they hoped I would enjoy myself."

She was thinking of those who had nodded to her in the doorway.

And Karl, walking along with his cigar hanging from the very extreme tips of his lips, said:

"Well, now we'd better give a bit of thought to what we're going to have to eat."

They both laughed.

They had reached the entrance to the Ørsted Park.

"We can go through the park; there's plenty of time," said Ida.

"But they'll be closing it," said Karl, following her.

They walked over the last fallen leaves, but there were still a few flowers left in the various beds.

"It's so beautiful," said Ida.

There could not be anyone else in the entire park, not a soul on all those paths, and as they walked along beside each other they could hear the sound of their own footsteps.

"They'll be going to sleep now," said Karl as he pointed to one of the silent statues.

They went over to a small terrace beneath a huge tree. Below them lay the slopes down to the dark, shining water.

Ida spoke more quietly:

"This is such a lovely place," she said.

Karl blew the smoke from his cigar in long rings, and neither of them spoke. It was as though the sounds of bells and carriages faded into the distance, and the light from the street lamps hung over the wrought iron gates like some resplendent wreath.

"Is this what it is like in big cities?" said Ida quietly.

Her eyes followed the slopes and the bridge down to the silent water.

"Yes," said Karl, and the rings from the cigar were dispersing.

"Nowhere more beautiful?"

"No," he said.

A swan silently made its way forward in the dark waters.

They stood there for a moment longer.

"But we are going to be late," said Ida in a quite different voice, and they turned to leave.

"Ah, good evening, old boy!" Karl nodded up to Ørsted's statue as they went past it, and they laughed again.

Ida was still a step in front of Karl now as they went through the park.

"We don't need to hurry," said Karl, who loved the "dusk" in the streets.

"Yes, but then we can see everyone arriving," said Ida, continuing to hurry.

But when they reached the theatre and entered dress circle, there was not a single person in the stalls.

"Well," said Karl. "Was this early enough for you?"

People gradually began to arrive, and they could hear the cheerful sound of seats being dropped and of the attendants' keys in the doors to the boxes, and from the foyer all the happy sounds of pushing and talking.

Ida raised her shoulders with a feeling of wellbeing as she shook her sleeves a little.

"Oh," she said, "it's the first time this play has been on."

"Yes," said Karl; "that's what is exciting about it."

There were gentlemen in tails standing in the stalls, and elegantly coiffured ladies were moving quickly to take their places. Karl recited their names: critics and authors and people she had read of in the newspapers.

Ida sat chatting, full of delight, and followed every name he mentioned. But suddenly she half rose and looked up towards the balcony with a little toss of her head.

"That's where we usually sit," she said and quickly sat down again.

"Who?"

"We," she said.

Some nurses had had subscriptions to the theatre last year.

As the noise increased, Ida sat down again smiling, with her back leant right back against her seat. But all at once, she said, quite frightened and turning scarlet.

"Oh, but suppose Mrs von Eichbaum were here."

"She isn't," said Karl. "She never goes to these private theatres unless she gets a decent ticket from someone she knows, and she hasn't got one this evening."

They again watched people continuing to stream in. Ida caught Karl's arm.

"Look, there's Mrs Lind. She's been in the ward."

That was the only person she knew.

The footlights were lit and bathed the curtain in their light. All heads in the stalls were bobbing about, and bright faces could be seen peering over the balcony rail.

Ida continued to smile.

"It's almost like going to a ball," she said quite quietly.

Karl sat with his legs wide apart, biting his moustache and looking as though it was something that tasted good.

The orchestra had been playing for some time.

"What's that they are playing?" said Karl and asked to see the programme. But Ida made no reply; she was sitting with her eyes half closed, listening to the music. Karl looked down on her forehead from the side. It was so small and so narrow. He felt the urge to stretch his fingers over it – like that – from temple to temple.

Ida sensed his gaze and opened her eyes fully.

"It's so lovely here," she said. "Don't you think so?"

The curtain rose.

People were pushing and shoving in the crowded rooms in the restaurant. Karl von Eichbaum went behind Ida Brandt, protecting her with his arms, but Ida was laughing all over her face as she turned round.

"We must sit where we can see people," she said, and her eyes were radiant.

"I've booked a table," said Karl.

It was in one of the small alcoves between partitions, and at last they reached it. But Ida remained seated on the sofa in there, with her hat and all her clothes on. She was looking at the ladies and gentlemen who continued to pour in.

Karl helped her off with her outdoor clothes and sat down.

"There," he said, stretching his legs out and wrinkling his nose:

"Now we're going to have some French food."

"Yes," said Ida, throwing her head back quickly. She did not know what she was saying "Yes" to.

Karl ordered and the waiter brought dishes and Karl served. Ida merely sat and watched them, observing everything they did and smiling; and she was so curiously cautious in the way in which she touched things, her glass, the dish and her bread, as though she were wondering at it all, at every single thing – the table cloth and the lamp and the green bottle in the cooler.

Then she spread both her hands out on the sofa and said with a quiet laugh:

"Just fancy that I'm sitting here."

Karl smiled happily at her and looked out at the people in the body of the restaurant who could scarcely find a seat at a table.

"Yes, we're sitting in the best place here, by Gad."

Ida remained seated in the same position:

"Hm," she said in the same voice, "it's just like having a picnic in the woods."

Karl, who ate slowly though with great appetite, laughed and said:

"Oh, I don't agree, the food you get is always so miserable on a picnic."

Ida continued to think of her excursions in the forest; the trips over there when a whole charabanc had gone to Stensballe and they had danced in front of the wheelwright's house and had rolling races down the high mounds.

"Yes," she said, "this is just like it was at home.

But Karl, who was beginning to feel he had had enough of this, said that she really must eat something and put a thrush on her plate.

"The food's damned good," he said; and as he thought of picnics in the woods, he sat there with his elbows on the table (and thought that by Gad she was good looking).

"I suppose you went on a lot of picnics in the woods?"

Ida sat for a moment staring up into the air.

"No, not all that often," she said in a quieter voice.

Karl continued to look at her:

"Now let us two Jutlanders drink to each other." He raised his glass to her with a smile.

Ida laughed and took hers.

"But you are not really a Jutlander at all."

Karl wrinkled his nose.

"Of course I am: all we Eichbaums are Jutlanders. That's where we once owned something."

And they drank.

Karl continued to sit and serve her, all the time with his elbows on the table: cheese and celery sticks, which he twice reached over and dipped in her salt cellar.

"They were all so nice at Ludvigsbakke," said Ida.

"Yes."

He continued to chew his celery while looking at her, and then he said:

"Ida, you should always wear yellow."

"Why?"

"Because," he said lethargically.

Karl went on chewing at his celery stick, and suddenly he thought of the Mouriers. He told Ida about them and how they might possibly buy "Ludvigs". "He's a butter merchant from Aarhus," he said. He lengthened the first syllable in the name of the "capital of Jutland" to signal his scorn, and then said with some satisfaction:

"But then we can get the Recks out."

"Why?"

"Well," said Karl in his dry voice, "because they're simply rabble."

"Yes," said Ida without thinking. She did not know herself why she felt so happy or that her face was radiant.

"And then we'll be able to go over there in the summer again," said Karl. "Cheers, Ida."

"Cheers," said Ida, still with the same expression on her face.

And Karl, who had put his glass down and stuck his hands into his pockets, said happily:

"But it can be very nice in our capital city, don't you think?"

They continued to chat happily and as it were came closer to each other. Ida spoke of Olivia and the villa and the Jørgensens – she always did this when she was happy – but suddenly she said:

"Oh, but he had such a loud voice..."

"Who did?"

"The suitor," she said.

Karl laughed.

"Well, you've got to be able to hear him."

Ida sat staring in front of her.

"Yes, but even so," she said more gently.

There were not many left out in the main body of the restaurant, and the waiters were whispering to each other over their bills.

Karl sat smiling and looked at the neck of a bottle.

"Have you ever been in love, Ida?" he said.

Ida looked up and shook her head a little sadly.

"No," she said in a tone that suggested that this was something that had passed her by.

"But" – and her voice trembled a little and she did not herself know why she said it or what she was really thinking of, if it were not the small house in Horsens and its three gloomy rooms.

"But," she said, looking across the table and trying to smile, "I suppose I have been sad rather often."

Karl had developed a kindly look in his eyes.

"That's damned hard to believe," was all he said.

And they sat silent for a while.

Ida looked out into the main restaurant, where it was half dark and most lights had been extinguished.

"But they've all gone," she said and was afraid.

"Yes," said Karl, sitting up indolently in his chair: "But we're damned well going to have a cup of coffee."

They were served with it and with liqueurs as well, which Karl poured. He continued to have such a gentle manner and tender voice as they sat there a little longer. But the waiters were beginning to lose patience and extinguished the last gas lamps, so that darkness forced itself in on them. The sole light now was that from the candelabra.

Ida looked at the darkness now closing in on them.

"It's all over now," she said.

"It'll be your turn next time," said Karl.

"Yes," said Ida quickly and happily.

"And that must be at home, in your room" said Karl as he helped her on with her coat.

"Oh no," said Ida with a laugh.

"Why?"

"It's not allowed."

Ida continued to laugh, but Karl merely passed her hat to her and said:

"Oh, never mind about that."

They went out through the hotel reception, and the porter made to close the door after them, when Ida, radiant with delight, said:

"Now, I must..." and put a krone in his hand.

Karl gave a hearty laugh.

"But, for God's sake, Ida, do you think that is a proper thing to do?"

When they had gone a little further down the street, he offered Ida his arm.

"I suppose I may offer the lady my arm," he said.

"Yes," said Ida as she took it, pressing her shoulders a little together. "It's night now, of course."

Karl walked up and down in his sitting room, smiling, for a long time before getting up into his big bed. The light was by the bed, and a yellow book lay there. But he did not read.

He simply lay there, looking up at the ceiling and wrinkling his nose.

"No," he said, profoundly reflective or wondering. "There's no understanding a woman after all."

And he stayed there and smiling amidst the smoke from his cigar.

∞∞∞∞

All was quiet in the block, and Ida went silently up the stairs. When she reached the first floor, she found Nurse Roed standing in front of the open cupboard.

"Good heavens, is it you coming home so late?" she said. "Where have you been, having a picnic?"

Ida suddenly smiled at the word "picnic". "I've been out," she said and made to continue. She was walking as though she was carrying some wonderful but invisible thing in her hands and wanted to bring it to safety.

"Good night."

But Nurse Petersen, dressed in elegant fabric slippers for the night, had heard her from behind the door and opened it. There was nothing that interested her as much as a detailed account from someone who had been "out".

"Ach, is it you," she said. Her voice assumed a quite special meddlesome quality when she sensed news.

Suddenly, Ida turned Nurse Roed around twice in front of the cupboard. "I've been to the theatre," she said so loudly that her voice suddenly resounded down the corridor and then she ran.

"Sshh, think of the patients," said Nurse Roed. But the two nurses merely heard Ida laugh up above; and they went in to where their dinner awaited them under the gas lamp.

As they ate, they could hear the deep breathing of the old patients and a few broken words from Bertelsen as he talked in his sleep, as though he was both obstinate and angry. There was the sound of footsteps to and fro in Ward A.

Nurse Petersen went on eating, and in the ward Bertelsen continued to talk in his sleep. Nurse Roed got up to see to him; but as always he lay tossing and turning, with clenched fists.

Ida was up in her room. She set the alarm clock and undressed. She was not really thinking about anything; she simply hummed quietly all the time until she was in bed.

Well, yes, it might be possible for Eichbaum to come for coffee if he could come up very quietly...

Ida's face radiated delight in the darkness.

But it would have to be a Tuesday when Nurse Roed was off duty...he could quite easily tiptoe up on a Tuesday, very gently.

Ida continued to smile as she thought about it. Then they would be able to use all the old things from "Ludvigs" and see whether he recognised them and set a real table...

Ida fell asleep.

It was midday a few days later. The four had come up from the basement and were walking round and round in the anteroom, alongside the walls as they waited for their meal (Bertelsen had developed a habit of constantly passing his hand over his eyes as though trying to wipe away something that prevented him from seeing). The jingle of keys was heard and Josefine came with the food.

"Good morning everyone," she said. "Here's your lunch."

She went into the kitchen to help Ida with the containers, while Bertelsen ceaselessly washed his hands under the tap.

"It's a shame about the head clerk," Josefine then said.

"What is?"

Ida spoke quickly. Josefine always referred to Eichbaum as the head clerk.

"They are after him for one unpaid bill after the other," said Josefine, "and everyone's talking about it."

"Here, in the office?" It sounded as though Ida had something stuck in her throat.

"Yes," said Josefine, putting down the container. "And the superintendent will be on him like a ton of bricks if it goes on."

Ida nodded mechanically.

"But of course, it's those women that are after him; we know all about that," said Josefine, proceeding to place potatoes on the six plates.

Ida made no reply; she simply went on to serve the food, while Josefine, who had finished her task, stood there with her hands on her hips.

"And he is certainly good looking," she said, staring ahead reflectively.

Josefine had a sympathetic eye for all male creation. Otherwise, she remained completely faithful to her conductor. *She* never left a "friend", and when *he* went off and she had shed copious tears, she then remained as it were in the same area. It was always a tram conductor. It was simply a different one.

"Yes," she said, "I know all about it, for Andersen has been a bad one." (Andersen being the current conductor.) "But now we've sorted it out."

It could not be seen whether Ida was listening, for she simply stood there moving the six plates around.

"Well, and then we went on," said Josefine.

There were always a few snatches of forbidden tunes, bits of variety songs, rather like a fanfare, when Josefine started.

Ida placed plates on the table in front of each of the four patients: "Now you must have something to eat, Holm," she said. "Now then, Bertelsen, you just stay where you are and have something to eat." She helped the two old men to get their food down, bit by bit, and she was finished and had cleared away while having but a single thought.

"That poor man, that poor man."

Comprehension was never established in her mind all at once, but only slowly and little by little until it grew out of all proportion and was all that was there.

What was to be done?

She served the gentleman in Ward A. He was bent over his never-ending papers, and she heard his "Thank you," and "Thank you," as he raised his head and watched her.

Ida went out again and sat down on the chair by the window.

And she had helped him to spend his money.

Her thoughts went no further than this: she had helped him to spend his money. All Josefine's words rang in her ears again and again, and suddenly she flushed scarlet. There was something she had only now understood. She did not herself know that she was not thinking about money any longer, but only about one thing, merely about that one thing...nevertheless each time skirting round it, skirting round that sentence.

Who had spent his money?

The porter fetched the four for work in the basement, and the old patients dozed in their beds. In Ward A, the gentleman measured the floor with his feet. Occasionally there came a cry from the "noisy" ward.

Ida went to and fro seeing to the old patients and then she returned to her chair until it grew dusk.

Nurse Kjær stuck her boyish head in from the women's ward.

"Good evening, nurse.

And suddenly Ida said:

"Oh, Nurse Kjær, could you take over for a moment? I would so much like to go upstairs."

"Yes," said Nurse Kjær, closing the door, "just for a moment."

Ida went out, down the steps, through the garden and hurried across the courtyard to the office. Karl was there alone by the desks beneath the gas lamp, with his legs drawn back under the office chair and his chin on his hands; he was whistling.

When he saw her, he raised his head and smiled at her:

"Good evening."

She asked about something or other – she did not know what – and she suddenly smiled as he went on talking and all at once stretched in the chair reaching up into the air with his arms.

"Heavens above, what a life," he said.

And Ida laughed.

She went back across the courtyard. She was no longer troubled and she smiled as she walked. All she was thinking was:

"It's only reasonable that I should help him."

And she no longer thought of anything else, simply because she had seen him.

When Ida reached the ward, Nurse Kjær was waiting just inside the door.

"The prof's there," she whispered.

Ida jumped and was horrified.

"Where?" she whispered.

"In A."

There was the sound of keys being gently turned, and Nurse Kjær was back in the women's ward. Ida went around lighting up, hearing the professor's voice through the door to Ward A, which was standing ajar. She started to tidy everything up ready for the round, at the same time hearing the porter and the four on the stairs and the keys that were turned in the lock.

"The consultant's here," she whispered to the porter, and the four patients, who heard her, crossed over timidly and sat down on the stools beside their beds, while a voice from the women's ward could suddenly be heard wailing.

Ida was standing in front of the stove when the door to Ward A opened. The professor remained on the threshold, slim and straight, in his long, black coat.

"Yes, just continue, doctor," he said, closing the door behind him..."Let the patient do as he wishes. And you can turn the gas down at night."

There was as it were no colour in his voice, and he scarcely opened his lips to speak as though it were a matter of keeping them as tight closed as possible around his white teeth and many secrets.

"Yes, professor."

He stood for a moment on the threshold to the Hall, while Bertelsen's eyes glinted as they wandered over his face.

"Nothing new," he said, moving on silently, in through the door to the women's ward. But one of the old men lying there in his bed started to complain, as he always did during the professor's rounds.

Ida went across and knocked on Nurse Petersen's door to waken her. Dr Quam had come in, but she had not heard him.

"Where's the professor?" he asked hurriedly.

"He went in to the women's ward," replied Ida, who was on her way to the Hall.

Quam was ready to rush across, but he nevertheless stood there for a moment and looked at Ida.

"Is it your birthday again today?" he asked.

Ida laughed:

"No, why?"

"Well you look so cheerful," he said. He was already half way into the women's ward. The woman's cry from before emerged clearly through the open door.

"Nurse Petersen, Nurse Petersen," Ida shouted.

She turned round; Bertelsen had his hands under the tap again.

"Come on, Bertelsen," she said, taking him by both wrists and waggling them as though she was shaking hands with him: "You are washed clean now."

And as she continued to shake the sick man's wet, red wrists for a moment, she thought with a smile:

"Poor Karl, he tried not to let me see that he was upset."

They were becoming more and more restless in the women's ward. Cry after cry, as though the cries were calling to each other and washing up against the closed door.

Nurse Petersen, who had emerged from her bower, put her head into the kitchen.

"Ach, how restless they are," she said. "But we have a change in the weather."

Nurse Petersen's feet were as good as a barometer when there was a change in the weather.

But after tea, Ida ran across to the post office with a registered letter for Mr Karl von Eichbaum.

It was Ida's last day on day duty.

Nurse Helgesen went through the ward checking; she had a look in her eye all the time as though she were adding something or other to a list.

"Will you take this report across?" she said to Ida.

"Yes," replied Ida. All the blood drained from her face.

"I have to stay here," said Nurse Helgesen, sitting down.

So Ida *had* to go across to the office. Her keys seemed to be reluctant to go into all the locks, and she failed to notice the ward sister nodding from her window. It was as though she had been overcome by fear the minute it had been sent yesterday. As soon as she emerged from the entrance to the post office, where she had been so delighted, so happy, as the postman sealed the letter and entered it and gave her a receipt and everything, she had been overcome by dread: suppose he was angry, suppose he was only angry? And she had not slept that night as the thought grew and grew in her mind: that he would be angry. But she ought probably to have written to him, to have said something and explained. But she had not been *able* to write. She had not been able to do it.

But perhaps he was angry now.

She went across the courtyard and in through the entrance and up the stairs. She immediately saw his face by the door; he looked pale. But when he saw her, he turned scarlet.

"I have a report," she said.

And he bent down towards her.

"It's simply damned incredible," he murmured in a voice that was a little broken.

"Thank you."

Ida drew her breath and made to go, but when they were outside the door – for he had followed her – she said (to help him over it or to comfort him; the thought of saying it had never entered her mind a second before):

"Now we'll have a cup of coffee on Tuesday."

It was as though Eichbaum winced. But pursing his lips, he said:

"I'd rather have tea."

Ida laughed:

"No," she said, still in the same hurried voice. "It's going to be coffee, and we are going to use the old pot."

And then she ran.

No, no, he was not angry.

Oh no, he had understood her.

Karl von Eichbaum went over to Svendsen's for lunch. He whistled as he went along the street; but there was nevertheless something, as though he could not really bring himself to think of the money or of the fact that he could now distribute it to plug the worst holes. And he also had something of an unpleasant feeling in his fingers at the mere thought of the envelope containing it.

But when he came to pay, he quickly took one from the bundle of large notes in order to change it.

Jensen, the waiter, stood there, half bowing in front of the envelope.

"Do you wish to pay it all, sir?" he said in a low voice down towards the sofa.

But Mr von Eichbaum did not reply. He had, as though timidly, taken out a card from among the notes. Ida was all that was printed on it and then there was a small picture of Ludvigsbakke in the corner.

Karl von Eichbaum continued to sit there with the card in his hand.

When lunch was over, both Svendsen's right-hand men, Messrs. Jensen and Sørensen, stood there each leaning on his own doorpost.

"There you see, Sørensen," (Mr Jensen spoke through his nose, which he considered a mark of distinction in the trade), "that I got the money. That sort of people always find a way out. *We* know that from d'Angleterre."

In the days when he was slimmer, Mr Jensen had been the wine waiter in the à-la-carte restaurant in the Hotel d'Angleterre.

"Aye, we do indeed," said Sørensen.

Mr Jensen made no reply. He was picking his teeth.

∞∞∞

Ida pretended to be asleep while looking from Nurse Roed in front of the mirror to the alarm clock in front of her bed through eyelids that were only a quarter open. She moved her feet gently up and down beneath the blankets. She could not lie still.

But Nurse Roed had her overcoat on at last and Ida pretended to be just waking up.

"Are you off to your sister's?" she said.

"Yes." That was where Nurse Roed was going. She always went to visit her sister, who was married to a clerk on the railways. They were the only people she knew in town, and in addition there was plenty she could do to help them, looking after their three children.

Ida suddenly had a picture of them, Nurse Roed and Mrs Hansen, as they sat sewing at home on the fourth floor in Rømersgade beneath the lamp in the living room, where the easy chairs – the backs of which were becoming worn – were covered with so many small pieces of embroidery and she suddenly laughed.

"What are you laughing at?" asked Nurse Roed.

"Oh, just something I thought of."

But suddenly, Ida threw the blankets aside and put her bare feet

143

on the floor.

"Oh," she said, "wait a moment." And she ran in her nightdress across to the dresser:

"I have something for the children." And standing in front of the open dresser so that Nurse Roed should not see the parcels and flowers in it, she tipped some French cakes out of a bag.

"They're so good," she said happily, putting one into Nurse Roed's mouth before jumping back into her bed.

"You always think of other people," said Nurse Roed.

But Ida simply laughed.

"No, I think of myself." And she lay looking up at the ceiling.

She heard Nurse Roed go down the stairs, and she got up again and very quietly turned the key twice as though she were afraid anyone might hear her. Then she started to dress as quickly as she could. There was something about her movements that resembled those of a schoolgirl about to carry out some mad scheme. Oh, there was plenty to do. There was a great deal to be seen to.

She pulled the drawers of the dresser out – they were so heavy from all the great number of things in them – and she took the damask cloth out and the old cups; and the silver coffee pot, which was wrapped in paper, she took out of the middle cupboard. There were also the old plates and the branched candlestick, in which she fixed candles; this was where he was to sit with the cigarettes by his place.

Hm, the last time she had put flowers on the table was for Olivia and the boys. Yes, that was in May. Fancy that it was no longer ago than the twentieth of May.

She lit the lamps and made sure the water was boiling. There must be a rose in his glass...

She went back and forth and she stood in front of the table: Yes, he would surely recognise the old things.

She started to listen while laying the colourful bedspreads on the beds. She looked at her alarm clock. It was not time yet and she sat down by the table, in his place, and waited. Someone was coming now, for she heard the door below: but it was only a porter.

144

Perhaps something had delayed him; perhaps he would not come. She became so convinced that he would not come as she sat there looking from one thing to the other as though she would at least print in her memory how lovely it was.

And as for the candles, she would let them burn, burn right down until they went out.

But the rose – she quietly took that out of his glass.

She had not heard anyone on the stairs when there came a gentle knock on the door, two knocks, in the way young men knock when on military service, and she opened the door.

"Oh, it's you," she said.

Karl von Eichbaum more or less tiptoed in. "I wasn't seen by anyone at all," he said.

"But Nurse Helgesen always sits just by her door," said Ida.

She locked the door – they had automatically both spoken in a half whisper – and Karl took off his coat.

"Well, here we are," he said as he shook her hand.

"Yes," said Ida with a laugh: "This is where you are to sit." She pointed to the big chair.

"It looks like Christmas Eve by Gad," said Karl, stretching his legs out as he looked at the white table.

"Yes, doesn't it," said Ida, who had felt just the same.

"And damn it, there are drinks, too," said Karl.

Ida poured the coffee in the old cups while Karl simply sat there looking happily at the array and talking about all the old things – the cake dish and the candlesticks. "They took care of their shells at home," he said.

"Yes, they were on an extension to the table," said Ida. In her mind she could see the old marble table in Ludvigsbakke with the shells and the fruit bowl from the court auction in Horsens and the two silver cups that were prizes from a couple of agricultural societies.

"But even so, we haven't any home-made cakes," she said.

Karl took liberal quantities of what cakes there were, and also of the liqueur. "Yes," he said, "we helped ourselves to some from

Schrøder." He was thinking of the dented cake tin from Ludvigsbakke. "It's great fun to go pinching like that."

"Yes, it was fun," said Ida, shaking her head, for Karl was looking at her; he always found it so amusing when she did that.

"Did you pinch things at home as well?" asked Karl.

"Yes, quite a lot," said Ida hurriedly, but suddenly she turned pale.

"How so?" asked Karl.

Ida stared up in the air and then, slowly and quietly, said:

"Because I had to."

There was silence for a moment.

Then she pulled herself together and raised her glass, and they chinked glasses.

"Cheers," said Karl. He continued to sit and look at her.

But Ida suddenly became uncomfortable or whatever it was, and she failed to think of anything to say, while Karl, who was perhaps also a little overwhelmed, sat silently, smoking and reading the inscription on the prize coffee pot until he suddenly blurted out:

"Aye, old Brandt liked his coffee."

They both laughed, and Ida fetched the old pictures. Karl took them and the ice was suddenly broken. He took his glass over to the sofa, and they pointed to the windows, remembering who had lived there, and to the roads, remembering where they led, and to the figures – *that* was so-and-so and *that* was so-and-so.

"That's you, Ida," said Karl, holding on to the photograph.

"Yes,"

"And there's the steward," said Karl.

"Yes, he's dead now."

Ida sat looking at the steward, with her head alongside Karl's.

"He died very suddenly," she said slowly.

"He shot himself," said Karl.

"No."

"Yes he did," said Karl, continuing to look at the steward's small face: "Didn't you know that? It was that wearisome Caroline Begtrup; she refused him. So he went up in the corn loft and shot himself just after setting all the folk to work."

"So where is she now?"

"She's married and lives in Næstved," said Karl, putting down the photograph.

He leant back and wrinkled his nose.

"I suppose it was really a very sensible thing to do," he said. "For, God help me, there's not much fun in living."

Ida looked up into the candles.

"Yes there is," she said slowly and quietly.

Karl, sitting with his hands in his pockets, nodded after a time towards the candlestick:

"Well, perhaps if you are a gentleman farmer."

"You can be one," said Ida, again tossing her head.

"Oh, thank you very much," Karl sniffed. "How?"

But suddenly his mood changed, and as he took his hands out of his pockets and rubbed them together, he said:

"It's rather nice in here, you know."

Ida was still gazing at the candles:

"But he was such a quiet person."

"Who?"

"Krog, the steward."

"Aye," said Karl and nodded: "but still waters run deep."

He got up from the sofa to stretch his legs, and he looked around from one piece of furniture to the other.

"There's the old bureau," he said. "That's amazing."

Ida had tears in her eyes; she did not know why; perhaps it was the tone in which he said this.

"Yes, look," she said.

And she opened the central section and pulled the old drawers out while he held the candlestick, and she showed him everything in it; she showed him Olivia's children and heather from the holiday and father's old account books with the faded writing and so many things, while they went on remembering and talking.

"No, you can't have that," she said, quickly taking one book from him; he had put the candlestick down on the flap. "No, that is my album."

"God help us," said Karl.

But he wanted to see the book.

"No," said Ida, holding firmly on to it. "You are not going to. People write so many silly things in them."

"But surely you can tell me what poem you like best," he said. It was mainly the fact that she blushed so prettily that amused him.

"Yes...I like this best."

And she showed him a page at the same time as holding firmly on the other pages; it was Solvejg's *Song*. Karl stood by the candlestick and read it.

"Oh, it's just a woman's poem," he said, but then there came something gentler in his voice:

"Why do you like it best?"

"Well, because it's the most beautiful. But," she added, "it was a long time ago. I wrote it down from a music book."

She put the album down, and a small photograph fell out of it. It was Her Ladyship's old white horse. And they stood and laughed at the time the old circus horse danced in the middle of the street in Horsens because a barrel organ played a tune it knew; and His Lordship could not keep his seat and the barrel organ went on playing and the horse went on dancing in the middle of the street.

"But it had been a splendid animal," said Karl.

"Now the butter merchant's been to have a look at the place," he said a moment later, putting the white horse away.

"Are they going to buy it?" asked Ida.

"They probably will," said Karl, looking into the candles.

"If only they keep it beautiful," said Ida and nodded.

"Yes. But no, they probably won't."

She grabbed Karl's hand. He was rummaging around in everything...They were mother's rings and her brooches and gold chain and father's signet ring, and he was poking around in them all.

"Mind the candles," she said.

The candlestick was rattling on the leaf of the table as she tried to keep hold of his hands.

"Those are the valuables, damn it," laughed Karl.

"And that is my bank book," said Ida happily. She held the greyish yellow book in her left hand and gave it a tap with her right. But suddenly she became quite pale and quietly put the book down.

Karl also stood silent for a moment.

"But can I never thank you, Ida?" he then said in a quiet voice.

"No," was all she said. It could scarcely be heard.

For a moment, Karl had placed both his hands down around her waist. Then he took them away. Ida did not move.

"Sshh..."

They could hear someone on the stairs.

"It's Nurse Petersen..."

"Put the candles out, put them out."

Karl managed to extinguish them.

"Brandt, Brandt," Nurse Petersen called out and knocked on the door.

And Ida replied, from over by her bed, in the dark.

"Yes, yes, I'm awake."

They heard her go again before Karl whispered, in a rather boyish tone:

"But I can stay a bit longer. We can sit by the stove."

Ida made no reply; but she sat down in front of the stove door, which Karl had opened. They heard no sound but that of the coal as it gradually fell, while the glow from it came and went over their faces.

"How quiet it is," said Karl.

"Yes," said Ida: "They are very quiet today."

They only spoke in low voices, and then they sat silent again. Karl looked at the fire.

"But you are far too patient, Ida," he said, looking at the embers.

"How?"

"Well, you could *demand* far more."

"How do you mean, demand more?"

They were sitting with their heads stretched half forward, each in just the same way, and the slow words came in the same tone.

"Well, I mean demand more of life," said Karl.

They fell silent again and heard nothing but the coals collapsing.

"Eichbaum, you will have to go now."

"Yes," said Karl: "In a couple of minutes." He actually *never* liked to get up from a place where he was sitting.

"Do you know what, Ida?" he said, continuing to look at the coals:

"I really am such a home bird."

"Yes." The word came quite softly.

Karl reached out his hand in the dark and took hers.

"Thank you for a lovely evening."

"And thank you," she whispered.

She got up and lit the lamps. She was strikingly pale as she did this – a pallor that almost seemed radiant.

Karl got his coat on and she opened the door without making a sound.

"Good night," whispered Karl and slipped out.

Behind the door, Ida listened to his steps: no, no one was coming and now he was down at the bottom.

She locked the door again. There was the same smile on her face as she opened and closed things and put everything away. But she was not going to extinguish the candles. They could burn; they were to go on burning until after tea.

Then she went down.

Karl was down in the street. His eyes seemed in some curious way to be bigger as he walked along, chewing at his cigar.

"Aye, she's a nice girl," he said, nodding his head.

He hardly realised that he went on walking up and down the bit of road that was overlooked by the lighted gable window.

Mrs von Eichbaum, who was working at her bed curtain, quickly got up and called:

"Julius...My son has come home."

Karl stayed in his own room until it was time for tea. Afterwards, he asked whether they should not have a game of bezique. They were still playing – in a room well filled with cigar smoke – when the general's wife came across to say good night.

"Oh," said Mrs von Eichbaum, "do sit down and have a glass of Madeira."

"Thank you," said the general's wife, taking a seat. "I wonder whether that is a good thing so late at night."

Julius came in with Madeira and French biscuits, and they enjoyed them together under the lamp in the corner of the room.

After Karl and the general's wife had gone, Mrs von Eichbaum went around opening windows: for smoke was unpleasant when it had been in the room all night.

The following morning, when Ida returned from her walk, Karl was standing on the steps leading up to the office. Ida had almost expected this. She went up a couple of steps and took a rose out of the buttonhole in her coat.

"You should have had that yesterday," she said.

∞∞∞∞

Mrs von Eichbaum and the general's wife took a last look at the Lindholm apartment. The Mourier family were due to arrive by the late morning train.

The sisters inspected the rooms and were satisfied.

"And, my dear," said Mrs von Eichbaum, "it is a good thing that we have put away some of the superfluous things."

The "superfluous things" were certain rather dubious silks that were "draped" in the Lindholm flat and which Mrs von Eichbaum loathed. "Good heavens, you only use that sort of thing to hide a stain," she said to her sister. "And then it just hangs there and gathers dust."

The general's wife nodded.

"Besides," she said, "fancy having all that in a house with a sick person like Mary."

Mrs von Eichbaum went into the next room before saying:

"It has been well aired in here."

"And," she added, "we are naturally not going to say anything about it." Mrs von Eichbaum was still thinking of that problem with Mary.

"Good gracious, Mille," said the general's wife: "We know what people's imagination can do for them. And these days, when people simply *insist* on being ill."

Kate's room was behind the small drawing room. It was empty. Miss Kate wanted to have her own furniture. Mrs von Eichbaum stood in the doorway and surveyed the bare walls.

"Well," she said, "Kate will have to arrange it all to suit herself."

Julius came and announced that the cab was there.

"Thank you, Julius. And then I suppose Ane will set a table for lunch, with boiled eggs."

The sisters went down to the porch and climbed into the cab, in which Julius was sitting on the box, wearing a top hat with a rosette and his own winter overcoat.

When the train drew in to the platform, a rather plump, fair-haired face popped out of a first class compartment. It was Miss Kate.

"There they are," she said. She had seen the two sisters waving their handkerchiefs exactly on a level with their faces.

Mrs Mourier and Miss Kate came out of the compartment, and hands were shaken and the three old friends kissed each other, all with tears in their eyes.

"Dear Vilhelmine," said Mrs von Eichbaum: "Just fancy our having you here now."

Her voice was truly trembling. Mrs von Eichbaum was always so emotional when she encountered "people from her younger days" again.

"And the weather's been good over the straits," she said.

"Oh, beautiful, simply beautiful. I sat on deck with my coffee while Kate fed the gulls."

Mrs Mourier, who gave the impression of being as broad as the two sisters together, had a rather more powerful diction, stemming from country estates in Jutland.

Julius brought out all their luggage on to the platform, finally a large woven basket with a huge handle.

"My dears," said Mrs Mourier, "this is for you from Mourier. He came with us as far as Fredericia...his orchids are his pride and joy."

"Then you'll take it, Julius," said Mrs von Eichbaum. "But where is Kate?"

"Oh, she is fetching the dogs," said Mrs Mourier.

"The dogs," said Mrs von Eichbaum. "Heavens above, Mine, have you brought those animals with you?" Mrs von Eichbaum had a nervous fear of all dogs.

"My dear, otherwise I would never have persuaded Kate to come."

The general's wife could see Kate approaching now, struggling with two frisky greyhounds on a double lead.

"There," said Kate, who was wearing a black costume resembling a riding habit and had an array of silver rings up her arm: "Come and say hello to your aunties."

On this command, the two hounds started to jump up at the general's wife and Mrs von Eichbaum, who defended themselves with their hands.

"Kate dear, they are a little rough."

They all emerged on to the square in front of the station, and Mrs Mourier and the sisters climbed into the cab, while Miss Kate stayed outside.

"Then I'll come with Victoria and the dogs," she said.

Victoria, a lady dressed in a grey costume and standing beside the carriage, was the "lady's maid".

The general's wife nodded "Good morning" and Mrs von Eichbaum said:

"Julius will bring the animals."

But Miss Kate was already over at another carriage, which she entered with Victoria at her side and both dogs on the back seat.

Mrs von Eichbaum looked at this arrangement rather nervously and said:

"Good heavens, Vilhelmine, you are going to have a problem

with those animals here in a town apartment."

"But," said the general's wife, "they are two lovely animals."

The two cabs moved off, Kate's bringing up the rear. She sat looking forward at the vehicle in front, with Julius sitting straight-backed on the box.

"There," she said, "now we're in."

When they reached the apartment, they surveyed the rooms while the sisters explained and demonstrated how things worked. Mrs Mourier said: "It is really delightful here," and immediately sat down on the sofa together with the general's wife while Kate, having first gained an overview from the dining room door, continued to go around with Mrs von Eichbaum.

"There is just room for my washstand here," she said as they stood in her own room. "And where is Victoria to sleep?"

"There is a room up in the attic," said Mrs von Eichbaum, "for the lady's maid."

Kate shrugged her arms and shoulders so that all her silver rings rattled. "Oh, well, yes, we can always see about that."

Mrs von Eichbaum, holding herself rather straight, turned to the lady's maid and said:

"Would you put the clothes in here for the moment, Miss Thora."

For some unknown reason, Mrs von Eichbaum had decided during the journey there that Miss Victoria should be called Thora.

Sitting on the living room sofa, the general's wife and Mrs Mourier were already engrossed in a discussion of all their winter plans, and the general's wife could be heard to say in conclusion:

"And Vilhelmine, then we have Petri on Sundays."

Julius announced that tea was ready and they rose to go in, but Kate really had to wash first. "Where is there a bathroom?" she asked. She had a certain matter-of-fact way of asking. But there *was* no bathroom.

"You know, Kate," said Mrs von Eichbaum: "this is a house that is let out, but at least we have our portable tub."

Kate disappeared with Victoria into her mother's bedroom while the others sat down at the table and the dogs before long began to howl and scratch at the bedroom door until Kate let them in. "I must say," said Mrs von Eichbaum at the table, "that will not be good for the varnish on the Lindholm's doors in the long run."

The three ladies turned to a discussion about Aline Feddersen. The general's wife thought she had been in Geneva.

And she was probably still there.

"Yes, you know," said Mrs von Eichbaum, "that is something that we cannot understand with the best will in the world."

Mrs Mourier, who had finished her second egg, said:

"No, but you know, Feddersen has never been anything more than a provider for his family."

"*Anything more than?* My dear Mine..."

"Yes, and Mourier is right: it is simply not sufficient to have a husband rationed out in daily portions."

There was just a brief pause before Mrs von Eichbaum said – and there was no telling whether the sisters had really understood:–

"Very well, my dear, but where do you think one will meet anyone else like Mourier?"

When Kate came in and sat down – she was wearing a pale blue cashmere morning dress – Mrs Mourier was talking about Ludvigsbakke. They had had a look at it and Mourier thought the price was reasonable.

"And what do you say, Kate?" asked the general's wife.

Kate, who was feeding the hounds on the finest white bread, thought that it could be quite adequate if some alterations were made to it, and Mrs Mourier asked after Karl.

"Good heavens," said Mrs von Eichbaum, "he is busy in the office."

And the general's wife added:

"He goes off and comes home with clockwork regularity."

Kate, who had finished feeding the dogs, now showed an interest in proceedings for the first time and asked:

"Where can one ride here in Copenhagen?"

After lunch, the sisters went home, just a couple of houses away.

They spoke little until they reached Mrs von Eichbaum's entrance hall and took off their coats.

"Dear Lotte," said Mrs von Eichbaum: "Let them get straight first."

"It is quite reasonable," the general's wife seemed to be smoothing something over with her hand: "The first day is always a little confused and noisy."

The sisters went inside and sat down and Mrs von Eichbaum, who nevertheless seemed as it were to be relaxing here on her own good sofa, said:

"And the clothes, dear, they are only the sort you put on when you intend to go to the shops."

The general's wife nodded and Mrs von Eichbaum stared into the air for a moment before saying:

"She dresses like a young married woman now."

"And the dogs, dear," said the general's wife, "they were just like a little procession."

And as though it had something special to do with the two hounds, the general's wife said after a brief pause:

"But you know, a husband will not have an easy time of it."

"And the lady's maid," – there was a touch of nervousness in Mrs von Eichbaum's voice – "Ane will show her how we do things. And then it will probably be best to leave them in peace today."

"Yes, dear," said the general's wife, getting up, "so that they can take stock and so on."

In the doorway she asked: "Are you coming for a cup of tea this evening?"

"No thank you, dear," said Mrs von Eichbaum: "The little Brandt girl is coming this evening, you know...I think Tuesday is her evening off."

"Oh, her...Well then, goodbye, Mille."

The general's wife was about to leave when the bell rang. It was the porter on behalf of Lindholm bringing the basket of orchids. There were some black grapes at the bottom of it.

"Mille," said the general's wife. "You know they are just like those you find in the vineyards. I think they will keep until Sunday, dear, and I had in any case thought of having the Schleppegrells round as well now that we have those four ducks from Vallø."

Mrs von Eichbaum arranged the orchids in two glass bowls. When she had finished, she stood looking at them.

"Yes," she said: "they are certainly beautiful, though I must admit I really do find these flowers unnerving."

"They have them in many country houses these days," said the general's wife.

She went off with her half.

Karl stood that evening waiting for Ida outside the hospital gate, as the soft snow fell over his elegant overcoat.

"Your hands are ever so cold," he said when she came.

They walked side by side as he talked in that drawling manner of his, and Ida made but little reply as though she were far away in thought.

"By Gad, I think you are frightened," said Karl with a laugh. "But I suppose I can quite understand that." And he put his arm through Ida's as though to indicate they would stand firmly together.

When they reached the rather modest middle building, Mrs von Eichbaum rose from the sofa and received Ida at the door to the sitting room.

"It was nice of you to come."

They all three sat down and Mrs von Eichbaum made a show of conversation, talking about the hospital and applying her finest pronunciation to everything; she said what a great blessing the institution was. Karl meanwhile sat with a twinkle in his eye, glancing at Ida, who gradually seemed to shrink and become smaller in her corner of the sofa.

"And it is so reassuring that they are young ladies from good homes. You know, Karl, Adelaide has also begun to train in the King Frederik Hospital, the private one, you know".

Adelaide was the daughter of a colonel of her acquaintance.

"Oh," said Karl, "that was probably the wisest thing for her."

"Good heavens, Karl," said Mrs von Eichbaum, "I just think it is immensely respectable."

There was a brief pause. But then Karl thought that it was now time to make a contribution, and he started to tell a story from the office (they really are a damned peculiar crowd, he said) about a mad father who wanted to have his sane son committed. The father turned up with his socks outside his boots and wanted to have his son in the mental ward.

"The son was wearing patent leather shoes," Karl explained, continuing his account while Mrs von Eichbaum laughed and Ida sat smiling: oh, she was so grateful, so really grateful, that he was talking. And Karl continued to tell stories (he could veritably see Ida growing in her seat) until finally they were all three merrily laughing aloud. Mrs von Eichbaum was always so happy when Karl was talking. "And he has such a fine sense of humour," she always said to her sister. Now she said:

"But Karl, this is not really anything to laugh at."

And Ida asked about the netting on the bed curtain:

"Was it difficult to learn how to do it?"

Mrs von Eichbaum showed her how it was done.

"You can try it," she said.

And she continued to teach Ida how to use the small needles, while Karl asked:

"Do you mind if I smoke, mother?" And with his cigarette between his fingers he sat looking at Ida's bent head alongside that of his mother."

Ida went on with the netting. There was the sound of the small needles clicking and rattling against each other, as Mrs von Eichbaum watched and Karl said:

"It's going fine," to which Mrs von Eichbaum added in a kindly voice:

"Yes. Young people have nimble fingers."

Julius came already to announce tea as Karl, who couldn't go on talking all the bally time, said:

"Aunt Charlotte could come over for a game of whist, mother."

"Yes, how right you are; there are enough of us for a game. I will ask her before we have tea."

When Mrs von Eichbaum had gone, Karl rose from his chair and went across to Ida's sofa corner:

"Well, what now," he said, smiling at her.

"Well..."

Ida looked up in his face, and she, too, smiled.

"You are so kind," she said. They were half whispering like children behind a teacher's back.

"Yes, of course I am," said Karl with a laugh.

In the dining room he opened the piano and started to play a waltz, pounding the strings to their limit.

Mrs von Eichbaum was over at her sister's. She invited her to a game of whist and said:

"She is really a delightful girl, my dear – well brought up and charming."

This could only please the general's wife.

"And she has really always been one of the circle."

Mrs von Eichbaum went across, and when she saw Karl at the piano, she said:

"That was a good idea, Karl; it is a long time since you played anything."

"Yes," said Karl. "And that's a good thing for the neighbours."

But he continued to play.

It was as though the waltz hung in the air while they ate, and Ida got up and asked if she might pour Mrs von Eichbaum's second cup of tea, and Julius had to put more bread in the basket because Karl had such an enormous appetite.

"Thank you," said Mrs von Eichbaum as she was served with her tea: "I must say that there is no meal to compare with my good tea."

They continued to talk until Mrs von Eichbaum said:

"I suppose you know that the Mouriers, the merchant family, are seriously considering buying old Ludvigsbakke. They are our very close friends."

Yes, Mr von Eichbaum had told her.

"But Karl," said Mrs von Eichbaum, "Kate doesn't like the main building."

"Oh," said Ida, "I just think it was so lovely."

"Hmm," murmured Karl, who was still eating, "I suppose she wants a couple of pig stickers above the door as a coat of arms."

Mrs von Eichbaum did not herself know why she did not reprove Karl for this, but all she said was:

"Well people's requirements are different, of course."

The general's wife arrived while they were still sitting at the tea table.

"Oh, let me not disturb you."

"Well," she said to Ida, "we have already heard so many nice things about you."

When they had finished, Ida helped Karl to set up the card table.

"No, no, that's not the way," said Karl, tapping her hands.

"Julius, would you please bring the candlesticks," said Mrs von Eichbaum.

"But I am so bad at playing cards," said Ida as they sat down. She was given Karl as her partner.

"Karl," said the general's wife, who had the lead and dealt the cards: "We do not talk when we are playing cards."

The sisters played slowly, looking long and carefully at the cards. One had the impression that they were playing chess. Ida, who sat biting her lip, flushed each time she put a card on the table, while Karl chatted ceaselessly to his aunt.

"Karl," said Mrs von Eichbaum, "when you play cards, you play cards."

Karl fell silent and looked across at Ida, who gained confidence and played her good cards suddenly, in the manner of a child, to take the tricks.

"It's you, Emilie," said the general's wife.

Mrs von Eichbaum only nodded in reply; it was as though both sisters were just showing signs of double chins as they played.

"That was ours," said Ida, involuntarily breathing in relief as her eyes shone.

"Miss Ida looks as though she has just come out of a Turkish bath," said Karl.

"Miss Brandt plays better than you do," said Mrs von Eichbaum.

"Yes. Oh well, congratulations," he said, and while winking he put his hand, with a raised thumb, in the direction of Ida, who put her thumb against his. "Congratulations," she said, and they both laughed.

Mrs von Eichbaum and the general's wife talked about the game and spread the tricks out on the table.

"But there was I," said Mrs von Eichbaum, "sitting there with my sole trump."

They played on, and Karl also became eager as Ida and he continued to win.

"Ida plays a fine game of whist," he said, forgetting to say Miss.

"Yes," said the general's wife. "This is really a delightful game."

Julius entered with the grapes and the Madeira, which they enjoyed in between two rubbers, talking about the old days, about Ludvigsbakke and about old Brandt. "He was an excellent man," said Mrs von Eichbaum.

Karl raised his glass.

"Yes," he said, "shall we then wish Miss Brandt welcome..."

"Yes, we must," said Mrs von Eichbaum; "it was really delightful to see you."

They all four took a drink, and then they had to change places, at which point Karl, who was so playful and happy, began to sniff at his aunt's back.

"Since when have you been using Patchouli, aunt?"

"Yes," said the general's wife, who also with some concern began to smell at her own sleeves, "I don't really understand it, but that smell persists all day."

"My dear," said Mrs von Eichbaum, "it is on me, too. It *must* be from Kate. I noticed it immediately, on the platform, in the *open* air. I, who have a horror of anything pervasive."

As he sat down, Karl said:

"It's Ess Bouquet. It's a gentleman's perfume, but it's actually very pleasant."

"Good heavens, Karl," said the general's wife: "You surely don't mean...a gentleman only ever smells of his clean linen."

"It is Ida's turn to deal," said Mrs von Eichbaum. This was the first time she had called her by her Christian name.

They played again. Karl became very engaged and silent with Mrs von Eichbaum as his partner.

"It's you, Miss Brandt," he said.

Ida sat thinking how much Karl resembled his mother after all. It was the same face.

After the two rubbers, they rose from the card table and Karl and Ida sat over in the corner sofa, while Ida looked in a stereoscope.

"Well," said Karl, momentarily touching her hand, which lay on the sofa: "You're a fine player."

"It's been so lovely here," said Ida softly.

"Yes," said Karl rather reluctantly "we've had a nice time this evening."

They remained seated beside each other, without saying much, while the lamp above them bubbled gently, and Ida looked at the beautiful, foaming waterfalls of Switzerland in the stereoscope.

Mrs von Eichbaum and the general's wife sat on the sofa.

"Oh," said the general's wife, "it is good to sit down. It has been quite an eventful day."

Mrs von Eichbaum nodded, and while the two sisters were both thinking of the same things, she said, after a brief silence:

"Good heavens, my dear, when I saw the dogs I cannot deny that I was horrified."

The two sisters sat in silence for a time, while Mrs von Eichbaum turned a kindly eye towards the two young people.

"A real pair of friends," she said, nodding and smiling in their direction.

Ida moved across to the table where the sisters were sitting.

Later, as he helped Ida on with her coat in the entrance hall, Karl opened the door to his own room.

"This is where I live," he said, stepping inside; the lamp was still lit in there.

"And here are a couple of the horses as well," he said, taking a few more steps and followed by Ida.

"Yes," she said.

And they were both silent as they stood, just for a brief moment, before the two pictures, which probably neither of them saw, until Karl said:

"Well, we got away."

And he closed the door behind them.

The sisters remained in the dimly lit dining room. Mrs von Eichbaum had an unusual flow of words in praise of Ida and the entire Brandt family.

"Yes," said the general's wife, "she is quite sweet and appreciative."

"Dear Charlotte," said Mrs von Eichbaum, who had detected something in the tone used by the general's wife that Mrs von Eichbaum almost corrected. "She comes from an excellent home. Her father was His Lordship's right-hand man and as good as his equal."

The general's wife stood for a moment before saying:

"Yes, she is really sweet and undemanding in spite of being so wealthy."

Mrs von Eichbaum made no reply; she had become as it were slightly preoccupied after Karl and Ida had gone. Suddenly her sister said:

"Do you think I should put my grapes in sawdust?"

Mrs von Eichbaum's thoughts seemed to be taking her in a completely different direction, but she said: "I wonder whether that would not spoil the flavour a little?"

The general's wife thought the same. She would simply, carefully, put each bunch in a little piece of tissue paper.

The following morning, while she was doing this, Anna Schleppegrell came in to ask whether she might be interested in some silk clothes. Mrs Schleppegrell, the admiral's wife, ran a small more or less private commission business for Printemps on behalf of friends. The general's wife told her about the whist:

"With Emilie, Karl and Miss Brandt."

The admiral's wife was not acquainted with Miss Brandt.

"Oh, my dear," said the general's wife, "a charming girl...her father, the bailiff, was His Lordship's right hand man as well."

"What is she doing working in that hospital then?" asked the admiral's wife.

"My dear Anna, she doesn't need to do that either. On the contrary, she inherited a pile of money."

"Oh, I see," said the admiral's wife, who suddenly looked as though she needed some fresh air.

∞∞∞

The gate to Mrs von Eichbaum's home had just closed behind Karl and Ida.

"Oh, I was so nervous," said Ida, waving her arms up and down like a bird flapping its wings.

"Yes, that was obvious." Karl put his arm under hers, but as though to excuse herself, Ida said:

"Yes, because I only knew her from Ludvigsbakke, when she sat at the top of the table and when she went for a walk past the pantry window."

"Yes," said Karl with a laugh; "I know mother when she has her outdoor clothes on."

"And in that big lace hat," said Ida.

"She still has that."

And they continued to laugh, not at that but as though they simply had to laugh now, out here, in the open.

"But it was so lovely this evening," said Ida.

They came to Grønningen, and the snow, which was no longer falling, lay among the silent trees like a soft carpet. Karl and Ida fell silent, as though they were walking through a forest.

"She is so fond of you," said Ida softly; her voice sounded so gentle.

"Yes," said Karl in the same gentle tone; and they walked on for a while before, slowly and almost reflectively, he said:

"But it's a mess all the same."

"What do you mean?"

"All of it."

"No," said Ida louder but not that loudly, and she shook her head. They walked on again and everything was just as silent.

"Look," said Ida with a smile. "We are the first ones to walk on the snow."

"Yes," replied Karl.

And they both looked down at the soft white carpet, on which their feet left marks beside each other.

"It's so lovely," said Ida, still smiling.

But when they reached the narrow corner by the tramline, she freed her arm from his and went on ahead, almost running. Karl followed her, looking at her fine, slender back. Then a snowball winged its way to the back of her head.

"There."

"Karl," she shouted. But he went on, and she received one more and then one more again, one on her ear and one on her cheek until she defended herself: "Here you are then," she said, and she pelted him with snow, loose snow, lots of snow, in his face, from the front, from behind and down his overcoat.

"Oh no, we're making a din in the street."

She shook herself suddenly and stopped: there was a policeman in the middle of the white avenue, standing there as straight as a post. But Karl went on, in high spirits, and once round the corner, he crowed like a cockerel.

"The people up there will think it's five o'clock," he said, laughing up at the windows of these respectable middle-class houses. Suddenly he started trotting, stamping his feet, with Ida alongside doing the same, as though they simply *had* to exert themselves, and Karl whistled all the while.

"It's Nurse Helgesen's birthday on Monday," said Ida.

"Are you going to have a party?" asked Karl, still tramping.

"Yes, we are going to make a pudding in the kitchen."

"What sort of pudding?"

Ida laughed. "It's supposed to be a rum pudding," she said, she, too, stamping her feet.

"Are men allowed in?"

"Yes, if you come with Quam," said Ida.

Karl nodded as they traipsed on, *there* beside each other, and Karl said:

"He wears huntsmen's underclothes."

Ida laughed, she was quite out of breath. "How do you know that?"

"I've seen them."

"We're home now," said Ida. They were at the gate.

"I'll go as far as the fence with you," said Karl.

And they walked, respectably, past the watchman, across the big, silent courtyard, where the passages were half lit and lay as though dozing and only half awake.

"Just listen to our steps," said Ida quietly. "They echo here in the courtyard."

They went past the doctors' corridor.

"Sshh, who's that?" she grasped Karl's arm; but then she laughed, quietly, though she continued to listen. There were the sounds of laughter and footsteps from the doctors' corridor. "It's the junior doctors," she whispered. There was a din in there as everyone shouted and laughed, and Karl sprang up the little staircase and opened the door.

"What's going on here?" he shouted in a sharp voice.

"The professor," someone shouted. It was Quam; and the doors opened and shut while Karl started to laugh so loud that it could be heard all over the yard, and Ida joined in as did the doctors up in the darkness; everyone laughed until suddenly everything fell quiet.

"The watchman," said Ida and started to go.

The night watchman came towards them, slowly and carrying his big lantern.

"Good evening," he said.

"Good evening."

"That was only Jensen," whispered Ida nervously and Karl took her arm.

They turned in at the middle gate, where it was quite dark.

"There are ghosts in here," whispered Ida.

"What do you mean?"

"Well, this is the way they go when they are going to die."

"Who says that?"

"The watchmen," said Ida.

And a little later:

"Because this is the way to the chapel."

"Are you afraid of that," said Karl.

"No, not now," Ida whispered, shaking her head.

They went past the laundry wing and as far as the lamp above the entrance to the mental ward. The building there was closed and silent. The trees in the gardens round it were all covered with snow. Ida stood there with her arm in Karl's.

"How lovely it is here," she whispered.

She looked around at it all.

"If all the stars came out," she said...

"Good night."

Karl heard the door open and shut.

∞∞∞∞

It was a few days later. Ida went over to the office with a report that evening. It was late, and Karl already had his overcoat on; he was the only one left and was about to put out the last lamp – the one above the counter.

"It's a long time since I saw you," said Karl.

"Yes."

"Why?"

"I can't always come," said Ida – she did not herself know why she said it almost in a whisper – and, bending her head forward under the lamp, she gave him the report.

Karl took it and touched her hand.

"Ida," was all he said; he had bent down and kissed her white neck.

"Ida."

Without saying a word, she had taken her hand away from his. Slowly and cautiously, almost as though she dared not walk there, she crossed the dim courtyard. All was so quiet in her heart.

Nurse Kjær was in the doorway to the dining room, where the ladies' voices could be heard loud and all talking at once, and she placed an arm around Ida's waist when she arrived. But Ida slowly pushed it away with her hand.

"Oh dear me," said Nurse Kjær, as Ida sat down by the door. "Am I not allowed to touch the young lady any longer?"

All the nurses were chatting and gesticulating along the table. Nurse Kaas, Nurse Boserup and Nurse Roed had moved their chairs out on to the floor and in loud voices – the most excited of all was Nurse Kaas, who was flushed right up to her bobbed hair – were eagerly discussing the new association that Nurse Boserup wanted to form, an association of nurses from both the King Frederik and the Municipal Hospital. A list had been circulated and a meeting was to be arranged.

"He would surely not refuse us the use of the lecture room," said Nurse Kaas. "He" was the professor, and the term was used as though heavily underlined, while Nurse Boserup started to gesticulate at Nurse Krohn from the easy ward and said that surely, despite them all being women, (this was one of Nurse Boserup's set phrases) it must be possible to summon up sufficient interest in their station to achieve some rights some time.

The three continued to discuss in loud voices while Nurse Helgesen, speaking from her permanent place behind the urn, said:

"It would surely at all events have to be done in consultation with the doctors."

Nurse Kaas, indignantly thrusting her breast forward in her blouse, but otherwise pretending not to have heard that, said:

"I would happily be secretary, at least if the idea is that we should be independent." Nurse Kaas was so to speak always the secretary, *first* for collections and *then* for addresses. And Nurse Roed said that what they should aim for was shorter periods on duty and then payment for holiday periods..."But I really believe, like Nurse Helgesen, in consultation with the doctors."

"The first thing is that we should have our food improved," said Nurse Øverud in her Funen accent.

But Nurse Friis, sitting with her shoulders hunched and leaning back in her chair, said to Nurse Berg:

"No, leave me out of this. Apart from anything else, it would mean being together with one's colleagues even when not on duty."

Ida had not said anything. It was as though, in the light from the flames and among all the others, she was all alone there, conspicuously alone.

Then Nurse Kaas suddenly said:

"What does Nurse Brandt say?"

"I'm listening," said Ida, the expression on her face unchanged.

But Nurse Boserup said:

"I suppose Nurse Brandt is not really interested. She's got money in the bank, of course." And she slapped her right hand down on her open left hand.

"Yes, Boserup knows all about that," said Nurse Friis to Krohn.

But Nurse Kaas had risen to go over to Ida. She had the discreet idea that Brandt could always advance the money for the preliminary expenses, whereas Nurse Kjær, who was of the opinion that Boserup had been ill-mannered, went across to Ida again and stroked her hair.

"Never mind," she said. "The one thing that is certain is that we shall have to pay a subscription."

Ida had simply not heard anything. She just looked up for a moment and smiled at Nurse Kjær.

"Have you seen their shadows?" she whispered, her eyes laughing. "They look so odd."

On the wall behind the excited ladies, their large, gesticulating shadows were dancing to and fro on the wall like jumping jacks.

And they both laughed, different laughs, Ida quite quietly, as though from far away, from a different, distant world until Nurse Kaas went over to her to talk about the association again. It was really of importance to the profession that they should work for some sort of independence.

But Ida continued to laugh, so very quietly.

Nurse Friis had also arrived and asked Nurse Kjær in passing what she was going to wear for Nurse Helgesen's birthday.

Ida looked up suddenly and a great smile gradually spread over her face:

"I'm going in a yellow dress," she said.

It came suddenly, so bright and so loud, that Nurse Kaas paused.

She had just repeated that they must assert themselves as a professional group.

Ida went upstairs.

The patients had settled down; only the doctor in Ward A was on duty, standing in front of the open window and staring out into the evening. Ida was looking in when the keys rattled. It was Quam, and he took up his usual position on the table.

"Do you think he's mad?" he said nodding in the direction of Ward A.

Ida shook her head.

"No, I don't think so," she said.

"No, I don't either," said Quam. "I'll be hanged if I would send him to the asylum."

"But," said Ida, still speaking in the same voice, a voice that seemed to come from other areas of the soul than the words she uttered, "why is he really here, then?"

"Well," said Quam, lazily crossing one leg over the other: "He's a statistician, of course."

"Really?"

"And then he has got a bee in his bonnet about the inevitable – the law of inevitability, as the great Norwegians would call it (Quam always spoke in a tone as though poking a little fun at his own words). You see, he wants to work it all out. How, for instance, each year about the same number of letter-writers make a mistake and put a seven instead of a nine when addressing an envelope, just in the same way as exactly the same number of people drown every five years by walking on thin ice. It is because they *have* to do it, just as those who hang themselves *have* to hang themselves and can't even be allowed to shoot themselves when they finish themselves off."

Quam was silent for a moment.

"And it would be rather tough," he said, "if you weren't even allowed to choose your weapon."

"But is it not true?" said Ida.

"Aye, that's the question," said Quam.

And shortly afterwards, changing his position:

"And it would be nice if you knew what task you had come into the world to undertake."

"Why?" That was all Ida could say; but her voice almost sounded as though she was feeling some secret joy.

Quam looked at her.

"No, damn it," he said, putting his feet down on the floor, "*that* doesn't really matter."

"Oh well," he said in conclusion, "I must go in with the syringe." He ruffled the hair up at the back of his head with his left hand. "That's what I like best to give those patients."

"But you never give them enough," said Ida.

And before long, for the thoughts came and went so clearly and quickly to her mind, which otherwise worked so slowly:

"You know, doctor, everyone really ought to be happy."

Quam opened the door to the women's ward, and a couple of cries met them.

"Well, we'll open the cage now."

But Ida did not hear him.

The gentleman in Ward A had flung his door open.

Standing up straight on the threshold, Ida said: "Coming, doctor." She had to close the shutters.

"Thank you."

Dr Quam went down the corridor in the women's ward.

"She looks like Frithjof when he's listening to music," he said to himself. He was thinking of Ida. Frithjof was a friend of his who was fond of Wagner.

When he had finished with the injections, he returned along the other corridor and gave a knock on Sister Koch's door as he went past. Sister Koch opened it. "Good evening, Sister Koch," he said.

He put his head inside, but when he saw Nurse Boserup, who had come to give an account of the meeting (late in the evening, Sister Koch usually also had baked apples standing on her stove), he said:

"Oh, it's a business meeting."

And then he went. "I am not particularly interested in 'members'" was his usual comment.

Nurse Boserup continued with her pronouncements. She spoke about Brandt and could not deny that she was really amazed.

"When all is said and done," she said, "she is one of us."

Sister Koch sat smoking her cigar. She smoked like an old seaman, and she had taken her glasses off while sitting there staring up in the air with her kindly, grey eyes.

"Aye, God help her," she said.

"But," Nurse Boserup said, "she will obviously join us later."

"Yes, probably," said Sister Koch.

And she continued to sit there and watch the smoke from her fat cigar appear and disperse and fade away.

Josefine could never get away again in the mornings when she brought the breakfast. She talked the hind leg off a donkey. "For Nurse Brandt," she said, "is a nurse you can talk to." Josefine herself talked constantly, and her sole subject was Andersen.

She was standing by the kitchen table beside Ida and had poured out her entire heart to her.

"For oh, nurse," she said, staring fixedly at the wall, "he's got such lovely skin."

Josefine remained standing.

"All over," she concluded.

Then she turned and went.

It was Saturday afternoon.

Nurse Krohn from the women's ward, who was off duty because of a cold, was sitting upstairs near the men's ward, as Ida was in the kitchen. She was the best at preparing food.

There was a fire burning in the kitchen in the basement, and it was warm. Josefine, busy making pastries, was spreading egg white on them with a feather, and Ida was so eagerly whipping the yokes for the pudding that she was out of breath.

Josefine was talking about her mother in Holbæk, where they used to make bread every Sunday.

Over in the basement corridor, where the four were at work, there was the sound of Bertelsen's saw as it bit into the firewood.

"And very good it was, too," said Josefine, referring to the splendid bread in Holbæk.

Ida went on beating, the metal clacking against the sides of the bowl.

"Be careful, they're burning," she said, and Josefine got the oven door open and moved and rearranged the pastries.

Ida rose and looked at them; such a lovely smell was rising from the browned cakes.

"We kneaded all the dough at Ludvigsbakke. Everything," she said with a laugh; "just Schrøder and I."

It was on summer mornings that Schrøder and she baked on their own; everyone else was asleep, and the windows were open to the dew-drenched fields. Then a long line of farmhands would come out of the farm gate and the steward would come across and say, "Good morning", and be given his coffee and freshly baked bread as he sat on the bench.

"And there was plenty of it," said Ida. She could not find bags that were big enough and deep enough.

"Oh," said Josefine, "I suppose they get fed here as well."

The door went. The nurses were coming off duty and came in to have a look. "Fingers off," said Ida, tapping Nurse Kjær's fingers. Boserup was over by the kitchen table, eyeing the food. She was given a little handful of blanched almonds in her back pocket before going.

"Be careful of the door," said Ida. "Watch out for the doctors."

The warm steam spread right up into the corridors.

All went quiet in the kitchen, while Bertelsen's saw could be heard as it cut through the large pile of firewood.

"Josefine," said Ida, "I'm going to give them some cakes in there after all." And she quickly put some pastries on a plate and popped down the corridor, into the basement, where three old men sat weaving mats quite automatically, as though they did not themselves know what they were doing, while Sørensen, the porter, sat leaning sleepily against a wall and Bertelsen eagerly and haphazardly sawed away through his firewood.

"Look what I've brought," said Ida, placing three buns on each of the mats, quickly, as though she had stolen them.

"Here you are, Bertelsen."

"These are for you, Sørensen." And she handed him the plate.

A voice was heard behind her:

"What's this?"

It was Quam, standing in the doorway.

"They are cakes." Ida gave a start and hurried past him.

But Quam followed her into the kitchen. "Oh, it's like Sunday in here," he said, sitting down by the chimney.

"No, it's Saturday," laughed Ida.

Quam also had a pastry and sat watching.

"Do you know what, Nurse Brandt," he said. "I really like you, you know."

Ida had finished in the kitchen. But Nurse Krohn nevertheless had to stay there for the whole of her time on duty: for there were a couple of things Ida had to go out and buy. Twilight was already gathering as she happily hurried across the courtyard. There she met Eichbaum, but she merely smiled at him and ran past.

"I'm in such a hurry," she said and hurried on.

Karl stood there and watched her. He had not spoken to her since that evening, and he did not really know how things stood.

But down by the gate Ida turned round and smiled, showing him her purse and shaking it.

Quam had just come out of the middle gate and stood watching Ida with his hands in his trouser pockets.

"Do you know," he said to Karl, "she'd be a damned nice wife to have in a country practice."

"You could ask her," said Karl, who had suddenly started juggling with his bunch of keys.

"Yes," said Quam reflectively, "but I would never have a wife with money even so."

Karl simply laughed and threw his bunch of keys up in the air.

"We'll have to see about that," he said and went in through the door.

He did not himself know how he ended in the basement kitchen together with Josefine, who was clearing up.

"It's lovely and warm in here," he said, stretching his legs and looking around at all the food that Ida had been frying.

Ida had taken a cab. There were more and more things that had to be bought for Nurse Helgesen's birthday. She was going to give her six bottles of really good wine in addition to that tray for visiting cards.

She could do that if she decorated the basket with flowers. And as for the flowers, they could use them on the table then, for there must be lots of flowers and plenty of light.

∞∞∞

It was Sunday evening, after dinner, at the home of the general's wife.

When Karl came back from his walk, Julius was just bringing in the tea urn.

A quiet game of whist was being played at two tables, while Miss Kate looked on with rather heavy eyes, sitting in the corner of a sofa together with Miss Fanny Schleppegrell, a lady with a very pronounced lower jaw, who was preparing to be a lady-in-waiting at court.

175

Karl sat down beside them, and Miss Schleppegrell asked whether it was still snowing. That everlasting slush made an appalling mess of one's shoes.

Kate suddenly said to Karl: "Do you know, I always imagined you to be quite different."

"Really?" said Karl without any real interest.

"Yes," said Kate. "I had quite honestly expected you to be much more fun."

She sat for a while and looked at the two whist tables and their eager players, and then she said:

"Does this go on every Sunday?"

Karl burst out laughing, so they both laughed together.

Julius announced that the tea was ready, but the general's wife said:

"We are expecting the admiral."

After coffee, Admiral Schleppegrell went to the Atheneum by way of Østergade, going there and back a couple of times and not arriving back on board before the exact time arranged.

But Julius said:

"The admiral is in the entrance hall."

They left the whist tables and in the midst of the discussion on the games Mrs Schleppegrell, who always spoke in a tone resembling a descant, was heard to say to Mrs Mourier:

"Good heavens, Vilhelmine, do you call that going to a lot of trouble? One always writes one's orders short and to the point on a postcard."

The admiral's wife was talking about Printemps.

The sound of a voice saying good evening could be heard at the sitting room door, and the admiral, who was standing there rubbing his hands after his walk, said:

"They say that Madame Aline is in a terrible mess now."

"Good heavens, Schleppegrell, how?" The general's wife took a couple of steps towards him.

"Well, Vedel told me that the chap has deserted her and she's left behind there."

Mrs von Eichbaum – in the ensuing moment's silence – put her hands to her eyes.

"Oh, poor thing," she said quietly.

"Yes," said the admiral, offering his arm to Mrs Mourier. "That's what Vedel said, too."

They started to go to table while, in the midst of the noise from the chairs, Mrs Schleppegrell was heard to say in her rather shrill voice:

"Yes, that is just like a man."

And Karl, pushing chairs forward for Miss Fanny and Kate, murmured:

"You have to blame the men, of course."

Kate, who heard this, started to laugh, and Karl said:

"What are you laughing at?"

"Hm," said Kate, tossing her head a little, "I simply thought that it must have been six of one and half a dozen of the other."

Up at the other end of the table, Mrs Schleppegrell continued to talk across the table in an eager but subdued voice until Mrs Mourier, who was drinking tea from a cup intended for use in an office, said:

"Well, it is no good denying it, Anna; Mourier is right: most people simply take what they can get."

The admiral laughed and said: "There's something in that, by Gad" and the general's wife, sitting facing Kate and Miss Fanny, by whose place there was a bottle of tuberculin-tested milk, said:

"Yes, I think, of course that..."

But Mrs von Eichbaum, who was still very upset and had tears in her eyes, ignored her sister and said in a voice as though she was taking a decision:

"But she cannot be left down there."

Mrs Schleppegrell gave a start and turned her head in a manner rather reminiscent of a wagtail, saying:

"Well then, but may I ask then where she should go? You surely can't imagine her coming home?"

Mrs von Eichbaum said slowly:

"I suppose that is something we shall have to think about. We all know Aline after all, when she is herself."

There was silence, and the admiral said: "Aye, it's a dreadful business," while Mrs Mourier, nodding vehemently, twice, down at her silken breast, said, in the direction of Mrs von Eichbaum, almost by way of a confession:

"I am fond of her."

And a further torrent of words could be heard coming from Mrs Schleppegrell. "Good heavens, you know perfectly well, Vilhelmine, that I don't throw stones."

Karl sat with his head a little on one side and looking over at his mother; there was something resembling a twinkle in his eyes.

When they had risen from table, Mrs Mourier found herself standing by Mrs von Eichbaum.

"You are the same as you always were," she said, firmly gripping her hand in both of hers.

"Dear Vilhelmine," said Mrs von Eichbaum: "One simply has to rally round. And if no one else will go, then I will."

Karl was standing behind his mother and he touched her shoulder with his moustache, almost as though he was caressing her.

"That was a lovely meal," he said in a quiet voice.

Mrs Schleppegrell also came across: "Emilie," she said, "I hope you won't misunderstand. You know perfectly well that if she were to come..."

"Anna, everything of that kind," said Mrs von Eichbaum, "dies down again provided no one talks about it."

Karl was in the dining room. He had suddenly found himself in wonderfully high spirits and had performed card tricks for Kate and Miss Fanny. Then he projected the cards on to the table in a double stream.

"Can you do that?" he said.

Kate took the cards and said:

"You are in high spirits today."

"Yes," said Karl, looking her straight in the eye while clapping one hand against the other: "because I'm going out with a lady tomorrow."

The Schleppegrell family went home after leaving Mrs Mourier and Kate at their door. The admiral's wife walked in front with Fanny. They were discussing Kate.

"Yes, Fanny," said the admiral's wife, "but in your place I would *nevertheless* take the opportunity to speak French. The girl has been in Lausanne for two years after all."

"Schleppegrell," she said, gathering her skirts about her as she stopped, "the ducks came from Malle Bardenfleth at Vallø."

Mrs von Eichbaum and Karl had arrived home, and Karl stood in the doorway to the living room.

"You know, Karl," said Mrs von Eichbaum, "Kate's a sweet girl, but she seems to me to be just a little restive."

"I think she's rather amusing," said Karl, tugging at his moustache.

"Yes, but she *must* be given a little polish."

Mrs von Eichbaum made quite a small dismissive gesture with her hand.

"She has quite an idiosyncratic way of sitting down on a chair and so on. But that reminds me of Mourier, with his rather daring ideas."

Mrs von Eichbaum covered her lace pillow over, saying:

"I suppose little Ida Brandt is not free on Tuesday?"

"No, they are only let out every third week."

"That is a pity," said Mrs von Eichbaum.

Karl went.

Mrs von Eichbaum pottered around for some time before putting out the light and going inside. She had obviously forgotten to shut the door between the living room and the sitting room. She had done this more frequently recently.

At home, Mrs Mourier and Kate had enjoyed a snack in their dining room.

"Heaven preserve us, we surely don't need to go there more than once a month."

Mrs Mourier made no reply, but Kate said:

"Oh, I suppose he's the best of them though. You can get to know something from him."

She was referring to Karl.

Kate gave her mother a goodnight kiss and went to join Victoria.

The following morning a telegram arrived from Mourier to tell them that he had bought Ludvigsbakke. Mrs von Eichbaum, who was going shopping with Vilhelmine, came just as Mrs Mourier and Kate were about to have lunch. She was not otherwise keen on eating in their apartment on account of the dogs.

"You know," she said to the general's wife, "one can never eat in peace with those animals around."

But today she stayed on account of the news.

"Well," said Kate, "so now it's been decided. But Engelholm would undoubtedly have been grander."

Nevertheless, Kate thought they should celebrate the event and she had Victoria fetch a bottle of the burgundy that had been stored in the cellar at home in Aarhus since her baptism.

The three ladies chinked glasses.

"Yes," said Mrs von Eichbaum: "Congratulations, Vilhelmine, congratulations."

Kate held her glass out.

"I suppose I shall be given the farm." She emptied her glass and went on.

"But at least we can have a couple of fillies over here, for the livestock is included."

"A *couple*, Kate?"

"Yes, I shall have to have someone to ride with me," said Kate. "I suppose Karl can do that when we get the horses."

"Yes, if only he had time for it from the office," said Mrs von Eichbaum.

Kate drank another glass of burgundy, to the arrival of the fillies.

∞∞∞∞

Monday evening arrived.

The nurses who had been on day duty had their party dresses spread out on their beds. But Ida, who had put candles in the candlesticks in Nurse Helgesen's room, had a lot to see to and was running up and down. There was always more with which to decorate Nurse Helgesen's table: plates and vases and three glass bowls and everything came out of the bureau as though from a magician's hat. There were also the five small lamps, which could be lit among the flowers. Ida brought them down and arranged them.

Nurse Helgesen, who was wearing a grey dress with a matt silk cape, said:

"Thank you, Brandt, thank you, well, in a way I suppose this is a joint effort."

"It's simply lovely that we can use them," said Ida, smiling and doing the arrangement. She needed some flowers now, to be arranged around each pudding dish.

"It's going to be lovely," said Ida, taking a step back to view it all. All the old silver shone so beautifully and it was so long since it had last been used.

Nurse Helgesen, out of a desire to set her eyes on something that was hers, extracted the crown-decorated card that had been inserted in the moss and commented:

"This tree from Mr von Eichbaum is quite a rarity."

Karl von Eichbaum's "Gloire de Dijon" stood proudly at the centre of the table. Nurse Helgesen had already protected each of the yellow flowers with small white paper trimmings.

"Yes," said Ida as she examined one of the yellow buds, "it's beautiful."

"But what time is it?" she said suddenly. All the nurses' presents were to be moved from the birthday table over to one end of the dining table. Nurse Helgesen took them across, and Ida arranged them. They formed a whole ring of plants and flowers around Nurse Helgesen's place.

"Those from Kjær are beautiful," said Ida.

"Everyone has been so kind," said Nurse Helgesen, who, as hostess, began to be all flustered and no longer really saw anything, but she said:

"Do you think there will be enough chairs?"

"We'll bring them down," said Ida, continuing to arrange things. Nurse Boserup had contributed a bleeding heart, a plant with a rather unpleasant smell that looked as though it had been taken up from a larger flowerbed and put in a pot that very morning.

"We'll put that on the worktable," said Ida.

There was a knock on the door, but it was only Nurse Kjær.

"Oh-h, this is fun," she said, standing at the end of the table. "It looks splendid."

All the candles were lit, and three lamps shone down on the flowers.

"Yes, don't you think so?" said Ida, happily shaking her head. "But just watch now," she said and she lit the small lamps, yellow and red, around the table.

"Oh, that's wonderful," said Nurse Kjær again, surveying the silver and the flowers and the puddings. "That's splendid."

"Yes," said Nurse Helgesen: "It's quite festive. And the room is not too small by any means."

Ida wanted to go, but there was a knock on the door again. It was a porter with compliments from Dr Quam. Dr Quam had at the last moment felt the need to contribute something and had bought a box of candied plums with a coloured picture of a Spanish dancer on the lid.

"They are princess plums," said Nurse Kjær, who knew the label. Nurse Helgesen put the fruit on one side.

"It's so nice of the doctors to show an interest in one."

Ida was up in her room, where her yellow dress still lay in its large muslin cover. She had just lit the spirit lamp in front of the mirror when there was a knock at the door. It was Nurse Boserup, who really had to "borrow something to have around my neck".

"Are you waving your hair?" she said suddenly from over in the middle of the floor.

"Well, I was just trying," said Ida blushing deeply.

Boserup had found a tulle shawl with long fringes in one of Ida's drawers.

"Are you going to use those two pins?" she said suddenly,

pointing to a solitaire that she took and fixed to the shawl while at the same time expressing the opinion that waving only made one's face look older.

"No, it really looks nice in the light," said Ida.

"Oh well, if you can be bothered. You wouldn't catch me doing it. But there's no accounting for taste. Goodbye, I'll see you later."

Ida locked the door; she wanted to be alone now that she was going to put her dress on.

The nurses had arrived downstairs, one after the other, each new arrival being greeted with exclamations at her dress. "Oh, just look at Friis, oh, just look at Friis," they shouted, and then they fell silent again; no one really knew what to say because they all felt they had to say something more than usual; and yet again they started to talk about the table standing in the middle of the room and looking almost *too* splendid, while Nurse Helgesen kept saying that they should sit down; and the nurses sat along the walls, with their shoes poking out from under their dresses, as though they had never been in this room before.

Only Nurse Friis, sitting in an easy chair a little away from the wall and with her hands crossed on her lap, reviewed it all and stopped at the outdoor plant on the worktable.

"That must be Boserup's," she said to Nurse Kjær. "Heavens, it's like her to limit herself to that sort of price. But the table looks nice."

"It was Ida who arranged it," said Nurse Kjær, going around to everyone and saying: "That's Ida." She always called her by her Christian name when she was not present.

Ida felt that she became all flushed as she stood outside the door and then opened it and entered and Kjær shouted:

"Miss has been waving her hair."

All the ladies rose from their seats and Nurse Kjær and Nurse Friis clapped their hands until everyone followed suit, while Ida stood there, blushing in the light, and a whole circle formed around her yellow dress.

"She looks wonderful," said Nurse Kjær, breaking out of the circle and embracing Ida as though she wanted to crush her.

Things had become a little livelier, and Nurse Helgesen was heard to say that perhaps they could begin, when there was another knock on the door. It was Eichbaum and Quam, who shook Nurse Helgesen's hand and said: "No, we've not been invited, but we assumed our honest faces would ensure that we could come in." Meanwhile, Karl went around making deep bows, dressed in a Parisian frock coat, the lining of which rustled a bit when he moved.

Nurse Helgesen, who was quite flattered by his formal manner, said:

"Mr von Eichbaum, it was so kind of you," and she took his long, cool hand before Karl bowed once more, while Josefine, high-bosomed and with hussar's braiding on her dress, offered the sauce around and the ladies, a little slowly and almost solemnly started to help themselves to the pudding. But Quam, who stood there looking around at all those tightly corseted nurses, said to Nurse Kaas:

"This is too damned formal."

And he took the Madeira and started to fill the glasses to liven up the mood. "Nurse Brandt," he said, "you must help me."

Ida emerged from the corner over by the bleeding heart plant, where Nurse Friis had until that moment been examining the yellow leaves like some kind of specialist, and she took the tray with the glasses.

"Have you provided this?" said Karl in a strangely quiet voice as he took a glass.

He stood there with his glass.

"You look so lovely," he said in the same tone, and she felt that she simply did not recognise his voice.

She spoke without looking up, presumably saying something about his flower.

"One has to do something to be welcome," said Karl, but it was as though he was giving her some secret message.

Then Nurse Kjær came from behind and put her arm around Ida.

"Yes, isn't she beautiful?" she said, as it were drawing her close.

"Yes, I can hardly recognise you ladies," said Karl.

"No," said Nurse Kjær: "We so rarely dress up."

Ida went on. She seemed to be so graceful in appearance, so delicate, as she bent forward over the nurses and offered them a glass.

"What did that dress cost you?" asked Boserup as Ida went past, and the nurse sitting beside her laughed. Quam was telling stories down at the end of the table and the ladies moved their chairs closer together and rose and helped themselves. Ida could hear that Karl was also laughing over there by Nurse Kjær.

"Brandt made the pudding," Josefine announced as she went round offering it to the others.

"There was a cry of delight when the door opened to Sister Koch, and Quam shouted: "Cheers, Sister Koch," while they all drank to her.

"Oh, there are men here as well," said Sister Koch, whose party dress was limited to a clean collar.

"Yes, two," said Karl with a bow.

"So I see," said Sister Koch, and they laughed again.

They started laughing at anything, talking in loud voices, talking past each other, while Nurse Boserup discussed the association and Nurse Kjær and Nurse Krohn made themselves corsages from the flowers on the table.

"Kjær's stealing, Kjær's stealing," came a shout from the other end.

"It's becoming lively here," said Ida; she was radiant as she went past Karl.

Nurse Boserup continued talking about the association: they were naturally not getting any backing from the King Frederik Hospital.

But Quam shouted from down at the end of the table:

"We don't want to hear about that, we don't want to hear about that," and he banged his spoon on his plate.

"We don't want to hear about that, we don't want to hear about that," they all chorused.

They all knocked their spoons on their plates – all except Nurse Helgesen and Nurse Kaas – and all the ladies laughed, while Boserup drew her chair back and said: "I didn't know there were children here as well."

"Well there are," said Quam, and they all banged their spoons on their plates.

"Sshh," said Nurse Helgesen.

There were two knocks on the door.

"Hush, the patients can hear us." It was the night watchman.

They suddenly all fell quiet, with the same expression on their faces; and they heard the door again, the door in to the "noisy ward".

"Never mind," said Quam: "*They* damned well make plenty of noise often enough."

But Nurse Kaas, taking advantage of the silence, rose, while Nurse Helgesen as though of her own accord moved up to the place of honour near the flowers, and Nurse Kaas tapped her glass.

Karl slipped past Ida. They had said little to each other, but it was as though he was always where she was.

"Are you not going to sit down?" he said.

And she seated herself on a chair close to where he was standing.

"Is it not hot in here?" she said, putting a hand to her forehead.

Although seemingly only speaking with half her voice, as though the night watchman's knock on the door was still resounding in their ears, Nurse Kaas made a speech in praise of Nurse Helgesen as one of those who raised the standing of their profession.

"Now we must give three quiet cheers," said Quam.

He beat the time with his hands and whispered "Hip, hip..." the others joining in, whispering in the same way, pouting their lips and laughing quietly.

"That was that," said Quam: "That's how loud you shout hurrah in Ward Six."

"Now we'll chink glasses," he said, and, walking on tiptoe, with his glass in his hand, he led the way while the others tiptoed after him, treading carefully on the floor, in single file, up to Helgesen.

"Hurrah," said Quam.

"And thank you for the Madeira."

Sister Koch said: "Oh, I suppose I'd better join in," and she stepped in behind Ida, with an empty glass. But from down in her place Nurse Boserup said:

"You must excuse me for chinking from my place."

"Well, it's you I must thank first of all," said Nurse Helgesen, chinking her glass with Ida.

"Oh," said Ida, surveying the flowers and candles and everyone there. "This is such a wonderful evening."

Josefine, who had been up to fetch more wine from Ida's room, was standing down by the door with Nurse Kjær.

"She really has such a lovely face," she said.

Sister Koch turned to her empty glass. "Have you got a drop more for me?" Josefine hurried to fill the ward sister's glass. "Yes, thank you for looking after me," said Sister Koch to Nurse Helgesen.

"This was where you were sitting," whispered Karl to Ida.

And Ida sat down as before.

But Sister Koch thought it was time for coffee now, assuming they were to have coffee. Quam offered her a cigar, and Karl passed the cigarettes around while they all, secretly, looked at his fine silver cigarette case. "*May* we?" said Nurse Kjær looking at Nurse Helgesen. But Nurse Friis was a gifted exponent of the art of smoking and could blow blue smoke rings down among the white candles before they were dispersed.

"Look at that," said Ida. She was watching the fine smoke.

"I think we should have a song now," said Nurse Krohn.

Nurse Helgesen wanted to raise objections, but Nurse Krohn said: "We'll only hum of course. We often do in our rooms."

"Ida," she said, "you lead. Let's sing 'Fly bird, fly'."

They moved the chairs a little further back, and, half humming as they looked into the candles, they quietly sang:

> *Fly, bird, fly, o'er the darkening lake*
> *Darkness descends on the ling.*
> *Now will the sun the deep forest forsake*
> *Day has once more taken wing.*

They continued to sing in low voices, as though far away behind a closed door. Nurse Kjær gently rocked backwards and forwards, and

Nurse Helgesen joined in, singing in her contralto voice. Josefine, who was standing at the door as though on guard, joined in as well, with her hands on her hips.

> *A singer am I and so must I know*
> *The joys and the sorrows of love.*
> *All that the heart can suffer of woe*
> *That must I sing of, my dove.*

The singing ceased, but no one moved.

"Now they've bought Ludvigsbakke," said Karl.

"Have they?" She turned half toward him. There were tears in her eyes.

"Yes."

They started to sing again.

"Are they going to pull the big house down?" asked Ida slowly and very quietly.

"Yes," said Karl.

The others went on singing, but Karl said, and Ida scarcely heard the words:

"We should have had it."

Ida did not move.

But suddenly Quam interrupted the singing:

"If we're going to sing, we must have less light in here." And he set about blowing out the candles in the candelabra, while Nurse Friis laughed and helped him. "Now," said Quam, "the big lamps as well. But the stars must shine." And he left Ida's small lamps to burn on.

"But then we must open the door to the stove," said Nurse Kjær. She failed to get it open and said: "Ida, come and help me." Ida got up and opened the door. "Sit here," said Nurse Kjær, pulling her down on the little pouffe.

"There," said Quam. "Now the lighting's right."

They started to sing again, perhaps rather more slowly, with their faces turned towards the glowing coals. Ida had closed her eyes.

> *Fly, oh bird, fly o'er the waters' dark surge*
> *Now draws the night its deep sigh,*
> *Whisper the trees with tremulous urge*
> *Telling that morning is nigh.*

The singing stopped. Round about in the darkness, the tiny glows of the cigarettes could be seen along with Sister Koch's cigar, which was like a sort of lighthouse.

"Don't you know a song about Jutland?" said Karl quietly but audibly over in the dark.

"Yes, Ida does," said Nurse Krohn.

"Oh yes, sing one," said Nurse Berg. Ida had not reacted.

"Sing," whispered Nurse Kjær.

Looking up into the darkness, clearly but very gently, while it looked as though she was only half opening her lips, Ida sang the song about Jutland.

> *Jutland here betwixt two seas*
> *Like a runic stone does lie...*

She hardly stopped after the first verse, but continued to sing. Nurse Kjær had leant her head on her shoulder.

"That's a jolly nice song," said Quam when Ida stopped; but Karl said nothing, he merely sat staring at her face.

"Come on now, Eichbaum," said Quam. "Now we're jolly well going to have a dance."

There was subdued laughter and shouting in the darkness. "Are you mad, doctor," said Nurse Helgesen, who loved to dance.

But Quam had lit a wax matchstick. "Be careful of all those things, be careful," shouted Nurse Kjær, who had got up as though she intended to hold on to them herself. And in no time the table had been moved aside and the chairs were gone.

Nurse Kjær and Nurse Krohn sang, still quietly, over by the stove, while Quam swung Nurse Helgesen so the steps could be heard in the dark.

"Shall we?" said Karl with a bow. He chose Nurse Friis.

Ida joined in the singing. It was as though her voice led the others in greater joy than she herself realised.

"This is fine," said Quam. He and Nurse Helgesen waltzed past in the semi-darkness like a pair of great shadows. *There* Karl glided past, so upright, with Nurse Friis.

"Let us," said Nurse Kaas to Nurse Boserup, and they started to dance. Nurse Boserup led.

Quam nudged Josefine who had come forward a little to watch the ward sister letting herself go.

"This is lovely," said Nurse Helgesen when they stopped.

No one was singing except Nurse Kjær and Nurse Friis now that Eichbaum had released her.

"Come on," said Karl, and Ida followed him.

They did not speak as they danced slowly, in the darkness. Nurse Kjær, who was still sitting on the pouffe, sang more gently. The wicks in the small lamps fluttered a little until they went out.

"They've stopped singing," whispered Ida.

All was quiet for a while, as though they were all tired, and the tiny lights from the cigarettes had gone out all around.

"Well, I think it would be best if we had our faces illuminated," said Sister Koch, starting to light the lamps again. The ladies blinked in the glare as though they had just wakened.

"Well," said Quam: "I think we should drink to Nurse Brandt. Damn it all, it was she who made the pudding."

He drank to Ida, and Nurse Kjær ran around to ensure they all had glasses in their hands.

"Yes, she deserved that," said Nurse Kjær.

Josefine, who was standing by the table putting the plates together, touched Ida's back from behind and also wanted to drink to her, in secret.

"This is my first glass," she said, and she had tears in her eyes.

Karl came over to Ida and chinked his glass against hers.

"Thank you," he said.

It was not long before they broke up, but Ida wanted to stay and help Nurse Helgesen prepare for the night. She said goodbye to Quam, who was already standing in the doorway, and to Karl.

"Goodnight," she said, taking his hand.

"Goodbye," said Karl, still in the same tone.

Ida stayed with Nurse Helgesen. They put the flowers in water and they cleared the table. Ida put the sofa down and made her bed. Then she went.

All was quiet in the noisy ward and there was a light on for Nurse Petersen who was on night duty. Ida went slowly upstairs with her candle.

"It's me," said Karl suddenly from up in the darkness on the stairs.

Ida started and made no reply; her face was merely pale against the raised candle, but she opened her door and closed it behind them.

"Was it all right I came?" whispered Karl.

Ida smiled at him:

"Yes," she said.

∞∞∞∞

Morning had arrived.

Karl sat on the edge of Ida's bed.

"Ida," he said: "Are you angry with me?"

Ida lay there with her eyes closed.

"Why?" was all she said.

And shortly afterwards she opened her eyes and said:

"I knew, of course."

Karl remained seated on the bed and perhaps he really believed that he was in love, that it was the first time in his life he had been in love.

"Good night, my love," he whispered.

Ida slowly moved her hand over her forehead:

"Kiss me *there*," she said.

191

She lay there again with her eyes closed.

"Thank you. And will you promise me one thing" – she opened her eyes, but closed them again as though it pained her to see him – "that you will tell me when you leave me one day."

Karl made no reply. Nevertheless, Ida took his hand and placed it against her cheek as though for a thousand caresses.

"Thank you," she said again.

∞∞∞

The snow creaked beneath Karl's feet.

"And why the devil shouldn't we be able to get married?" he kept on saying to himself.

III

The real frost had arrived.

The mornings were bright with clear skies, with snow on the road and snow far out over the frozen lake. Ida stepped out confidently on the path – it was as though she asserted her presence more now – as she walked towards the sun, and the Nørrebro steam whistles were sounding and the machines clanking as though they were the bright morning's pulse, while riders came in their twos and threes, trotting quickly from Østerbro on panting horses.

"Ooh," said Ida to a boy who had fallen off a slide.

"Ooh," he replied and then he was up and off again.

Two elderly gentlemen had also been watching.

"Up again," said one of them, laughing to Ida: "Young people."

All the elderly gentlemen taking their morning walk had to chat with Ida if there was anything at all to be said; and Ida nodded.

"Yes, Your Honour," she said. She knew all these elderly gentlemen.

The two old gentlemen continued their walk, and one of them – he was wearing ear muffs – said slowly and clearly:

"You know it is really lovely to see a healthy face."

The other stood there for a moment and watched Ida as she walked. It was as though there was a certain proud bearing about her, about her hips.

"Indeed, young people look splendid in the sunshine."

Over by the working-class houses, Ida met Boserup and Kaas, who were wearing large galoshes.

"You are out on your walk rather late today," said Nurse Kaas as she went past.

"Yes," said Ida without stopping: "I prefer to go out when the sun is shining."

"But isn't it a lovely morning?" she said; she was already a few steps away from them.

"Yes, at minus eight," shouted Kaas, who was wearing black mittens.

"Oh, the cold warms you up," shouted Ida back.

"Not to mention the fur coat," said Boserup, who had not stopped and was already some dozen trees further on. She said something to the effect that one ought to dress a little according to one's position in life.

"Yes," said Kaas, who was thinking about Ida as she went. It was as though Ida never had anything to say to her colleagues any more, and that hurt them.

"I must say she's been putting it on recently."

When she had almost reached Østerbro Ida turned and raised her veil. Yes, the channel was free of ice; and she went back, with the sun on her back, and dodged round the corner at Rørholm. The toothless old man opened the door to a private compartment as though he had been expecting her.

"It's warm," he said.

"Yes, thank you."

"I think we'll have the usual." Ida took off her coat and had the table moved forward and the door of the stove opened to show the coal burning.

The toothless waiter nodded and had closed the door, quietly letting down the flap (when Ellingsen, the waiter, was carrying out his tasks, there was something about him rather reminiscent of a subservient verger during divine service opening the pews for those who rented them) before going off to order the lunch.

Ida laid the table herself and put some violas in Karl's place, and she unwrapped the cake. How lovely and fresh it was. There came the sound of a walking stick knocking on the door.

"Good morning," said Karl. "By Gad, you always seem to have something to unwrap."

"Good morning."

He kissed her cheek and hung up his overcoat.

"It's lovely and warm in here," said Ida, moving her cheek against his, and earnestly looking up at him all the time. She so wanted to stand like this for a moment and look into his eyes.

"It's jolly nice here," said Karl, sitting down and setting about the lunch while the fire roasted his legs.

Ida sat there laughing.

"You are all right now," she said.

"Yes," said Karl, dipping his toast in his egg and looking across the table at her.

"This is the best meal of the day."

Ida cut a piece of cake. She made rather a lot of small movements when she was so happy.

"It's from the court baker's," she said, tossing her head, a movement she had really learned from Olivia.

"Good Lord," Karl took a piece. "Aye, I must say you get around," he said in a rather soft voice.

"Yes," laughed Ida with a nod. She had developed the habit of opening her eyes curiously wide when she was happy.

Stretching his long legs out in front of the fire, Karl went on eating, slowly, one piece after the other. But Ida pushed her cup and her plate aside to make room and tell him:

"Oh, you must hear this, it is incredible."

It was a story, a long story about a bottle of "drinks".

"Oh, I see," said Karl. "Aye, you go through a few small glasses over there, I must say."

"I don't," said Ida, taking his hand across the table.

"No, I suppose you don't need it. You presumably don't need to have it both ways."

"Karl."

"It was a bottle of Dôm, and Nurse Friis had – incredibly – just put it in the cupboard in the corridor, straight in front of the door and then the prof came while Petersen was standing there...with the cupboard open. And he saw it straight away and oh, how he carried on; you have no idea."

Karl had finished and now sat puffing great rings of smoke up in the air from his cigarette.

"So I don't think Friis will be made a sister now," concluded Ida, with a frightened look in her eyes.

"That's a pity," said Karl. "But Friis is probably one who can look after herself."

"But," and Ida nodded twice, "she only earns twenty-five kroner a month."

She had risen and was standing behind Karl, rubbing her chin on his hair, while he seemingly sat there gently humming.

"But the prof damned well ought to have a job in Rome," he said. Ida put both her hands round his cheeks.

"Why?"

"Well, because all those round the Pope have faces like that."

Ida went on laughing, sitting on the floor with her elbow resting on his knee. They were silent for a while until Karl said:

"Do you know what, mamma is going away, probably."

"Going away? Where?" Ida gave a little start.

"To Geneva." He clicked his lips.

"Grandma Aline's jolly well got to be brought back home."

"Mrs Feddersen? And your mother is going to fetch her?" She looked up and then down again. "That is so kind of her."

It was as though Ida's voice had suddenly trembled a little, and Karl nodded thoughtfully as he continued to stare at the fire.

"Yes, that's what she's like."

The coals in the fire collapsed:

"Well, so she doesn't judge her...so harshly." She spoke gently, and there was a special ring to the word "judge", as though she had learned it by heart.

Karl continued to look at the coals.

"I don't know, damn it, she condemns her like all the others, I suppose, but she's fetching her."

Ida did not move; it might almost be thought she suddenly had tears in her eyes.

Karl nodded at the fire again.

"And she'll get her reinstated in all her old glory," he said.

Ida made no reply, but she had taken her hands away from his knee.

"What are you thinking about?" he asked.

"Your mother."

It came from deep down inside her, and she laid her head against his side, while Karl stroked her hair and the coals continued to collapse, little by little.

"You are so nice when you sit there so silently," he said, still stroking her hair quite gently, but there was nevertheless something about his caresses as though he were stroking a hound.

"And there was so much I wanted to say."

"What did you want to say?" he said, not taking his hand from her hair.

A moment passed:

"Thank you," she whispered quite quietly.

There came a slight twitch at the corner of his mouth, and his hand went in under the hair at the back of her head.

"And I'm never allowed to thank you."

"Yes, you are," she said, no longer looking at the fire – if you – one day would say thank you...for yourself."

Karl bent down over her: there was something about his eyes that made them look like velvet.

"Dearest," he said.

Ida did not answer his caresses, and she did not look up while saying in a voice he could scarcely hear:

"For I always wonder what your mother would think."

A second passed.

"There's no point in that, damn it" said Karl, changing his tone.

But Ida had risen and fetched his overcoat (managing to dry her eyes the while) and spread it out to warm the lining by the fire. She sat smoothing the soft silk with her hands. She was very fond of that overcoat.

"The lining is wearing well."

"Yes."

"Hm," and Ida smiled: "You were so pleased when you got it."

Karl got up and shook his long legs.

"And it was about time, too," he said, putting on the coat with the aid of Ida, "that I had something warm to wear on these morning walks."

Ida also put her outdoor clothes on. "Goodbye then," she said, putting her arms round his neck before ringing for Ellingsen. Mr Ellingsen had a way of coming in through a door as though he were entering by way of a crack. The purse was already over by Karl's plate (it was a Russia leather gentleman's purse that Ida had bought), and Karl paid while Ida was putting her fur collar up, and Mr Ellingsen went out to change the large note, while Ida snatched the purse.

"Goodbye, dear," said Karl again, rocking her gently backward and forward, with his hands round her waist, while Ida smiled.

"Goodbye."

She stood for a moment.

"Do you know, I'm always so happy when I leave."

"Really," laughed Karl, letting go of her.

"Yes," said Ida, standing close to his shoulder, "for then I *know* everything – again."

"Goodbye."

The door to the corridor closed. Ida always went first, and Karl waited until she had gone a good way ahead. Mr Ellingsen gave the change to Karl, and Eichbaum put it in his pocket, and the toothless old man began to clear up, with his head on one side; two places had been reserved for quarter to eleven.

"You get a lot of people in here, by Gad," said Karl, who was still waiting.

"Yes, we have quite a number of people here in the mornings," – Mr Ellingsen pronounced "quite" as "quate" – "during business hours."

"Good morning."

Ida walked past ladies and gentlemen and past trees that were truly radiant; she knew that Karl had come round the corner now and was walking on the path some way behind her, sauntering along, with his walking stick over his arm and with Ida's back in front of him, at a respectable distance: this was by Gad the best cigar he would have all day.

Some horsemen rode by, and some ladies went past: the smoke from a Havana cigar was simply beautiful when the air was as still as this.

A couple of lieutenants rode up alongside Karl and stopped their horses with a "Morning."

"Morning," murmured Karl.

"You are walking along looking like some wealthy landowner," said one of them, a member of the Knuth family.

"Yes, I'm doing some calculations," said Karl.

The lieutenants laughed and stopped alongside him. They talked about the animals' croupes and stayed with him until there came the sound of fresh hoofs behind them and the two uniformed men saluted. It was Kate with her servant, and she, too, stopped her horse.

"Good morning. Is your mother leaving tomorrow, then?" she asked, looking down at Karl.

"That was the idea," said Karl, his eyes on her steed.

"Bon voyage," said Kate, flicking her whip.

The two lieutenants growled something or other about accompanying the lady, and Kate said:

"Why, of course," (Knuth had been garrisoned at Aarhus) and they all three rode on, slowly, Kate between the two officers.

"Oh, that was what you were waiting for," said Karl as he watched them; Kate was now nodding down to Ida.

But she rides damned well, he thought with a nod. He whistled between his teeth; he had a curious whistle that could be heard half a mile away and Ida, who was walking quickly ahead, slowed her pace until he reached her: it was as though he needed to talk to her a little. But all he said was:

"She rides damned well." And he continued to look at her twenty-year-old waist, *there* on the horse's back.

"She's very pretty," said Ida. And her eyes shone at Karl's.

They turned off further down the road while Karl was still watching them. The lieutenants' bodies had become so flexible as they leaned towards her.

"I suppose the butter profits will benefit the hussars as well now," said Karl.

They had reached the slide where the boy had fallen off earlier and suddenly – perhaps in sheer joy because Karl had called to her – Ida started to go down the slide. She positioned her legs a little too youthfully apart as she laughed.

"You wouldn't be particularly elegant on skates, by Gad," said Karl, and Ida smiled again.

Then they parted on the corner.

Karl went on, thinking that he might really just as well ride with Kate in the mornings, for in any case he was not going to go to that damned office any earlier.

"And it's a lovely animal," he said.

When he reached the office, he found Sister Koch there. She had taken her glasses off – she had just met Ida by the middle door – and was watching von Eichbaum.

Karl took his books out and adjusted his office chair.

"Oh, so the cavalry has its eye on the butter," he thought. He started on the books.

Ida did not fall asleep; she lay in the greenish light and thought of Mrs von Eichbaum, who was to travel all that way. That was so nice of her. She was going to fetch her and was not judging her.

Ida lay there without moving, staring out into the pale green light. Her thoughts took her so far away.

Down below there was the sound of doors being opened and closed.

Ida would send some flowers to Mrs von Eichbaum when she left. Indeed she would send a bouquet out to the station.

∞∞∞

Mrs von Eichbaum and the general's wife were in the dining room, sitting in front of the closed trunk when Mrs Mourier arrived together with Kate.

"But Emilie," said Mrs Mourier: "Are you wearing silk for the journey?"

"Good heavens, Vilhelmine, I always do. It's the only practical thing. You can shake the dust off silk."

The general's wife took up the theme while Mrs von Eichbaum called for Julius, and said:

"Oh no, fancy travelling in woollen clothes, we who hate dirt."

Kate, who had a large folder under her arm and was standing in the dining room with her lips pursed as though she wanted to whistle but was keeping the sound to herself, asked if they would like to see the design for the main building at Ludvigsbakke.

"Dear Kate, just fancy looking at the designs now," – it was Mrs von Eichbaum speaking – "only minutes before leaving."

"You are not leaving for another hour," said Kate.

Mrs von Eichbaum always unfailingly left home at least half an hour early, "as though one knew what could happen at the last minute."

They all went down to the cab and drove off, with Julius on the box. Mrs Mourier was saying that she would probably also have to leave within a few days, for Aarhus. Mourier had written to say that they were simply *obliged* to give those two dinners.

It would not matter about the actual farms. But there were the tenant farmers and bailiffs that Mourier thought should be invited as they were accustomed to..."And he is always very dependent on them, of course," said Mrs Mourier, "these days when there is so much competition."

"I entirely agree with Mourier in that," said Mrs von Eichbaum. "There is no point in upsetting that kind of people."

"Yes, that is exactly what Mourier says," said Mrs Mourier.

When they arrived in the main hall at the railway station, they found Mrs Schleppegrell waiting together with Fanny, who was wearing a bonnet tied with dark red ribbons under her pointed chin. Mrs Schleppegrell went across and embraced Mrs von Eichbaum, saying: "Oh, thank God it was possible to arrange something, my dear and, how grateful Line must be to you."

"Dear Anna," said Mrs von Eichbaum, "it is not really worth talking about the two-day journey when I am travelling on a modern railway train."

They all sat down by one of the round tables around the pillars, while Mrs von Eichbaum put on her newly washed silk gloves for the journey and Fanny brought a greeting from Miss Juul, the lady-in-waiting.

"Yes," said Mrs Schleppegrell: "Emma (Emma was Miss Juel's Christian name) actually said to me yesterday: 'Dearest friend, it will be a relief for the entire group'."

But Mrs Mourier had tears in her eyes as she said:

"Seeing you again, Emilie, will nevertheless be awfully difficult for Aline."

The waiting-room began to fill up as Kate peeled an orange and the general's wife and Mrs Schleppegrell talked about Geneva chocolate. "Yes, Emilie," said the admiral's wife, "if it would not be too much trouble for you to order twenty pounds for me to be sent direct. Geneva chocolate is what Fanny likes best of course."

Karl appeared among the travellers with his stick under his arm and leaning slightly forward. "Oh," he said, "I suppose you've been here for an hour already."

He kissed Mrs von Eichbaum on the cheek and gave her a small bottle of eau de Cologne in Russia leather for the journey. "A little present for you," he said. Karl was managing his money remarkably well recently, and he was really very attentive by nature. He greeted all the others, and Mrs Mourier said with a smile:

"He is an attentive son. I'm sure he will be a good husband."

"Are you sure of that?" said Karl, who was standing between Mrs Mourier and Kate, and he wrinkled his nose.

"Hm, what are the qualities of a good husband?" said Kate.

"That he is a real man," said Karl.

Kate looked up, and something appeared in her eyes for a brief moment that made Karl as it were move closer to the back of her chair.

"Yes, Karl is right in that," said Mrs Mourier.

The door to the waiting-room opened and Julius gathered the smaller pieces of luggage.

"But in Geneva," Mrs von Eichbaum was heard to say to Mrs Schleppegrell, "one can always attend the Reformed Church."

Fanny, who was looking at Karl and Kate through her pince-nez, said to the general's wife: "Yes, they have a new minister now, and he is said to speak in such a beautiful way."

Mrs Mourier, who was the last to rise, said: "Oh, I am never keen on hearing ministers I do not know."

They all emerged on to the platform and Mrs von Eichbaum found a compartment. There was something about Mrs von Eichbaum that immediately persuaded conductors and the like to shower her with attention even though she did not exactly give the impression that she would be giving a tip. She got in while all the others except Karl and Kate clustered together around the door, so that Nurse Kjær, who came running up, quite out of breath, with Ida's bouquet could hardly reach the step.

"There are just a few flowers from Miss Brandt. She could unfortunately not come herself."

Mrs von Eichbaum took the flowers and expressed her thanks: it was so kind of Miss Brandt. And Nurse Kjær disappeared again just as suddenly and embarrassingly flushed as when she had arrived, while Mrs von Eichbaum, sitting with the bouquet, said:

"My dears, that was really kind of her, but flowers are *simply* one of the least practical things I can imagine for a journey. Take them home with you, Vilhelmine, and put them in some water."

And she handed the roses to Mrs Mourier:

"I would only put them in the luggage rack here and find them withered in the morning."

The flowers were passed to Kate, who stood there holding them.

"They are beautiful," she said, looking down with supreme

indifference at the long La France roses.

"Yes," said Karl, smiling suddenly and so nicely down at the pink flowers. "She meant well, damn it."

Then he returned to his theme – they had been talking about Knuth's riding skill – and he wrinkled his nose at the thought of the count.

"No, he's a fine jumper, by Jove. Where did you come across *him*?"

"He has been garrisoned at Aarhus. And you refuse to ride with me."

"It's a lovely animal," was all Karl said with a vague nod.

The conductors closed the doors and the latecomers rushed out of the waiting-rooms, followed by panting hotel porters. Doors were opened and closed again, and suddenly, for a moment, it was as though everyone was quarrelling, porters, conductors and travellers.

"My dear," said Mrs von Eichbaum, standing bolt upright at the window of her compartment, "I cannot understand that people who are about to embark on a journey can never arrange their time better."

∞∞∞

The train had left and they only saw Mrs von Eichbaum's white handkerchief once more before all turned and left.

When they reached the main hall, Karl said:

"I could actually come riding tomorrow."

"But Knuth's coming now," replied Kate.

"Well then, he can come with us," said Karl.

That was agreed, and Karl left.

Mrs Schleppegrell and Fanny decided to take the tramcar home, while the others took a cab. They spoke about Aline, and the general's wife said:

"We do not condemn her. But you know there are things one simply does not comprehend."

"Well," said Mrs Mourier, staring straight ahead, "there is a little of it in all of us, and when you don't become closely attached to the one you have."

"Yes, dear," replied the general's wife, "but, there are things, you know, that one has to restrain."

Kate sat watching the Schleppegrells. They were stepping into the tramcar now. Mrs Schleppegrell always had the conductor take a really firm hold around her waist.

"Fanny," she said when they were both safely aboard, "I do not think we should tell anyone that we were at the station."

Mrs Mourier had arrived home and had collapsed in a chair still wearing her outdoor clothes. Her thoughts were with Aline.

"Well," she said, "the worst is still to come for her." She was thinking of Aline and her arrival home.

"Kate, will you put those flowers in water."

Kate looked around.

"I forgot them in the cab," she said, and went in to Victoria.

Mrs Mourier remained seated with her outdoor clothes on. She smiled: she had thought of Karl. She so liked him. There are no airs and graces about him, she always said to the general's wife.

∞∞∞

Ida was in the café, by the fire, beside the well-laid table, when the door opened and she rose – flushed right down over her neck – but it was only Mr Ellingsen bringing a note.

Ida opened it and read it, immediately, while standing in the middle or the floor, and there came such a strange sudden pain in her breast.

"I am afraid I shall have to go riding with the butter this morning. Will see you soon. Karl."

"Is the gentleman ill?" said Ellingsen, very quietly. He had only taken one look at her face.

"Yes," said Ida, almost without realising it.

She just took a look at the table.

"Let me pay you," she said, suddenly smiling (it was all so reasonable: it was naturally Mrs von Eichbaum who had arranged it yesterday evening at the station) but she suddenly realised that Ellingsen would recognise the purse, so she said:

"Oh no, it can wait." And she went on to talk to Ellingsen as he helped her on with her coat and said goodbye to him without turning round.

Ellingsen closed the door and cleared the table and smoothed the serviettes a little. There was something about the movements of his hands as he did this that suggested concern, as though he were distributing black-edged hymn sheets in a choir loft.

Ida walked along the road, erect and quick, smiling once more. It was so reasonable and Karl was so fond of riding. (The thought of Karl's name brought the smile back to her eyes, which had been as it were round and stiff, although there was plenty of radiance in them.) She continued to smile. Yes, he rode so elegantly.

But – yes – she would walk quickly, for if they were riding and came this way...She was nevertheless reluctant to meet them.

However, for whatever reason, she walked slowly every now and then and it was as though the heads of the old gentlemen who were taking their walk only came into sight suddenly, when they were right upon her, so that she hardly managed to nod to them. But the old judge stopped her and held both her hands tight between his knitted mittens. What lovely weather it was today, he said, and so bright.

"Aye, it's a wonderful air for those of us who are hard of hearing," he said. But at that moment Ida heard the sound of horses trotting behind her, and she simply *had* to leave him: it must be them, though it sounded as though there were three horses...

Ida did not herself know why she took such a deep breath when she had half turned to see Knuth come trotting along – there, on the other side of Kate.

The horses came ever closer, and Ida was about to acknowledge them when Kate Mourier reined in her horse.

"Good morning, Miss Brandt," she said, up on the animal, and the others stopped like her.

Ida flushed and then turned pale.

"Good morning," she said, and the stiff expression that had been there before returned to her eyes.

"You can be sure we have been for a long ride," said Kate, while Karl, who was close to Ida and had been unable to catch her eye, allowed, as though by chance, the furthest tip of his riding whip to touch Ida's cheek quite lightly, causing Ida, with the speed of lightning, to look up for a second.

"Ugh," said Kate, looking out across the lake (Knuth did not take his eyes of Ida) "It must be awful to work in the madhouse on a day like this."

She nodded again and they rode off.

"She's quite sweet really," she said as they cantered along.

"Yes," said Karl slowly: "She's so lovely when she's upset."

Kate laughed, "Good heavens, that's so like you. Is she not lovely when she's happy?"

"No," said Karl.

"Why?"

Karl rode on a little. "I suppose she's not used to being happy," he said and nodded.

Knuth had come half a horse length behind the others: he turned around twice in the saddle to look back.

"Come on, Knuth," Kate called, and Knuth quickened his pace. Shortly afterwards, he asked:

"Is she in the Municipal?"

"Yes," replied Karl.

"Allez-y."

They broke into a sharp trot.

During each break in the barracks that morning, Knuth went around in a strange manner, chewing at the knob on his whip.

Brahe stood there with his legs apart, grinning. He knew what was wrong when Knuth chewed at his whip and his eyes took on, as it were, a darker shade.

"Nonsense," said Knuth. But he continued to chew at his whip. She had had a lovely smile by Gad, as she stood there looking up at that fellow.

207

Ida was at home. She had nodded to the porter and spoken to Josefine on the stairs – Josefine's skirts swished wonderfully during these days – and up in her room she had closed her window: she was conscious of only one thing, all the time: the gentle touch of Karl's whip on her cheek.

∞∞∞

"Blast, oh, I don't think he saw me." Karl jumped around the corner of the stairs up to Ida's room at about five o'clock just as Dr Quam opened the door on the first floor. He stood by her door for a moment until he heard Quam's steps die away down the corridor.

Then he knocked twice on the door, as was his custom.

"You looked so lovely this morning," he kept saying to Ida; and he stayed with her until the very last minute.

But when he came down, Quam was standing outside the ward with the noisy patients, talking to Sister Koch.

"Good evening," he said softly as he went past.

Sister Koch made no reply, but she gave him such a furious look, and her conversation with Quam came to a halt.

"I really do wonder," she said suddenly, in the midst of something else: "what people like that are *thinking* of..."

Dr Quam stood for a moment:

"I suppose there are people who never think very far," he said. "And things are easier for them when they don't think further than they want to."

Sister Koch closed her lips so tightly that they were no more than a line.

After a slight pause, she said:

"Tell me, doctor, what is really to be done with this world?"

Quam whistled.

"I've no idea, unless a certain number of men were to be treated in the same way as stallions and turned into work horses quietly pulling a big cart."

He was silent for a while:

"In that way," he went on: "The excellent result would be achieved of depopulating the earth as far as possible."

"You are a sensible man, doctor," said Sister Koch.

"Well," said Quam: "God knows. I suppose you become bitter by going around in a lunatic asylum, most of all when you think of those who have not been confined to one."

∞∞∞

The cab stopped outside the door in Toldbodvejen, and Karl emerged:

"Right, now get the shawl down over your ears."

Ida was to act the part of the general's wife as she passed Svendsen, the porter, walking on tiptoe to look the right height and laughing, with the lace scarf covering her face.

"He's there, damn it," said Karl, glancing at the porter's hatch as Ida went past on stretched feet.

"There."

They were safely inside the courtyard, and they both laughed, quietly. But nodding towards him, Karl said:

"But it was his confounded fault the admiral's family moved out."

"Why?"

Karl smacked his lips. "The admiral's an old rogue," was all he said. They crept up the stairs, and Ida stumbled and laughed again before they reached the door.

"You're trembling," said Karl as he helped her off with her coat.

"Yes," said Ida, laughing but trembling nevertheless. But Karl, opening the door to the dining room, simply said: "They're in bed," as though it was for this reason she was trembling. Ida waited for a while in his room until Karl came back.

"They're asleep," he said, and he took Ida, who still walked cautiously, inside to the living room, where the lamps were lit and the wine was on the table.

"Oh, it's so lovely," said Ida, laying her head against his shoulder.

"Yes," said Karl: "You're the daughter-in-law this evening."

For a moment Ida gave him a radiant look while blushing at the same time, and Karl, who had met her eyes drew his shoulder away just a little, something of which he himself was perhaps not aware, but which she nevertheless sensed.

"It's the navy's Madeira," said Karl.

They drank a little until Karl stretched his legs right out in the big chair and Ida brought him a stool, and they heard nothing but the gas hissing.

"It's nice here," said Karl.

"Yes."

Ida lay with her head against his legs, and her voice still trembled a little, but suddenly she became high spirited simply by feeling the tender desire in his fingers against her neck and she looked around, from below, and pointed to the lace pillow, laughing the while, though she did not know why.

"She didn't take that with her," she said.

"No," said Karl, raising her up; but Ida freed herself and took the work from the pillow and started playing with the needles. "Be careful," said Karl, who had bent down and was blowing at her hair until she came close to him again and stood behind his chair with her chin on his hair. Then, with her eyes closed, she said in a voice so gentle that it was only just audible:

"We're going to get married this evening."

Karl looked up into her eyes, which had opened wide, but his look was different from hers and he had given the same tiny, imperceptible start as before.

"We've done that before, love," he said in a rather louder voice than hers and her chin was lifted from his hair.

"But damn it all, we're not drinking anything," said Karl. They had been silent for a while, and he handed her the glass up above his head; she took it but did not touch it.

"Ah, we've got the drawings over there, by Gad." Karl suddenly caught sight of the parcel on the marble-topped table in the corner.

"What drawings?" Ida asked, scarcely aware of what she had said.

"The ones of Ludvigsbakke," said Karl, who had risen. "Let's have a look at the damned things."

"Good heavens, where have they come from?"

Ida was over there like a shot.

"It's Kate that has left them around," said Karl, who had taken the package and pushed the lace pillow aside.

"What a lot," said Ida. There was sheet after sheet.

"They unrolled the plans and held them down with their elbows while sitting beside each other on the sofa.

"That's the main building," said Karl. "Oh, it's going to be some size."

"And there are towers on it," said Ida.

"Yes," said Karl, nudging her. "All you need to see is a tower."

It was in the Italian style with towers and flat roofs. Ida lifted the plan up and supported it on the lamp. "But it will be lovely," she said.

Karl sat and sniffed. "Yes, it will suit the surroundings fine by Gad," he said and wrinkled his nose. He sat waving one hand in front of the plan while Ida continued to look at the building.

"You know," she said: "You will be able to see the whole of Brædstrup from that tower."

"Damn it all, what they want is to see as far as Horsens," said Karl. He sat nodding in front of the plan. "And there are no terraces, but the fact is that people always build in such a way that it is obvious they don't really have the money for it after all."

They went to the next sketch. This was the plan of the first floor. Ida traced the way from room to room with her finger and Karl checked the letters at the bottom of the plan. *That* was the sitting room – two sitting rooms – and *that* was the room for tea.

"And all that is the dining room," said Ida.

"Thirty-six feet long," said Karl. "There will be a splendid view from there after dinner."

He started to find it interesting; he followed the letters and measured the rooms, stretched his fingers over them and nodded. Walls had been broken through, and there was plate glass everywhere.

"Yes, she's got hold of some designs from abroad," he said.

Ida had let go of the plan; she had never seen such a house.

"What a lot of space they will have," she said, looking at all the rooms. "But we won't recognise it."

Karl continued to measure and study.

"Yes, the inside's all right." He clicked his tongue. "It's damned good."

"Yes," – and almost a little shyly she put her head down on his shoulder – "They have the money."

Karl nodded and looked up from the plan into the lamp.

"Yes," he said.

He went on looking in the light from the lamp for a moment:

"It was us who should have had the damned place," he said then.

Ida suddenly smiled.

"Yes," and she, too, looked into the light from the lamp.

"Because we were born to it," said Karl.

"Yes, *you*..."

"You, too, damn it," said Karl, lowering his voice a little.

He took the next plan. This was of all the bedrooms and bathrooms with tubs and wardrobes. The entire alphabet from A to Z was at the foot of the sketch. Karl sniffed and rubbed his hands.

"Good God," he said, "she's furnishing this for when she gets married."

"And six guest rooms."

He counted them up:

"With a bathroom to each of them."

It amused him, almost as though Kate had been studying interior decoration under his direction."

"It's English," he said. "It's good." And he scratched his head: "She's a devil; she's really got hold of some designs."

Ida continued to sit with her head against his shoulder, following his hands and looking up into his face: it was as though she was not really able to encompass all those rooms.

"Yes, they are going to have a lovely place."

"Of course they are going to have a lovely place." And he shuffled a little in his eagerness: now came the next plan, the stables.

"Wonderful, wonderful," he said. "She's a devil, she really is."

The stables were also English (as he explained) with stalls for the animals like they had for the great racehorses in England.

Ida admired it in silence – she knew nothing about stables – and while looking out across the lawn, she suddenly said:

"But it's a good thing that my father is dead."

Karl laughed as he bent over the sketch.

"No," he said, "there wouldn't have been anything for the old man here."

And he went on laughing at the thought of seeing old Brandt in Kate's English stables.

Ida had risen and all of a sudden she said, without knowing why it suddenly occurred to her, for a minute previously she had never thought of it:

"Do you know, I'm going to rent a flat now."

"What do you say?"

"Well, I'm going to rent a flat."

She had been thinking for a long time that she would really like to have a flat.

"Where?" was all Karl said.

And suddenly, Ida knew where it was to be, in Ole Suhrsgade, for that was so convenient; and she knew what sort of a flat she wanted: four rooms; she had always had this idea, a flat like the one the Kristensens had.

She stood on the other side of the table and leant forward beneath the lamp so that the shadow of her head fell on the sketch of the stables.

"And the furniture is all standing unused out at Horsens."

She was so enthusiastic that her cheeks flushed.

"Yes, that's a good idea," said Karl; he was still sitting with the sketch in his hand. Ida went over to him and pulled his head down to her.

"And then you will always be able to have lunch at home," she said.

Her voice had the ring that he loved.

"Tell me, chick," he said, and she looked up into his face: "How long can you stay?"

Ida merely smiled and closed her eyes.

Karl rolled the plans up while Ida went across to the corner sofa with the stereoscope as though she were here for the first time.

"And we'll have gentleman's furniture in the big room," she said.

Karl was sitting on the sofa with the back of his head against the wall.

"No," he said: "We are going to sleep in the big room."

They sat in silence for a time while the gas bubbled, and Karl looked across at Ida sitting right under the light until he suddenly said in a low voice:

"It must be horrible to sit there and keep watch."

And Ida shook her head and said in the same tone:

"No, not now..."

She was silent for a moment.

"For I can sit there and remember everything," she said.

There was silence again for a moment until Karl went across to her. He did not make use of pet names, but simply sat and stroked her hands, quite tenderly (thinking to himself: this is going to be difficult one day) until she kissed his cheek.

"Are you going now?" he whispered.

She got up and he heard the door quietly open and close.

"Have you put the light out?" he asked when he came into his room.

"Yes," she whispered.

And the hands she reached out to him were trembling and cold.

"Are you frightened, chick?"

"I'm going soon," she said, and she continued to be nervous and cold.

She had to go when morning came.

Karl was in a bad mood.

"You need only to take me down to a cab," said Ida.

And that was all he did, and when Ida was in the cab, she bent her head down and kissed his hand as it lay on the carriage door.

"I was afraid after all," she whispered.

"There, chick," said Karl as though to comfort her. For it was as though she was on the verge of tears.

Karl wandered back.

Shortly afterwards he was stretched out at full length in his French bed. He took a couple of final puffs at his cigarette, while staring up rather dubiously at the ceiling.

"But I mustn't give her any ideas," he said, nodding his head on his pillow.

Ida was home and went in through the doorway. Porters and doorkeepers were costing her a great deal in tips. Once up in her room she lay down on her bed.

Yes, she would have that flat and then she would never go over there any more. No, she would never go over there again.

The day had started with rain and sleet. The doctors had been there, cold in their white coats, and the professor's fingers had been white and dead to the knuckles as he rubbed his hands over the patients' beds.

Daylight should come now, but it did not come.

The porter turned out those who had jobs to do and moved them towards the door, shouting at them as though they were a herd of cattle. And the keys rattled and the doors were shut.

"Why aren't I going?" said Bertelsen probably for the tenth time, raising his watchful eyes while the tap water ran down over his hands.

"Because your mother's coming, Bertelsen," said Ida.

"Now Bertelsen, you're clean, you're washed now."

Bertelsen looked at his hands and every chewed nail before, with his head down, going across and settling near the stove, languid and with his eyes half closed until he again said to Ida as she passed:

"Why wasn't I going?"

Ida repeated:

"I've told you, Bertelsen; it's because your mother's coming."

And as Ida went about her tasks, there was no sound but the groaning of two patients from the Hall and the footsteps of the gentleman in Ward A as he walked about on the floor.

There came the rattle of keys in the door to the women's ward. It was Quam returning.

"It's rather dull in here," he said.

"Yes," said Ida; it was as though she either could not or did not really dare to wake up.

"And it would really be better if they made a din," said Quam, "for if they become too lethargic, this place begins to look like the confounded underworld itself."

He sat down on the table beneath the window while Nurse Petersen called to Ida from the kitchen to see whether she could help with the hem on her dress.

"Do you go out in this weather?" asked Quam.

"Oh," Nurse Petersen was going to the sales. When there was a doctor present, Nurse Petersen always adopted some strange movements with her arms, not unlike a wader flapping its wings. There was a sale on of table linen.

"Oh," said Ida, kneeling behind the kitchen door to help with the hem, suddenly adding in a high-pitched, excited voice: "In that case you could perhaps keep an eye open for upholstery material."

Quam raised his head.

"Are you getting married?" he asked.

"No, but I'm going to rent a flat." She stood up.

Quam got down from the table.

"Yes," he said: "That's probably far more sensible."

He went across past the kitchen door and nodded back towards Bertelsen.

"Are they *his* clothes?" he asked in a low voice.

"Yes."

"Good morning."

Quam went; but Nurse Petersen sat down. She had to know: *where* it was going to be and *when* she had decided.

"Oh, I've wanted to for a long time," said Ida, and she started telling them about the flat and the furniture she was going to have, and the fabrics she would choose, making up all the things she had never thought of and she herself believed she had been thinking of it for a long time.

"And I'm going to have leather upholstery on the furniture in the main room," she said.

Bertelsen suddenly raised his head.

"What time's she coming?" he asked.

"Eleven o'clock, Bertelsen."

Nurse Petersen had become quite sentimental at the thought of the flat.

"Then you'll have a whole home of your own," she said.

Ida smiled at this word and was silent for a moment, though the smile did not leave her.

"Yes," she said and, silently, stared into the distance.

Nurse Petersen was gone – carrying the news with her for general distribution – and Ida took water to the patients in the main ward and tidied their pillows. Then she sat and crocheted at the table under the window. From the noisy ward there came a subdued groaning, as though the entire building was filled with some secret and subdued complaint.

"When is she coming?" asked Bertelsen again.

"She'll soon be here, Bertelsen." And she continued with her work: when she was not talking to anyone about it, it was as though she was edgy and unable really to grasp the ideas relating to her "home".

There were two hesitant knocks on the door from the corridor and Ida opened it. It was Mrs Bertelsen whose face showed the first signs of tears even on the threshold. "Come in, Mrs Bertelsen," Ida said, "he's been expecting you." And Mrs Bertelsen went across to her son, who did not get up. "Hello, Jakob," she said in a curious mixture of humility and nervousness, to which he only answered with a grunt. Then he moved across to the table, and his mother went with him. Her face, on which all flesh seemed to have disappeared, and her hat – a summer bonnet covered with some old material – stood out in contrast to the grey wall.

Ida left; from the kitchen she could hear Bertelsen constantly talking in something resembling an irritated and suppressed snarl and his mother's nervous: "Yes Jakob, but, yes Jakob, but..."

The door to the women's ward flew open. It was Nurse Kjær, who first looked round the anteroom and then ran out into the kitchen.

"Good Lord, nurse, when is it going to be?" she said. "You're going to rent a flat?"

She had to hear it all at breakneck speed, and Ida told all about it again although it was as though her own words encircled her as she spoke; and Bertelsen went on talking, louder and more intensely, scarlet-faced, holding both his clenched fists out in front of him, at the same height all the time, as though they were bound by a chain.

"But Jakob dear, Jakob dear."

"You'll be having quite a doll's house," said Nurse Kjær out in the kitchen. "My word, how I'm looking forward to it."

Suddenly, nodding her head and in a different tone, she asked:

"Is she here to say goodbye?"

"Yes, poor thing."

Bertelsen pushed the chair away and got up; through the doorway they could see his mother grasp his arm, but he shook her off.

"You bloody bitch," he screamed. From the door to the Hall he continued to pour a stream of abuse at her, while the emaciated mother stood there, motionless in the centre of the ward, trembling a little, like a target in a hail of bullets.

Then she turned round – Nurse Kjær had gone and quietly closed the door – and Ida went across and took her hands.

"Yes, Mrs Bertelsen," she said, "but it will be better out there."

Mrs Bertelsen made no reply. What had once been a breast rose just a little, and she started for the hundredth time, for the thousandth time, to tell how it had come over this son in the same way as over his two elder brothers.

"He was in an office, you know, like his brothers. And everything was well until one day he *left* his office and came home, just like his brothers: he had left; he'd got up from his chair; he had put all his pens carefully in place (I saw it myself) and the ruler was in its place and his books had been made up (I saw it myself) before he left and came home, and it was all finished for him like it was for his brothers."

She was unable to weep, but it *sounded* as though she was weeping.

"Just like his brothers."

"But it will probably be better out there," said Ida again.

But Mrs Bertelsen merely shook her head, and with an expression in her eyes as though they were blind, she said:

"And it's all my fault."

These words had been Mrs Bertelsen's first and last thought ever since the day when the consultant had said to her in anger: "Why on earth do people have children when their husband's a drunk?"

"And it's all my fault..."

Ida had not heard the door open, but suddenly she turned round and found the gentleman from Ward A standing in the doorway: he was smiling and looking at them both.

Mrs Bertelsen freed her hands from Ida's and went towards the door to the corridor.

"Aren't you going to say goodbye?" asked Ida, and Mrs Bertelsen looked into the main ward, where her son was huddled on the edge of a bed.

"No; leave him," she said. And Ida closed the door to the corridor while Mrs Bertelsen turned round at the last moment with her eyes on the door to the main ward and went.

"Do you want anything, doctor?" Ida asked.

But the gentleman from Ward A merely stood there with the same smile on his face. (Yes, I'm sure he's mad after all, thought Ida).

"No thank you," he said, though he did not move.

Dusk fell.

Throughout the day, the ladies had rattled their keys and had been rushing in and out to ask about the flat, and Ida had replied almost hectically, describing everything, *first* this and *then* that.

Now Nurse Kjær was sitting at the table with Ida for a moment, and, with interruptions, they were discussing the same subject.

"Hm," said Nurse Kjær: "Then you'll get somewhere where you

can sleep."

Ida nodded. Today, she was constantly catching herself sitting with her eyes closed. Now she opened them. Bertelsen was drifting past the door to the main ward, backwards and forwards like a shadow, and suddenly, far inside her head, she heard Mrs Bertelsen's voice again, a sound that had pursued her all day.

"Poor Mrs Bertelsen," she said.

They sat in silence for a while. From the noisy ward there came the same dull groaning as had been audible throughout the day like some indeterminate, distant complaint, while Bertelsen continued to glide past the door like a shadow that was being washed away in the darkness.

"Yes, I wonder what a woman like her does with her life?" said Nurse Kjær, thinking of Mrs Bertelsen.

And then she was silent for a while again.

"Oh, she'll die some day," she said in reply to her own question.

The gentleman in Ward A went about as usual. It was as though the subdued groans from below were heard in waves coinciding with his steps.

"It's miserable in here today," said Nurse Kjær, getting up.

Ida shuddered involuntarily.

"Yes," she said: "Let's get some lights on."

Nurse Kjær went, and the patients from the basement came back, and some time later Josefine hurried in with the food, while Ida knocked on Nurse Petersen's door to wake her.

Josefine was simply in a bad mood these days. Not so much as a snatch of a melody was heard on the stairs, and now she stood there deep in her own thoughts as she dished the food up.

"No, nurse," she said: "You ought never to do anything for a man."

"For they're dogs, the lot of them," she declared, and she set about the unpacking.

When Ida came down to the dining room, Nurse Friis was there alone. She was turning some old black lace into ruches for a silk underskirt. Nurse Friis attached increasing importance to modern, up-to-date underclothing.

While Ida was drinking her tea, Nurse Friis said:

"Oh, I hear you're going to have your own home; when are the banns going to be read?"

She started to laugh as she pulled at the ruches.

"Well, I assume it will be from a pulpit."

Nurse Friis hummed as she went on working with the ruches.

"I must say I hadn't thought you were so sensible," she said suddenly, nodding to Ida. Then she said no more. But the cup shook in Ida's hand.

When Ida was on her way upstairs, she met Nurse Boserup.

"I suppose you'll be resigning," said Boserup.

Ida had simply not thought of that.

"Oh," said Boserup: "Thank goodness, it will be some time before you go. Jørgensen set about furnishing a flat a whole year before she got married as well."

Ida flushed suddenly. Then she turned quite pale.

"I suppose I can be allowed to furnish my own place to live in," she said. She had never spoken so harshly before, and she did not herself know why she did so now.

But when Boserup got down into the dining room, she said:

"Good Lord: don't talk to Brandt about the flat. That little dove has claws as well."

"But when you can afford to rent a flat and furnish it with leather upholstery, you oughtn't to do others out of a job."

Øverud said in her Funen lilt:

"Leather upholstery, that's what they had in the smoking room at Broholm. It looked so nice and it was so cool to sit on after a meal."

Ida had lit the lamp up in her room. She did not herself know why all this sense of nervousness and anxiety had come over her. But suddenly, she started to write to Karl:

"But you *must* not be angry, you hear, you must not because of you know *what*. I simply became so afraid, as I am sure you can understand. But I only want the same as you do all the time: do you not realise that? And it was only because I felt as though your mother was there all the time. But you must not be angry, my own, own dear, surely you will not?"

Karl was putting his riding breeches on when Julius came with the letter the following morning.

He stood for a moment and looked at it, wrinkling his nose a little before opening and reading it, still with the same expression on his face. Then he dressed. But when he had finished and come down into the street, he smacked his whip against his thigh:

"Women damned well always think about things for such a ridiculously long time."

Kate was already in the saddle when he arrived.

"Nom d'un chien," she said, "vous n'êtes pas matinal."

Karl pursed his lips:

"I've been reading some business letters," he said, putting his foot in the stirrup.

Kate waved her whip up at her mother. Mrs Mourier always came to the window in a dressing gown to watch "the two young ones" ride off.

∞∞∞∞

It was Wednesday after lunch, and the general's wife wrote to her sister, Mrs von Eichbaum:

Dear Emilie,
I am writing because it is my turn and we have agreed that I should write on Wednesdays. For nothing has happened here apart, naturally, from the fact that we miss you with all our hearts, Mille. Your house has been cleaned throughout and only awaits you and your return (the hyacinths between the windows are in flower; two of them are red, although Asmussen had promised faithfully that they would all be blue, but actually it is quite a pretty colour, as I told him when I ordered flowers for the birthday reception at the Schleppegrells). It was really very pleasant (we were given maraschino mousse,

you know, but it was not a success, Anna is always keen to try new recipes), although there were not enough seats for all of us. The young people left when the time came for the desert – Karl was with Kate – and partook of the sweet mousse in the cabinet. Unfortunately, I do not think that Fanny has any good prospects. Miss Juel told me the other day at the Reverend Jørgensen's lectures (he has finished with Baggesen, and, fancy, he spoke for three quarters of an hour about Sofie Ørsted, something that was rather superfluous for us who are related to her, as we know better) that the princess in all probability is not to have a lady-in-waiting. The fact of the matter is presumably that they expect the Prince of Saxony to marry her soon, which would make it all superfluous. Moreover, it is natural that they wish to economise. Now Anna is talking of the possibility that Fanny might learn massage. It is only a question of strength in her arms, and they say she has that in spite of her stomach, which continues to be a problem to her. The best thing would naturally be if Skeel finally married her. I suppose Karl will have written to you. I do not see much of him, but hear him in the house at his good, regular hours. Dear Mille, it is as I have always said, that if he started on a fixed routine, the family calm would descend on him. We are not, thank God, capricious by nature. He and Kate go for a long ride every morning now across the bridge (it seems to me that she grows quieter and quieter and more and more like Vilhelmine) and converse a great deal in French: they have all their memories in common from Lausanne. We have reached Chateaubriand in the French lectures. It is very interesting, but he must have been a restless creature. Vilhelmine is reading "Attila" now. You know how thorough she is. As soon as the spring puts in an appearance, they are going to start on the main building at Ludvigsbakke. Karl and Kate are for ever changing the plans together, but the house will be lovely (Mr Schmidt from Aarhus, you know, who was here for the birthday, also told me that Mourier earns a couple of barrels of gold each year now) with bathrooms like those in Aix-les-Bains. Little Brandt is said to have been here the other day to ask whether she should see to your flowers. It was very thoughtful of her, but quite superfluous to my mind for that is what we have Ane for. Ane said she looked drawn and strangely old. But I suppose she will soon be at the age when young girls become old maids. There has been some smoke in the kitchen, so I finally sent for Petersen (he had just got a grandson, so I had him inside for a glass of Madeira), but he said it was the weather, so there was nothing to be done about it. Give my love to Aline; it is a pity she has problems with her legs. Bruun (who looks worn out, poor man, he is terribly busy in his practice) says that it must be some sort of paralysis and that is not surprising. Good heavens, my dear, just fancy people of that age exposing themselves to all those emotions. All here send their love.

Your loyal sister
Lotte

P.S. The other day, Vilhelmine brought us a picture of Kate and herself – framed, lovely and with their signatures. For the moment I have put it on the big étagère. Kate is lovely, with her slender figure. It was taken at Hansen's, as I suggested. For Fanny was taken somewhere else recently, and it was awful. I think Anna is looking forward to the chocolate.

Mrs von Eichbaum answered on the Saturday:

Dear Charlotte,
Thank you for your letter and all that delightful news. All goes fairly well here (I will not deny that I am longing to be home in my quiet surroundings), but for Aline's sake we shall probably remain here until the end of the month, for I believe after all that it is best she should only come home when she is completely in a state of balance. Her legs are a little better (Dr. Brouardel, a really clever doctor, who has also given me a kind of ointment or something to combat dry hands, to be applied morning and evening, says that it is a weakness in her knees) though not entirely right; it is as though they will not really carry her, although she has become much thinner. When the sun shines, however, we regularly sit on the terrace in

the morning to enjoy the fresh air. We naturally never talk about the person concerned or, you will understand, anything at all about how it all happened. That sort of thing is something you have to struggle with on your own. The maid says that madam often weeps in the mornings, something I pretend not to notice. If she is weeping, it is best she should carry on undisturbed. You know I am of the opinion that people often grow tired of weeping if no one sees them. But I imagine we shall be leaving in a fortnight, and after a few days Aline will go home to the estate. And when she has been home for a month or so, she will come to town, quite quietly, just as she usually does in the spring. But it would naturally be best not to talk about all this. Here in the hotel they still think that she is having follow-up treatment after Vichy, as I told them immediately on our arrival. Vilhelmine wrote to me (I also had a letter from Anna, she is often rather a bother when one is travelling with the many tasks she wants one to perform; that Fanny did not become a lady-in-waiting came as no surprise to me, they do not take them so young out of consideration for the impression it would make) and was full of praise for Karl. It gives me great delight that he can be something for Mine and Kate, as she wrote, provided he does not neglect his office. One thing I would ask you is that for heaven's sake you will make sure the apartment is still well aired. They would never forgive me if they caught as much as bronchitis. You know that when one is away one can get ideas that tend to disturb one's peace of mind (and being together with Aline every day does not leave one's nerves untouched) and I can wake up in the night perspiring at the thought that there can have been any infection left after Mary. One can never open a newspaper nowadays without reading something about these bacilli. Karl writes that little Brandt has rented a flat outside the hospital. It is my opinion that she ought to have been content with a room; she has somewhere to live, and she has not been used to more. But that must be up to her if that is what she wants (she has rented a flat in Ole Suhrsgade; you know the apartments from visits to the adoption society, three rooms with parti-coloured wallpaper on the walls) for one must never interfere in other people's affairs. It struck *me, Lotte, that if you saw her you could perhaps ask her about some effective disinfectant. She must know about such things, as she works in the hospital. And the thought of infection gives me no peace, and I worry in case that healthy family could be struck by any kind of infection. I would like you one day when you have time to take my savings bank book (it is in the desk drawer opposite the window) and draw a hundred and fifty kroner to give to Karl. It naturally costs him something to look after Vilhelmine, who gives no thought to money, and things are not expensive down here if you live reasonably economically. In order to make sure she does not forget, would you ask Ane to cover the furniture in the cabinet with a couple of sheets. Pressed velvet fades so easily in the sun now that it is beginning to shine on it longer (it is almost spring here with violets in the street) from the south, as it does. Thank Vilhelmine for the picture – indeed, Kate has quite the same figure as her mother did when she was a young woman. Aline sends her best wishes, and I send mine to all.*

Your devoted sister
Mille

P.S. If you should see Bruun, perhaps you would ask him whether there could be any question of infection, as the walls are all painted in oil paint. I have been to the Reformed Church. The language was beautiful, but the sermon I thought was bombastic and without the firm, religious train of thought and the solid construction we expect of Petri. Nevertheless, it was a delight, as I say, because of the language. Ask Karl whether he is taking care not to catch cold after riding, as can so easily happen. Anna will be receiving a consignment of the chocolate we drink here every morning. It goes further than that from Cloetta.

∞∞∞∞

Ida slipped through the corridor in the Rørholm Café; quickly, she dodged into the private room; her shoulders were strangely narrow.

No, he was not there – not yet.

The lady at the counter, still wearing a net over her hair, had seen her come along the corridor:

"Hm, you can bring it all back again now, Ellingsen," she said.

Mr Ellingsen made no reply. He never indulged in staff conversations, but he had today and for the future decided only to set the table when "the gentleman" had arrived.

"It doesn't really matter in any case whether he comes or not: we're sure of the money," said the lady at the counter in a shrill voice as Ellingsen went past with a table cloth. In the corridor he encountered a young couple who were fooling around and laughing. The lady, a chubby woman with red cheeks, banged the flap down on the door opposite Ida's room.

"Occupied," she shouted.

"Occupied," said the gentleman, knocking the flap with his walking stick; and the younger waiter, who had already seen them, shouted from the counter:

"Tea, butter, toast, four soft-boiled eggs..."

"Six," shouted the gentleman, and the door banged shut.

"Six," the sound was blared out from the counter to the kitchen like a fanfare; while Ellingsen, with a napkin over his arm, opened the door to the private room where Ida hastily hid a couple of small packets under her coat.

"You are busy here today," she said.

"Yes," said Ellingsen, laying the cloth on the table and smoothing it with his wrinkled hands so that his celluloid cuffs could clearly be seen: "We must not complain, thank goodness."

Ida had sat down (it was as though she had felt a kind of stitch recently when entering Rørholm) and Ellingsen said:

"But early spring is always the best time here."

"Yes," Ida replied. She seemed not to have heard what he had said, but she had recently talked to all the staff, to Ellingsen and to the lady at the counter, to all of them almost as people involuntarily spoke in hotels when they are frightened of not being able to pay one day.

"It is such lovely weather," she said.

"It is the season for it," said Ellingsen. He was about to go when the sound of laughter came from further down the corridor, and Ida said, "They sound happy."

Ellingsen held his head on one side and smiled. "Yes, it is the young people; they have just started to come here." He went over to the door and added before gliding out – Mr Ellingsen had a way of opening and closing doors as though all the doorsteps in Rørholm's were covered with felt:

"We will wait a little, then."

Ida sat there. Her eyes had taken on a strange stare, and she thought the one thought she had had since arriving: If only he would tell me when he's not coming. But suddenly she smiled as she envisaged Karl's ever carefree face.

"But he doesn't think about it," she said, continuing to smile.

She started when there came two knocks on the door.

"Is it you?" she said. Her voice broke and there was Karl standing in the doorway.

"So you *are* here?" he said.

"I have someone with me." And he stepped aside to make way for Knuth. Ida had stopped and turned scarlet, and Karl said – perhaps a little too suddenly and cheerfully:

"Knuth was hungry as well, you see."

There was a slight pause and Knuth said: "Yes, I'm sorry for barging in, Miss Brandt," before Ida held out her hand, mechanically, without knowing that she had tears in her eyes.

"I know you of course, Count Knuth," she said.

And after another moment's hesitation, she said, as though she simply *had* to get away:

"I will go and order some coffee." And she went.

Neither of the men said anything before the door was closed and they were alone.

"Oh hell," said Karl, and it was as though he was shaking something off: "She'll get over it. Take your coat off."

Ida had gone. For a moment, only very briefly and only with her elbow, she supported herself against the wall. But when she reached the counter and saw the waitress' rat-like eyes looking at her, she suddenly said in a happy voice:

"There are three of us today, Miss..."

And there she stayed, talking and laughing, without thinking, until Ellingsen started to take the food in and she followed him, into the private room, where Karl and Knuth sat waiting. Sometimes looking up and sometimes with his eyes turned down, Knuth started to talk in a quiet, respectful voice about the lovely mornings and the barracks. "Of course, you also live in a kind of barracks, Miss Brandt," he said. "Yes," Ida murmured. Although rather more hesitantly, Knuth continued speaking in the same respectful tone about the theatre, which would soon be closing, and spring, which would soon be coming.

Ida answered yes and no. And no sound was to be heard other than the chinking of their cups as Ellingsen served them and the sound of a silver bracelet that Knuth was turning round his wrist.

"Now let's see about getting some of this food down us," said Karl even before Ellingsen had gone.

And they started to eat while Ida held her egg cup up from the table as though she was afraid that her spoon would not reach her mouth, and Knuth continued to sit rather far away from the table, in the same respectful manner. But Karl felt for Ida's cold hand under the table and pressed it.

"Are there no cakes?" he said, speaking almost as though caressing her and, although not aware of it, he avoided calling her by her Christian name, "Miss Brandt always has cakes with her."

Ida rose and took the parcels from under her coat.

"Oh, of course there's a cake by Gad," he said, and while Ida was cutting it he put his hand on her wrist still in an attempt to be kind to her, but Ida took her hand away.

"Do have a piece," she said, handing the plate to Knuth, who took it with a sudden rather jerky movement.

"The cake's lovely," said Karl, "but we need some port wine with it; it clears the throat."

Knuth stood up, a little too quickly, to order it. "May I?" he said.

Hardly had he gone before Karl rose and stood behind Ida.

"Surely I can bring someone with me," he said, bending over her.

Ida made no reply. Framed by his hands, her face was as pale as a sheet.

"You don't need to be so damned upset about it, chick," he said, continuing to look down on her until he suddenly kissed her behind her ear.

Ida had not made a move, but suddenly she rose and, trembling all over as though she was cold, she clung to him.

"But I've given you everything," she said. There was something about her tone like a shriek that had not been uttered.

"There, there, there."

The tenderness in his voice was genuine, and there was something in it that almost sounded like pain:

"There, there."

A smile passed over Ida's face. "I'm all right again now," she said, drying her eyes. "It's all right."

And she suddenly ran over to her coat and took the purse out and put it down in his pocket.

"I've got enough," he said and seemed almost to shake himself.

But Ida stroked his hair.

"He is very charming," she said.

Karl laughed:

"He's one of those who start behaving like a woman when they are in love."

Karl continued to laugh. "And it's damned obvious he's in love," he said.

Knuth returned with Ellingsen carrying the port wine, and Karl said:

"We're laughing at you, Knuth."

"What for?" said Knuth.

"Cheers," was all Karl said, and he emptied his glass while Ida, too, said: "Your health, Count Knuth," and Knuth drank his wine, jerkily as before. "Thank you, Miss Brandt," he said. Karl laughed again, winking at Ida and stretching his legs out:

"It's lovely here, by Gad. To hell with the ride."

Ida poured more coffee, taking the cups and handing them round. The sun fell on the tablecloth and on her hair as she bent down, and she started to talk about Jutland. About Aarhus, where "Count Knuth used to live, of course."

She had been there the year before last, for two days with Franck and Olivia, during the holidays. Oh, it was so beautiful in Riis Forest.

As she herself started to drink, Ida went on talking about her visit to Aarhus and about the Francks and about the esplanade. She probably did not herself realise that she was perhaps looking to these memories as though for a little social support.

"Yes," she said, "it was lovely on the esplanade. We used to go there in the evenings, Olivia and I."

"Oh," said Karl. "Now we've got to Olivia."

But Knuth, who probably did not hear much apart from the sound of her voice – as his eyes seemed to confirm – and for whom the mention of Aarhus only produced a vision of the dry, sun-drenched cobblestones in front of the cathedral, said quite absent-mindedly:

"Aye, I spent a couple of years in that place."

Karl, sat rocking astride his chair, in front of the two of them, with his cigarette between his lips, glancing at Knuth and winking at Ida.

Then he said:

"By Gad, you're quite one for the ladies, Knuth," and he laughed in a profound sense of wellbeing.

Ida blushed but managed to smile as she hurried to say:

"But we didn't get as far as Marselisborg."

And Knuth, who was perhaps blushing more than she, said:

"Aye, we often went there from the barracks."

Karl went on rocking on his chair, his eyes directed contentedly across the table at Ida, who was shading herself a little from the sun with her hand; there was always a maidenly beauty about her when she talked about the Francks.

And Karl, suddenly nodding and pursing his lips at the same time as his eyes were smiling, said:

"*Mais il n'a pas tort, monsieur le comte; madame est bien jolie.*"

She did not realise it, but a cloud suddenly passed over Ida's face at the sound of the French words (Karl had been using so many French expressions recently), but then she smiled again, happy in front of Karl's eyes, which "encompassed" her, and she raised her glass and took a sip with her eyes lost in his.

Until (after all three had been silent for a moment) she spoke again, the final three syllables came suddenly and with an almost melancholy ring:

"But that was so long ago." She had again been thinking of Aarhus.

Karl, who was also lost in a completely different train of thought, was brought back by the mention of Aarhus and, blowing out his smoke through his nose, said:

"But those Aarhus merchants are a damned clever bunch."

Ida did not register this, but she turned a pair of radiant eyes towards Karl and said:

"I wonder where the next holiday will be."

And, as the smile returned to his eyes, Karl replied:

"Aye. God knows."

But Ida had to go. It was getting far too late. Knuth rose. "Thank you, Miss Brandt," he said, chinking his glass against Ida's. There was something strange about Knuth's movements, almost those of a jumping jack, when he was suddenly called back from whatever was preoccupying him.

Karl, too, rose.

"Oh well, *allez-y*," he said, and while he helped Ida on with her coat, he said to Knuth, perhaps continuing the train of thought from Aarhus or perhaps simply because of the French expression:

"Hell, the way she made Beauté jump yesterday in the Deer Park."

He stood there with his cigarette hanging from his lips.

"Aye, she's got steel in her back, by Gad."

Knuth went out into the corridor, and Karl put his overcoat on. He held Ida before him for a moment. "Well, chick," he said and his voice suddenly became tender when he saw the expression in her eyes: "That was a lovely day."

"Yes."

She leant against him.

"If only you come," she said, and with a smile she whispered, though the corners of her mouth were trembling a little:

"Because it is so difficult to go out of that door when I have been waiting here alone."

It was almost as though Karl suddenly blushed. But all he said, very gently, was:

"Thank you for a lovely time today, chick."

And quickly, with the same look of fear in her eyes as before (but perhaps only because they were each going off in their own direction now), Ida flung her arms round his neck.

"Oh Karl..."

Then they went out. In the street they all three walked side by side. Ida was pale, as could clearly be seen now she was out in the open. But Karl, who was whistling gently as he walked, said happily:

"Now we could have a look at the flat."

Ida blushed and made no reply; but Karl continued in the same tone:

"Miss Brandt has rented a flat. We could go up and have a look at it now."

"It's not been done up," said Ida; her voice so harsh that it broke; Karl looked at her in amazement:

"All right, then we can leave it."

They separated soon after this.

"Thank you Miss Brandt," said Knuth as he released her hand.

Karl and he walked along the pavement side by side. Karl was smoking and Knuth was chewing at his walking stick.

"You're a fortunate man, Eichbaum," the lieutenant said.

Karl puffed his cigarette smoke out, but Knuth said in the same dreamy tone:

"You see, it's the gentle girls one should have."

Karl went on a bit before saying:

"Aye, they're probably the best to have." He placed a hesitant emphasis on "have" as though he was stopping before some unspoken "but" and they went on a little before he said in that drawling voice of his:

"But damn it all, you're a dreamer Knuth and you just worship women."

"Well, what else is there?" he said.

"There's life as well," said Karl, screwing up his nose. "And so we have to work things out, unfortunately."

Knuth walked on, looking straight ahead.

"Yes," he said: "We work them out all right but I don't know, at times I feel almost as though someone else were adding the figures up."

"Are you a philosopher as well?" asked Karl dully.

But Knuth walked on and continued to stare ahead and, still in the same tone, said:

"But I ought to have gone in the navy."

And a little later:

"For then I could at least have gone to Siam. And *there* they fight."

"Knuth, you're drunk, damn it," said Karl, throwing away his cigarette. And, following his own train of thought, he said as he stopped at the corner:

"You see, you don't take a girl for all eternity."

"And that's that," he said decisively, waving goodbye with his whip.

Karl arrived at the office far too late, and the bookkeeper had a few unpleasant things to say to him. This he had had plenty of reason to do recently. But Karl made no reply and simply sat at his desk, where he opened his ledger. It was full of designs for the stables in Ludvigsbakke on all the blotting paper:

"Oh hell, he was going dancing again that evening."

He suddenly smiled. He was thinking of Knuth.

"When he gets near a skirt he looks like that chap who swam across to his girlfriend."

234

And suddenly he had a sense of longing, a purely physical longing for Ida, stronger than he had felt for a long time.

Ida had gone up to her flat and taken off her outdoor clothes. All the new furniture was there and the old as well, wrapped in canvas: she would have to set to work. But suddenly, surrounded by the old furniture, the edges of which could be seen protruding from behind canvas and cords, she threw herself down on her new bed and with her face buried in the pillows and her arms outstretched as though they were nailed to this new, wide couch, she wept and wept.

Karl had been with her that day, during the afternoon, up in her room; and now he was to go and he was in love and excited now, too.

Ida stood with her arms around his neck.

"What are you going to do this evening?" she said.

"Stay at home."

He scarcely knew he was lying before he had said these words.

"Goodbye, chick," he said, kissing her hair.

And then he went.

Ida remained seated for a long time on the disordered bed.

But when she came down into the tea room, Nurse Kjær said:

"What's wrong with you? Your eyes are all red."

From behind the urn, Nurse Helgesen said something about the gentleman in Ward A. Now the professor would surely soon have to make up his mind.

"The patient has now worked out," said Nurse Helgesen, "that there are just as many people every year who write a T instead of an F."

And Nurse Friis, who was ostentatiously darning black silk stockings, one of which she had pulled high up on her arm like a glove, said:

"Ugh, that horrible man, he's just like a ghost."

Looking into the gas ring on the table, Nurse Kjær said:

"No, that's not right but there is something about him as though he knew that he would get the better of us after all."

But Nurse Øverud, who was making sandwiches, said on the subject of the red eyes:

"They are the result of being awake so much at night. I have the same problem. But I have a remedy to use against it.

Ida went to her night duty.

∞∞∞

Julius opened the carriage door at the station, and the general's wife emerged.

She went through the main hall into the waiting-room, where she found Mrs Mourier sitting on a sofa.

"Good morning," she said. "Oh it's dreadfully raw this morning."

But Mrs Mourier, who every moment had tears in her eyes, said that she had not had a wink of sleep all night. "For just imagine her in that bunk, Lotte, listening to every stroke of that steam engine."

She was thinking all the time of Aline, whom they had come to meet.

"And then, you know," she said, "we can't be too kind to her either."

"My dear Vilhelmine," said the general's wife, sitting down beside Mrs Mourier: "I say the same as Emilie: We will get over that problem mainly by taking things quietly and pretending throughout that nothing has happened." But, without realising it, the general's wife smoothed her Randers leather gloves up from her wrists, thereby showing the whole shape of her nails.

"Yes, my dear," said Mrs Mourier shaking her head a little, "but one thinks of her nevertheless."

And in a slighter harsher and quite decisive tone, the general's wife said:

"But, my dear Mine, if she has *gone*, she will have to come back *home*."

She started to talk about the change in climate that Emilie after all would encounter when she heard a slightly out-of-breath Mrs Schleppegrell arriving with Fanny in her wake. "My dears, what dreadful weather. I can feel the damp going right through me in spite of my French vest."

A torrent of words came from the admiral's wife as she seated herself: "But as I said to Vilhelm today, we are meeting..."

Fanny had taken up a position by the door to the platform. She was wearing the expression she had when on behalf of the admiral's wife she made her weekly visit to the welfare association and remained at a distance from the others.

The admiral's wife started to talk of the chocolate she had received and about Emilie, who was always so considerate, until she suddenly looked around at the walls (perhaps she realised that no one was listening to her) and said:

"My dears, how unpleasant it is in here. It is as though we were waiting in a criminal court of some kind."

"Yes," said the general's wife, "this waiting-room really is a scandal in a city like Copenhagen."

They fell silent again, and suddenly Kate and Karl, dressed in their riding clothes, were out there on the platform in front of the glass door.

"There we have the young ones," said the general's wife, and they all smiled as they nodded out there, while Fanny looked at them through her lorgnette.

Kate nodded back, again with her riding cloak over her arm.

"*Voilà l'église triomphante,*" she said, pouting her lips, a habit she had caught from Karl.

"Aye, there we have the aunts, by Gad," said Karl. He walked with both hands in his riding breeches as they sauntered on.

But suddenly Kate turned back and shook the waiting-room door. "Hang it all, I'm going in to see them," she said.

She made to go inside, but the door was locked. "Oh," she said abandoning the attempt. "The hordes will come out here." Karl, who was also looking in at the aunts, laughed aloud. The distance and the fact that the two of them were unable to hear the conversation meant that there seemed to be something about the whole group slightly reminiscent of a stage performance.

They continued to look in through the glass doors and, standing close together, they both laughed at the family in happy understanding with each other.

There came symptoms of noise and disturbance, and ladies and gentlemen put their heads in through the doors when the admiral arrived. He had a cold and greeted the ladies before sitting down close to Mrs Mourier and blowing his nose.

"Ah, my dear," he said, "here we are now, provided with both lifebelts and a gangplank."

"Oh yes, indeed, admiral," said Mrs Mourier. It was as though she had expected more response from him. "I'm all of a tremble."

The heavy baggage trolleys started to rumble along the platform, and unfamiliar ladies and gentlemen congregated by the doors, though not by Fanny's: she had an ability to establish an invisible circle around herself creating an empty space in her vicinity when the conductors came and opened the doors.

"There they are," said the admiral's wife, leaping up from her chair as though she were leading a charge.

The general's wife had almost convulsively grasped Mrs Mourier's arm and said in a voice that was suddenly trembling with emotion and which she was struggling to calm down again:

"Oh heavens above, Mine, this is such a happy occasion."

They had all gone over to the door.

"Fanny," said the admiral's wife: "Are you coming?"

And corpulent and with the energy of someone arranging a party, she said to the general's wife:

"We ought to be together. Where are the young ones?"

"Here comes the cavalry," said Karl.

The admiral brought up the rearguard, with a look on his face as though, from some elevated position in Frederiksberg, he was "following" some highly-placed colleague representative of the infantry.

People crowded on to the platform, where the flock herded by the general's wife was standing, rather nervously watching the locomotive glide forward, while the admiral's wife twice moved her arms as though she was already opening them to embrace the two who were returning home, and Mrs Mourier made the most of the opportunity to dry her eyes.

"Can you see them?"

"Can you see them?" said the general's wife as compartment after compartment moved slowly past them. "Are you there, Vilhelm?" said the admiral's wife.

Kate flicked Karl with her switch. "Just look at the court masseuse," she whispered. There was not the slightest movement in Fanny's face as she surveyed the first class compartments through her lorgnette.

"Kate," called Mrs Mourier, who was quite overcome with emotion and wanted to have her daughter with her.

"*There* she is," said the general's wife and she started to wave, and then they saw Mrs von Eichbaum sitting erect in her compartment.

They were all waiting to see the other face as they waved. Mrs Mourier did not know that two large tears were running down her cheeks.

"Now," whispered Kate to Karl.

"You are not expecting Aline, surely?" said Mrs von Eichbaum in a loud voice from the compartment. They had all started to move along with the gliding train as though drawn by a string and suddenly they came to a standstill. No one said anything until, after a second's hesitation, the general's wife again started to wave her hands and the train came to a standstill.

"She left the train at Ringsted," (Mrs von Eichbaum's first glance had sought Karl and found him in his riding clothes alongside Kate) "and went home in the landau with Feddersen."

Kate had turned on her heel. "*Quelle blague,*" she said to Karl, "I won!"

"Doesn't count."

"Oh? Never mind, wasn't the bet supposed to be about your mother putting her foot on the ground?"

And suddenly they heard the admiral's wife, who had required a moment to gather herself, say: "Good heavens, Emilie, it's for your sake we have come." And the general's wife all at once started to weep as she embraced Mrs von Eichbaum, and Mrs Mourier said: "Oh, then she will be at home by now."

All of a sudden they started to talk in loud voices, quite loud voices, about the journey and the chocolate and the steamship, as though Aline had never existed, while Mrs von Eichbaum stood in front of Kate for a moment holding both her hands in hers.

"My word," she said almost emotionally, "you look quite radiant."

The admiral and his wife had already departed. The admiral's wife and Fanny had had to take a cab. They were going to visit the distinguished Miss Juel.

The admiral's wife had so far made no pronouncement on the event, but said:

"Kate Mourier is putting on rather a lot of weight."

Fanny, who was looking at Kate and Karl through the carriage window as they took their horses from the man who had been left in charge of them said, without any explanation: "She is a bitch."

Fanny had heard Kate's remark about the court masseuse.

The admiral's wife did not contradict her daughter. "But," she said merely, "you'll see she will get what she wants. That sort of girl always find themselves provided for nowadays."

"If they can provide for his needs," said Fanny.

Mrs von Eichbaum and the general's wife had also taken a carriage; they were on their own on account of all the luggage.

"Oh dear, Emilie," said the general's wife: "there was a moment when I ran all cold – when no one saw her – until I recognised the sense in what you had done."

"My dear Lotte," said Mrs von Eichbaum, "that was the only right thing to do, provided it could be arranged."

Mrs von Eichbaum suddenly nodded and smiled: Kate and Karl were trotting past the carriage and waving.

"It suits her so well," she said, still watching them, and her eyes suddenly became damp. "I just hope Karl is not neglecting the office."

"My dear, Karl has become as regular as clockwork," said the general's wife. And shortly afterwards, she added:

"And besides, I suppose he is not going to be sitting in that office for ever."

The two sisters sat holding each other by the hand.

They were home, and Mrs von Eichbaum was sitting in her old place on the sofa after having had Ane in to curtsey to her.

"Oh, my dear, it is such bliss to be at home again within my four good walls. For you will understand of course that there are things one does not send by post and, between you and me, it has not been an unalloyed pleasure."

The general's wife did understand: "Of course, I admired your letters which said nothing at all."

"The worst thing, you know, was that she talked to *me* incessantly, and I believe that one never knows what one does not wish to know. But Aline simply has to bare her soul. Just imagine that last night she was simply overcome by her urge to talk in a cabin on the way over from Kiel, where every word could be heard out in the corridor. I finally gave her some chloral and told her that she was likely to be seasick otherwise."

Mrs von Eichbaum was silent for a moment, staring into space.

"But," she said, "the things you are exposed to if you abandon your permanent bulwark."

Mrs von Eichbaum fell silent again and gazed as though into a far-reaching prospect of the inconceivable. "But," she said, "a journey abroad always refreshes your languages."

The general's wife rose: Mrs von Eichbaum must need some rest. There was a bouquet in the small drawing room. It was from little Brandt. Mrs von Eichbaum looked at it. It was lovely.

"But heavens above, my dear, all this courtesy," she said, "it is just a little embarrassing."

The general's wife said:

"Yes, dear, but it is only quite reasonable that the girl wants to show her appreciation."

And suddenly a new thought struck her. She said: "On her advice, I thought up some excuse to fumigate the Mouriers' apartment with sulphur the other day...But, Mille, you need some rest."

She held out her hand to her sister, and suddenly overcome with emotion, the sisters kissed each other with tears in their eyes.

Karl was in the office. He was thinking about the game of snap. The prize was a riding switch; and it had to be one with a gold knob. He nodded over his ledger. But he would wait until after the first, when his wages had been paid.

Ida had kept a report until the evening. When she arrived, Karl had his overcoat on and was standing beneath the lamp.

"Has your mother come?" she said.

"Yes," said Karl. He had taken the report and put out the light.

"I'm sorry, chick, but I'm in such a hurry."

"Do you think I should pay her a visit?" said Ida from in the darkness.

"Yes, why not?" Karl was groping his way in the dark.

"Well, I didn't know."

She was speaking so quietly.

"Can you find your way out?" said Karl, opening the door to the lighted corridor.

But on the handle, her hand touched his for a second, briefly, helplessly.

"Good night," she said.

"Good night, chick."

The gate out to the street opened, and there was the sound of bells from countless tramcars when Karl went out into the lights illuminating the throngs of people.

It could be seen that Ida had become thin when she reached the light from the lamps on her way back through the silent and almost dark courtyard.

Mrs von Eichbaum was taking a cup of tea together with the general's wife. The lamps were lit, and they settled down to talk about things both old and new. Mrs von Eichbaum had changed the place for the picture of the Mouriers. She thought she would have it on the writing desk for the sake of the light.

"Do you know," she said, "I sat there before dinner and looked at Kate's picture for a really long time. She seems to me to have changed. It is as though she has acquired something more reflective in her expression."

∞∞∞

Karl and Ida drove out towards Christianshavn. The lights out there had become few in number, and they could hear nothing but the determined trotting of the horse on the uneven cobblestones.

"This is such a dismal place," said Ida who was quietly following the scant patches of light from lamp post to lamp post.

"And it's cold," said Karl. They shrunk each in their own corner.

The carriage rumbled on, and they fell silent again.

"But he's driving as though he were going to a funeral," said Karl.

And they sat in silence once more.

"I went to see your mother," said Ida, from her corner.

"Oh," murmured Karl.

"But she wasn't at home."

Karl chewed at his cigar and – presumably without thinking of it – he said:

"She damned well was at home."

Ida no longer heard the horse's hoofs. This was what she had thought and thought about ever since. She was at home; ever since she had stood there as the door closed in front of her, she had known: she was at home.

They heard the sound of some fiddles and wind instruments. "There we've got the whole menagerie, by Gad," said Karl sitting up. There were crowds of people and noise and the light from gas-filled torches.

"Now we'll have a look at what they've got to show us," said Karl, stretching his legs in the gaslight and seeming to be at home.

"Two." He handed the money to the girl at the entrance to the tent while – he had again acquired the habit of looking up under every woman's hat – he looked up at her face.

"What are you sighing about?" he said, turning to Ida.

"Oh, I'm cold," she said, seeming to give a start.

Karl took her by the arm at the entrance. "Oh," he said – a lady wearing a flowered skirt was already diving through hoops and all the seats were full of people, some locals and some from Copenhagen – "The air from the stables will soon warm you up for heavens' sake."

"There are such a lot of people," said Ida.

"Yes," said Karl, shrugging his shoulders as the music blared out. "But it's always a change."

"It's damned good by Gad," he said after a few minutes, and with a nod and a single glance he scrutinised the nag, the floral-skirted woman, the seven musicians and the audience.

"It's jolly nice here," he repeated, rubbing his hands so vigorously that his seat creaked. (After the lone rides in cabs, he was usually overcome by a certain sense of wellbeing when he found himself among other people again).

A couple of clowns were gambolling around while the graceful lady was regaining her breath. They bounced each other on the ground and tumbled all over the place.

"They've got cushions on their bums," said a gentleman behind Karl, and everyone around laughed and sniggered.

"People are out to enjoy themselves here by Gad," said Karl, rubbing his leg and suddenly knocking his stick up on Ida's chin (it was as though she was sitting so completely on her own).

She started; then she smiled, and for a moment, with her hand, she held the silver knob firmly against her chin.

"Yes," she said.

A couple of musical acrobats had started to play "The Last Rose of Summer" on a *single* violin, and the audience settled and quietened down a little. Karl clamped his cigar between his teeth, rocking it up and down in time with the melancholy song.

"Well," said Ida suddenly, in a quiet voice: "Perhaps I have been there too often."

Karl turned to her: "Good God, are you still thinking about that?"

And, suddenly guessing her secret anxiety and thoughts, he tapped her hand cheerfully (he had in general sought to console her a lot recently):

"Mother never understands a damned thing."

Ida held his hand tight. "Oh, my dear," she whispered. But Karl sat up in his seat with his legs outstretched.

"Oh, there's the baron," he said, waving with his left hand.

The "baron", the circus manager, led out two horses. They danced a waltz and jumped over an array of barriers; their brown skin was tense and shining as they sprang, and all faces turned towards them and followed them. Then, suddenly, a voice was heard from the back of the tent:

"Damned good, baron."

And everyone laughed, hilariously, while the men banged their walking sticks against the chairs and a lady over on the other side laughed so much she was turning and twisting in her chair. "Just look, just look," said Ida. But two burly men over by the side of the tent, mimicking the horses' least movements, said:

"Wonderful."

People started to laugh again so much that they shook their heads and laughed at each other because they were laughing at nothing.

"They do jump beautifully," said Ida, holding her left hand to her breast and supporting her right on Karl's knee.

Karl, who had been watching the show keenly, to the accompaniment of tiny puffs at his cigar, nodded and said reflectively:

"That's a horse that would suit Kate."

Ida had not understood him at first but now Karl rose: "I must just go and have a talk to the boss," he said, and her hand dropped from his knee, down on to the chair arm.

Then she saw a lady up on a tightrope, a lady all in pink, and she again heard people laughing and saw Karl nodding to her from down by the entrance to the stalls (he never liked it when she was sitting in such a way that she could not move) and she smiled again as he approached her.

"What a wonderful lot they are there," he said, putting his arm under hers.

Ida sat for a moment with her head against his shoulder: "It's like at home down by the harbour," she said in a voice that trembled a little.

"But Schreiber was damned good," said Karl.

"Oh," said Ida, "Olivia kept a portrait of him in her workbox."

The impressive lady was brought back time after time. Finally she was given a flourish by the musicians, for the applause refused to die down.

"Goodnight, dear," said the gentleman who had spoken before and gently waved the lady off the arena.

But the drums continued to beat as Ida grasped Karl by the arm.

"There's Nurse Friis," she said. She had grown as stiff as a corpse.

"Oh, what the hell," and Karl turned his head rather quickly. "Yes, there she is," he said.

But Nurse Friis, who was coming straight towards them, simply gave them a cheerful, familiar nod.

"Good evening, so you've come out to Amager as well?" she said and went on holding her skirt up. There was something about her carriage and gait as seen from the back that suggested she felt at home and was happy to be here. When she had reached her seat and sat down, she said to the small man with the large nose who had followed her:

"They are childhood friends."

"Oh," he said slowly, "then it's criminal."

"He's a nasty piece," murmured Karl as the couple passed them. He remained in his seat and stared at the tip of his cigar until he said – it was as though his hands had nevertheless shrunk further up into his sleeves – like someone who has just settled an unpleasant account:

"Well, she'll probably keep her damned mouth shut."

Nevertheless, he remained silent, sitting with an expression as though the cigar did not suit him.

Idea leaned forward – a gap had grown between their seats – and with a smile she whispered to him (through lips that were trembling slightly):

"Karl," and this was the first thing she had said, "I don't like this."

And she started to talk, a little more eagerly and a little louder, surrounded by a buzz on all sides; the fat women from the tightrope had now entered on a horse.

"Couldn't you sit a bit more still," said Karl.

Ida suddenly had tears in her eyes, but she smiled at him again (she understood him so well, of course) and she whispered once more, turning her face to his:

"Karl, I simply don't like this."

"I don't suppose it would be much use," said Karl, still in the same voice. And suddenly making a move to get up, he added:

"I'm going out to see the boss, damn it."

"Are you going again?" It came so quickly, and Ida perhaps raised her hand just an inch to stop him (and probably did not realise that it was ultimately also out of vanity).

"Oh, I can stay then," said Karl.

"Your childhood friends are not enjoying themselves," said Nurse Friis' escort, who twice nodded to Ida.

There was a fanfare. "Here comes the jockey," said Karl, sitting involuntarily up in his seat along with all the others as the rider galloped past. "He rides well."

Ida was leaning forward and simply nodded – there was something about her reminiscent of a child stuffing its fingers into its ears when it is simply *determined* to read – and she did not take her eyes off the bare man taking a leap.

People clapped and clapped.

"He jumps well," said Karl.

And Ida, who involuntarily went on watching the bare figure, said in a quiet voice, blushing before she had finished her sentence:

"He's not as good-looking as you are."

Karl suddenly looked down at her face.

"You're developing an eye for men by Gad," he said.

And he laughed and suddenly stretched out his legs.

"Shall we go," he said when the jockey had finished, and they got up. Not until they were over by the exit did they wave to Nurse Friis.

They drove again in silence. Ida had stolen Karl's hand, though it was not particularly responsive in its glove:

"Couldn't we go to the Dagmar today?"

"I suppose so," said Karl, adding:

"One meets people everywhere in any case."

And suddenly rubbing his hands, he said in a different tone, like a man who has taken a decision:

"Then we'll *have a proper meal* by Gad."

He said he wanted lobster. "But you'll have to have a glass of stout along with it," he said, and he became talkative and exuded a sense of wellbeing as though he was already sitting before the red delicacy and the salad accompanying it.

"We'll have something to drink this evening," said Ida.

"We'll drink to Nurse Friis," said Karl from his corner; and they fell silent again, each staring out of their own window.

"We've reached Højbro now," said Ida.

"Oh, thank God," said Karl, and he did not change his position until the carriage stopped and they had reached the restaurant where the waiters were running to and fro in the bright light among a large number of guests, and they were given a separate room.

"It's the usual one," said Ida in a strikingly bright voice, and she took off her coat.

"They are all alike, damn it all," said Karl, already deeply engaged in perusing the menu. But when the dishes came, he woke up and threw his head back in physical wellbeing. "One needs food," he said, and he started eating with his serviette tied around his neck. He talked about all manner of things. About Knuth: "He's completely mad," he said, winking at Ida: "But he's a great chap." And as for the admiral: he had gone off the rails again; he simply couldn't leave women alone. And the bookkeeper: "God help me, he gets worse and worse," he said, wrinkling his nose and continuing to eat.

But Ida, sitting watching him, said with a smile:

"You look so nice when you are eating." And she inserted her hand under his cuff and up his sleeve.

"Yes," said Karl with a laugh, "if I'm having a good meal. And he pressed his arm down on her hand.

Ida sat staring before her. "We'll soon be able to eat at home now."

"Yes," was Karl's only reply.

But Ida continued to talk about the flat: How lovely it was, now the carpets had come to cover both floors. Oh, the pattern was so beautiful, decorated all over simply with autumn leaves and the door curtains were in the same pattern.

She continued to tell him about the sheer yellows and browns in the pattern in the carpet until she suddenly became aware that Karl was saying nothing. And she wanted more than anything else to go on talking and fell silent.

"But when will all this be ready?" asked Karl in a tone suggesting that he was working something out.

"I don't know," said Ida, supporting her head on her hand and in a voice that suddenly trembled.

The Russia leather purse had already appeared at the foot of his glass. He took it without thinking and opened it. There was a letter in the front compartment.

Ida grasped his arm: "That's not for you."

But Karl had already opened the letter: "It's from Franck." And in a tone as though it were a demand sent to him, he said:

"Of course it's about the money."

Ida made no reply and she put the letter away, but Karl said:

"I simply don't understand what you do to get all that money out of him."

"I lie," said Ida, suddenly looking down at the tablecloth (she had blushed scarlet) and in the same breath – as though to say that he should not be so upset about that – she looked up and said:

"I always have done."

Karl, who was touched and scarcely knew why, murmured:

"But to lie your way to a complete set of furniture isn't all that easy."

Ida smiled again, while considering the endless tissue of all her excuses.

"Yes," she said, almost laughing: "Once you've started, you can always go on to lie more."

"You're turning into a fallen woman," said Karl. It was a long time since he had last grasped her hand so firmly and tenderly.

"But why do we need to talk about it?" said Ida, shaking her head. "Now we're going to have a drink." And she took her glass.

When they had emptied their glasses and put them down, she suddenly, although she did not really want to, said:

"The worst thing they can do is dismiss me."

"Surely they wouldn't do that," Karl exclaimed.

"Well, then that would be the end of it all," said Ida.

But Karl made no reply until, with the same expression he had had in the circus, he said:

"But for God's sake, she'll surely keep her mouth shut."

He beckoned to the waiter for the bill.

"Are we going already?" said Ida. It was as though she always had a sense of fear when they were to leave; and she looked across the table and the glasses.

"It's jolly well about time," said Karl.

He did not himself realise that he sighed a couple of times as he took a fifty kroner note out of the Russia leather purse.

But it was as though he had no wish to leave her, and in the carriage he said:

"Now we'll go to the flat."

"But it's not ready," said Ida.

"Surely something's in place," said Karl, and he called out the street and the house number to the coachman.

"You mustn't inspect everything," said Ida who had lit a little lamp in the passageway and now opened the door. But as she raised the lamp up in front of her, she pointed straight at two large rolls leaning against the wall:

"They are the carpet."

"There's a lot of it," said Karl, standing and thinking that the furniture was too big for the living room.

"Yes," and she nodded to him: "But you can't see the pattern."

"I'm dreadfully thirsty," said Karl, taking off his overcoat.

Ida had some red wine and went to fetch it. Karl walked up and down alone, with a cigar that had gone out; lost in thought he rattled the furniture like the bars in a cage. The empty windows gaped at him like a pair of staring eyes.

Ida came back with the wine. "Thank you," he said and was about to drain the glass.

But suddenly emotional, or desperate – at that moment he could gladly have smashed all that furniture – he said, and his voice was low:

"Well cheers, chick."

"Yes," said Ida, looking up into his face from the sitting room, where the furniture that was not yet in place cast long shadows: "This is our first glass here."

And she drank the whole glass, her eyes fixed on his face.

Karl had gone.

"Thank you, I'll stay here a little longer," Ida had said.

Now she was alone. Her head was devoid of thought. She merely wanted to be alone when she put on her coat and her hat and when she left. But when she reached the street, she almost ran. She thought: supposing she met Nurse Friis at the gate, or outside, and she ran as though this would help her to avoid that.

But she reached her room without meeting anyone.

She took her outdoor clothes off. But she continued to walk up and down the floor. Then she opened the door. She wanted to see Roed and Nurse Petersen, to see them before they got to know about *that*. She went down. The entire building was silent. The first signs of day could be seen against the window in the corridor, and the patients were asleep. Quietly, she turned the key and went in. Roed and Nurse Petersen were sitting each on their own side of the stove, their eyes stiff with sleep.

"Gott, Gott, is it you?" said Nurse Petersen.

"I wanted a little chloral," said Ida, and absent-mindedly, or nervously, she smoothed Roed's hair with her hands.

"Oh, you're cold," said Roed in the strangely indifferent voice of those who have been awake too long.

"Yes."

Ida left her and went to the door to the Hall. The patient in the nearest bed moved and Ida went in. A bearded man wearing blue glasses lay staring up at her.

"Good evening, nurse," he said in such a humble tone.

"Good heavens, Lauritzen," said Ida: "Is it you?"

The patient made no reply. He was a drinker who was here for the third time and merely lay there wringing his hands.

"Yes, it's me," he said then and he went on wringing his hands so that his knuckles shone white.

And while he looked up in her face and his arms fell back at his sides, he said with the look a man must have when about to be crucified:

"I can't help it."

Ida leant against the bedpost. Quietly, without a sound, she sobbed in desperation.

Karl had arrived home. Half undressed he paced up and down the floor.

"It's incredible," he said.

"It's just damned incredible," he continued; he stopped his walking up and down and stared into the lamp.

"But damn it all, women are simply blind," he said, nodding into the light.

Finally, he sat down on his bed.

"Hm." And he twisted his face as though this was extremely unpleasant for him: and Knuth must naturally have been cooling his heels in the Café Vienna and waiting for him.

At last, he got down under the blankets. He lay on his back, staring at the ceiling.

"It's strange, but they damned well all end up being simple when you get them into a bed."

Karl von Eichbaum put out his light. But in the darkness he lay for a long time tossing and turning and shaking his head, and his hands were also curiously restless like those of a man pestered by troublesome flies.

Nor was he in a good mood when he got up, and he failed to part his hair straight as he sat there working away with his comb and the brushes in front of his mirror. But suddenly, raising his face and looking himself straight in the eye in the looking glass, he said just audibly and with a nod:

"Aye, that's it: a man damned well does what he has to do."

Ida had waited for a long time up in her room. Now she had to go down to the tea room; she simply must. She went through the noisy ward into the quiet one. Never, she thought, had she ever walked with such an upright gait. All that was left now was the door to be opened, and the threshold to be crossed.

"Good morning."

She was there now. And for a moment she had listened to her own voice and seen in everyone's faces that they knew nothing; and she had seen Nurse Friis sitting nearest the door and rising quickly from her chair to embrace her.

"Good morning, pet," she said.

And as she kissed her, she touched Ida's cheek lightly with her tongue.

Ida blushed scarlet...

And she heard Nurse Helgesen say:

"Two patients have died during the night."

∞∞∞∞

Ida had waited for perhaps half an hour. She would leave now.

Perhaps no one was coming, so she could go.

But Ellingsen was at the door to "assist madam".

He took her coat and hat and she put them on.

"Thank you," she said. "Goodbye."

But Ellingsen, standing by the door, with his lips very moist, said:
"You are forgetting your parcels, madam."

Ida took them, and Ellingsen also opened the street door.

"Goodbye," she said and went. The outer door was one of those
that quietly close of their own accord. Mr Ellingsen returned to the
private room. He still had a sympathetic look on his face. He took
a serviette to brush away a little dust that he thought had gathered
on the tablecloth, after which he used the same serviette to dry his
mouth. Mr Ellingsen had really seldom received less that sixteen or
eighteen kroner a month from "those people".

Someone rang from the buffet.

But the business was doing well.

Mr Ellingsen went out. A lady and a gentleman were coming
towards him in the corridor.

Ida walked – she probably thought she did not herself know where –
along the path, towards Østerbro, further and further out.

There she met them. She saw them a long way off. *There* they
were.

She had to go past them. Her small parcels seemed to hang loose
on her limp arm and she did not know how she managed to bend her
neck in greeting.

But Kate stopped her horse for a moment.

"Good morning, Miss Brandt," she said, greeting her with her
switch. "Lovely weather."

"Yes, beautiful," said Ida, suddenly staring up at her face.

"You can really feel the approach of spring," said Kate.

Karl stopped a little way from them. It looked as though he was
having difficulty controlling his horse.

"Well, allons...Good morning."

They rode off.

"She had come a long way out of town," said Kate.

And after a short while, looking out over her horse's head, she added:

"It doesn't matter in the least to me, by the way."

Karl would have liked to ask *what*, but he was suddenly silent and looked bewildered.

"I'm no match for you by Gad," he said then after they had trotted for a time.

Ida had turned round. It was as though she had suddenly awakened. She saw every face she met as though it was strangely radiant, and every gateway and every house and every tree, as though everything was in some way sharply defined. And she clearly heard every snatch of conversation and every carriage and every sound as though she had a thousand senses.

But most of all she saw the soil and the yellow crocuses and the rose trees, their cover having been taken off them now. For now spring would soon be coming.

She could have walked ten miles, but nevertheless she turned down by the corner of the lake out of habit.

On the road close to Rørholm, she met Nurse Friis, who started to shout from a great distance and then kissed her, as had recently become her habit. "But," she said, "I really must see your flat today, love." Nurse Friis went on pestering Ida to let her see the flat: it was only just round the corner now.

Ida suddenly felt so tired, or perhaps she felt the need to savour one final pain.

"Yes," she said quietly "we can go up."

She mounted the steps as though she was climbing a mountain. Nurse Friis went before her, reading all the names on the doors.

"What a lovely quiet building," she shouted. (The residents were all state employees or minor officials plus a Baptist minister.) She could hardly wait for Ida to open the door and say, as though she had forgotten:

"Oh yes, there are some men working here."

But Nurse Friis was already in the living room, shouting:

"Oh, my hat, this is nice." She flew out into the passageway again and had to kiss Ida in sheer enthusiasm before dancing in again. She felt everything and saw everything and she talked until she suddenly sat down on a chair arm.

"But, my dear Brandt, this must have cost you a fortune."

Ida sat down. Motionless, she sat there and looked at it all, piece by piece: now it was all in place.

She did not hear Nurse Friis or notice that her torrent of words suddenly ceased; she only felt that she was alone, for a moment, and raised her hands from her lap when Nurse Friis appeared in the bedroom door.

"Brandt," she said, and she spoke the name in a tone (there was a touch of admiration in it) which she had never used before: "You know how to arrange things."

Ida had suddenly risen, and at the sound of her name her cheeks flushed.

"Well, we'll go now," she said and had almost forgotten her pain.

But Nurse Friis was in the bedroom again, bouncing on the big bed.

"We are going now," Ida repeated.

There was something in her tone that persuaded Nurse Friis to get up rather quickly.

But Ida waited in silence first at the door to the living room and then at the outer door and finally at the street door until Nurse Friis was out. Nor did their conversation really resume out in the street. Nurse Friis was also quiet, thinking her own thoughts as though she had discovered something. But when they reached the hospital entrance, she said before continuing on "an errand":

"For heaven's sake, Brandt, do be reasonable, this is only for those of us who are broadminded."

Ida silently pushed her hand from her arm.

"Goodbye," nodded Nurse Friis.

When, still carrying the two small parcels, Ida came down the stairs in the Pavilion, she met Nurse Kjær.

"Oh," she said in her happy voice – she was so used to Ida's bringing something home with her – "You've got some cakes."

And she ran ahead up to Nurse Petersen: "Miss has some cakes," she said, and they quickly gathered for a picnic in the kitchen.

Ida sat and watched the cake disappear between Petersen's teeth.

When the two had had enough, there was still a piece remaining. They offered it to Josefine, who came to fetch the buckets.

"Well, someone's got to have it," said Josefine.

But Nurse Petersen said:

"Oh, we ought to have kept them to have with the coffee."

Ida had risen and left.

∞∞∞

Kate Mourier had developed the most remarkable habit. She wandered up and down through all the rooms followed by both the hounds.

"My dear Kate, why all this marching up and down?" said Mrs Mourier from her sofa.

"I'm thinking," said Kate and marched on.

"But couldn't you do it in just one room?" said Mrs Mourier.

Suddenly, Kate had sat down with both dogs in front of her, and then she got up again. Over by the door, she stretched her arms up along the door frame.

"Is it this evening we are going to a concert?" she said, staring up in the air.

"Yes."

"That's nice. Because I need some music," she said; and she went in.

Mrs Mourier continued to sit there. The pages in her "Peters Edition" were left untouched. She was thinking that it was good that Mourier was coming at last. He would be company for Aline.

For Mrs Mourier did not really know what was going on in Kate's mind.

The bell rang; it was Mrs von Eichbaum. She came merely to ask whether Mourier was also bringing their butler to town with him.

"Because, you see, Mine, it is best to know that," she said.

Mourier's butler was to help at the reception that Mrs von Eichbaum was arranging for the recently returned Mrs Feddersen.

They discussed it for a while, and Mrs von Eichbaum said then, in a different tone:

"The children have been riding, you know."

"Yes," said Mrs Mourier, staring ahead. She would so much have liked to have a "straight talk", but she refrained.

Nurse Friis's "errand" was a minute's dash across to Svendsen, to find her large-nosed friend having lunch. The nurse was all hot and bothered after what she had seen that morning.

"Heavens above," she said, "I would never have believed it. It was so splendid."

Her large-nosed friend viewed his sandwiches.

"It's always like that with those very gentle girls," he said.

Nurse Friis sat for a while; she could still picture the bed and the big washbasin and the broad sofa.

"Yes, it must be that," she said thoughtfully, and then she nodded. But shortly afterwards she said:

"But, good Lord, it must be lovely to have money."

"Well," said her large-nosed friend, "the most important thing, when all is said and done, is to know what you want with each other."

He offered Nurse Friis a glass of beer, which she lifted her veil to drink.

But, once more quite heatedly, she suddenly said:

"Frederik, she'd moved the bed right into the middle of the flat."

"Aye, *that*'ll probably be left where it is," said the large-nosed friend.

∞∞∞∞

Mrs von Eichbaum was sitting with the general's wife in front of the well-laid table in the latter's dining room, where Mrs von Eichbaum's guests were to eat today. All was ready.

Mrs von Eichbaum looked over the decorations, consisting of crocuses from the estate, and said:

"And then little Brandt is coming. I was out there myself this morning."

And when the general's wife made no immediate reply, she said:

"There was no sense in leaving the place empty, and she has been here a good deal during the winter. Besides, she will help a little with the tea."

"But it is quite reasonable to invite her," said the general's wife, "as there is an empty place. And precisely," she said, stopping just a little too suddenly after having said it, "under present circumstances."

But Mrs von Eichbaum, appeared not to have heard, for she simply rose and said:

"And now all that remains for Julius is to light the lamps."

The general's wife also rose, but over by the door Mrs von Eichbaum stopped.

"And then I would also," she said, rather more slowly, "like Aline to come a little earlier, for Lotte, (Mrs von Eichbaum performed a gesture with her hands as though she were putting something in place) then it would be as though she is really *here*."

The general's wife nodded as Mrs von Eichbaum opened the door.

"But good heavens my dear, the young ones are coming after dinner."

They went down the corridor to the general's wife's kitchen.

"Those screens, Lotte," said Mrs von Eichbaum as she went through the kitchen, where some grey screens both concealed and adorned the kitchen table and the stove, "those screens are a blessing."

They separated, and Mrs von Eichbaum went over to her own small corridor where, in a rather commanding voice, she said to Julius, who had his gloves hanging to dry on a cord over by the stove:

"And Julius, I suppose you will take care of the visiting butler."

Julius appeared, smelling slightly of petrol, and said he would take care of him.

Mrs von Eichbaum went in. She did not speak to Ane before the dinner.

The three rooms made a quietly comfortable impression, and the coal, which had been put on rather sparingly, was burning gently. Mrs von Eichbaum settled down in the sofa. She was going to make lace until it was time to dress. The bed curtain would soon be finished – within a few weeks. But Kate, that dear child, had really also been an eager lace-maker during the evenings and she did it very competently.

It really was as though those beautiful fingers had quietened down.

The lace bobbins slipped out of Mrs von Eichbaum's hands, and she became lost in thought. The rooms were beginning to grow darker. Mrs von Eichbaum thought of so many things, of this winter and the many winters before it, of Aline and Kate and Karl. And suddenly she thought of one of the sermons preached by the chaplain to the royal household.

The subject had been faithfulness and a day's work and the peace that was its reward.

Mrs von Eichbaum suddenly became very emotional, and she took out her handkerchief in the half light. Her eyes had alighted on Mr von Eichbaum's picture above the desk. He was still visible in the half light.

His widow had folded her hands.

Then she was awakened from her thoughts. She had heard Karl. He opened the door from the dining room and came in.

"Have you dressed, mother?" he asked.

"No, I've simply been sitting in my corner for a while," said Mrs von Eichbaum from the darkness: "But everything is ready."

"Are we having Christensen then?" said Karl, who had collapsed on to a chair.

"Yes."

They sat for a while in silence, until Mrs von Eichbaum said:

"And I have invited Miss Brandt."

She had perhaps expected some comment from the gloom, but the word did not come, and all that was heard by either of them was the ticking of the clock.

"She's been here a good deal during the winter after all," came the voice from the sofa.

And Mrs von Eichbaum's tone changed almost imperceptibly: "And so I have thought of this as a kind of final visit."

The clock went on ticking perhaps for a minute.

"Will you light the lamp in the corner," said Mrs von Eichbaum. Karl lit the lap, and Mrs von Eichbaum rose.

"It is probably about time," she said, and as she went past her son she suddenly laid her arm on his shoulder:

"I have been sitting here looking at the portrait of your father."

Karl could feel she was trembling.

And suddenly moved, like her, he said:

"You are so kind, mother." And he kissed her forehead.

"And now we must dress," said Mrs von Eichbaum: "Julius has put the seating arrangements on your table."

Karl stood in his room studying the "seating arrangements". He felt something of a relief: Ida, who was to have the research student next to her at table, had been placed on the same side of the table as he himself.

Over in the dining room, Julius had finished lighting the lamps when Mourier's Mr Christensen arrived with his dress shirt covered for protection by a velvet cloth. Julius treated the stranger with a great deal of ceremony and said that he "might perhaps be allowed to explain the situation to him".

He took Mr Christensen into the general's wife's guest room beside the dining room, and Mr Christensen divested himself of his outer garments while looking at the two beds.

"This is where we dish up," said Julius.

Julius had been thinking that Mr Christensen could pour the wine.

Mr Christensen – who wore gold cufflinks and had three square gold buttons on his shirt front, had served in the guards and during Mr Mourier's annual visit to Karlsbad had zealously trained in the international style – studied the bottles.

"Of white wine," said Julius," we usually pour twelve glasses per bottle."

Mr Christensen, who looked like a man who would not be surprised by anything, started arranging the bottles with a pair of very well-groomed hands. He wore a broad gold ring on the little finger of his left hand.

Mrs von Eichbaum had dressed and now sprinkled the rooms with "just a drop" of eau de Cologne.

The porter had taken up his post in front of the gate so as to give orders to the carriages. They were to stay on in the street. The "courtyard" between the two parts of the building was too narrow to allow them to turn with ease.

But the first guest came on foot. This was the student who was regularly given a meal here. He always came first because of an excessive fear of arriving too late, and as he divested himself of an array of strange garments he said to Julius:

"I suppose no one has arrived."

Then, his head slightly bowed, he went in to Mrs von Eichbaum. Mrs von Eichbaum rose and said: "How nice to see you, Henrik; I take it you are reasonably well." The student seated himself and thanked her. When sitting in the middle of a room, he looked as though he had been put in a corner, and he kept his legs curiously close to each other as though he had them in a foot muff. Hearing someone out in the corridor, Mrs von Eichbaum said:

"Yes, spring is a bad time for ailments of that sort."

The research student's "ailment" was a stomach upset.

"But have you had a lambskin rug under your table during the winter?"

Mrs von Eichbaum got up without waiting for an answer. The Schleppegrell family was making its entry into the small drawing room.

"Good lord, my dear," said Mrs Schleppegrell, who was quite out of breath: "Fancy our being so early and I have been rushing around for hours."

Mrs Schleppegrell had spent four hours of her day in the custom house, as she immediately told everyone.

The admiral had greeted the research student – in roughly the same way as he would have addressed a ship's cook – and Mrs Schleppegrell moved across to the general's wife, who usually came when she had heard the first carriage and had perhaps been hoping it was Aline. Karl, who had come in and was going round bowing and clicking his patent leather heels, had stopped before Fanny, who had a lace veil over an older salmon-coloured robe from a court ball, and, as a contribution to the conversation, Mrs von Eichbaum called across the room:

"I suppose you went to Father Dominique this morning, Fanny? *What* did he talk about?"

The priest had spoken on the subject of authority.

The admiral, who was truly religious every Sunday and attended service in the Naval Church with the Roskilde hymn book in his pocket, said:

"I don't like all this enthusiasm for Catholic churches..."

"Good Heavens, Schleppegrell," said the general's wife – there was a certain staccato quality to the conversation – "for someone so firm in her faith as Fanny, it can only broaden the mind."

And Mrs von Eichbaum, rising again, said:

"No, Schleppegrell, I can't agree with you in that either – we are just talking about Catholics, Emmy – after all Catholics have a breadth of vision that is a source of inspiration."

And hearing the door to the small drawing room open again, the general's wife added as Fanny armed herself with her lorgnette:

"After all, there is a quality of permanence to Catholicism."

For a second, while everyone was speaking, all eyes had lighted on Madame Aline, who had appeared in the doorway.

"Good morning, Aline," said Mrs von Eichbaum, reaching out both her hands to her, and Mrs Feddersen, dressed in silk, without a word and supported by her walking stick, entered the room. Mrs von Eichbaum remained by her side as her friend shook hands with everybody – while shaking hands, Mrs Falkenberg instinctively stuck out her arm like a child learning to waltz – and the admiral (who was still talking about Catholicism) was heard to say:

"Well, damn it all, I don't think it's healthy."

Mrs Schleppegrell had risen to embrace Aline, while over by the étagère Lieutenant Colonel Falkenberg was heard to say to the student: "Yes, that's as it is, you go out in the sunshine, and then you find a cold wind blowing." And the general's wife, taking Mrs Feddersen's walking stick, said:

"Sit here, Aline."

While Mrs Feddersen was seating herself it was as though the group closed around her in the corner of the sofa.

But Mrs von Eichbaum, returning to the door to the small drawing room, said with a laugh:

"Yes, of course, the fine folk are the ones to come late."

The Mouriers and Miss Rosenfeld had arrived together.

"No, Andreas," Mrs. Mourier had said at home, "I do not wish to be there to see her arrive."

Now, not having the courage to go in, she stood in the cabinet whence she could see Aline in the corner of the sofa.

"Good Lord, but she has gone grey," she said to Fanny, who was standing closest to her, and Mrs Mourier had tears in her eyes.

"Who?" asked Fanny.

Karl, going past the end of the table, suddenly found Ida, behind the others, over in the corner by the rubber plant.

"So this is where you are, Miss Brandt?" he said, clicking his heels, slightly pale.

And Mrs von Eichbaum, who had completely forgotten her, but had extremely sharp ears, came towards her. "Good day, dear Miss Brandt," she said and introduced her to a couple of those closest to her. Mrs Lindholm suddenly sailed into the small drawing room in front of her distinguished husband who was redolent of eau de Lubin, so there was quite a squeeze, while Kate, in a tone suggesting she was standing at the entrance to the Ark, said, as she tapped Karl's arm with her fan:

"Well, there are eighteen of us now."

264

They were already beginning to move out of the living room, while Mourier continued to shake hands heartily with all, and they went out through the doors, couple after couple. The research student bowed to Ida, whom he had never met before, and they were the last to go in.

But as they went in past the screens, Karl, accompanying Mrs Lindholm, scraped past Ida and, as though there were not sufficient room, put a hand on her waist for a moment.

"We are bringing up the rearguard," he said.

And Mrs Lindholm, who was the daughter of the Purveyor of Glass to His Majesty, said with a glance at the screens:

"It is so convenient that you live in the same house as your aunt."

"Yes," said Karl, who had followed her eye: "The screens are one of the family treasures; I think we inherited them."

Mrs Lindholm laughed and, as they went along the corridor, raised her skirts a little as though crossing a farmyard. When they reached the dining room, Karl cast a host's eye over the table. It was as though his face suddenly became older and adopted a certain official look.

They were all seated, the mother at the bottom end of the table, the admiral at the top, with his symbol of knighthood around his neck, alongside Madame Aline.

Julius started to serve the soup as solemnly as though he were bearing a pair of sacrificial vessels.

The conversation centred on dining rooms and on seating.

"We have enough room here, thank God," said Mr Mourier, who was tying his serviette around his ample chest.

The conversation built up, though still on the subject of dining rooms, and, while Mrs Mourier bent forward to hide Madame Aline, whose hands were trembling so that she was spilling her soup when raising her spoon to her mouth, Mrs von Eichbaum said:

"But there is no dining room to rival that at Korsgaard."

And Madame Aline, speaking as it were in a deeper tone than the others, said:

"It is cool there at least."

Miss Rosenfeld had for a moment listened to the timbre of Madame Aline's voice, and she gave an absent-minded answer to a question put to her by Lindholm:

"Yes, we have a hundred pupils in the school now."

Which gave the admiral's wife the occasion to raise her bosom in a rather splendidly low-cut dress as she said:

"Yes, it is incredible; everyone has to have something to do nowadays."

But the general's wife said:

"Good Lord, it's just a result of all this impatience. There is no one these days who is calm enough to sit quietly somewhere and knit a sock."

Mr Mourier declared that it was an excellent halibut, and while Mr Christensen, who had removed the ring from his little finger before serving, poured the white wine, Lieutenant Colonel Falkenberg caught the word "calm" and said:

"Yes, but what is the reason for that madam? We (and the lieutenant colonel's voice became sharper), *we* have two opposition newspapers in our house. If it were up to me, they would never be allowed inside the door."

Mrs Falkenberg, who only ate a little but was constantly looking up at Madame Aline as though staring at a miracle taking place close to her, said:

"But, Falkenberg, we cannot prevent the children from reading."

"But we don't have to discuss things with them," replied the lieutenant colonel.

Almost as though to place herself between the two of them, Mrs von Eichbaum said:

"Well, Emmy, *there* I agree with Falkenberg: these everlasting discussions give rise to nothing but disagreement."

Mourier, who was still eating, was of the general opinion that it was necessary to know what those people were thinking: Damn it all, he reads the "Social Democrat".

"My dear Mourier," said Mrs von Eichbaum, who now, with some relief, could hear Madame Aline talking in a brighter voice about her home at Sølyst: "I think that wrong..."

Mrs von Eichbaum meant "for the sake of the example it gives". It was dreadful the way things were going at the moment:

"Just imagine the other day, I discovered that Ane and Julius – just imagine Ane – subscribe to one of those little newspapers. It is difficult to understand where they get it from."

Mourier laughed, but the conversation on journalists had now reached Lindholm, who said that those people were sometimes seen in the theatre, and he often wondered about it. "For they are really well dressed," he said in a tone suggesting he had expected that everyone writing in a newspaper would turn up with holes in their jacket elbows.

The admiral told how he had once had a gentleman from a newspaper on board the "Heligoland", and he had spoken quite sensibly by Gad, but the admiral's wife, who had continued with her argument that everyone felt a need to do something, said across the table to Mrs Mourier, speaking of the daughter of one in their circle:

"My dear Mine, didn't you know – yes, she wants to start as a midwife."

The research student, who had eaten his fish without sauce because of his diet (he was the son of a famous figure from the middle of the century and had for ten years been busy arranging his father's "Memoirs" while growing ever thinner), said to Ida:

"It must be a very rewarding task to be able to lessen other people's suffering."

"Yes," said Ida, and her partner's conversation came to an end again. She had acquired two red patches, one over each eyebrow, as though she had just come straight from a frying pan.

Mrs von Eichbaum looked out across the table with her hostess' eye.

"Oh, Miss Brandt, dear, would you take that dish and pass it on."

Ida gave a start. She had only heard all the conversation as an alien hum, and now she heard Karl's voice addressing Miss Mourier again.

"Yes," she said, and took the dish.

"Thank you," said Mrs von Eichbaum.

Mrs Lindholm spoke to Fanny Schleppegrell about the princes: one of them had given her a paperknife. And the conversation in general came to centre on the royal family.

As the conversation became increasingly animated and the admiral had approached as it were a little closer to Mrs Feddersen, the general's wife and Lieutenant Colonel Falkenberg spoke about a family friend who was the prince's governor and was preparing him for an examination.

"But he is very constrained," said the general's wife, "having to sleep in the room front."

The lieutenant colonel replied with some words on the excellent example this was and turned to Miss Rosenfeld.

"Well," he said: "You are naturally a radical like my wife."

"I don't understand what you mean by that word," said Miss Rosenfeld, "but I am actually very fond of the king because I consider him a very noble person."

Karl and Kate started to laugh at the word "person", and the general's wife said to Miss Rosenfeld:

"My dear Betty, that is presumably not the only thing about him."

But Mrs Falkenberg, who had two red patches on her cheeks – she easily acquired them, as though they were the result of a suppressed or secret agitation – said without addressing her words to anyone in particular, though they were probably intended for the lieutenant colonel:

"But people nevertheless think..."

And the lieutenant colonel replied:

"Yes, they think...they think until they are laid in their graves."

Mourier, who had heard this, laughed and said:

"You're damned right," and he chinked glasses with the lieutenant colonel.

The word "think" suddenly led Mrs von Eichbaum on to the subject of Martensen's *Ethics*. She was reading the book at the moment. She was savouring it slowly.

"But," she said, "he is not difficult to follow, thanks to the clarity of his style."

Suddenly, the general's wife said across the table to Ida (She is sitting as though she doesn't belong anywhere, Her Ladyship had immediately noticed):

"Is there much sickness this year, Miss Brandt?"

"Yes, a considerable amount," Ida managed to say. All she was hearing was Karl and Kate's laughter. They were laughing as though far away. And then she sat keeping an eye on the dishes, almost frantically, as though from a long-standing habit that had suddenly recurred – the habit she had had at Ludvigsbakke.

Mourier, sitting surveying the table, let his eye rest on Ida and leant across to Mrs von Eichbaum:

"Who is she?" he asked in a subdued voice, and Ida heard Mrs von Eichbaum in the midst of a longish explanation say:

"And her father was His Lordship's land agent. A truly estimable man."

Ida did not perhaps herself realise she was fighting to prevent tears coming to her eyes.

Up at the other end of the table the conversation was rather more light-hearted. They had continued to talk about "Sølyst", and Mrs von Eichbaum started to join in, while the admiral's wife had once more reached the subject of customs and the customs authorities, finally saying to Mrs Lindholm:

"But, my dear, I am hoping to get some pieces of silk home with your mother-in-law and Mary...good heavens, when you put them at the bottom of your case..."

The conversation about "Sølyst" also caught her, and she abandoned the subject of "silks". Mrs Mourier talked so happily and loudly, for she was so truly delighted because things were thawing out completely with regard to Aline; and Mrs Feddersen sat bending forward with her face fully illuminated.

"Yes, it was a lovely time," said Mrs Mourier. "Do you remember, Mille?" – she was addressing Mrs von Eichbaum – "When we drove to Marienlyst to dance. That was in Brix's day. It is ages now since I was there."

Mrs von Eichbaum said something, suddenly with tears in her eyes: *that* was where she had met Eichbaum for the first time.

And they all continued to talk about those days: about the soirées and the lieutenants from Kronborg barracks and the trips to Gurre and the hours spent bathing when they drove on a hay cart down to the beach at Hellebæk, and the great expeditions into the forest, when they went to Grib Forest, which was so huge and quiet.

All their faces became quite radiant and they all – including Madame Aline – started to speak in almost the same way.

"Oh yes," said the admiral's wife: "We were after all far better people in those days."

But the admiral, whose cross of chivalry was by now a little skewed and who was sitting thinking that it was damned incredible how Aline had kept her good looks, said:

"Yes, I can remember how it was giving you a swing."

Karl and Kate had started chatting in French, but suddenly Karl bent forward – they were still talking about Grib Forest over there – and raised his glass:

"Miss Brandt," he said.

Ida started and scarcely raised her eyes. Then she drank.

But Karl sat there for a moment, quite preoccupied. A sad look had come over his eyes.

"Little Miss Brandt" said Mrs von Eichbaum – her words seemed to come rather hastily – "Perhaps you would be so kind as to pass the jam round."

But it was Miss Rosenfeld, who replied in a rather loud voice.

"I will see to that, Mrs von Eichbaum."

Everyone joined in the lively conversation, while the light from the candelabra flickered a little in the warm air. Lindholm entertained the student on the subject of memoir literature. He had to say that memoirs as a whole were his favourite reading, especially when they concerned Napoleon.

"While you are reading memoirs you feel so to speak," said Lindholm, "that we are all human beings."

Lieutenant Colonel Falkenberg started to talk about Napoleon's

270

marshals and Marshal Ney's tomb, which, he said, was simple as befits a soldier's grave; while Mrs Lindholm asked Fanny whether she knew how much Mrs Verdier had asked for a trimming of old lace.

Almost everyone was talking more or less at the same time. Miss Rosenfeld compelled Ida to join in. Mourier, who was flushed, put his hand down on Mrs von Eichbaum's and said:

"It's damned nice here."

"Dear Mourier," said Mrs von Eichbaum with a smile: "It is so easy when you only have your own circle around you."

They were finished with the grouse, which was a present from Mrs Mourier, and Mr Christensen poured the port.

Up at Madame Aline's end of the table, they were still talking about times at Sølyst, when Mrs Mourier said:

"We must all get together again at Ludvigsbakke."

And Mourier, hearing this, said happily:

"Aye, that's right, damn it, you're all welcome when we get it built. I think the last wall in the old place is due to come down today."

The word Ludvigsbakke had awakened Ida, but she did not realise that, leaning forward, pale, she was staring directly into Mr Mourier's face.

"The old walls have otherwise been tough," said Mourier. "But now we'll be able to use the old bricks for the new stables."

"But the old house was nice after all," said Mrs von Eichbaum.

"Of course it was nice," said Mourier quietly. "But the younger generation are never satisfied."

"But you spoil Kate," said the general's wife.

"No," Kate suddenly broke in with a kind of vulgar emphasis on the word: "One could not possibly have moved into those old buildings."

Kate suddenly became the central figure at the table as they talked about the new rooms, the staircase, the billiard room and the bathrooms and the gazebo and the terraces, for which the granite vases were to be carved in Italy.

Mrs Lindholm was extremely interested and bent forward over

the table to ask a question while Fanny withdrew her thin bust and looked as though she were smelling at concentrated vinegar, and Kate continued to talk about banisters and parquet floors and a room in which to drink tea as they did in England.

The conversation grew in intensity and Mrs Mourier said to the general's wife: "Yes, people want more, you know," looking with loving admiration down at her daughter while Karl started telling Lindholm all about the stables, eagerly and deeply engaged, explaining that they were being constructed to the English pattern, with the horses free in their stalls, large rooms, with marble floors and water conduits.

"Wonderful, you know," said Karl. "I have done the drawings myself."

But Kate told Mrs Lindholm about the bedrooms, all of which were to face north, for you had to be able to sleep in a cool room.

Ida was not aware that Julius had offered her ice cream and that she had some on her plate.

But the two young people were speaking ever more eagerly because Kate's father was teasing her, and Colonel Falkenberg started to criticise the stalls in the stables. Somewhat excited by the heat and the wine, they both spoke at the same time, each in a different direction, Kate down to her father and Karl up to the colonel concerning bedrooms and horses and central heating and stalls, so much so that it sounded like a duet. Even Mrs Feddersen became caught by the conversation and leaned forward, and some brief, quick glints came into her grey eyes at the mention of all that comfort and the marble bathtubs.

And suddenly Mrs Mourier nodded to Mrs von Eichbaum with tears in her kind eyes.

But Mourier took off his napkin and said:

"Aye, the young ones must have their fling."

When things had quietened down a little, Miss Rosenfeld said in a low voice:

"But, you know, there were so many lovely memories from the old house."

Karl heard the words and suddenly he stopped his explanations and made no reply to Lindholm.

Mrs Falkenberg sat trying to catch Falkenberg's eye, but the lieutenant colonel was enjoying a biscuit and talking to the admiral about remounts.

Mrs von Eichbaum said that she thought it was time to leave the table now.

Ida had not heard this, and she did not rise until the research student offered her his arm. As though only half awake she sat for a moment and surveyed the table with the remains of the meal and the slightly smoking candelabra and then her own plate at the table. The blood red ice cream had melted and turned into some coloured, dirty water in her bowl.

The admiral made to hand Mrs Aline Feddersen her stick. But Madame Aline thought she could manage without it. And, supported by the admiral, whose enamel cross shone in the light from the Eichbaum candelabra, she walked, with some difficulty but nevertheless upright among the other couples, past the screens over to Mrs von Eichbaum's apartment, where Mr Christensen started to offer them coffee.

Ladies and gentlemen were speaking in loud voices in groups here and there. Mrs Mourier was standing with Mrs von Eichbaum and holding her dry hands in her own.

"That was delightful," she said: "I don't know anyone who understands the art as you do."

Mrs Mourier omitted to explain what she really meant by the art, or perhaps she was not even aware of it herself.

But Mrs von Eichbaum replied:

"My dear Vilhelmine, it all takes care of itself."

"Yes, when you understand these things," said Mrs Mourier.

Ida had quite mechanically – or perhaps as a kind of unconscious defence – taken sugar and cream and was gliding around offering them to the guests. Now she reached Mrs Mourier.

"Ah, Miss Brandt, you are going around as though you were the daughter in the house."

"Yes," said Ida, and glided on.

"I think she is rather nice, you know," said Mrs Mourier, who had an indeterminate feeling of sympathy, perhaps on account of the strangely old-maidish quality that had come over Ida's personality. It was as though the yellow dress was too big for her so that there was no real living body in it, and her waved hair over her small forehead looked strangely like a wig or as though it had been glued on.

"Good Lord, my dear, wonderful," said Mrs von Eichbaum: "And one of those rare people who always know their place."

The gentlemen had gone into Karl's room to smoke, all except the admiral, who was taking care of his health by going for his usual walk up the road. Lindholm said something to the effect that Copenhagen was a damned fine capital city, a city in which it was impossible to get a decent shirt in the entire place.

But Mourier had met Karl in the entrance hall.

"I have really been going to write to you for some time but, you see, well, I know what it costs for a young man to accompany young ladies throughout the winter. But now (Mr. Mourier was quite embarrassed) we are going to make a deposit in the local branch and that is all settled, so you need only go across and draw it."

"Oh, don't mention it," he concluded brusquely. Karl had turned blood red, and Mr Mourier turned away, much relieved.

"Should we not rather move into the dining room?" he said: "The air's a damned sight better in there, and it's nice to be away from the ladies while we have coffee. "

Before long, the gentlemen broke up and went into the general's wife's dining room, where Mr Christensen and Julius were clearing the table.

Mr Christensen had acquired something of a twitch in his nose on reaching Mrs Feddersen's place, where her perfume could still be detected.

"I must say she is still an imposing lady," he had said to Julius.

A certain silence had come over the ladies after the coffee and now the gentlemen had gone. The admiral's wife was half asleep on the sofa after the morning's exertions (and in addition she always ate a great deal when she was out), but in the corner beneath the gas light there was a group talking about books and reading. Mrs Falkenberg, who was nervously rubbing one cheek with her clenched fist while looking up in the air, said:

"But reading so often makes one restless."

At which, Mrs Eichbaum, over by the étagère, speaking to Mrs Lindholm about Mary, said:

"My dear Emmy, one reads in order to rest."

But Mrs Falkenberg, still rubbing her cheek, said quietly:

"But surely also to get to know life?"

"I do not think that is often what one finds in books," said Miss Rosenfeld.

The general's wife, who had persuaded Ida to sit on the edge of a sofa, seemed to interrupt and said:

"Dear Miss Brandt, you have a task to fulfil." And she gently raised Ida's arm. It was so strangely lifeless as it fell back on the marble table, or perhaps it was as though it had been crushed or was out of joint, that the general's wife suddenly looked at her.

"But of course, it makes demands on you," she said in a different voice.

The admiral's wife, who had awaken and heard they were talking about reading, said from over in the sofa:

"But, my dears, you have to go through the lot to keep up. Fanny and I read ourselves to sleep every evening."

In the small drawing room, Mrs Feddersen had settled down for a moment. Perhaps she was rather tired, for she had closed her eyes and was supporting her head against the wall. She was directly in the light, and the red links of pearls falling down on her bosom almost looked like blood flowing down into her lap. She had not noticed Mrs Mourier coming and sitting down beside her.

"I have been thinking such a lot about you," said Mrs Mourier, quietly taking hold of Madame Aline's hand.

Mrs von Eichbaum had the windows in the dining room opened as they already were over in the general's wife's apartment. The gentlemen's laughter and Mr Mourier's voice could be heard over in Mrs von Eichbaum's rooms, as though the entire house was one single source of festivity harmonising with the brightly lit courtyard. The front-door bell rang and Julius went to open it. It was the younger members of the family who were starting to arrive, girls in bright dresses and young gentlemen in freshly starched shirts, bowing in turn to the older guests.

A small pianist, beardless and slightly flustered and asking for a cushion for his chair, finally sat down at the piano, and a couple of young people started to dance on the dining room floor, while the gentlemen's laughter mingled with the music.

Mrs von Eichbaum went to and fro. Now she came from over in the gentlemen's room into her own kitchen:

"Julius."

Julius came, followed by Mr Christensen, who was in his shirt sleeves with stiff cuffs.

"Julius, would you please put the screens in place," said Mrs von Eichbaum as she passed by.

Mr Mourier had overturned one of them on his way through the kitchen.

Just at the door to her own dining room Mrs von Eichbaum met Ida.

"My dear Miss Brandt," she said, rather flustered: "I am so worried about cups, whether there are sufficient, because the young people need to have some tea. Would you be so kind as to make sure..."

Ida's words were lost in the happy music, and Mrs von Eichbaum only saw that she bowed her head and went.

Out in the kitchen, she took an apron (there are drunken people who do nothing but sensible things in this way, quite quietly, and afterwards are unable to remember what they have done) and she tied it on. In the gaslight, she washed cup after cup.

Mrs Mourier was standing in the doorway to the living room, watching the young people dancing. Now Karl, who had actually been drinking rather heavily, had come over into these rooms and was dancing with Kate.

"Oh it is lovely to see so much happiness," said Mrs Mourier, putting her arm in under Mrs von Eichbaum's. And standing side by side, they watched their children.

There came sounds of laughter and noise from the gentlemen's room when the music stopped. The admiral had come home, and a couple of the young people had also gone over there unnoticed.

At the middle of the table, the colonel was talking about a sense of morality and the defence forces.

Lindholm had asked the research student who the little lady really was that he had sat next to at table, and the student had explained and said:

"Actually, I think she is a very cultured young lady. But – " and the student made some strange movements with his hands – "one sits there, sir, and says to oneself that such a person could be a source of infection."

The lieutenant colonel remained standing at the middle of the table, speaking ever more loudly about His Excellency the Minister of War as the central figure in the entire patriotic movement when the admiral, who along with Mr Mourier had sat looking as though he were listening, and who perhaps was a little tired of his colleague, said to Mourier:

"But why did you refuse the opportunity of going into parliament?"

"Well," said Mourier, wriggling slightly: "I don't really know, damn it. I'm a natural conservative of course," he repeated. "But you see, admiral, I lack the ability to be outraged, confound it, and that ability is necessary in public life in this country."

"Ah," said the admiral: "Thank God there is not so much outrage at sea."

And laughing merrily as they drank a glass of liqueur, the two gentlemen started walking up and down the floor, talking about Madame Aline.

"Aye," said Mourier," I agree with my wife that that kind of thing doesn't happen provided the husband remains strong and healthy."

But the admiral scratched his head and said:

"We-ell, but I remember up at Sølyst when I used to give them a swing as little girls, she had a way of getting up in the swing and gasping for breath."

"No," and the admiral looked almost satisfied, "she's one of the restless kind."

Over in Mrs von Eichbaum's apartment the piano could be heard again, and Lindholm, standing by the window looking at the dancers, said to Karl von Eichbaum, who had come across for a fresh glass of liqueur:

"I say, Eichbaum, shouldn't we go for a stroll?"

But the lieutenant colonel suddenly said to Mr Mourier:

"But, my dear Mourier, how is it you have never been given a decoration?"

"Because my wife refuses," said Mourier.

Ida had returned and was sitting beside Miss Rosenfeld when Karl came over to her. He was flushed and his voice was rather unsteady.

"Miss Brandt," he said, "we must have a dance."

Ida made no reply, and she rose with difficulty. Karl thought she felt quite thin in his arms.

They only danced round the room a single time. "Thank you," said Ida, and her lifeless hands failed to sense the almost desperate pressure with which he held them.

"She ought to go in and smooth her hair down," said young Falkenberg when Karl took Ida back inside.

Miss Rosenfeld had risen and Ida stood beside her.

Then Miss Rosenfeld took her hand:

"My dear Ida, what on earth do you want here?"

Perhaps Ida did not understand these words, but nevertheless she said:

"I am going home now."

She saw no one as she went through the rooms, where the music had ceased, and she did not know that she suddenly curtsied to Mrs von Eichbaum almost as though she were a child, and she managed to say:

"I have to get up early."

There was no one in the corridor, and she took her own coat. Nothing hurt her except the light. That hurt her eyes. She took a couple of steps until she was standing on the threshold of Karl's room.

Then she turned and left.

It was blowing and raining, but she did not notice. She quickly made her way against the wind. She had not heard a voice addressing her.

It was Knuth, who came along with another officer in uniform.

"Hello, is it you, Miss Brandt," he said. "Are you walking home in this weather?"

And when he suddenly saw her pale face, he said:

"Are you not well? I'll get a carriage for you."

Ida made no reply, but Knuth simply ran while Ida remained standing there. There was something in his voice that softened the blood around her congealed heart.

The carriage came and Knuth helped her in.

"Thank you," she said, and they exchanged no further words.

∞∞∞∞

Karl had reached the general's wife's dining room. He took another glass of liqueur, while Lindholm preferred a mineral water.

Karl sat staring into the almost finished candles in a candelabrum.

"Living's damned expensive," he said suddenly.

Lindholm laughed and said:

"Well, but you'll be able to afford it, Eichbaum."

But Karl probably did not hear this, for he went on staring into the candles until he clicked his tongue and said:

"But I suppose one is of benefit to society."

The admiral and Mr Mourier broke up and went down through the corridor and the kitchen, where the admiral chanced to knock over a screen.

"What rubbish to have in the kitchen," he said.

"But they hide the stove," laughed Mr Mourier.

Over in the living room, the rather tired older ladies had settled down around Mrs von Eichbaum's bed curtain.

"Yes," said Mrs von Eichbaum: "all that is needed now are the bows. But Kate has promised me to tie them."

The young people were dancing a quadrille, and the ladies and gentlemen wound almost wildly around. The lieutenant colonel's voice could once be heard over the music. He was talking about tradition.

∞○○○∞

Ida opened and closed gates and doors so quietly.

But as she passed the door on the first floor, Dr Quam was just opening it.

"Is it you?" he said. "Oh, what a night, two attempted suicides, and they have both had to be pumped out."

Petersen had heard Dr Quam speaking to Ida, and she put her head out:

"Och, have you had a good time?" she said, pulling Ida into the ward, where Nurse Roed was sitting under the gas lamp eating her dinner.

There were loud voices from in the women's ward, and from the main ward came the sound of the patients' groans.

"Ach, ach," said Nurse Petersen, who had to run back and forth: "They are restless tonight."

Dr Quam looked in the direction of Ward A and asked Nurse Roed:

"Is he not in bed?"

"No."

"And he's being sent off tomorrow?"

"Yes."

Dr Quam opened the door leading in.

The gentleman in Ward A was sitting up on the windowsill, with the window open, and looking out into the gale. The rain had passed and the stars were out again.

"Are you sitting *there*?" said Dr Quam. "That is rather against the rules."

The gentleman in Ward A turned his head half way, stared at the doctor through his heavy eyelids and said:

"I am sitting here in defiance of the regulations."

And as though he was talking to himself, he said in that strange voice of his that always sounded as though it was laden with sympathy:

"I am looking at the stars. The stars that are so high in the heavens."

He was silent for a moment.

"When I was young, I looked at them because I wanted to pull them down. Now I look at them to learn patience."

Dr Quam had come closer. From where he was, down on the floor, he looked up at the gentleman from Ward A: this face registered something of great sorrow.

Then the sick man looked down from the windowsill:

"But let us bow to the laws," he said and closed the shutters.

Quam remained standing there.

"Yes, but who wrote the laws?"

The gentleman from Ward A smiled:

"Was it not the prof?" he said.

But his fleeting smile disappeared, and he asked:

"Am I to go tomorrow?"

"Yes, tomorrow morning."

The gentleman from Ward A stared ahead for a moment.

Then he shrugged his shoulders:

"Well, perhaps that is a good thing, doctor."

And as he fixed his eyes on Quam, he said with a new smile that had the character of a farewell:

"Your world does not tempt me."

Quam was suddenly moved and said in a rather gentler voice:

"But life has to be lived."

"Yes," said the gentleman from Ward A, "by those they don't lock up."

"Let me say goodbye now," he said, opening the door.

Outside, Sister Koch from the women's ward had come in to fetch Dr Quam.

Ida was standing on the same spot, near the door, leaning against a wall. Her waved hair had been ruined by the rain.

The gentleman from Ward A shook hands with each of them.

"Goodbye," he said.

Finally, he took Ida's hand, and then he raised his eyes.

"Goodbye."

Then he went in again and closed his door.

There was silence for a moment after he had gone. Then Nurse Koch looked at Ida who was standing on the same spot.

"So the party is over, I suppose."

And Quam, suddenly looking at her, said:

"Yes, Nurse Brandt. I think you need to sleep it off."

The keys could be heard rattling in the door. Dr Quam and Sister Koch went in to the women's ward.

"Good night," said Ida gently.

There was the rattle of keys again. Ida Brandt was going up to her room.

The cries from the restless patients could be heard coming up through the pavilion, as though they were coming from far, far down, from under the ground.

Translator's Afterword

Herman Bang was one of the group of writers representing the advent of modern literature in Denmark. Words such as realism and naturalism are associated with this movement, but Herman Bang was the impressionist par excellence. His novels contain very little by way of authorial comment, but leave readers to pick up the countless hints as to what is really going on.

Social criticism was also a feature of the new movement, and although Bang avoids taking a political stance, his criticism of a society in which social class, snobbery and insensitivity are dominant features is plain to see. Ida Brandt is a victim of this society, brought up on the fringes of the wealthy landowning class, but never quite a part of it and never quite accepted by some of the nurses with whom she subsequently works and who think that, as she has money, she is merely taking up a job that someone else could do with. Good looking and gentle, generous and kind, not endowed with the sharpness to understand what is actually going on around her, she is the outsider, the obvious victim. And victim she is.